SECRETS AND LIES

"So you and Whitney were fighting about a boy. That's what this whole thing was about, the whole reason why the two of you stopped talking?"

"Mom, please, just stop." She looked at her phone. "I'm going to be late."

Her mother's phone pealed again. She scoffed. "I have to take this. Jordan, we're not done with this conversation—"

Jordan didn't say a word as she stormed out of the house and sprinted toward the bus stop, barely making it. She flopped back against her seat, her head swimming from the impromptu interrogation.

She had lied. About everything. Where she was on Saturday, the imaginary boy named Alex. All of it.

She wasn't worried about her mother. She'd just boo hoo a little and suck up to her and her mom would get out of her face.

The cops were a whole different thing, though. But honestly ... could they really figure out she was lying?

No. Probably not. Everything she said was so vague.

Besides, Whitney was dead, so she wasn't talking.

And just like Whitney, she'd take her secrets to the grave.

PRAISE FOR BIANCA SLOANE

WHAT YOU DON'T KNOW

"Riveting and terrifying! The very definition of a thriller! This is what I call, "an all-nighter." Once you start, you won't be able to stop! *What You Don't Know* is what nightmares are made of."
−@ELIZABETH.NESS.56

"[*What You Don't Know*] was a 5/5 for me … Brilliant."
−@MOMFLUENSTER

"It was pure joy to read and edit *What You Don't Know* by Bianca Sloane. Alternating between the violence unfolding at the Gilbert's and investigative interviews with their friends and family, Sloane transports us into a terrifying, brutal home invasion while constructing a brilliant plot that reads like an episode of *Dateline*. I was mesmerized and petrified through every page. Masterful and gripping, this is a suspense novel that any thriller lover will devour."
−SAMANTHA M. BAILEY, #1 BESTSELLING AUTHOR OF WOMAN ON THE EDGE

"Sloane creates complex characters within multi-layered plots that will have you flipping pages to the very end."
−CINDY READS & WRITES

"I read [*What You Don't Know*] in roughly 24 hours, and . . . near the end I was carrying my Kindle around the house so I could sneak in a page or two because . . . I had to know what happened. I actually turned the shower on and stood in the bathroom so I could read the last few pages. This book is that good."
−@THE_TOWERING_TBR

"[What You Don't Know] . . . [was] such a thrill to read . . . We have been looking for a thriller that captures our attention from the first page and holds it until the last. Bianca Sloane's ability to plot and pace such a universally scary event was masterful. We were absolutely petrified reading this book. . ."
—@AUDIOSHELFME

"My favorite thing about being a book reviewer is discovering new authors and Bianca Sloane was a new to me author who has me ready to read more of her books after devouring this one in just two nights. I was quickly hooked on this story [and] Sloane's writing style is fast-paced and totally gripping."
—GRIPLITGRL

THE LIVE TO TELL SERIES

"Bianca Sloane sure knows how to make a page turn."
—WHATISTHATBOOKABOUT.COM ABOUT **TELL ME A LIE**

"...Once again, [Bianca Sloane's] fast-paced, nail-biting, on-the-edge-of-your-seat style of suspense had me gripped from the first page to the last."
—GOODREADS REVIEWER ABOUT **LIVE TO TELL**

"...You will sail through these fast-paced thrillers."
—ASHLEY GILLAN, EBOOKNERDREVIEWS.WORDPRESS.COM ABOUT **LIVE TO TELL** AND **TELL ME A LIE**

EVERY BREATH YOU TAKE

"...Will have you chewing your fingernails down to the quick. The author has a deftness for building suspense and tension, leaving you wondering what's coming next."
—THE HAPHAZARDOUSHIPPO.BLOGSPOT.COM

"Once you start reading this book, you won't want to stop."
–IONIA MARTIN, READFULTHINGSBLOG.COM

"The character buildup … is beyond perfection. Highly recommended."
–SAN FRANCISCO BOOK REVIEW, 5 STARS

SWEET LITTLE LIES

"It is impossible for a reader to relax their grip on *Sweet Little Lies*. The story elements are crisp and exciting with multiple twists and turns."
–NIGHT OWL REVIEWS

"The mystery [of *Sweet Little Lies*] deepens from the very beginning and comes to a satisfying but shocking ending. I feel that anyone looking for a good thriller would be hard pressed to find a better one."
–GREEN EMBERS RECOMMENDS

"From the first few pages, you get instantly hooked. When you first read about the premise … you think you know exactly how the story might unfold. There is no amount of predictability that would have foreseen all the twists and turns that came from reading [*Sweet Little Lies*]."
–WHATISTHATBOOKABOUT.COM

"Once again, Bianca Sloane has written a fast-paced mystery that is the perfect choice for some exciting reading escapism."
–SHETREADSSOFTLY.BLOGSPOT.COM

"I could not put this down until … I found out what would happen. The ending was a big shock. I loved this and would recommend it to any thriller fan."
–WILOVEBOOKS.BLOGSPOT.COM

KILLING ME SOFTLY

Thriller of the Month by www.e-thriller.com (May 2013)
"2013 Top Read" by OOSA Online Book Club

"[A] cross between 'Sleeping with the Enemy' and a superb murder mystery."
—A CrimeReadersBlog.Wordpress.com

"*[Killing Me Softly]* is a book that will leave the reader scratching their head trying to figure out the villain. And, just when the reader thinks they have it all figured out - think again - AND AGAIN!"
—Examiner.com (New Orleans)

AND WHEN I DIE

BIANCA SLOANE

Cover design by Damonza: www.damonza.com

Cover image by Gabriel Hohol via Pexels: www.pexels.com

Bianca@BiancaSloane.com

http://www.biancasloane.com/

Bianca on Facebook

Bianca on Twitter

Bianca on Goodreads

Bianca on Pinterest

Bianca on Instagram

To sign up for the author's newsletter, visit www.biancasloane.com

ISBN: 9798357075031

First Paperback Edition

V2 - FIN

BOOKS BY BIANCA SLOANE

STANDALONE NOVELS

Killing Me Softly (Previously published as Live and Let Die)

Sweet Little Lies

What you don't know

And when I die

THE EVERY BREATH YOU TAKE SERIES

Every Breath You Take

Missing You: A Companion Novella to Every Breath You Take

The Every Breath You Take Collection (Box Set of Every Breath You Take and Missing You)

THE LIVE TO TELL SERIES

Live To Tell

Tell Me A Lie

White Christmas (A Live To Tell short story)

AND WHEN I DIE
Family Trees

The Mitchell Family

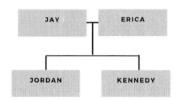

The Ewing Family

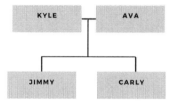

The Dean Family

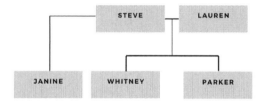

AND WHEN I DIE

PROLOGUE

So, this is how she dies.

She's sixteen. She doesn't think about how she'll die. She thinks about what color to paint her nails. What she'll wear to Skip Lane's party next weekend and whether Mikey Gold will notice. Her English comp paper on *The Scarlet Letter* that's due in four days and how she's only halfway through the book. SATs, college, being a lawyer, or maybe a fashion designer. A husband—a cute one—kids—also cute—and a big, beautiful house.

Those are the things she thinks about.

She doesn't think about how she'll die.

She knows she will. Die, that is. Everyone dies. Like her Grandma Joanne who had a heart attack last fall at the age of sixty-five. Or Mrs. Lupico, her fifth-grade teacher, who died from breast cancer two years ago. Or the really bad car accident Stacy Keaton's dad was in the year they turned twelve.

No one she knows has ever been viciously stabbed to death.

With each gasping breath, her lungs swell with blood. Blood coats her eyes. Blood pounds in her ears. Blood streaks down the length of her hands. Blood runs from the strands of her hair like rain.

Through the haze of blood, she sees a house. A white house with black shutters, a red door, and a light in the window. A house where there'll be people. At least she won't be found in the street. At least her parents won't have to wait too long to find out what happened to her.

At least she won't die alone.

She blindly zigs and zags toward the white house with black shutters and a red door. She staggers up the front walk and commands the heavy brick of her hand to pummel the red door, ready to beg whoever is on the other side to let her in.

The door swings open to reveal a woman. A horrified, shrieking woman in a beautiful, shimmering white silk blouse. At least she thinks it's silk. She falls against the horrified, shrieking woman in the beautiful white silk blouse, hoping the blouse wasn't her favorite. The woman screams orders at someone and she feels the two of them sink to the floor. The woman in the beautiful, shimmering white silk blouse cradles her, tries to hold the chasm in her chest together with one hand as she claims help is on the way, if she'll just hold on.

It's a nice thought. Holding on. Being saved. It's a thought the horrified, shrieking woman in the beautiful, shimmering white silk blouse needs to cling to. It's not a thought she herself can clutch at. There's no point.

Because this is how she dies.

1

AVA

Ava Ewing tapped her index finger against the steering wheel as she glanced out the driver's side window, her eyes peeled for her daughter. The harsh yellow-white glare of the late afternoon, late September sun blasted into the car like a cannon. She looked at her watch for the third time in a minute, her brain plowing through the details of the conference call she was leading in a half hour.

She should have let Carly catch a ride home with one of her teammates. A day like today was one more reason why, trite and selfish though it may have been, she missed her son, Jimmy, being at college, because she could have had him pick up his sister after school.

She was feeling guilty, she supposed, which is why she'd insisted at breakfast she'd pick Carly up after practice, even though it meant taking a bite out of her work from home day. Ava had been home approximately five out of the last thirty days. This after-practice pickup was her woeful attempt at spending a few stolen minutes with her child. It was pitiful really, since she'd be back on her laptop after dinner, then up at five tomorrow to be in the office by seven thirty.

And soon, Carly would be sixteen, getting her license and a car all in one day. She'd passed the written test six months ago and had shown herself to be a diligent, easygoing driver. She and Kyle had already picked out the seven-year-old BMW they were going to give their daughter on the big day. A shiny new ticket to freedom.

She'd be lucky to see Carly at all.

Ava sighed and looked out the window again, relieved to see her daughter emerge through the gates of the football field in what looked to be semi-serious conversation with her pom squad teammate, Whitney Dean. It wasn't hard to miss the naked adoration on Carly's face as she listened to Whitney, the girl with all the boxes checked for "Most." Beautiful. Talented. Congenial. Outgoing. Confident. Intelligent. "Most Likely to Succeed" stamped across her forehead in bold red ink. Both girls were laden with sparkly maroon and silver pom-poms, water bottles, protein bars, duffel bags, and purses that cost more than the rickety green Pinto Ava had bought with her babysitting money when she was sixteen. Ava wrinkled her nose as her daughter finished off the last of her protein bar, crumpling the silver wrapper in her hand and shoving it in the side pocket of her duffel bag. Her daughter used to turn her nose up at them, calling them gross and weird. But since Whitney Dean lived off them, so too must Carly. In fact, Carly was fixated on just about everything to do with Whitney. When she wasn't obsessing about what the girl was saying, doing, eating, or wearing, she was obsessing over her own wardrobe, hair, makeup, complexion, and diet.

Ava's eyes narrowed behind her sunglasses as she watched Whitney's free hand slice through the air as she explained something of clearly vital importance to Carly, given how solemn her daughter looked as she hung on every syllable.

It baffled Ava, this unyielding fascination with Whitney.

Then again, Carly was a puzzle whose pieces Ava was convinced she'd never put together.

She'd never understand Carly, because she'd never *been* like Carly. Endlessly lacking in confidence, no matter how many wins she scored, prone to idol worship and following the crowd. The classic people pleaser.

Nothing at all like Ava. At forty-seven years old, Ava wasn't much different than she'd been at sixteen, because even then, she hadn't really given a shit. She'd always kept her nose clean or as her Aunt Matty would say, stayed on the right side of righteous. Ava was one of those women almost stubbornly free of vanity, inclined toward throwing on what was clean and close, cheap and easy. She dutifully went to the salon every six weeks to trim the wild curls of her mostly dark mane, resisting her stylist's suggestion she color the few sprigs of gray sprouting from her temples, or the wiry strands woven into the back. She washed her face with the Noxzema of her youth and covered it in drugstore makeup. Her bottom teeth were crooked, a slow failure of the braces she'd worn all through junior high. Even though her dentist told her that new technology could permanently fix the problem, she'd decided not to care.

Ava's one acquiescence to vanity were her mind-numbingly expensive clothes, in particular, the rows of designer suits populating her closet, worn not just because that's what was expected of a senior VP at a global consulting firm, but because they were well made and lasted a near lifetime. Because wearing a suit required no mental gymnastics about what matched and what didn't. She didn't have the time or patience to stand in her closet for a half hour each morning dithering about which blouse went with which skirt.

Which made her own daughter's slavishness to such impulses hard to stomach.

Since she came screaming into this world, Caroline Gene Ewing had been a pretty little girl. Very pretty. Large, luminous dark eyes, shiny black hair, button nose, and round, glowing cheeks. Then, geeky adolescence visited with a vengeance, depositing an explosive case of acne, her mother's warped teeth, and frizzy hair in its wake.

Whitney and Carly had been playmates as children, attending the same skating parties, ballet lessons, and tumbling classes. However, once gawky puberty descended, Carly seemingly fell out of Whitney's orbit. It's not that Carly became an outcast—she was well-liked with a good number of friends, if the amount of sleepovers and skating parties she was invited to were any indication. However, pretty, glossy girls flocked together and Carly was no longer considered pretty or glossy.

The next shift came at the start of sophomore year, with geeky adolescence slinking away, leaving behind glowing skin and envy-inducing straight white teeth in its wake (hopefully the braces worked better for Carly than they had for Ava). Whitney and her crew took notice, and Carly was back in, receiving invitations to hang out and engage in incessant, obsessive texting, messaging, and chatting and whatever other forms of non-verbal communication teenagers subjected themselves to these days. Whitney had even encouraged Carly to try out for one of the open slots on the pom squad at the end of last year.

It worried Ava, this hero worship of Whitney Dean. Putting someone like Whitney on a pedestal could be problematic. The truth is, Ava needed to do a better job of keeping on top of Carly, or, do her best to in between jetting to London for weeks at a time and quick overnights to New York.

There were times when Ava wondered if the lifestyle was worth it, if they should have opted for simpler careers, a less pretentious existence. They'd moved to Lake Forest, just north of Chicago, when Jimmy was three, Carly on the way. Ava tamped down her jitters about being one of a handful of Black families in this old money suburb, populated by slender, seventy-something blond-bobbed women with gargantuan gold Rolexes affixed to their knobby wrists, the hems of their skinny white jeans hovering far north of their veiny ankles, cashmere cardigans tossed carelessly across their tanned, freckled shoulders. She allowed herself to get swept up in Kyle's confidence they were doing right by their little family, giving their kids every advantage, allowing them the room to thrive like sunflowers. The kind of posh, idyllic childhood Kyle had enjoyed in the English countryside. The kind of place where mildly paunchy dads piled their sticky-faced children into shiny red wagons and hauled them to town on balmy Saturday afternoons for dripping cones from the local ice cream parlor. The type of town where quartets of teen girls in matching tennis whites and bopping ponytails hogged sidewalks as they stalked toward Starbucks and waiting lattes. The kind of Rockwellian wonderland where an American flag proudly billowing in front of your house was as much of a requirement as a mailbox. Where every corner boasted the tasteful brick facades of financial institutions promising wealth management if you simply came in and said hello.

In Lake Forest, you weren't trying to keep up with the Joneses because you were the Joneses.

Her daughter glanced at her out of the corner of her eye and Whitney turned and started walking, still talking, Carly jogging to keep up with her. Whitney stopped in front of the car, smiled at Ava, and waved. Ava nodded and waved back as the teammates said their good-byes before Whitney caught up with Madison Fowler and Peyton Knowles, also drowning in pom-poms and gear, one blond, one brunette, both still carrying their summer tans, both pretty and shiny, engaged in another conversation, all three ambling toward the student parking lot.

Carly lumbered over to the car and threw her gear into the back seat.

"I told you this morning you didn't have to pick me up," she said. "Madison could have dropped me off after Peyton and Whitney."

"It's no problem," Ava murmured as she scratched her scalp through her curls.

"Can I drive at least?" Carly asked breathlessly.

"That is an excellent idea," Ava said as she unbuckled her seat belt so they could switch places.

Carly smiled and slid behind the wheel, re-positioning the seat and carefully adjusting her mirrors. She had her hand on the gear when she stopped, smiling at something that caught her attention out the window. Ava looked up to see a young guy swinging his briefcase and smoothing down what looked to be a red knit tie as he headed toward the teachers' lot.

"Oh my God, so hot."

"Is that one of your teachers?" Ava asked.

"Mr. Byrne. He teaches American lit and he's super cute."

Ava winced, wondering how big a deal she should make out of this. She'd only ever had one teacher she thought was cute—Coach Lansing, who did double duty as the social studies teacher and assistant football coach. Most of her teachers had been crotchety old women.

"He's a new teacher?"

"Yeah, it's his first year here. I think someone said he used to teach in the city," Carly said, before putting the car into drive and pulling away from the curb. "So, are you going to give me this car when I get my license?"

"Very funny," Ava said, drumming her fingers against her thigh as she watched the traffic.

"Dad gave Jimmy his car when he got his license."

"Dad's car was ten years old. Mine's only two."

"So, that means I'm getting a new car?" Carly smiled.

"Like I said, kid, you're funny. How was practice?"

"We got to learn a new routine today. It was the first one Coach K let Whitney choreograph."

"That's good, right?"

"What?"

"That Whitney got to choreograph."

"Oh, my God, yeah, it's good," Carly said. "It's awesome. She's the best dancer on the team. Her moves are sick."

"Sick. That's also a good thing, right?"

"Mom. Stop. You're beyond embarrassing."

Ava shrugged. "Sorry."

"You remember that her Sweet Sixteen is next Saturday, right?"

Ava adjusted her sunglasses against the late afternoon glare. "Whose—Whitney's?"

"Yeah, Whitney's. Who else would I be talking about?"

"So much to remem—yes, yes, you told me. Whitney Dean's Sweet Sixteen. The social event of the season."

"So, I need to go shopping."

"For what?"

"I don't have anything to wear."

Ava twisted around in her seat, her jaw slightly agape. "Carly, you just dropped three hundred and fifty dollars at the mall for back-to-school clothes. You're telling me you didn't buy something then?"

"Mom." Carly scoffed and rolled her eyes as though she was about to explain a simple concept to a moron. "I can't just buy something at the mall for the Sweet Sixteen party for the most popular girl in school. I gotta come correct."

"Whatever 'correct' you're coming, you better 'correct' it out of your closet."

"Oh my God, Mom—"

"Carly—"

"I'm seriously going to be the only girl there looking like a straight-up hobo."

"You'll live." Ava's phone dinged from her purse and she dug around for it. "What about that red, kind of flouncy dress you wore to Uncle Frank's birthday last year? That's cute. You've only worn it that one time."

"Oh, yeah." Carly made a left-hand turn, the wheel snapping back expertly beneath her hands, now snugly back at ten and two. "I totally forgot about that dress."

"Well, maybe if you didn't have so many clothes crammed in that closet, you could actually see what you have," Ava said, sighing to herself as she scrolled through the chapter-length email from her new boss, a recent transfer from the Dallas office and a raging psycho from what she'd seen so far. Rumor had it she was being groomed for eventual reassignment to Japan. Ava couldn't wait to spring for the kimonos.

"Ugh." Carly smacked her lips. "Not this again."

"Tell you what," Ava said, throwing her phone back in her purse, deciding to deal with the email after her conference call. "You give me the dress tonight, I'll take it with my dry cleaning tomorrow. We'll have it back by the end of the week, plenty of time for the party."

"Awesome. Thanks, Mom."

"So, Whitney Dean's turning sixteen. I guess she's the first to turn sixteen this year, huh?" Ava asked.

"Like, four girls turned sixteen over the summer."

"So hard to keep track," Ava mumbled.

"It's going to be straight fire. They're turning the Palisade House into a nightclub with a red carpet, a photo booth, a step and repeat. It's going to be so cool."

Ava snorted. "God, when I turned sixteen it was in our basement with pink streamers, a fake disco ball, ham salad sandwiches that Granny and my Aunty Judy made, a bowl of Ruffles, and an ice cream cake from Carvel."

"That's pathetic."

"I loved it," Ava said, laughing. "Granny let me charge a dress to her Dayton-Hudson account—pink, my favorite—and some really pretty strappy silver heels to go with it. Uncle Frank played DJ. Bobby Benson gave me my first kiss. One of the best nights of my life."

"That still sounds pathetic."

"While you're over here giving me a hard time, did you manage to remember to buy Whitney a present?" Ava asked.

"They're not doing presents," Carly said, her eyes lighting up as she looked at Ava. "They've asked for donations to Rosie's Club instead. How cool is that?"

"Well, that's a very nice thing the Deans are doing," she said, the irony not at all lost on her. Throw what was likely a million-dollar party for your daughter, but benevolently ask for charitable donations. She wondered whose idea that was. Whitney's probably and Lauren just went along with it. "Rosie's Club can always use any extra help."

"Whitney always does the coolest stuff."

"So, who's going?"

"Everyone. Everyone who's cool, I mean." Carly bit her bottom lip. "Except for Jordan. She's probably not going."

"Why not?" Ava asked.

"She and Whitney had some fight or something. They're not talking."

Carly signaled to turn onto their street, and their house, a comfortable Georgian, came into view. It wasn't grand or sprawling, but a beautiful, warm, and spacious home draped in warm earth tones and outfitted in quality furniture that, much like Ava's wardrobe, lasted forever.

"Huh." Ava scratched her nose. "I thought those two were thick as thieves."

"Whatever happened, it's definitely nuclear." Carly pulled into the driveway and cut the engine. "Level twelve."

"Well, whatever it is, I'm sure it will blow over."

"I don't think so, Mom. I think they're done."

Ava shrugged. "With teenage girls, you never know."

2

ERICA

E rica Mitchell gripped her sweaty palms around the handles of the elliptical, the heart charm of her gold Tiffany bracelet clanging against her wrist. Her gaze drifted down to the white terry cloth towel obscuring the machine's digital keypad. She'd gotten on right as *General Hospital* danced across the flat screen TV on the wall above her, watched on occasion these days out of mild curiosity. Not like when she was growing up, when the goings on in Port Charles and Pine Valley had consumed her. Using her babysitting money to buy soap magazines, reading them like a religion, the covers and pages smudged and wrinkled from her constant handling. In the days before DVR, OnDemand, YouTube, and streaming services. When a VCR was a luxury, not a right. When summer vacation and sick days were the only chances you got to watch your soaps.

She pumped her arms, sweat sluicing down her back as she ticked through her to-do list for tomorrow. Packages to drop off, annual eye and teeth appointments to schedule for everyone, the simple black cocktail dress to alter in anticipation of Jay's holiday gala in December, dry cleaning to pick up, and three client projects that only needed a few tweaks to finish. With time to spare for a two-and-a-half-hour session at the gym. All in a day's work.

She glanced over at the woman who got on the elliptical next to her, a little disappointed it wasn't Lauren Dean. On occasion, she was here in the afternoon and Erica thought she might catch her today. Calling Lauren had been a nagging weed on her to-do list for the past few weeks. Normally, she wouldn't put something like this off so long, but Jay kept telling her to give it time and not to make a big deal out of it. Of course, *he* didn't think it was a big deal. He was a man. Anything that didn't have to do with football or cars was no big deal. A casual run-in at the gym would have made the situation with Lauren a bit more relaxed, a little less awkward than a pointed, deliberate phone call at nine-thirty tomorrow morning, the time Erica designated to cross that item off her to-do list.

Well, the clock was ticking and Erica couldn't wait any longer. Nine-thirty tomorrow morning was D-Day.

The *Jeopardy!* announcer's voice boomed out of the TV and Erica slipped the towel off the machine and around her neck before jamming the down arrow button to decrease the intensity for sixty seconds before hopping onto the treadmill for a brisk power walk through the first commercial. Her cool-down done, Erica wiped down both machines with a handful of antibacterial wipes from the cylinder near the door and took a gulp of water from her bottle, her entire body burning with calories gone. She mopped her face with the towel, not seeing the woman she bumped into.

"Excuse me," she said as she pulled back, pleased to see none other than Lauren Dean staring back at her. Ask, believe, receive.

"Oh. Hi, Erica," Lauren said.

"Well, hello. Gosh, I feel like it's been forever since I've seen you. Not since the end of last school year. How are you?"

"Fine. Busy. You know how it is. How are you?"

"I'm great. How was your summer?"

Lauren, who fit the template of a glamorous suburban real estate agent to an aching, clichéd T, with her streaked blond hair, trim, muscular body and sparkling white teeth, flung her towel over her shoulder and looked around, seemingly distracted. "Oh, you know. Summer."

"I guess you guys must have done a lot of traveling this summer. So did we. You know we went to Singapore and Hong Kong."

"Wow. I'll bet that was amazing."

"Oh, it was. It was. We should have a drink soon and I'll tell you all about it."

"Sure. Of course."

"We also spent a bit of time at the house in Door County. You did such a great job finding that for us."

"I'm glad you're so happy. With the house."

"You know we told Jordan that Whitney was invited to come up for a week or so, but she didn't show." Erica tapped her water bottle. "I guess because you guys were so busy."

"Yeah, we, uh…" Lauren shrugged. "We spent a lot of time in California this summer. Steve's older sister lives in Malibu, so, sun. Surf. You know. The beach."

Erica nodded. "Malibu. How lovely. Really. Really, really lovely."

"Yes," Lauren said. "It was … lovely."

"That's wonderful."

"Well, I should snag a machine." Lauren went to step around her. "It was great to see you—"

"I'm glad I ran into you," Erica said, positioning herself in front of Lauren, blocking the woman's escape. "It actually saves me a phone call."

"Oh?"

"I was looking at my calendar and Whitney's Sweet Sixteen is around the corner."

Lauren pursed her lips. "That's right."

Erica pulled her ponytail holder out of her hair, the damp, honey blond strands falling to the glistening, bronze slopes of her shoulders, courtesy of regular professional spray tans. "Well, Jordan hasn't gotten her invitation yet."

"Um, well—"

"I mean, I'm sure it's an oversight, but I did want to ask you about it." She chuckled. "After all, we've been hearing about this Sweet

Sixteen since the girls were ten. I mean, the way Whitney's been planning it for all these years, it's almost like a wedding."

Lauren clicked her tongue against her teeth. "Yes, I did notice Jordan wasn't on the invite list and I asked Whitney about it—about inviting Jordan to the party—and, well, I guess the girls aren't really getting along at the moment."

Erica smiled. "I'm afraid I don't follow."

"It's just ... you remember how it is at that age. Everything's the end of the world, everything's life or death."

"Okay...?"

"I just think Whitney would be more comfortable if Jordan wasn't there." As the damning words rushed from Lauren's mouth, it was hard to miss the red splotches crawling up the woman's neck.

"So, you're saying Whitney doesn't want Jordan at her party?"

Lauren tucked an imaginary chunk of hair behind her ear. "Yes, that's what Whitney said. Yes."

"Lauren." Erica smiled again, cocking her head to the side. "That's just completely unacceptable."

The crimson exploded across Lauren's face as she attempted to surreptitiously scratch her thigh. "Well, it's Whitney's choice and I try not to interfere in these things."

Erica opened her mouth to speak before moving aside to let someone pass. She sighed, letting her lower lip droop. Time for a different tack.

"It's ... well, Jordan is just devastated. I know the girls have had their troubles lately, but not getting invited to the party? She feels awful."

Lauren frowned and scratched her thigh again. "I don't think Whitney ever intended for that."

"The girls have been friends since the monkey bars and they've always been invited to each other's birthday parties and this is obviously such a special time in a young girl's life." She put her hand across her chest and shook her head. "I mean, we only turn sixteen once and I would just hate for the girls to look back and regret they didn't get to share this experience together."

"Erica, it's really not up to me."

She could see the storm brewing across Lauren's face. Time to go in for the kill.

"Isn't it?"

Lauren blinked. "I'm sorry?"

"As mothers, isn't it up to us to set the example and teach our children that sometimes you have to be the bigger person and take the high road? Isn't that our job? In this case, your job?"

Lauren's chin trembled as Erica's words hit their target. As she knew they would.

"Well, I mean, it's just ..." Her voice trailed off as she bit her bottom lip and nodded. "Of course."

"You and I know in time they won't even remember what they were fighting about."

"We'd love to have Jordan come to the party," Lauren said, squaring her shoulders as though some surprise backbone suddenly slithered up her spine. "It wouldn't be the same without her."

Erica smiled. Mission accomplished. As she knew it would be. She grabbed Lauren's damp hand with her own and squeezed it. "I can't tell you what this means. Jordan will be thrilled."

"I'll drop the invitation by tomorrow. Make it official."

"That's wonderful," Erica said. She straightened up her own shoulders, smiling as she mentally drew a red line through the item on her list. Always have a plan. "Why don't you stop by tomorrow morning. Say around ten?"

"Okay. Yes. Ten. I, I'll see you then."

"Excellent," Erica said. "Have a good workout." She smiled one last time before heading into the women's locker room, the high of her workout and securing Jordan's invitation to the party a double whammy of euphoria.

She hummed to herself as she gathered her things from her locker to head home to shower, smiling as her phone alerted her to an Amazon package waiting for her filled with new versions of her standard wardrobe of skinny black pants and a monochromatic rainbow of black, beige, and gray fitted t-shirts. Erica shunned the ostentatious clothing displays many of the women around here indulged in. There were no designer labels or couture gowns crowding her closets, no towering high heels fighting for prominence in the shoe rack. She didn't need to wear her prosperity, because wealth didn't scream, it whispered. She had other ways of wielding her station in life.

Erica threw her phone back into her purse, her exhilaration about the party warming her insides. Jordan was going to be so excited. She'd wait until she had the invitation in her hand before telling her. It would make for a nice surprise. They'd go shopping this weekend for a dress. There would be hair and makeup to get, manis and pedis. The works. On her way out, Erica glanced at Lauren, having taken her place on the elliptical. Her phone rang and she smiled seeing it was Jay.

"Hello, darling," she said as she switched to Bluetooth in the car. "Ready for your investor dinner tonight?"

"Flight grounded because of weather in Dallas. We'll do it tomorrow, so I'm actually on my way home now."

"Guess what?"

"Chicken butt."

Erica burst out laughing. "You're such a boy sometimes."

"Only sometimes."

Even at fifty-two, Jay Mitchell hadn't quite outgrown being class clown. The hulking, beer guzzling, future frat boy bro who bulldozed his way through high school by balancing bottles of Bud on his head and holding a cigarette in the folds of his forehead. The bull in a china shop who carried whoopie cushions like talismans and thought *Porky's* and *Animal House* were mantras to live by. For teenaged Jay Mitchell, school was a necessary evil between weekend rages and hangovers. Adult Jay Mitchell channeled his fascination with technology into building global software empires many times over, making him one of the wealthiest men in the world. These days, instead of infantile party tricks, he spent his time laughing all the way to the bank.

"Anyway, I saw Lauren at the gym today and … Jordan's in," Erica said.

"In where?"

"What do you mean 'in where'? Whitney's Sweet Sixteen," she said. "Remember, I told you Jordan hadn't been invited, which was ridiculous. I mean, there is absolutely no reason why she shouldn't be going to that party."

"I thought they weren't talking to each other."

"Oh, I'm sure it's just silly teenage girl stuff," Erica said as she hit her turn signal. "I bet you anything they kiss and make up at the party like nothing ever happened."

"I don't think so."

"Well, I do. Lauren's bringing the official invitation over in the morning, so I can surprise Jordan with it tomorrow when she gets home from school."

"You should have stayed out of it."

"Oh…" Erica scoffed and rubbed her eye beneath her sunglasses. "You don't understand. Being snubbed from the biggest event of the year is the kind of thing that can have a major impact on a girl's social life. These things can stick to you like gum to your shoe."

"Jordan's fine," he said. "Stop worrying about her so much."

"But these things can turn on a dime, Jay. One minute, you're best friends with the most popular girl in school, people want to be your friend, people want to be around you and the next minute, you're a freak and everyone turns on you."

"Listen, babe, I know you were 'Most Popular' and homecoming queen and all of that in high school and this kind of stuff is important to you, but Jordan could give a shit. Let it go."

"No." She shook her head. "Trust me, Jordan's going to thank me for this."

"Said the iceberg to the Titanic."

"Now you're just being negative."

He sighed. "All right, just don't say I didn't warn you."

"Don't worry. I know what I'm doing. Now, what do you want me to pick up for dinner?"

3

WHITNEY

W hitney swabbed her mouth with Pink Pow, then applied a dot of Gold Glow gloss to the center of her bottom lip. She'd read somewhere doing that made your lips look sexier in pictures or something. She pressed her lips together several times as she examined her reflection, mock-frowning as she leaned back in her desk chair. She subconsciously arranged her hair over the barely visible dime-sized purple splotch of birthmark high on the back of her neck, and snapped a selfie, her stainless-steel water bottle in front of her. Within seconds of posting the picture to Instagram, it lit up with likes, fluttering hearts, emojis, bitmojis, and comments wanting to know what she was drinking, what lipstick she was wearing, Evan Collins commanding her to hit him up later. She smiled when Peyton's post with a dancing Beyonce gif about how she couldn't wait to see her killer choreography at pom-pom practice next week popped up. She posted a kissing emoji and liked the post. Lexi and Madison liked the post too and her comments were flooded with people saying they couldn't wait to see her moves at the next home game.

As her Spotify playlist droned quietly in the background, she wrote down her volunteer schedule at the public library for next week, excited they were going to let her do two children's story times a month with games and crafts. The kids were so cute the way they called her Miss Whitney. She was still waiting to hear back from the community center about teaching a few dance classes a couple of Saturdays a month. After updating her calendar, she flipped open the spiral-bound choreography notebook adorned with flowers laying on the desk in front of her. She scribbled some notes alongside rudimentary stick figures for the routine she was working on, humming to herself as she went over the moves in her head, excited to show them off at practice tomorrow.

Without even thinking, she stopped, picked up her phone, and pulled up a *#ThrowbackThursday* post from about this time last year of her and Jordan from the night of the eighth-grade dance, with their matching black and white dresses and same curly updo and red nails, one girl brown, one girl peaches and cream. She couldn't help flipping through the mountain of photos she hadn't been able to bring herself to delete. Pictures from pom camp, selfies from hanging out at Jordan's house in Wisconsin, movies they'd seen together, sleepovers, pool parties, the beach. A lifetime of memories.

Whitney's finger hovered over the trashcan icon, wanting so badly to delete Jordan out of her life forever. She'd ripped up everything that reminded her of Jordan: movie and concert stubs, notes passed in class. Even the silver chord friendship bracelet had gone in the trash.

One reminder of that girl had been one too many.

But for whatever reason, she couldn't bring herself to delete the pictures.

As Whitney secured her hair with a yellow ponytail holder, there was a soft knock at her door.

"Is dinner ready?" Whitney asked as her mom entered the room.

"Almost," her mom said, hanging back in the doorway before edging into the room and sitting on the corner of the king-sized bed. "So, how was school? How was practice?"

Whitney wrinkled her nose. Something was up. Her mom's eyes kept ping-ponging around the room and she had a kind of dazed, distracted look on her face. Hopefully she wasn't about to give her a hard time about the pom gear everywhere or why her shoes weren't in the closet or how come the corners of the hot pink duvet were sagging on the floor because Whitney hadn't made the bed. It was so aggravating when her mother hassled her about cleaning her room. It was *her* room. She could do whatever she wanted.

"School, you know, school. Practice was amazing," she said slowly. "And so, remember I told you Coach K and Lizzie were going to let me start choreographing some routines?"

"Yes."

"So, I got to choreograph my very first routine at practice today. Isn't that awesome?"

"That's wonderful, honey. I'm so proud of you."

Whitney nodded, still waiting for whatever bomb her mom was about to drop. "Thanks."

Her mom bit her bottom lip, then smiled. Whitney realized she was holding her breath. It had to be something about the party. Something she wanted that her parents were now saying she couldn't have. Whatever it was, they'd just have to figure it out and make it happen.

"Honey, listen, there's something I need to talk to you about."

"Is this about the party?"

Her mom hesitated. "Yes."

Whitney folded her arms across her chest. "What?"

"I ran into Mrs. Mitchell today."

Whitney shook her head slowly, knowing where this was going. "Don't even say it."

"Listen, Jordan is really upset you didn't invite her and … you girls have been friends your whole lives and—"

"Mom, I already told you under no circumstances is Jordan Mitchell invited to my party. She's totally void."

"Okay, Whitney, I understand you two got into it about something—"

"We will never *ever* be friends again. I am done with her. So done." Whitney grabbed her water bottle, which was full of Gatorade, taking a healthy swig.

"I told Mrs. Mitchell Jordan could come."

Whitney lowered the water bottle, narrowing her eyes. It was on the tip of her tongue to ask if her mother was high. Her parents thought she didn't know that they huddled together in the hot tub in the backyard a few times a month and got completely toasted, giggling and falling all over themselves like wobbly toddlers.

Instead, she asked, "You did what?"

"Whit, listen, it's one night. One party. It's not that big a deal—"

"Are you kidding me?"

"Whitney, calm down."

"I will not calm down. No. No way—"

"Whit—"

"I told you, I'm totally, totally done with her. Like, are you deaf or something?"

Her mother unfolded herself off the bed. "Look, Jordan's invited and that's the end of it."

Whitney threw her water bottle across the room. It exploded against the wall, bright green Gatorade tears weeping down the length of the hot pink and white striped walls.

"How could you do this? I hate you!" Whitney screamed.

"You keep this up, there won't be a party." Her mother cocked her head. "Got it?"

Whitney stood in the middle of the room, her arms still locked across her chest, tears poking the back of her eyes. She wouldn't give her mother the satisfaction and instead, sniffed them back.

"Clean up this mess," her mom said, heading out to the hallway. "Dinner is in ten minutes."

Whitney shook her head, her face pinched in disgust, tears brimming in her eyes as she sat down at her desk and stared at the blank spot on her wall where Jordan used to be.

4

CARLY

Carly twirled in front of the full-length mirror as she examined the flouncy red dress she'd found at the back of the closet her mother suggested—insisted—she wear to Whitney's party. It was a cute dress, even if it was a year old. At least no one at school had ever seen it, so she could totally pass it off as new. Maybe Whitney would also think it was cute.

She took off the dress, and laid it carefully on the full-sized bed before turning on her phone's flashlight. Still in her white cotton bra and panties, she bent over the dress, running her fingers along the soft fabric in search of stray threads, ripped seams, weird stains, or anything out of place. She couldn't afford to have even one tiny little thing wrong with this dress.

Her phone chirped in her hand. Her heart leapt at the text from Whitney. She smiled in spite of herself and took a few deep breaths to calm down before reading it.

W: My mom is a total bitch.

Carly screwed up her face.

C: What happened?

W: She fucking invited Jordan to my party.

Carly chewed her bottom lip, her heart pounding. Jordan? Jordan was going to be there? That would ruin everything.

C: Are you serious? Why would she do that?

She waited, the phone staying agonizingly dark and quiet.

Finally, it pinged.

W: I told you, because she's a bitch. You're so lucky your mom's so cool. She'd never pull any shit like that on you.

Carly wasn't sure what to say to that. It's true, her mom was kind of like the cool mom. Everyone was always saying it. Weirdly gorgeous with her big brown eyes, smooth skin, and snub nose. Okay, she wasn't all the way perfect. The bottom row of her teeth was super crooked and she was missing the tip of one index finger, accidentally cutting it off with a kitchen knife when she was thirteen while slicing potatoes. And she could be all kinds of snarky sometimes. But beyond that, she was funny and awesome. A cool job that required her to travel all around the world. Tall and pretty with a kind of careless chic. More than once in her life, her friends would say she was so lucky to have Ava as her mom.

She weighed her phone in her hand as she contemplated what to say to Whitney. She took a deep breath.

C: Just because your mom invited Jordan doesn't mean she'll come.

Carly chewed on her bottom lip as she waited for a response, growing less confident in her answer as time ticked on. It seemed like a good thing to say. Just because somebody asked you to do something didn't mean you had to do it. Kind of like when her Aunt Benny asked her dad to call their dad more often and he'd always lie and say he would, then wouldn't. Grandpa *was* kind of mean, so Carly totally got why her dad avoided him as much as possible.

But maybe Whitney didn't think that. Maybe she thought it was a stupid thing to say and would tell her so. Maybe she would say she really couldn't believe Carly would say something so completely and utterly moronic.

Her phone pinged.

W: You're totally right. That bitch knows better than to show her face at my party.

Carly's heart stopped its gallop as she read and reread Whitney's text. Everything was okay. They were still cool. She smiled and responded with smiley face and thumbs-up emojis.

W: I gotta jet. Bitch is calling me for dinner. Hit me up later and we'll rip on the new season of Black Mirror. You're all caught up, right?

She groaned. *Black Mirror* was Whitney's favorite show. Like, obsessed. So, when Whitney asked her over the summer if she watched it, gushed about how she totally had to if she wasn't already, she lied and said she'd seen every episode. Whitney was so wrapped up in talking about the show, she didn't notice Carly barely said two words about any of the episodes. Carly promised herself she'd set aside one whole Saturday to binge some episodes.

Except she hated it. Absolutely hated it. A man fucking a pig? People as roaches? Mechanical dogs? It was straight-up bizarre and she could not get into it. Sci-fi was so not her thing and after a few episodes, she gave up. Instead, she skimmed recaps and analysis of different episodes so she'd know enough to make Whitney think she was totally up on it and totally into it. Anything she wasn't sure about, or couldn't remember, she just agreed with Whitney that *yeah, that was so weird* or *no, I totally didn't see that coming either*, or *OMG, how crazy was that?* Truthfully, she'd rather be watching Lifetime movies.

She'd started the lie and now she would have to keep up the pretense.

C: Yeah, totally caught up. I'll text you later.

Whitney sent back a string of dancing bitmojis and Carly grunted. The last thing she wanted to do was waste time texting about *Black Mirror*.

But for Whitney, she would.

It was crazy that she and Whitney had gotten back to being friends. They'd been kind of friends when they were kids. Not super close—Whitney and Jordan had always been besties—but Carly had been invited to sleepovers and birthday parties at the Dean's and Whitney had been to her house many times after school to swim in her pool or do homework.

All the alliances shifted in junior high and as Carly got uglier and geekier, Whitney completely lost interest in being around her, which meant the whole crew did. No one made fun of her or anything like that. She just stopped getting invitations to slumber parties or the mall on the weekends for a slice of pizza and a Coke after getting spritzed with perfume samples at the makeup counters. Carly joined band and French club, while Whitney did cheerleading and pom, being named Queen of the Court every year in junior high to boot. Carly still had friends, but her childhood ties to Whitney Dean were a distant memory.

Then, like magic, right before sophomore year, Carly blossomed. That's what her mom called it. Blossoming. The braces were gone and the acne cleared. She had to settle for blowouts every couple of weeks to tame her naturally curly hair, as her mom wasn't going for any keratin treatments. And Whitney noticed. She'd say hi to her in the hallways, asked her to sit at her table at lunch, invited her to hang out at the mall. At first, it was Whitney, Carly, Jordan, Madison, Peyton, and Lexi, and it was generally understood that Jordan and Whitney were the queens. The rest of them just followed along and did whatever the queens wanted. What Whitney and Jordan said was the law.

Both girls made her nervous, but for different reasons. Whitney, because she was always afraid of saying or doing the wrong thing and she'd realize Carly was still the geeky little baby with pizza skin and frizzy hair, that she wasn't nearly as cool or together as she tried to pretend she was. Because everything about Whitney was perfect, from her clothes to her hair, her teeth, everything. Even her house was amazing, all glass and steel, and modern. Not like her house, which was definitely nice—really, really nice, since her mom believed in buying quality stuff—but it wasn't a showplace like Whitney's house. And her room! The big king-sized bed with the silky hot pink duvet, pink and white striped walls, furry white throw rug, and Chinese lantern chandelier—so cool in comparison to the pale blue walls, plain lamps and beige carpet runner of Carly's bedroom. Everything about Whitney's pretty perfectionism intimidated her.

But Jordan wigged her out for a whole other reason.

She kind of scared her.

Jordan had this edge to her, a hardness that petrified Carly. Moody, sarcastic. What her mother would call a tough cookie. Carly just thought she was a straight-up bitch.

The two had never been close. They were all in the same class, went to all the same birthday parties, play dates, and carpools. And while she and Whitney would hit up the mall or linger over lattes at Coffee City, she and Jordan would never call each other up to hang out. They definitely weren't curling each other's hair or painting each other's toenails. Jordan had never gone off on her or anything like that. They were friendly-ish, but Carly would never say she was Jordan's friend.

And she definitely didn't want to be on her bad side.

Still, Carly had always kind of envied Whitney and Jordan's friendship. Even though Hayley Clayton had been her best friend all through junior high, it just didn't feel like they had the same bond as Jordan and Whitney. She knew they spent every weekend together, shared clandestine lipstick and eye shadow, passed dog-eared copies of *Teen Vogue* back and forth to each other, went out together for cheerleading in elementary school and junior high and pom in high school. They went on double dates, wore matching outfits, and styled their hair in the same bouncy ponytail tied with red ribbon.

And then, something happened over the summer and almost overnight, Whitney Dean and Jordan Mitchell went from BFFs to mortal enemies for eternity. And no one knew why. Neither one of them would talk about it. Jordan was out and Whitney had decided Carly was her new best friend, calling her, confiding in her, asking for her opinion on her shoes or purse or complaining about her mother. It was like a dream come true. Even Hayley seemed to understand when Carly drifted away from her. Who wouldn't want to be Whitney Dean's best friend?

She hoped Jordan and Whitney never became friends again. And if Jordan came to the party, the girls might make up.

And where would that leave her?

Carly's breath quickened and she grabbed her phone, tapping her favorite meditation app, letting her eyes slide closed as she tried to force herself to calm down and stop thinking about Jordan.

5

JORDAN

Jordan Mitchell picked at the dry grilled chicken breast and limp asparagus in front of her. Next to her, her nine-year-old sister, Kennedy, happily dipped her cheeseburger into a pool of ketchup, while her father wolfed down his burritos, and her mother speared a cherry tomato from her side salad and popped it in her mouth. She looked around the table, disgusted as always by her freak show of a family. What in the actual F? Why did they all have to eat something different? Why couldn't they just all eat the same thing for dinner like normal people? Why didn't her mom cook?

Because she refused to cook, as she liked telling whoever would listen. No slaving over a hot stove for Erica Mitchell or worries about menu planning every night or grocery shopping for the week. She took the attitude that everyone should be able to eat whatever they wanted. And her dad? Forget it. He could barely work the microwave. No, this all fell on her mother. So, if her father wanted to feed his beer gut and eat four grande burritos from Taco Bell, then he should eat four grande burritos from Taco Bell. If her sister wanted to have Burger King every fucking night of the week, then she should get to eat a Whopper every fucking night of the week.

Her mother's preference was salad. Literally all day, every day. A fruit salad or Greek yogurt for breakfast, an apple and a handful of almonds for a snack, another salad at lunch, celery with peanut butter in the afternoon, and a salad for dinner. In her entire sixteen years, Jordan hadn't ever seen her eat a piece of chicken or even a wet, nasty sliver of tofu. Just salad. Even at the holidays, the one time of year when everyone gorged on turkey and stuffing, there was her mom in a corner with a sad little pink Tupperware of dry lettuce.

Since she was at least six years old, she'd wondered if maybe she was adopted. Not only because she was nothing like the rest of them, but because of how she looked. She didn't resemble either of her parents—her basically obese father with his fleshy, ruddy cheeks and beady eyes and her ludicrously thin mother and her flat nose, huge hazel eyes, and stout lips. Kennedy looked exactly like their father, except she was also skinny like their mother. But Jordan's gymnast physique, beak nose, high cheekbones, and wide-set eyes were a mystery to her.

"Did you know that the highest point in Africa is Mount Kiliman-jaro?" Kennedy informed them as she dragged a French fry through the puddle of ketchup on her plate.

"Yes," her father said.

"Did you know that the highest point in Asia is Mount Everest?" she said, popping the French fry, now drenched in ketchup, into her mouth.

"Yes."

"Daddy, how come you know everything?" Kennedy asked, laughing.

"Because I'm Daddy." He winked at her before picking up his second burrito and taking a huge bite out of it, grains of rice dribbling from the tortilla, one getting stuck in the corner of his mouth, a smear of refried beans wedged against his chin.

"So, Jordan, I keep meaning to ask if you talked to Coach K about getting back on the pom squad," her mother said as she chewed on a slice of cucumber.

"No."

Her mother set her fork down. "I thought we decided you were going to talk to her?"

"No, you decided. I told you it wasn't happening."

"Why not?"

"I've told you a hundred times, I don't want to do pom anymore."

"Jordan, I just don't understand where this is coming from. You're so good and—"

"Mom, seriously. Stop."

Her mother opened her mouth to say something else and her father shook his head, indicating she shouldn't press the issue. She didn't miss the look that passed between her parents. Jordan had seen this look a lot lately. Her father silently trying to warn her mother to back off. Her mother, looking perplexed, as always, when talking to her these days.

"Did you know that a foot is twelve inches?" Kennedy demanded.

Jordan threw her fork down. "Oh, my God, will you shut up?"

"Jordan," her father said, his voice teetering on an edge she knew all too well—one that meant shut the fuck up. "Enough."

Kennedy stuck her tongue out at Jordan before she took a sip of her milk, humming to herself.

"But weren't you in line to be captain next year?" her mother pressed on, ignoring the little drama that had just taken place. "Doesn't all this time off the squad ruin your chances?"

"I'm not talking about this anymore."

Her mother shifted in her chair. "Okay, but you were up for it, right? Well, I guess she'd have to make you and Whitney co-captains, since you're the two best girls on the squad—"

"Mom, give it a rest."

"Jordan, sweetheart—"

"Why do you always have to do this?"

"Honey, I just want to understa—"

Jordan heaved a sigh and pushed back from the table, picking up her nearly full plate. She hadn't even wanted this dry, stringy chicken and bland asparagus. She'd only made it in defiance, as though she could set some sort of example for her whacked out family to be normal. Her friends thought it was cool that she could eat whatever she wanted for dinner, that she wasn't subjected to meatloaf or casseroles or whatever. She found it mortifying.

Kennedy started reciting multiplication tables and Jordan could hear her father whisper something to her mother as she took her plate into the kitchen, dumping the hardly touched chicken into the garbage. She rinsed off her plate, put it in the dishwasher and went upstairs, glad her dad had intervened and kept her mom from running after her.

Jordan went into her room, a neat, almost utilitarian space of hard black and white furniture with accompanying stark, arty photos on the plain walls. Much like her mother, Jordan preferred order and precision. She closed the door behind her and flopped onto the white comforter spread efficiently across the California king, staring up at the ceiling. She half-expected her mother's timid knock followed by an endless merry-go-round of what was wrong and why won't she talk to her and what could she do and she only wants to help and why wouldn't she let her help and how come she hates her so much?

And on and on and on.

Jordan dug her phone out of her purse, mindlessly scrolling through her Twitter and Instagram accounts. She'd blocked Whitney months ago (though she, weirdly, hadn't done the same), but was still following Peyton, Lexi, and Madison, mostly out of habit, mostly because she had no beef with them, even though they didn't hang out like they used to. She was surprised they still followed her and hadn't blocked her either. Apparently, Queen Whitney hadn't commanded them to do so.

Out of some bizarre voyeuristic she-didn't-even-know-what, Jordan pulled up Whitney's profile, scrolling through her ridiculous, totally unoriginal selfies, her filters and snaps completely stolen from reality TV stars. Even her post from earlier fangirling over the most recent season of *Black Mirror.* Jordan was the one who'd discovered the show and told Whitney all about it. Jordan was the one who'd scoured the web for painstaking dissections of each episode, sending the links to Whitney so the two girls could riff on all the Easter eggs and deeper meanings. Whitney couldn't even be original in the things she liked. She always had to crib from someone else.

And here was Carly Ewing's post congratulating Whitney for the awesome routine she choreographed at pom practice today. All hearts and bitmojis and smiley faces and just … gross. Had Carly always been this much of a kiss ass? Her memories of Carly when they were little were … blank. A white spot. As far as she could remember, Carly existed on the fringe. In the background. Quiet. Begging not to be noticed. A completely unspectacular person. How she made pom was beyond Jordan's comprehension, as the girl was a total void. She must have been a better dancer than Jordan realized. Now, the way she fawned all over Whitney made what little dinner Jordan had in her stomach churn.

Her phone pinged with a new text message.

Speak of the fucking devil.

W: FYI, I dont care what my mom says or ur mom says, u r SO not coming to my party I will have u thrwn out u fucking skank.

Jordan frowned. Party? What was she talking about?

She reread the text a few times until it hit her.

Mom. Her mom had done something.

She jumped off the bed and flung open her bedroom door, screaming for her mother as she flew down the stairs.

"Jordan, what—?"

"Did you say something to Whitney's mom about inviting me to her birthday party?"

Erica's face faltered for a moment as her lips flapped and she trembled. "Well, I, I—"

"You what?" Jordan spat.

"Okay, I did run into Whitney's mother today at the gym and—I just mentioned that I thought it would be nice if you were invited—"

"Oh my God, Mom, just stop. Stop, all right?" Jordan's hands trembled as they pushed chunks of hair behind her ears. "We're not friends anymore. I don't *want* to be friends with Whitney anymore and I do not want to go to her stupid party."

"Jordan, that's enough—"

"Why do you always have to keep butting your nose into things?" Jordan demanded, ignoring her father's warning. "I don't need you hassling me about Whitney or pom or anything. I'm fine. Better than fine. So stop!"

"Hey!" her father yelled and Jordan twitched, realizing she'd edged a little too far over the line. "I don't know where you think you are, but enough!"

"Sorry," she mumbled.

Her mom tried again. "Honey—"

Jordan ran back upstairs before her mother could finish whatever she was about to say. Slamming her bedroom door would have felt great, but she didn't want her father running up here to yell at her either, so she closed it quietly instead. She paced back and forth, heaving, repeatedly winding and unwinding the ponytail holder from her hair as she tried to bring her jagged breathing back to normal. She looked down at her phone on the bed and snatched it up, her blood boiling all over again as she reread Whitney's text. She couldn't let that go. She had to respond.

J: Trust me, bitch, I won't be anywhere near your whack ass party.

W: Whatever. You totally wish you could be there you trash skank

J: Back up off me, bitch ... or did you forget what I know about you????

Silence.

Jordan held her breath, waiting.

W: You wouldn't say anything.

Jordan smiled.

J: Wouldn't I?

6

WHITNEY

W hitney loved walking through the hallway at school each morning.

As she pushed open the heavy metal door, sunglasses still affixed to her face, she saw the looks. They were hard to miss. For just a second, time would stop, sunlight flooding in behind her, the whoosh of air fanning her hair back and, in that moment, everyone would stare, blinded by her appearance. She'd push the shades to the top of her head and smile as she made her way down the hall.

As she sailed past the shiny blue lockers, girls she only sort of knew would say "Hi" and wave. Girls who wished they knew her would either avert their eyes, embarrassed at potentially being caught staring, or give her longing looks. Guys who'd she'd known since the first grade would yell out, "Yo, Whitney." She returned every "Hello," or "'Sup, Whit?" or "Good morning, Miss Dean," (because, even teachers weren't immune) with a smile, a joke, or a "Hey, girl," an "Oh, my God, that dress is so cute," or something flirty for the guys, unless they said something disgusting, which only ever happened once in a while.

Whitney saw her morning walks through the halls of East Lake Forest High School as a pep talk. Kind of like orange juice, her multivitamin, and the antibiotic she took every morning to control her fungal acne. An essential start to her day.

There was no disputing that Whitney was the queen of East Lake Forest—the prettiest, the most popular, the girl everyone flocked to. She was one of seven Black kids in the whole school—Carly included—and even though she was mixed, she, of course, still considered herself to be Black. When she was little, she once over-heard her dad's cuckoo clock sister telling someone Whitney could have easily passed, which sounded weird to her. Passed what? A test? A car on the road? When her father explained what it meant to pass, it made Whitney sad and confused. She couldn't ever imagine denying a part of herself. Her grandparents—or as she thought of them—her mom's parents—lived in Morton Grove and they didn't seem to have any problem denying a part of themselves. The last time she'd seen them, she was seven, some crazy Christmas when they were ranting about children in Africa. In the years since she'd last seen her mother's parents, Whitney's heart would twist a little at ads or commercials she saw with loving, doting grandparents fawning all over their grandkids. They never even sent a birthday card. She thought grandparents got off on that kind of thing. Her mom said the only Black people they knew were either the hired help of their friends or the drug dealers, maids, crackheads, and gangbangers they saw on TV.

Evan Collins yelled out her name, stretching out the syllables as he slammed his locker shut and puckered his lips. She flashed him a smile and flipped her hair over her shoulder, her own locker a few feet away.

At the opposite end of the hall, Jordan rounded the corner and Whitney's smile melted into a scowl. Jordan glanced over, her own glare smearing her face as she reached her locker.

It was weird to hit her locker and Jordan not be there. Ever since middle school, the two would always meet at Whitney's locker at exactly seven thirty. That was the natural order of things. They'd bitch about school, homework, parents, siblings, then shift over to boys they thought were cute, shows they watched, music they listened to. As kids passed them, it was always, "Hey Whitney, hey Jordan," "'Sup Jordan, sup Whitney?" "Jordan, hey, how's it going? What's going on, Whitney?"

Jordan Mitchell and Whitney Dean. The queens of the school.

Whitney snuck another glance over at Jordan.

Now she wanted to bash her fucking face in.

"Hey, Whit."

She turned to see an out-of-breath Carly behind her. Whitney smiled. Carly was so sweet, even if she could be a little annoying sometimes. At least she was loyal.

"Hey, girl."

Whitney looked over again to see Jordan slam her locker shut and her snarl returned.

"What's the matter?" Carly asked. "What's wrong?"

Whitney stacked her chemistry and history books in her locker, glancing at Jordan. "That's what's wrong," she muttered.

"Did you talk to your mom about the party? Is Jordan coming?"

"Yes and no," Whitney said, peering into the mirror affixed to the inside of her locker and running a swipe of gloss across her lips.

"Oh. So, she's not coming?"

"Absolutely not."

"But didn't your mom say—?"

Whitney slammed her locker shut. "I don't care what my mother says."

Carly nodded and clamped her mouth shut as she followed Whitney down the hall toward the American lit class all three girls shared. Beside her, Carly's jaw cranked as she cracked her gum. One of the girl's super annoying habits that Whitney couldn't stand. So aggravating. Beyond irritating. She'd have to talk to her about that.

Of course, she'd take Carly's gum cracking over having to look at the back of Jordan's head for fifty minutes.

"Hey, sorry, I meant to call you last night, but I fell asleep while I was watching *Black Mirror*," Carly said.

"What?"

"*Black Mirror*? Last night. I was going to call you, but I fell asleep. I was rewatching the new season—"

"That's great," she murmured. Whitney bit her bottom lip as they reached the doorway of the classroom. Jordan was scribbling something in her notebook and her heart lurched. Was she writing about her?

Jordan glanced up and the two girls locked eyes briefly. Jordan scoffed and shook her head before turning her attention back to her notebook. Whitney flipped her hair over her shoulder as she sashayed past Jordan and took her seat two rows back and seven seats over. The final bell rang as Carly scooted into the seat next to her and pulled her English notebook out of her bag.

Whitney tuned out as Mr. Byrne started droning on about how everyone should have read the first five chapters of *The Scarlet Letter.* She hadn't, but she wasn't worried about it. She'd be done before the test or paper or whatever. Mr. Byrne then launched into a monologue about imagery or something and right on schedule, Trish Sellers, sitting in the front row, center seat, raised her hand. Every year it was the same with her. Had been since elementary school. Always front row. Hand always first in the air, lips always glued to the teacher's ass.

Mr. Byrne turned to write down what Trish said on the board and she couldn't help but to let her eyes drift down to his ass. It was nice. Hard as a rock from what she could tell beneath the tragic khakis he wore. Maybe he didn't realize he was in Lake Forest now and needed to step it up. At least he had being a stone-cold fox going for him— even if he did dress like a Salvation Army reject, images of him rummaging through the bin for the rumpled slacks, stained tie, and threadbare button-down shirt he wore floating through her mind. From a distance, his creamy bronze skin made him look mixed like her. She wondered if he felt weird about being the only teacher of color on staff. Maybe she'd ask him next time he kept her after class. His muscles hung nicely on his average height, and the tiny mole that disappeared into the cute little dimple on the right side of his face, chiseled cheekbones, close-cropped black hair with the slightest wave, and smooth brown eyes were sweet and sexy all at once.

She twirled the ends of her hair around her index finger, the end of her pen clamped lightly between her teeth as she watched him write down a bunch of mumbo jumbo on the board about character and scene and setting and Puritans and prison doors. Next to her, Carly scribbled in her notebook, dutifully writing down everything he said. Whitney didn't say anything, her eyes flicking between him and Jordan, who was slouched down in her seat, doing slow, bored doodles in her notebook.

"Miss Dean?"

Whitney blinked, not having realized he was talking to her.

"Yes?"

"I asked if you would tell me what you think the prison door represents in the story?"

"I'm sorry?"

Mr. Byrne perched on the corner of his desk, shaking the metal chalk holder in his palm as he watched her. "What do you think the prison door is a metaphor for, particularly as it relates not just to Hester, but society as a whole?"

Her mind groped for something to hold onto, something she could say to dazzle him while simultaneously hiding that she had yet to read the book. She cleared her throat and opened her mouth, hoping something brilliant would come out.

"Well, I think what the ranch, I mean, what the prison door probably really means in the larger context of the book, of the story is—"

Jordan's hand shot up and Mr. Byrne pointed to her. "Hang on a second, Miss Mitchell. Miss Dean was just about to give us her thoughts on the meaning of the prison door to the story."

"I was just going to say, Mr. Byrne," Jordan said, plowing on, "that I think what the prison door represents in the story is the restrictions of this new world that the Puritans are in now. They have to be perfect, like role models almost. It's all about judging other people. And everyone is judging Hester because of what she did, which goes against everything in this new society. And the rosebush is supposed to be the thing of beauty, but it's in front of this super harsh door, which is all about punishment. Which is what Hester is being. Punished."

Mr. Byrne nodded slowly, seemingly impressed. "Very good, Miss Mitchell. The two things are in direct contrast with each other and

Hester is caught in the middle." He got up and scribbled down bits of what Jordan said on the board. He turned around and tapped the chalk in the palm of his hand, his eyes finding Whitney again. "Anything you'd like to add, Miss Dean?"

"No, that was exactly what I was going to say," she said, flipping her hair over her shoulder, her fingers trembling, hoping no one saw the flames of humiliation leaping across her face.

Mr. Byrne turned his attention back to the board as Carly leaned over, lowering her voice. "Her answer wasn't that good. She probably read that online or something. She couldn't even come up with something herself."

Whitney shook her head, fuming as she watched Jordan return to doodling her slow circles in her notebook. "Yeah, probably."

"Since we don't have practice, we can study together after school, if you want," Carly said. "I can catch you up. I'm almost done—"

"I'm fine," Whitney said, louder than she intended. All eyes turned toward her, and Mr. Byrne stopped writing on the chalkboard and looked at her. Jordan smirked.

"What was that, Miss Dean?"

Jordan's sneer ignited something in her. What she wouldn't give to shove that smug bitch's face in the dirt.

The bell rang before she could answer and she made a big show of shoving her notebook into her book bag and slinging it over her shoulder, her face on fire now.

"All right everyone, read the next five chapters by Friday." He paused as he put his chalk down. "Miss Dean? A word?"

Carly gave her a questioning look and Whitney indicated she should wait for her outside. Whitney bit her bottom lip and tilted her head to the side as she approached Mr. Byrne's desk. "My next class is on the other side of campus, so I really can't stay," she said, her voice breathy.

"All right then, after school. Three-thirty sharp."

She smiled. "Yeah, sure. Three-thirty sharp."

"It's very important that you be here," he said. "I can't stress that enough."

"Of course, Mr. Byrne. I wouldn't miss it."

"Good. I'll see you then."

"What was that all about?" Carly asked as Whitney exited the classroom and they fell in with the other students moving by rote through the hallway to their next classes.

Whitney cracked her gum and smiled, about to answer, when she spotted Jordan halfway down the hall, heading toward what Whitney knew was chemistry. Fresh anger tore through her and she ran up behind her, flinging her around by the shoulder.

"What was that, trying to embarrass me like that?" she hissed.

Jordan looked her up and down. "You don't need me for that. Mr. Byrne already knows you're a complete fucking moron."

"Why don't you shut the hell up?"

"What are you going to do about it, bitch?"

Whitney opened her mouth to say something, but was distracted by a nervous-looking Carly sidling up next to her.

"Hey, Whit, we should get to class," she said, tugging on her arm. "We don't want to be late."

Jordan continued standing there, cracking her own wad of gum, a smug smile on her face as Carly gently guided Whitney down the hall toward American history. The sting of tears buzzed behind her eyes. Was she about to cry?

"You okay, Whit?" Carly asked, frowning.

"God, I wish she would go away. I wish I could just get rid of her."

"After school, we could go to Coffee City and hang out for a little while, talk about *The Scarlet Letter*."

"I'll be busy."

"Are you sure? Because it's really not a big deal—"

"I said, I'm busy."

"Are you crying?"

Whitney blinked back the threatened tears, back in control. "Jesus, of course not. I'd never cry over that THOT."

"Is she … I mean, is that…?" Carly asked, her face turning red.

"What?"

"You know." Carly lowered her voice and leaned over to Whitney. "A ho."

Whitney glanced over her shoulder to see Jordan had been swallowed up by the crowd. She pushed her lips into a thin line and stared straight ahead.

"Whatever you do, don't trust Jordan Mitchell with anything. Ever."

7

LAUREN

L auren's SUV whined as it came to a stop in front of the Mitchell's house. House wasn't the word for it really. Mansion, even, seemed to understate it, though castle was perhaps a bridge too far. With eight bedrooms and eight bathrooms, almost nine acres, and close to thirteen thousand square feet, currently worth fifteen million, a massive commission was what it could be. The city condo and Door County cabin she'd sold the Mitchells were tolerable consolation prizes, but if Jay ever put this one up for sale, she'd pucker up and kiss whatever he wanted her to for the listing.

And if she was being shamefully honest, some miniscule part of Lauren had bent to Erica's whim about the party for just that reason. Yes, it was a good lesson for Whitney to learn—sometimes, you had to suck it up—as Steve had said when she called him last night to fill him in on their daughter's predictable meltdown. But … piss off the wife, face the wrath of the husband. Of course, when you were a billionaire like Jay Mitchell, you could get away with it.

Besides, if she really thought it was that big of a deal, she wouldn't be inviting Jordan. It was just a party.

She glanced down at the large purple envelope on the passenger seat next to her and sighed as she picked it up, tapping the sharp point into the index finger of her other hand. Lauren knew she was being over-the-top with Whitney's party. It was because she'd never had a Sweet Sixteen. She'd never had much of anything. Not because her parents couldn't afford to get her the best of everything. The two doctors in a thriving dermatology private practice were loaded. Misers, to be exact, buying the cheapest house they could, wearing the same ratty clothes year after year, driving their deathtrap cars into the ground. It wasn't even that they were saving for something fun, like exotic vacations or unique, crazy experiences like skydiving or parachuting or ziplining like her girlfriend Emmy's family did a few times a year. They just had a literal mental block against spending money. Her father refused to buy a washer or dryer, instead handwashing all the laundry in the bathtub, draping it over dirty lawn chairs in the backyard to dry. He stole condiments packets from fast food restaurants by the pocketful, squeezing the contents into the crusty, decades-old bottles of mayonnaise, ketchup, and mustard he refused to throw away, much less wash once in a while. Her mother stole paper products from public restrooms to avoid buying toilet paper, Kleenex, or rolls of Bounty. She even emptied sanitary dispensers of their cheap tampons and pads. Rinsing off dental floss after she used it and hanging the wet strings over the towel bar was a nightly ritual, changing out the stiff strands once a month.

And that was just the stuff Lauren told people.

She vowed to never be like that in her life, much less with her children. Truthfully, she'd probably gone a little too far in the other direction with indulging her kids. She wanted them to have the best of everything, showering them with designer clothes and shoes, throwing over-the-top birthday parties with Cirque du Soleil performers for Parker's circus-themed bash when he turned six, or turning the backyard into a mini spa for Whitney's fourteenth. Lavish vacations, enrollment in a million different activities through the years, each one seeming to cost more than the last: horseback riding, ice skating, tennis, pageants.

She knew it was too much, but she didn't care. Her kids were good kids. Parker was charming, Whitney an all-around star. Both seemed appreciative of the opportunities they'd been given. Sure, Parker could be a little bratty, but he'd grow out of that. Yes, Whitney could be temperamental and a little snotty at times. However, she hadn't given them any trouble, never falling prey to drugs and alcohol, or running with a bad crowd like Lauren had. She was just confident and let it show. There wasn't anything wrong with that. At times, Lauren thought maybe she could learn a thing or two from her daughter.

She swung her car door open, clearing her throat several times as she made her way up the front steps, accompanied by the insistent chirp of birds and the aggressive mid-morning sun. She eschewed the heavy brass knocker in favor of the doorbell, peering over her shoulder as she waited, twitching a little at the blanket of pink parfait roses draped across the massive, rolling green lawn.

The front door flew open and she was face-to-face with a slightly frazzled, slightly askew Erica. Lauren found herself blanching a bit as she always did at Erica's gaunt appearance. Petite and jittery Erica was as sharp, and thin, and angular as a wire hanger. Constantly clutching at her neck, her hair, her jewelry, her standard uniform of bland fitted t-shirts, cropped, skinny black pants and black suede loafers. In fact, Lauren didn't ever remember seeing Erica wear a color of any shade. Painfully thin body, painfully white teeth, and a strained, clipped way of speaking. Everything about the woman screamed agony.

"Lauren," she said, her voice sounding slightly surprised and distracted. "You're here."

"Yes." She thrust the envelope toward her. "I brought Jordan's invitation to the party."

Erica looked down at it for a moment, something—Lauren wasn't sure what—flickering across her face, before she carefully took the envelope from her.

"Thank you," she said. "Jordan will be so pleased."

"Just one quick thing." Lauren gulped, gesturing toward the envelope. "There's a QR code imprinted on each invitation. Jordan will need to show that at the door in order to be allowed in. You wouldn't believe..." Her voice trailed off, uncomfortable, but grateful she'd stopped herself from ranting against the hangers on who'd petitioned her for weeks and months for an invitation.

"I'll make sure Jordan understands," Erica said, her gaze dropping to the ground before flicking back up just as fast. "Do you have time for a quick coffee?"

"Oh. I—" Lauren wracked her brain for an excuse to get out of this impromptu invitation. She could say she had a showing. The pretext was on the tip of her tongue when something in Erica's eyes stopped her. It was one cup of coffee. She'd drink it fast.

"Sure," she finally said. "I do have to leave no later than ten-fifteen, though. I have a showing at eleven in Highland Park. The Gilbert place." That was only half a lie. She'd closed on that last week and the only thing left was to schedule the demolition the new buyers had requested as a condition of purchase.

"I've got a conference call at ten-thirty, so that's perfect."

Lauren gripped the handle of her red Birkin as she stepped into the foyer, overwhelmed as usual by the opulence of the house, which always smelled of an intoxicating blend of lavender and lemons and something exotic Lauren couldn't quite place. Grand sweeping stair-cases, the banisters gleaming as if they'd been freshly polished that morning, which they probably had been. Venetian glass and imported Italian onyx sparkled across the house like jewels, with Erica's seeming fondness for plush blue velvet couches dominating the living room. Each room dripped in crystal chandeliers, each floor shiny imposing marble, every window stretching floor to ceiling, offering expansive, gasp-inducing views of velvety green grass and the blue sweep of Lake Michigan. The décor, though beautiful, wasn't Lauren's taste, but she could appreciate the money behind its majesty. It wasn't an intimate home, though it wasn't austere and foreboding either, landing in some odd space in between.

She followed Erica into the near commercial size kitchen, outfitted in the requisite stainless-steel appliances and gleaming marble, sliding onto a bar stool as Erica rubbed her eye and blinked several times before she poured steaming cups of coffee for them both.

"Cream, sugar?" she asked.

"A little of each please, thank you," Lauren murmured, watching as Erica tugged at her eye again. "You okay?" she asked.

"Hmm? Oh. Just an eyelash or dirt or something. At any rate, thank you again for bringing the invitation by," Erica said as she placed a bottle of hazelnut creamer, which Lauren hated, and a jar of multicolored sweetener packets down on the counter in front of her.

Lauren poured a little cream into the coffee to be polite and stirred in one packet of raw sugar. "Of course."

"I'm really hoping … well, I think this could be a fresh start for the girls, you know, get their friendship back on track."

"Oh. Well. High school can be a brutal time."

Erica scoffed. "You know I hear people say that and I don't get it. I loved high school."

Lauren tried to avoid wincing at even the tiny mouthful of hazelnut-laced coffee she'd taken. "Really?"

"Oh, yeah. Parties and football games and school trips? So much fun."

"No wonder you have such good memories." Lauren took another tentative sip of her coffee. "I was kind of a stoner."

Erica plunked her mug down on the counter, a few drops of steaming liquid jumping over the lip. "I don't believe it."

She chuckled to herself, wondering what sixteen-year-old Lauren with her ratty, bleached blond mullet courtesy of dollar bottles of peroxide and orange-handled fabric scissors, ripped jeans, rotating supply of concert t-shirts with cut-off sleeves, and scruffy hi-top Reeboks would think of forty-four-year-old Lauren. Forty-four-year-old Lauren and her obviously expensive blond highlights streaking strategically through even blonder hair. French tipped acrylics. Bright white veneers. Couture her constant companion. The coveted red-soled pumps. Tanned. Toned. And a Black former football jock for a husband and two biracial children to boot.

Sixteen-year-old Lauren would probably shrug her shoulders before taking another drag on her joint.

"I was I guess what you'd call stoner-lite. I wasn't a pothead— well, maybe a little bit of one. Okay, maybe a lot of one. I basically lived under the bleachers smoking and drinking every day. Gettin' high, the latest Crüe album, and my boyfriend were about the only things I was thinking about in high school."

"I never would have guessed," Erica said.

"Well, with any luck, none of us are the same now as we were in high school." Lauren looked at her watch and took another tiny slurp of coffee, her mouth itching for one of the Altoids in her purse in order to banish the hazelnut taste. "I'm sorry, but I really do need to get going."

"Of course." Erica slid off the stool. "Let me walk you out."

The two women made their way to the foyer. Lauren opened the door before turning toward Erica.

"Thanks for the coffee and ... tell Jordan we're looking forward to seeing her next Saturday."

"I will," Erica said. "And thank you."

Lauren grabbed her car keys from her purse and slid behind the wheel, her shoulders loosening a little as she started the engine. She was a lot less apprehensive about this whole situation after talking to Erica. As a mother, she could even see the situation a little from her side. It was a hard pill to swallow thinking your child is being left out of something, especially when it comes to her oldest friend. She couldn't say she wouldn't have done the same thing if the situation was reversed.

She popped a mint as she headed toward Green Bay Road, the lump of stone that had been sitting in her throat since yesterday at the gym dissolving. This would be okay. There were over two hundred people expected, a crush of people surrounding Whitney with love and light. Jordan could be a little on the bitchy side, God knows, but she wasn't a troublemaker.

Lauren smiled, relaxed.

It was going to be a great party.

8

RON

R on Byrne hoped the sigh of relief he felt as the last bell of the day sounded wasn't audible as twenty-six bored juniors fled his classroom, not thinking about the fact they'd have to do it all over again tomorrow, only glad they were done for today. He quickly erased the blackboard and refilled his chalk holder with a fresh stick, before sitting at his desk to wait for Whitney as he wrote out his notes for tomorrow's classes while he thumbed through his well-worn copy of *The Scarlet Letter.* He should really get a new one, having carted this around since his undergrad days at Michigan. Better still, maybe he'd finally jump on the e-book craze and make that his first purchase, a copy forever free from aging. However, this musty, dog-eared, disintegrating, pencil-scarred paperback was like an old friend. He wasn't ready to give it up.

Four o'clock came and went with no sign of Whitney. He continued glancing up at the clock as the minutes ticked past, annoyed by her no-show. Thirty more minutes passed as he finished up with his notes and did a quick check of his school email on his phone, before gingerly placing the book in his briefcase and straightening up the papers on his desk. He took a quick look around to make sure he hadn't forgotten anything before flipping off the light and closing the door.

The halls were empty as he made his way to the office to check his box for any messages. He nodded at a few teachers leaving for the day who only offered tight, polite smiles in return. Things certainly were different here in the suburbs. At least at this school. Back in the city, as the new guy, he would have already been to half a dozen happy hours and been taken under a flock of wings as the old timers showed him the ropes.

But not here. This was a quiet and dignified school, less prone to raucous happy hours, more inclined toward rushing home to husbands and wives and bottles of Merlot and wheels of Brie.

Still, he was grateful for the job. The fresh start. He hadn't expected he would get one. Not after the brutality of the last two years.

Ron shook his head to wipe away the nightmare of the past couple of years. He wondered if there would ever come a day when it wasn't with him every minute, every second.

Probably not.

The stout, dark-haired school secretary with the fuzzy, dime-sized mole on her cheek waved and said *"Hola"* as he entered the office and they chatted in Spanish for a few minutes before he grabbed his mail and told her to have a good night. That they were both Latino was probably why she bothered. Granted, he was only half, courtesy of his Puerto Rican mother, his European side owing to his Irish-Italian father, but he didn't care. He was happy to have at least one ally at East Lake Forest High School. Even after coming in during the last two weeks of the previous school year, the other teachers still hadn't exactly been warm and welcoming to him. It wasn't his fault that the first-year teacher he replaced had finally snapped and quit by walking out in the middle of fourth period, never to return.

Ron smiled to himself as the warmth of the fading afternoon sun washed over him and he made his way to his dilapidated, salt-stained black Corolla, surrounded by a trough of luxury brand name cars—the proverbial weed in the garden. He wondered if the teachers snickered behind his back as they mused about who on earth would drive this blight. Someone who couldn't afford anything else. At least for now.

He threw his briefcase into the passenger side of his car, relieved when it started right up. These days, it was a guessing game. He rotated his head around to relieve the knots in his shoulders and rolled the window down to compensate for the busted air conditioning. Winter would arrive in due time, so he'd suffer with his hot box of a car until the spring, when he could hopefully afford to get the AC fixed.

He made a quick stop at the grocery store, loading his little red basket with a loaf of bread, peanut butter, package of deli meat, a box of pasta, and tomato sauce, deciding at the last minute to splurge on a pint of Häagen-Dazs Chocolate Chip Cookie Dough and a bottle of Shiraz. A night of vegging out on the couch for a few hours while binge-watching *Black Mirror* was calling. Thank goodness his brother let him use the password.

When he pulled into his apartment complex, there was an empty spot right in front of his unit. He gathered up his briefcase and small bags of groceries, thoughts of the wine and ice cream sliding down his throat making him shiver in anticipation as he climbed the steps to his apartment. He juggled his keys as he fumbled to get the door open.

"Hey, baby."

Ron gasped and turned to find her standing there. Right in front of him. The bags and briefcase slid out of his hands to the ground, the bottle of wine shattering as it smashed into the concrete.

"What the—" He hustled her inside, hoping no one had seen her before scrambling to gather up his briefcase and the sopping plastic bag of wine and glass. He slammed the door behind him, dropping everything to the floor.

"I was going to come by after school, but—" She jumped on him, smothering him in kisses. Like fire. "I thought this would be better."

"Jesus … you can't be here," he panted, trying to pry her groping octopus arms from his body, wanting so badly to give in, knowing he couldn't.

"Oh, come on. This is better, right?" she moaned, that tight, lithe body squirming against him, her Bubblemint gum and strawberry shampoo driving him to distraction.

Ron grabbed her and slammed her against the wall, rattling the cheap frames of the pictures, staring at her. Her bottom lip quivered, her eyes drowsy half-slits. Everything in him wanted to throw her down and bang her until the sun came up, melt into those silky legs, bury himself in all that soft, sweet, wild hair of hers. God, how bad did he want that.

No. It was wrong. All of it. He had to be the adult. He had to be the one in control.

He straightened up and sighed, his head hanging down. "Go home."

"Come on, *Ronaldo*—"

"Don't call me that."

"You know you love it when I call you that."

"Look … go home. This has to stop. Do you understand?"

"But I love you, baby, I can't—"

He dug into his pocket for his phone. "Do you want me to call your father? Huh? Have him come and get you?"

"Don't," she said, grabbing for his phone, which he held out of her reach. "You wouldn't."

"I'm giving you three seconds to turn around and go home and don't come back," he said, surprised and proud of the control in his voice. "Or, I will call your father."

She folded her arms across her chest, pouting. "Fine. I'll leave. For now."

She blew him a kiss before opening his door, careful to avoid the puddle of purple wine pooling on the concrete. She slammed the door shut and for several moments, all he could do was stand staring at it as he waited for the storm inside of him to die down.

9

CARLY

"Hold still, Whitney."

"Mom, stop. Let the woman do her job."

Carly looked between Whitney and Mrs. Dean as the seamstress gathered a few inches of the glittery material of Whitney's party dress at the waist and tugged at it. "You've lost a little weight since the last fitting, yeah?"

"She only eats protein bars," Mrs. Dean said apologetically to the seamstress. "I try to get her to eat some actual food—"

"You can totally take this in, right, so that I don't look like a cow? And have it back in plenty of time for the party?" Whitney asked as she preened atop the wobbly platform stationed in front of the bank of mirrors outside of the small fitting area.

"This is no problem," the seamstress, a rotund Polish woman with short, curly red hair, said. "I take new measurements, we do right away."

"Okay, Carly, tell me honestly, how do I look?" Whitney asked.

"It's beautiful, Whit, really. Every girl is going to be so jealous."

"Good." Whitney turned back to look at herself in the mirror. "Mission accomplished."

Whitney and the seamstress continued to chatter on while Carly turned her attention back to her phone. She'd been shocked when Whitney asked this morning if she wanted to come to the final fitting for her dress. Whitney had been so snarky with her yesterday after the whole confrontation with Jordan, and then claiming to be too busy to hang out after school, and not texting her at all. Whitney was secretive sometimes. Like a locked diary. It scared and worried Carly how Whitney would clam up. Carly had stressed out all night she truly was on the outs with Whitney this time. Whitney hadn't shown the dress to anybody, wanting to wow everyone when she made her grand entrance on Saturday night. And now Carly was getting her own sneak peek. The dress, which Whitney designed herself, was based on somebody's Oscar dress from a few years ago. Carly had no idea who, since she didn't really keep up with award shows or things like that. But the dress was gorgeous. Whitney looked like a princess—a queen. Carly wondered how it was possible to be that perfect and still be so nice.

Carly snuck a peek over at Mrs. Dean, her own concentration on her phone seemingly unbreakable. If her mom was the cool mom, Whitney's mom was like the movie star mom. She was a big-time real estate agent—practically anybody who was anybody in Lake Forest or Highland Park had bought their house from her. Where her mom had this kind of effortless style, this, 'I just threw on these skinny jeans and random Tory Burch top and look like I walked out of a magazine,' Mrs. Dean actually put in serious effort to look glamorous. She always wore expensive suits, lots of perfume, and high heels. Even her jeans and casual tops were elegant. Always a strand of pearls, chip-free nails, and red lipstick that never faded. Her blond hair always shiny and smooth, like she went to the salon every morning for a fresh blowout. Adding to her allure were the glimpses of tattoos Carly had spied over the years: an infinity symbol on her wrist, a small coiled snake on her shoulder, the tiny butterfly at the base of her neck. All of it made her even cooler.

"It was really nice of you to come with Whitney today, Carly," Mrs. Dean said as she tapped the screen of her phone, the tip of one acrylic clacking against the screen.

She shrugged. "No problem, Mrs. Dean. The dress is beautiful."

"I just hope the seamstress gets it done in time."

"She seemed pretty confident."

"So, how's your mom? I haven't seen her in forever."

"She's okay," Carly said. "She's out of town right now. I mean, again. Always."

"Tell her once all of this party chaos is over, I'll reach out to her so we can grab dinner."

Carly nodded. "Sure, yeah, okay."

Mrs. Dean looked up and smiled at her. "I'm so glad you and Whitney have been spending more time together lately."

"Yeah, it's been pretty cool," Carly said. "Pom squad's been a lot of fun. Whitney is such a good dancer. I'm learning so much from her."

"Well, that's wonderful. I'm happy to hear it's worked out with you being on the squad." Mrs. Dean flipped her hair over her shoulder. "I guess you took Jordan's spot, then?"

"No, I tried out at the end of last year. Jordan was still on the squad. She only quit right before school started."

"Oh, that's right, that's right." Mrs. Dean fingered the long strand of pearls around her neck. "So hard to keep track sometimes."

Carly laughed. "You sound like my mom."

Mrs. Dean chuckled. "Yes, trying to keep up with all the comings and goings can be exhausting. At any rate, it's good for Whitney to expand her circle while she and Jordan are taking a little bit of a break. All relationships need a little breathing room."

Carly's heart fluttered. "What do you mean?"

Mrs. Dean gave a careless wave of her hand. "Just that whatever is going on with those two will blow over sooner rather than later."

"Oh ... you think they'll make up?"

"I do, I do. I went through something like this with my best friend during my junior year. We had this huge fight over a guy and didn't talk for six months. Then, we ran into each other at Sam Goody one Saturday and picked up right where we left off, like no time had passed. We're still best friends to this day. And I can't even remember the guy's name."

Mrs. Dean's words were like a dagger through Carly's heart. Her mom had said the same thing the other day, but her mom was always saying weird stuff like that. Coming from Mrs. Dean, though, that was different. It made it feel real, as though Whitney and Jordan making up could actually happen.

The seamstress slung her blue tape measure around her neck and scribbled some more in her notebook. "Okay, we get measurements, we fix super quick, you have beautiful dress in time for party."

"Nadia, thank you so much," Mrs. Dean said. "I know the dress is going to be perfect."

"It's no problem."

Whitney stepped off the dais and headed toward the dressing room. "Mom, come help me with the pins and everything with the dress."

"Excuse me, Carly," Mrs. Dean said as she rose to head back to the dressing room with Whitney.

Carly's heart continued to slam across her chest, Mrs. Dean's words reverberating in her ears. Whitney and Jordan becoming friends again would suck. It would absolutely suck. She didn't want Jordan around. At all. It would ruin everything. Besides being a little afraid of her, she didn't want to give Whitney up and that's what Jordan coming back into Whitney's life would amount to. No more hanging out at the mall on the weekends, no more texting each other fifty times a day, or lattes at Coffee City.

No more Whitney and Carly. Carlney. Whitley.

"Hey, Carly."

She looked up to see Dionne Cruise standing in front of her, her long red hair fluttering behind her, the wedge of makeup she wore only sort of covering the blanket of freckles across her face. She smiled at Carly, a sliver of peach lip gloss slashing one tooth. A bundle of clothes sheathed in plastic sleeves slung over the crook of both arms. Dionne Cruise. The biggest gossip in school. The last person you wanted to be alone with. Ever.

"Hey," she said as Dionne took Mrs. Dean's seat. "What's up?"

"My mom sent me over here to pick up some of her tailoring. What are you doing here?"

"Whitney wanted to show me her dress for her Sweet Sixteen," Carly said, straightening up in her chair, throwing her shoulders back. "She wanted my opinion on it."

"Oh my God, is it the sickest thing ever?" Dionne asked, her eyes wide.

"So sick."

"Okay, okay, okay, tell me exactly what it looks like."

"I can't do that. You'll just have to wait to see it like everyone else," Carly said, smugness lacing her words.

"This is going to be the party of the year." Dionne squealed. "I'm so stoked."

Carly still didn't understand how Dionne scored an invite. Maybe Whitney wanted it spread around school to anyone who wasn't there how awesome it was.

"Yeah," Carly said. "It's going to be pretty amazing. Totally surreal."

"So, you will never guess what I heard about Jordan."

Carly squirmed in her seat. "What?"

Dionne tossed her hair over her shoulder, before glancing around quickly, her gaze swiveling back to Carly. "I heard her mom totally cornered Mrs. Dean at the gym and demanded that she invite Jordan."

"Who told you that?"

"My cousin works there, she heard the whole thing. Anyway, so is Jordan going?"

"I don't think so."

"Ugh. Could you imagine?" Dionne smacked her lips. "It would be beyond ridic for her to be there."

"Yeah, that would be pretty crazy."

"You totally know what happened with them, don't you?"

Carly opened her mouth, intending to say she had no idea.

Instead, she saw an opportunity. A way to solve the potential problem of Jordan and Whitney patching up their friendship.

And Dionne's big mouth was going to help her.

She cleared her throat and leaned over. "I think it had something to do with a guy. Maybe."

Dionne's eyes lit up. "Seriously?"

"I mean, don't quote me on this or anything, but Whitney told me Jordan's a skank and a THOT and not to trust her." She wasn't telling an actual lie. That's really what Whitney said. She just didn't have all the details. Carly shrugged nonchalantly, her heart racing. "That's all I know."

"Whoa." Dionne leaned back and Carly could see her wheels turning. "I'll bet that's exactly what happened. Jordan totally hooked up with someone Whitney was going out with."

Carly stayed silent. The less she said, the better.

"I'm trying to figure out who it was." Dionne turned to her. "Who was it?"

"That's all I know." She lowered her voice to deliver the boom. "But don't say anything, since like I said, I don't know much."

"Carly, seriously. You can totally trust me." Dionne pinched her thumb and forefinger together and drew it across her lips. "Sealed. Totally."

"Cool."

"I gotta bounce." Dionne stood, adjusting the batch of clothes in her arms. "See you at school tomorrow."

"Yeah. See you."

Dionne winked and left the shop just as Whitney's voice floated out from the dressing room. Carly quickly picked up her phone and started scrolling, hoping she looked casual as everyone came out, the seamstress with the dress draped over her arm and Whitney back in her skinny jeans and Free People print top.

"Mom, Carly and I are going to walk over to Coffee City," Whitney said. "We've got some pom stuff to talk about. We'll split an Uber home."

"All right, be careful. Dinner's at six-thirty," Mrs. Dean said as she came over and planted a kiss on Whitney's cheek, then smiled at Carly. "Thank you for coming today."

"No problem," Carly said, beaming.

Mrs. Dean took her keys out of her purse. "Okay, girls, have fun," she said before she breezed out of the shop.

Whitney linked arms with Carly as they followed behind. "I am so excited about my party, I can't stand it. It's going to be perfect."

"Yeah. So on fleek," Carly said, thinking about Dionne, hoping she'd given her enough ammunition to keep Jordan far, far away from Whitney.

10

JORDAN

Jordan tapped her nail against her MacBook as she reread what she'd just written for her American history essay. It wasn't actually due for another few weeks, but she was trying to get ahead on a few things. It was amazing how much time she had now that she was no longer on pom squad. It was an added bonus that when she got home after school, her mom was out meeting with a client, her dad was still at work, her sister at soccer practice, meaning she had the house to herself, something that almost never happened. She'd propped her feet up on the coffee table, which would have driven her mother nuts, and binged three episodes of Kimmy Schmidt while scarfing half a bag of pita chips and hummus, which also would have made her mother crazy. She couldn't wait to have her own place. She'd do stuff like this all the time. Just sit back and check out for a few hours.

Actually, it was amazing how much time she had in general since her friendship with Whitney had ended. She never realized how wrapped up they had been in each other's lives, spending all their time talking, texting, messaging, giving each other breathless updates on the most tedious of details minute by minute. For so many years, that unending connection had felt like a lifeline, a natural extension of herself.

It was funny that they'd even been best friends at all, since they were so different from each other. Whitney was sparkly. Social. A people person. She cared what people thought about her, so her whole vibe was about striving to be the best, the most, the top. She thrived on attention and people sure did love giving it to her. People gravitated to Whitney because she portrayed sweetness and light, like a bottomless bottle of frothy bubbles.

That's not why people wanted to be in Jordan's orbit. They loved her sarcasm and endless bag of one-liners. Unlike Whitney, she didn't care if people liked her or not, which made her even cooler, because she gave zero fucks. Her father always said she was one cigarette and a leather jacket away from being James Dean, whoever that was.

Despite the polarity in their personalities, Whitney and Jordan had balanced each other out, becoming a one-two punch in popularity, from elementary school onward. Two peas in a pod, who giggled endlessly over their many inside jokes and had each other's back. They'd planned to attend college somewhere on the East Coast and be roomies. They were supposed to be best friends forever. At least that had been Jordan's plan.

Which made the bullshit Whitney pulled on her over the summer all the more stunning. Worse, Whitney hadn't thought it was that big a deal—had laughed about it and told Jordan to grow up and stop acting like a baby.

If Whitney had only apologized, told her it was a stupid mistake, that she was sorry, that she hadn't been thinking, Jordan would have forgiven her.

But she couldn't—or wouldn't.

So, Jordan had to walk away.

And it broke her heart.

She picked up her phone and finished archiving her text messages for the day on the secret cloud account she had. When Jordan was eleven, she'd caught her mom looking through her diary. It had made her furious, especially when she didn't even apologize, saying that as her mother, she had a right to know what was going on in her life. It was beyond humiliating. Not that there was anything in it—mostly about boys she thought were cute, or how much she hated when it was fish stick day at school. It didn't matter. Her privacy had been breached, so Jordan threw the diary in the trash. The following year, when she got her own phone, she'd gotten in the habit of deleting her text messages, only leaving anything she wasn't worried about her mother seeing. When she found out she could archive them, she started doing that every night. There were just no lines her mother wouldn't cross to poke around in Jordan's life.

There was a timid knock on her door. Jordan rolled her eyes. Her mother's knock, which meant peace was shattered and she was home. She quickly exited out of her account.

"What?"

The door creaked open and sure enough, her mother was peering around it. "Honey, do you have a minute?"

"No," Jordan said, her eyes never leaving her computer screen.

"I have a surprise for you," she said.

"I said I was busy."

Her mother came over and stood next to the desk, barely able to keep from smiling. "It's important."

Jordan heaved a sigh and leaned back in her desk chair, arms crossed. "What?"

Her mother thrust a large purple envelope in her face, the smile no longer contained. Jordan's heart sank. She knew exactly what this was.

"Mrs. Dean came over yesterday morning to drop this off and she said they'd love to have you at Whitney's Sweet Sixteen." She beamed. "See? It's official now."

Jordan stared at her mother, her jaw hanging open in disbelief. "Are you kidding me?"

"I know, I know, there's not a lot of time, but I can take you shopping tomorrow after school and—"

She shot out of her chair until she was face-to-face with her mother. "Seriously, what part of leave it alone, give it a rest, *stop,* do you not understand?"

"Jordan—"

"Why can't you let this go?"

Her mother sighed. "All right obviously you're too worked up right now to appreciate what a really nice thing Mrs. Dean did for you. What *I* did for you. Why are you so ungrateful?"

"I never asked you to do this!" she screamed as she went to step around her mother. "I'm not going."

"I'm so disappointed in you, Jordan." Her mother's voice wobbled and tears ran down her face. "When did you become such a spoiled brat?"

"Why are you always butting into everything?"

"All right, you know what? Your father is at his dinner tonight," her mom said, digging her phone out of her pants pocket, holding it up. "You want me to interrupt him so he can talk to you?"

The image of the blistering vein on her father's forehead and creeping red stain on his neck whenever he got angry flashed across her mind. And it wouldn't just be being pissed about the interrupted dinner, though that was enough to make the lava erupt with roaring fury. If there was one thing they all knew, it was that you didn't mess with her father's business.

It was about her mother. He always took her mom's side. Always. He'd stand in the middle of that restaurant and rip her a new one. Then, he'd come barreling through the door when he got home to scream at her some more—even if it meant waking her up—to yell at her about treating her mother with respect, no matter what asinine, nosy thing she did. His blind devotion to her mother's lunacy pissed her off almost as much as her mother's lunacy.

She folded her arms across her chest and looked away. "No."

Her mother cocked her head to the side as she shoved the phone back in her pocket. "I didn't think so."

Jordan clucked her tongue against her teeth, venom burning inside her. Tears threatened to slip out of her eyes, but she held them in. Sometimes, she hated her mother so much.

"Well?" her mother asked.

"Well, what?"

"Are you going to apologize?"

Jordan exhaled, pinching her face together to keep the tears in. "I'm sorry for yelling."

"Good. I accept your apology." Her mother stood in the doorway for a few more seconds before slamming the door behind her.

She flopped down on the bed, her breath roiling in her chest as the tears exploded. She pushed her face into her pillow, the wetness soaking into the pale white cotton.

Across the room, her phone dinged with a new tweet. She looked up at the ceiling, debating about whether she even wanted to deal with Twitter or anything right now. Turning out the light and crying herself to sleep seemed like a better idea.

A flurry of pings bombarded her phone, so she swung her legs over the side of the bed and stumbled toward her phone on the desk next to her laptop.

Hey, @itsJordanBaby Who'd you bang?

Her heart jumped, her eyes narrowing.

@itsJordanBaby - Ho

@itsJordanBaby - Trash

@itsJordanBaby - Skank

@itsJordanBaby THOTTHOTTHOTTHOTTHOT

@itsJordanBaby will sleep with your man. Watch. Your. Back.

She jabbed at the screen, stunned as she scrolled through the barrage of garbage clogging her Twitter feed. Tweet after tweet. Because of pom, she had been required to keep her account private and had never gotten around to changing the setting. So, she knew these handles.

She knew every last one of these bitches.

And she knew who the head bitch was.

Her phone continued to ping as she threw it down, her breath coming in short, heavy spurts as she paced the length of her room. She undid her ponytail holder, running her hands through her hair repeatedly. She had warned Whitney, had made it clear she couldn't start stuff and not have it come back on her.

And now this. Like she was taunting her, daring her to do something about it.

Jordan snatched up her phone, finger hovering over the screen to fire off a series of angry, seething text messages, to let Whitney know her time was up.

Her gaze landed on the sparkly purple envelope her mother had just delivered. Jordan sniffed as she picked it up, tracing the embossed silver letters. She'd already told Whitney not to mess with her. She didn't need any more warnings.

It was time to teach her a lesson.

11

CARLY

Carly scrolled through her Twitter feed, lit up with Jordan's handle and all kinds of super nasty things. She had to give Dionne credit. The girl worked fast. There was no way Jordan would want anything to do with Whitney now. She'd be mortified. Totally humiliated. Maybe it would get so bad, she'd have to transfer to another school or her family would have to move.

No, Whitney and Jordan definitely wouldn't be making up.

As long as no one found out she'd been the one to turn Dionne loose, she'd be fine. Totally fine. She didn't do anything. Not really. Dionne was the one with the big mouth.

Carly bit her thumbnail, her whole body shaking. If Dionne got the chance to throw her under the bus to save herself, she'd do it in a heartbeat. Everyone would be mad at her. *She'd* be the one in trouble.

But she didn't tell Dionne to go blab all over social media. She'd barely said anything. And technically, she hadn't lied. Whitney had said Jordan was a skank and that she couldn't be trusted. She was simply repeating what she'd heard. Dionne jumped to her own conclusions.

That would have to be her story. Dionne totally got confused about what she was saying. So, really, this would still be Dionne's fault.

Everything would be fine.

Her phone dinged.

W: WTH?

C: This is sooooooo crazy!! What happened??

W: No clue.

C: Hav u heard frm Jordan?

W: Not yet. But I will. Trust that.

C: U think so?

W: Of course I will cuz she'll think it ws me.

C: But you didn't do anything.

W: Jesus, like that will stop her. Seriously, think.

Carly bit her lip and swallowed hard. The last slot she wanted to occupy in her life was next to Jordan on Whitney's shit list.

C: Totes just thought of this ... maybe she'll die from humiliation and then you'll never have to see her again.

W: I wish.

Carly's breath eased out of her slowly like a tire hissing air. Everything was good. They were still tight.

She responded with a laughing emoji and waited a few minutes before Whitney texted back to say she was wiped and going to bed and would talk to her in the morning. She couldn't help herself. She went back on Twitter to see Jordan's feed had virtually exploded with endless variations of "ho," "skank," "thot," and "trash."

And Jordan hadn't responded to a single tweet.

Carly slowly put on her pajamas, her heartbeat thundering in her chest as she kept an eye on her phone. As she crawled into bed, she continued scrolling through Twitter until she fell asleep and her phone thudded to the floor below.

12

ERICA

Erica grabbed her coffee mug with both hands, taking a slow sip. The fight with Jordan kept her alternating between crying and tossing and turning throughout the night. Jay slipped his arms around her, holding her close, whispering soothing words into her ear before she drifted into a light, troubled sleep around three. She finally pushed herself out of bed at five, sitting glumly in her office and staring out the window, watching the sun swallow the mist of early morning, Jordan's fury repeatedly slicing into her like a million little paper cuts.

She'd been so disappointed when Jordan told her last year she didn't want to do a Sweet Sixteen party. At first, Erica thought she didn't want the competition with Whitney, even though Jordan's birthday was in August, Whitney's in September. Turns out, she didn't want to do anything, opting instead for a movie and dinner at Old Orchard with two friends whose names Erica had never even heard before. Jordan had allowed the family to give her a small cake and candles beforehand, and had, of course, accepted the gift of the brand-new BMW, though she grumbled the whole time before slamming out of the house to meet the two mystery girls.

She really hoped Whitney's party would be a turning point back to her old self. Jordan had always been spirited. Feisty. Funny, no-BS

Jordan, a one girl Greek chorus who called it like she saw it. Erica could do without the surly, put-upon creature who had moved in over the summer, the one who snapped and snarled at the wind blowing the wrong way. She'd even quit the pom squad before school started, saying she wasn't into it anymore, which Erica could not comprehend. Jordan was a phenomenal dancer. Powerful and athletic with a flair for the dramatic, she executed every move with flawless precision and played to the crowd like a natural. Coupled with Whitney's natural grace and poise, they would have made for formidable co-captains their senior year.

Until this past summer. Whispers of a falling out echoed across the Mitchell house and suddenly the lifelong friends were mortal enemies. She didn't think it had anything to do with a boy, though she supposed it was possible. It could have even been something as stupid as fighting over who wore a lipstick when. A borrowed sweater. An overblown social media slight. Teenage girls were trivial and melodramatic that way. Whatever it was, Whitney was persona non grata in the Mitchell household. No more parties, sleepovers, hanging out, texting, or phone calls—nothing. Every time Erica attempted to ask her daughter about it, an explosion of sound and fury detonated, followed by stomps and slammed doors. At times, it was frightening, this flip in her daughter's personality. Jordan had always been a confident girl, verging on cocky at times, but never mean. These days, however, she was venomous. Erica could only hope her fits of rage were due to the unfortunate condition of being sixteen and saddled with the world.

Kennedy's soft, yet insistent footsteps sounded on the stairs before she padded into the kitchen, dressed for school, humming quietly to herself as she parked herself at the kitchen table.

"Cereal, please," she said, beaming, her hands folded in front of her.

Erica cocked her head. "You know, Kennedy, I've seen you feed yourself cereal a hundred times. I have every faith you can make it a hundred and one."

Kennedy gave her a solemn look before bursting into laughter.

"Gotcha!" she yelled, before sliding from her chair and heading for the pantry and the cereal.

"Your smoothie is in the fridge, sweetie," Erica said as Jay lumbered down the stairs behind her, the clean, crisp spice of his after-shave racing into the room ahead of him. He leaned down, nuzzling her neck.

"How are you feeling, sweetheart?"

"Terrible."

He kissed the top of her head before coming around to stand in front of her. "Try not to let it bother you. You were only doing some-thing nice for your daughter. Nobody can fault you for that."

She scoffed. "Jordan can."

"Don't worry about her. One day, this won't even matter."

"Jordan's a terrible, terrible daughter," Kennedy said solemnly as she resumed her spot at the table, her blue glass bowl teeming with Cheerios. "Just terrible."

"Hey!" Jay snapped. "You be nice to your sister."

Kennedy shrugged, unfazed as she lifted a spoonful of cereal to her lips. "Well, she is."

Erica stopped herself from agreeing with her youngest, instead resting her forehead against Jay's shoulder, pressing against him like the life preserver he often was. They both turned at the sound of Jordan shuffling into the kitchen, a sheepish look on her wan face, dark crescents of her own sleepless night beneath red, droopy eyes. Erica cleared her throat and looked down into her coffee mug while Jay poured himself a cup, as Kennedy continued eating her cereal, not even acknowledging her sister's appearance.

"Good morning," he said.

"Good morning." Jordan set her book bag down onto the empty bar chair next to Erica before reaching into the refrigerator for a blueberry Greek yogurt and a bottle of water. She plucked a banana out of the green glass bowl on the counter. Erica resumed sipping her coffee, the tension stretching across the room like a rubber band bound to snap loose at any minute.

"Did you know that the Great Pyramid of Giza is located in Egypt?" Kennedy asked.

"Did you know the most annoying sister in the world is named Kennedy Mitchell?" Jordan spat.

Jay slammed his hand against the kitchen counter, causing the sisters to jump in unison. "Hey! Both of you, shut up!"

Both girls complied and for several moments, the only sounds in the room were the insistent clank of Kennedy's spoon against her cereal bowl, the slurp of Jay and Erica's coffee, and Jordan's quiet chewing of her banana.

"I'm sorry about last night, Mom," Jordan finally murmured as she picked at the foil flap on the yogurt, her eyes pinned to the table.

Erica's insides melted, runny as ice cream at this more sincere apology as she looked over at her oldest child, the child she'd desperately wanted for so many years, the child she thought would be denied her. Wordlessly, she set her coffee mug on the counter and pulled Jordan into a bear hug. Tears of happiness pricked her eyes as she inhaled the Juicy Couture perfume lining the folds of her daughter's neck and strawberry shampoo woven through her hair.

"Oh, honey." Erica leaned back, cupping her daughter's face in her hands. "Thank you. That means so much."

"So, so, sorry, Jordan," Kennedy chirped as she carried her bowl to the sink. "Jordan is so sorry."

"Shut up," Jordan hissed as Kennedy stuck out her tongue.

"Kennedy, wait in the car for me," Jay said. "Now."

The little girl giggled then kissed Erica's cheek before picking up her bag and running outside, slamming the door behind her.

Jordan pursed her lips and took a deep breath before resuming. "I was thinking, and you're right. You and Mrs. Dean did a really nice thing and … I should go and celebrate with Whitney."

Erica gasped and turned to Jay, who smiled and winked at her as he took a sip of coffee. She pulled Jordan back into her arms, hugging her tightly. "Sweetie, I'm so glad to hear that. Listen, we'll go shopping this afternoon and I'll make you an appointment with Delia at the salon and she can do something extra special with your hair and makeup."

"I thought I'd wear the dress you bought me for my birthday a few months ago." Jordan smiled. "I haven't had a chance to wear it yet and since it's for a special occasion, I thought this would be perfect."

"Oh, honey, I think that's wonderful. Just wonderful." Erica beamed. "And we could get manis and pedis and go to lunch after. How does that sound?"

"That all sounds great, Mom." Jordan slung her book bag over her shoulder. "I should get going. Don't want to be late."

Jay came over and kissed Jordan on her forehead. She smiled before hugging Erica and heading out the door.

"Can't say I saw that one coming," Jay said as he finished the last of his coffee.

"I told you I knew what I was doing," Erica said, wiping a tear away with her fingers.

"Maybe now we can get some peace around here," he joked, pulling her into another quick kiss. "I was starting to think I'd have to move."

"No such luck, sailor," she said, patting his shoulder as she hopped off the bar stool. "You're stuck with us."

"Apparently," he said, leaning down to kiss her goodbye before he slammed out of the house to take Kennedy to school before his trek into the city. Erica couldn't keep the smile off her face as she finished cleaning the kitchen and throwing in a load of laundry before heading into her office at nine on the dot. There was so much to do. Call the salon to make the appointment, a reservation for a light lunch at The Gallery, and of course, their mani/pedis.

She couldn't wait.

13

JORDAN

Jordan adjusted her sunglasses as she slammed the door of her cherry red BMW. A warm breeze rippled through the filmy material of her black and white striped shirt dress. She cracked her gum as she made her way to the main building, ignoring the titter of whispers as she approached. Trish Sellers, who she totally couldn't stand because of how fake she was, who actually still braided her brown hair into short pigtails, thinking it ironic somehow, was chatting animatedly with her crew, stopping when she saw Jordan, before bursting into a suppressed giggle and leaning over to whisper something to Dionne Cruise, who also started laughing. The hairs on Jordan's neck stood up and she came close to stopping, ready to whirl around and go off.

But she kept going. She had a mission to complete.

The furtive whispers, sneaky glances, and embarrassed laughs continued as she stalked down the hallway toward her target. Not one person said hello to her, not one person said good morning. They just stared and whispered and laughed.

Whitney and her little minion, Carly, stood in front of Whitney's locker, their heads bent together, frantic whispers passing between them. Whitney's eyes went wide once she saw Jordan approach and she straightened up. Jordan could feel everyone around them hold their breath as they waited for the inevitable showdown between the two girls.

She cleared her throat and reached into her book bag. She could see Whitney tense and she wanted to laugh. Did she think she was going to pull a gun or knife on her or something?

"Happy birthday, Whitney," she said, handing her the pink envelope she'd picked up at Walgreens before school.

Whitney exhaled and everyone else seemed to do the same, although they couldn't take their eyes off the two, ready and waiting for it to pop off.

"Really," Whitney narrowed her eyes. "You shouldn't have."

Jordan smiled sweetly. "It was no trouble. Believe me. I want you to have this."

Whitney handed the card back. "No, thanks. I'm not accepting any presents for my birthday."

Jordan shoved her hands in her pocket as she leaned closer to Whitney and lowered her voice. "Hope you enjoy your little party tomorrow night."

"You fucking nasty skank—"

"Come on, girl," Jordan said, getting in Whitney's face. "You got something to say to me now? Huh? Huh?"

"Get out of my face."

"Jordan, you should totally roll out of here," Carly said.

Her head whipped around at the squeaking sound of that mouse, Carly. "Excuse me?"

"I'm just saying, you should back up," Carly said, before taking a noticeable gulp and shrinking away a little. "Don't start any trouble."

Jordan laughed. "Wow, the thirst is so real." She turned her attention back to Whitney. "So now you've got this little kiss ass doing all your dirty work, huh?"

Whitney rolled her eyes. "Please, bitch, nobody's worried about you."

"Keep talking shit, bitch, keep talking." Jordan pointed her finger in Whitney's face. "I will fuck your shit up and you know it."

Some of the color drained from Whitney's face. "You better keep your finger out of my face," Whitney said, backing up a little, her voice sounding a little less confident.

"What are you gonna do, huh? Huh? Spread some more lies about me, huh? Talk some more shit about me on Twitter?"

"I didn't say anything about you, bitch." Whitney smiled. "But if it walks like a duck and acts like a duck, it's a ho."

"What's going on here, ladies?"

Everyone stopped and turned at the sound of Mr. Byrne's voice from the doorway of the classroom, his hands on his hips, brow furrowed. The crowd scattered, a few of them filing into the classroom. Whitney and Jordan scowled at each other, while Carly's gaze fluttered around everywhere but on the two girls.

"Come on, everyone, let's get to class." Mr. Byrne clapped his hands together twice rapidly.

Jordan glared at Whitney as she slowly backed away from her.

14

WHITNEY

Whitney's father, a former college football player, always said pros played hurt. Coach K said the same thing. Whitney had never felt it more than tonight during the game against St. Edwards as she did her best to perform the routines she'd been practicing diligently for weeks, to get lost in the frenetic roar of the crowd and the insistent brassy boom of the marching band's fight songs, as she frantically tried to scrub Jordan from her mind.

But she was always there, waiting to lower the boom over her head, waiting to ruin her life.

She should have played it cool with Jordan that morning. She should have stayed calm and let that girl look like the lunatic instead of taunting her, calling her a ho, since that was only going to make her more mad. She had to admit though, she kind of liked seeing Jordan get trashed all over Twitter. After the way she'd treated her over the summer, she had it coming.

But the other part of her was scared, because now Jordan was all riled up, which meant she was coming after her. The match had been lit and it was only a matter of time before everything exploded.

She had to figure out a way to stop her.

Whitney still couldn't believe how screwed up everything was.

Junior year was supposed to be her year of years. She was turning sixteen, getting the car of her dreams. She was practically a shoe-in for pom captain next year. She and her mom had been planning her Sweet Sixteen since she was twelve and it was going to be *the* event of the year. She was starting to think about colleges. She and Jordan had planned to go somewhere on the East Coast, where she'd always figured she'd meet a cute boy from some super rich, old money family who'd take her to Cape Cod on the weekends or something and eventually, put a big rock on her finger that came from his ninety-year-old grandmother's safe.

Everything was supposed to be golden.

And then one mistake, one stupid, stupid mistake. Actually two. First, doing what she did and two, telling Jordan, who'd been holding it over her head since. Every. Fucking. Day.

To her, it hadn't been that big a thing. But she also knew if it got out, she'd be in major trouble. With everyone. Honestly, she figured Jordan would be the one to back her up by agreeing it really wasn't that big a deal.

Instead, she turned on her. A complete and total one-eighty. Instead of being her girl, her ride or die—like Whitney would have done if the roles were reversed—she said she didn't want to be her friend anymore, told her how disgusting she was. And just like that, Jordan was out of her life. She quit pom, requested a new locker on the other side of school so they no longer had adjoining lockers like they'd had since junior high, blocked her on social media, and stopped calling and texting her. Whitney had been stunned, the knife of betrayal twisting in her gut every time she thought about Jordan icing her out. There were times she still couldn't believe it.

Jordan had never threatened to tell anyone what she'd done and Whitney didn't think she would. She couldn't hate her *that* much.

And then everything with the party and their mothers. And now suddenly, the one thing Whitney stupidly believed Jordan would never do—betray her—was exactly what was about to happen. Her best friend in the whole world was threatening to blow her out of the water.

Jordan was going to tell everyone what she'd done and totally ruin her life.

From the corner of her eye, Whitney spotted Mr. Byrne walking down the bleachers, a Coke in one hand, a red and white striped box of popcorn in the other, his long-sleeved navy and white striped polo and cargo shorts so much better looking than the rags he wore to class every day. She knew she was in trouble with him, that he was super mad at her, but she wasn't too worried about it. The next time he kept her after class, she'd calm things down. She could sweet-talk her way out of just about anything with anyone.

"You okay, Whit?" Carly asked for at least the tenth time in the last five minutes.

God. She'd been asking her that all damn day.

"I'm fine."

"I wanted to ask you something." Carly looked over her shoulder, lowering her voice. "What was Jordan talking about earlier?"

"What?"

"This morning, by class. What did she mean when she said she was going to fuck your shit up. Was she … was she threatening you?"

"Forget about it," Whitney said.

"What did she mean?" Carly pressed.

"Okay, you're getting really fucking weird. Just shut up, all right?"

Carly shrank away from her and for a moment, Whitney thought she was going to cry. She rolled her eyes and looked away, not feeling all that sorry about knocking the girl down a peg. She could be so fucking annoying sometimes.

"I—I just wanted to say I've got your back, Whit. I'll always have your back."

Whitney sighed and looked back over at Carly, a twinge of regret replacing her irritation. "Thanks," she murmured.

"I'm so psyched for tomorrow night," Carly said. "Seriously, it's going to be the best night ever."

"Yeah. Totally."

"And I wouldn't worry about Jordan." Carly's leg jiggled. "I bet she won't have the nerve to show up tomorrow night."

"Yeah."

Carly sighed, playing with the glittery plastic strings of her pom-poms. "Listen … if Jordan has something, or thinks she has something on you … maybe I can help."

Whitney scoffed. "Can you make her go away?"

"What?"

"Nothing." Whitney shook her head, turning her attention back to the game. They'd just tied the score and the entire stadium was on its feet, thundering with elation. They were going for the field goal and as the kicker's foot smashed into the ball, sending it sailing into the air, for just a moment, she pictured Jordan's face on the receiving end of her own vicious kick.

15

RON

I t had started innocently enough, as these things usually do.

She was a marvel of a student, the kind he wished he could have been, the kind he puzzled over every year when he got one. Often (always) unprepared in class. Incessantly attempting to bullshit him when she didn't know something. Monotone answers to his queries about the text he'd assigned. Endless bored doodles in a notebook or folder. A sheen of tedium coating her skin, draped across her eyes. Several times he'd held her after class to admonish her for her flat-footedness. She'd smile, laugh, tell him he was right, she should take her studies more seriously. And then the next day, she'd be back to scribbling in her notebook during class, popping her gum, giving stuttering, nonsensical answers to his questions. And yet, the one paper and two tests he'd given were near perfect. Crisp analysis, insightful observations, inspired use of quotes and passages from the text. It was like two different girls. The one droopy with boredom during class. The other, an underrated source of literary and academic brilliance who could have held her own with graduate students in the upper echelons of the finest universities.

It occurred to him she might be cheating. She had to be. That she'd purchased tests and papers. Of course. He'd be stupid to think otherwise. So, he'd done his due diligence and checked all the usual suspects and then some for evidence of plagiarism and had found none.

It seemed she was just that good.

It made him squirm to realize that it heightened her appeal.

That she was gorgeous didn't hurt. He'd have to have been blind not to notice the glossy dark hair and the careless tosses of those smooth strands over her shoulder every few minutes, the light catching a silky swell. The doe eyes outlined by long, luscious lashes. The full lips, always sparkling with something pink and shiny. The strawberry shampoo wafting over to him whenever she entered the classroom.

Forging a relationship with a student had never crossed his mind. Ever.

But she was hard to ignore.

And then, *that night*. He and a few buddies at a local restaurant, one of those with arcade games and pool tables. She stumbling in with her friend, another student. It was all laughs and OMGs (the girls) when they realized they were running into each other outside of school. Comfortably uncomfortable. The game of pool in the back room, everyone laughing, shooting, sipping beers (his friends), and pop (his two students). During a quiet moment, she asked him about his ethnicity, fascinated by the combination of Irish and Puerto Rican. He teased her about deceiving him with her disinterest in class. She laughed, twisting one of those dark strands of hair around the tip of her finger. Purring that she was full of surprises.

The horror at realizing they were flirting.

And yet against his better judgment, he didn't stop.

Nor did he stop when they were pressed against each other in the tiny hallway between the bathrooms, out of sight of everyone, advancing hesitant and tender at first and later, aggressive and needy kisses toward each other.

He didn't stop her from giving him her phone number.

He didn't stop himself from calling her.

He didn't stop himself from meeting her on the beach that night.

He didn't stop any of it. Ever.

Mistake after mistake after mistake.

16

AVA

A va tapped her tablet to turn the page on the book she was reading and took a long swig of her papaya, banana, kiwi, kale, and cucumber smoothie as she glanced at the time. Every few minutes, the jaws of the gym café's monster blenders pulverizing fruits and vegetables drowned out the clank of weight machines and muffled hip-hop from the cardio class upstairs. She'd had her pick of tables after her early morning circuit training class and to sit by herself, uninterrupted with her book club book and a smoothie—a rare occurrence in her world—was akin to a mini-vacation. She'd have to leave soon, as it wouldn't be long before the café was overrun with the late morning Saturday crowd in search of wheatgrass shots and fresh-squeezed green juices. Ava still needed a minute before she went home to face the madness of Whitney Dean Turns Sixteen.

The whole thing was driving her nuts, as if she was the one with the daughter at the center of the biggest party of the century, which considering Carly and Whitney were glued together these days, may as well have been the case. Carly's anxiety over the looming event was all-consuming, threatening over the last couple of days to gobble her whole. Yesterday morning before school, she dove headfirst into the tailspin, crying that the red dress wasn't good enough after all, her shoes were stupid, in between moaning about the seeming emergence of what she predicted would be a monster pimple on her chin. The tirade continued when she got home from the game last night. Nothing was right, Whitney would hate her for looking so hideous, her life was over. A befuddled Kyle could only stand in the kitchen, feeble offerings of strawberry ice cream the only weapon in his arsenal, muttering to Ava it had always worked when she was six. Ava rolled her eyes at Kyle and behind Carly's back, dispensing mildly weary assurances that the party would be great and she should concentrate on having fun.

In the light of day this morning, the dress was gorgeous, the shoes were amazing, and the overnight dab of toothpaste had obliterated the looming pimple. She would make Whitney proud.

Ava glanced at the clock again. Fifteen more minutes of enjoying her book and smoothie before heading home to greet one of the Three Faces of Carly. Hopefully, Excited Carly would be the one waiting for her.

"Ava?"

At the sound of her name, Ava looked up from her tablet and groaned inwardly at the sight of Erica Mitchell wielding a fresh smoothie as she approached her table. Erica was nice and Ava got along with her well enough. However, she didn't necessarily view her as a girlfriend. Friendly, but not friends. Erica was not someone she'd call up for a random Thursday happy hour or an afternoon of shopping followed by apps and margaritas. It was the trying too hard, the 'like me, like me,' vibe Erica radiated at times, that irritated Ava.

Qualities, she hated to admit, her own daughter displayed on occasion.

She plastered on a smile and stood. "Erica, hi. How are you?"

"Look at you hiding back here," Erica said as they did the dual cheek kiss. "I'm good. You?"

"I've been traveling like a demon the past few weeks." Ava sat back down, purposely not inviting Erica to take the seat across from her, mildly annoyed when she did anyway. "Leaving again on Monday to head to New York for two days," Ava said. "Did you take a class today?"

"Oh, no, I always do the treadmill and the elliptical. I had to cut it short, though, since it's an absolutely insane day."

Ava chewed on a seed from her smoothie. The last thing Erica needed was to burn any calories. As her mother would say, the woman was thinner than half a stick. "What's going on?"

"Well, Whitney's party tonight," Erica said, traces of smug indignation spiking her words. "Carly was invited, wasn't she?"

"The social event of the season? Yes, trust me, it's all Carly's talked about."

"We've got so much to do to get Jordan ready for tonight. Hair, nails, the whole thing." Erica drummed her own short nude nails on the side of her smoothie cup, which Ava couldn't help notice she had yet to take a sip from. "So, Carly's definitely going?"

"Hmm? Oh, yeah, she'll be there." Ava nodded, hoping her look of confusion and surprise didn't show. She could have sworn Carly told her Jordan was persona non grata from the party. Of course, that was a week ago, a lifetime in teenage years. "She wouldn't miss it."

"Well, that's just wonderful. It's so nice the girls get to share this moment. You only turn sixteen once. Thirty-five is another matter." Erica winked and laughed. "And I'm assuming Carly's got a whole look planned for tonight?"

"Actually, Lauren is springing for some of the girls to get blowouts and all of that later today, so kind of like you, I snuck over here for an early cardio class before the craziness begins."

Erica's face fell momentarily, resurrected almost as quickly. "That's so nice of Lauren to treat some of the girls to an afternoon of pampering. So nice. I'm guessing it's Lexi, Peyton, Madison, the usual crew?"

"Honestly, I have no idea. Probably."

"Oh, well, that would make sense, of course. All of those girls were always joined at the hip, weren't they?"

"Personally, I thought it was a bit much, this whole mini spa day, but Lauren really wanted to do it and Carly's excited about it, so I'm staying out of it." Ava fingered the straw of her smoothie and rolled her eyes. "So glad I'm not sixteen anymore."

Erica finally took a barely perceptible sip of her light pink smoothie. "I don't know, it's kind of exciting, remembering what it was like."

"I was telling Carly the other day my Sweet Sixteen was way different than this production. In my basement with a Carvel cake, my brother on the turntable, and a kiss from Bobby Benson at the end of the night."

Erica laughed. "Well, yes, that would be pretty hard to beat. Now, I didn't have anything like what Whitney's doing, either, but I had a big party at the country club, huge cake, tons of presents. No Bobby Benson, but there was a shiny new pink Carmen Ghia with a big red bow outside."

"So much for me and Bobby Benson."

"I suppose you know Jordan and Whitney have been on the outs recently," Erica said.

Ava winced inwardly as she shook her smoothie cup before taking a hearty sip. Erica always was one for gossipy asides, even if it was about her own daughter.

"Carly had mentioned something, but didn't know what it was about," she said.

"Neither do I. Something ridiculous, I'm sure. Anyway, tonight is the perfect opportunity to put all this silliness behind them and get back to being best girlfriends. There's nothing like a party to bring people together. Especially best friends."

"I'm sure it will all work out."

"Well, it's just nonsense. I mean, the girls have been like sisters for all these years and then to all of a sudden say she isn't invited to your Sweet Sixteen over what I'm sure was something trivial." Erica shook her head. "Do you know I had to make a direct appeal to Lauren to get Jordan on the list?"

Ava choked on her smoothie, mortified for Jordan. She couldn't see any scenario where she'd ever finagle a party invitation of all things for Carly. It wasn't that serious.

"Are you okay?" Erica asked.

She coughed and nodded. "Yeah, just uh … went down the wrong pipe. Did you say you asked Lauren to invite Jordan?"

"You bet I did. I had to."

Ava coughed again. "I hadn't heard that." She made a mental note to get a happy hour on the books with Lauren ASAP for the scoop.

"You know how it is in high school. One girl doesn't like you, then everyone stops liking you. Especially the most popular girl in school." Erica shuddered. "Now I've got to work on getting her back on the pom squad."

"What uh—" Ava coughed again then cleared her throat. "What made Jordan decide to quit?"

Erica scoffed. "Oh, I don't know. Again, I'm sure it was something ridiculous. Anyway, I'm going to have a talk with Coach K, see if we can't get all of this straightened out. She's far too talented and worked way too hard to just give it up."

"I have to say, Jordan has always struck me as someone who has the courage of her convictions." *Like mother like daughter.*

"High school is just so much easier when you fit in." Erica jiggled the heart charm on her bracelet, seemingly agitated. "Unless you're popular, then it doesn't matter."

"Well, listen, you and I both know one day, none of this will matter. I mean, all the shit that meant so much in high school, when you get to be our age, nobody even cares."

Erica smiled. "Except at their age, everyone cares."

Ava glanced at the clock on her tablet. Time to wrap this up. She flipped the cover over the screen and put it in her gym bag. "I'm sure all the girls will have a great time."

"They will. I know they will." Erica clapped her hands together. "I can't wait to see the pictures."

"I should get going." Ava stood. "I told Carly I'd drop her at the salon by eleven and if I'm even thirty seconds late, she'll have a melt-down and God knows there's been enough of those this week."

"Oh, don't I know the feeling," Erica said, laughing as she stood up. "I'll walk out with you. Jordan and I have to be at the nail salon by eleven ourselves."

"Don't forget your smoothie." Ava gestured to the practically untouched pink concoction sweating on the table.

Erica gave a careless wave of her hand. "It wasn't that good anyway," she said, leaning over to pick it up before tossing it in the trash. "Besides, I'm too nervous to eat. Oh! Before I forget, when are you back next week?"

Ava's heart raced, knowing where this was going. Erica was always extending invitations to drinks and lunches and dinners and Ava always found a way to wiggle out of it, hoping Erica would take the hint, but in all these years, no dice. At times, she had succumbed out of guilt, usually managing to corral one or two of the other moms into going too so it would be a festive group outing versus an uncomfortable and grating one-on-one. "Late on Wednesday."

"Why don't we grab a drink when you get back, download on the festivities?"

Ava's phone chirped from the bottom of her purse as they walked out the front door, saving her from having to put forth a lame excuse. She smiled at Kyle's face on the screen.

"Oh, it's Kyle. Probably wondering when I'm coming to rescue him."

"Of course, of course. I'll text you about a drink next week?"

"Sure, yeah, that sounds great," Ava said, acquiescing. Maybe it wouldn't be so bad. This little run-in hadn't been the end of the world. "Let's figure out something."

"Great." Erica smiled and mouthed 'goodbye' before heading to her car parked close to the entrance.

"I'm leaving now, English," Ava answered, her nickname for her husband, a nod to his British ancestry. "I'll be home soon."

"Right, because she might be speaking in tongues."

"Why, what's happening?"

"Hell if I know. She's talking a mile a minute about blowouts and CD Nails and Greek prints and it's all gone to pot and now I've got a bloody headache."

Ava got behind the wheel and put the phone on Bluetooth as she started the car. "Speaking of headaches, I just ran into Erica Mitchell."

"Nice one."

"Get this. She made Lauren invite Jordan to the party."

"It's that serious then?"

"No, it's not that serious," Ava said as she backed out of her space, watching Erica's car exit the parking lot. "I shouldn't be surprised, though. It's exactly the kind of thing she'd do."

"Well, you've always thought she was a bit dodgy."

"I need to text Lauren when I'm back in town and get the lowdown. Unbelievable." Ava adjusted her sunglasses and shook her head. "I mean, it's a fucking birthday party. Who cares?"

17

CARLY

This party was the sickest thing Carly had ever seen.

When they pulled up to the Palisade House in the stretch limo Mrs. Dean got for them, the eight photographers she'd hired were lined up along the red carpet, cameras poised for a barrage of pictures. Two searchlights stamped *#WhitneyDeans16* against the inky purple sky. One by one, the girls exited the car, flashbulbs popping, blinding them temporarily as they posed and waved to the small cluster of kids crowded around the entrance, who cheered their arrival as they waited for the main attraction. Whitney was the last one out and as soon as she emerged, everyone went crazy, screaming her name and whistling. Carly had even seen one girl crying. Whitney smiled and waved and blew kisses as she sauntered solo down the red carpet, stopping at the step and repeat to turn and twirl for both the cameras and the adoring crowd. The five of them posed for pictures as a group and at one point, Whitney pulled Carly over for photos of just the two of them. The gesture pricked tears of happiness.

Once inside, her jaw dropped at the transformation of the Palisade. The light boxes, Lucite dance floor jammed with kids, wall drapes, five-feet-tall flower arrangements bursting from every corner, tables overflowing with filet sliders, truffle fries, chicken skewers, meats, cheese, fruits and veggies, waiters passing by with trays of wontons and sushi rolls stuffed with lobster and caviar. Carly knew there would be a sweets table later and they'd roll out the multi-tiered birthday cake with pink frosting—Whitney's favorite color—at the end of the night.

It was beyond bananas.

Carly had lost count of how many songs they'd danced to. They were smack in the middle of the dance floor, the disco ball twirling overhead, the music pumping, and colored lights exploding seemingly every thirty seconds. The DJ did not disappoint, spinning out jam after jam after jam. She was a little hungry and wanted to load up on the sliders and truffle fries. She'd wait until Whitney was ready to eat, even though it didn't seem like she planned to slow down anytime soon.

As a result of staying rooted to the dance floor, she didn't see Jordan right away. One minute, they were all dancing, singing, having a great time. The next, whispers detonated around the room as people noticed Jordan, the tight aquamarine dress hitting her mid-thigh, her long black hair done up in a genie ponytail, Kendra Scott drop earrings bouncing against her ears.

Carly gulped as Jordan made her way around the room, seeming to survey it, but not saying anything. She winked at a few people and smiled at a few others, though nobody smiled or winked back. She glanced over at a fuming Whitney, her own heart racing. Jordan headed for the food table, filling her plate with two sliders, a mushroom puff, and a handful of truffle fries, before grabbing a Whit-tini—cranberry juice, lime juice, simple syrup, and crushed raspberries—from one of the trays moving past her. She stood next to the table, staring at Whitney while she nibbled on her food and sipped her mocktail.

"I can't believe she came," Whitney said, more to herself than to anyone else. "That she had the fucking nerve to actually do it."

Carly grabbed her arm. "You should just ignore her. If you go over there and talk to her, that might get her all worked up."

Whitney shrugged her off. "If I want to talk to her, I will."

"I think Carly's right," Peyton said. "Like, this is your party. Blow her off."

Whitney didn't say anything as she kept dancing, her eyes glued to Jordan, who also kept her eyes locked on the birthday girl. They all watched Jordan wearily, who continued to sip, eat, and stare, not saying a word, not acknowledging anyone.

Carly's heart leapt when she saw Dionne sidle up to Jordan. It looked like Dionne was doing most of the talking. She squinted, wondering if it would be possible to read Dionne's lips, to see if she was spilling the beans to Jordan about what she'd said that day in the dress shop.

She had to go over there. She had to know what Dionne was saying.

"I'm gonna grab something to drink," she said to Whitney. "I'll be back."

No one said anything as Carly pushed her way through the throng on the dance floor, getting lit once again as the DJ pumped Rihanna. She smoothed down her hair as she reached the table. Dionne stopped talking and glanced at her, smiling as Jordan continued to sip her drink.

"Hey," Carly said as nonchalantly as she could with her heart pounding against her chest like a freight train gone wild. "What's up?"

Jordan clicked her tongue as she slurped down the last of her Whittini. "Wouldn't you like to know?" she said, stepping around Carly and heading toward the bar.

"What was that all about?" Carly asked, irritated at the nervous squeak of her voice. She lowered her head toward Dionne. "You didn't say anything about … you know…"

"What?" Dionne yelled as Lizzo came on, the DJ seeming to have turned the volume up.

"Did you say anything to Jordan about—?"

Dionne's boyfriend, Tommy, came up behind her and yanked her in the direction of the dance floor. She mouthed 'sorry' as the two suctioned themselves together.

Panic flushed through Carly as she looked around for Jordan, freaked when she couldn't see her. She continued to thread her way through the horde, her eyes desperately peeled for even a flash of aquamarine from Jordan's dress. Carly slowly spun around in a distressed circle, the pulse of the music and the elated screams from the dark crowded dance floor pushing against her.

Whitney. She needed to get back to Whitney.

Carly pivoted in the direction of where she'd left Whitney, not even noticing when someone spilled a drink on her, the cold liquid splashing against her shoulder and dripping down the sleeve of her dress. Nor did it register when someone else stubbed her toe. All that mattered was getting back to Whitney.

Just as she broke free from the crowd, from the corner of her eye, she spotted Jordan standing alone, her hands on her hips as she stared Whitney down from across the room. In slow motion it seemed, Whitney turned from her conversation with Peyton to face Jordan. For what felt like an eternity, the two girls stared at each other, the heat of rage emanating from both like fire. Peyton whispered to Whitney while holding her arm, but she shrugged her off as she took a defiant step in Jordan's direction. Carly shook her head in silent fear as she rushed toward Whitney, blocking her advance.

"Whitney, why don't we dance?" Carly said, breathless from the anxiety, the fear of what was about to happen. "Forget about Jordan. Please?"

Whitney stepped around Carly, her finger pointed in Jordan's direction. "You need to leave. Why are you even here?"

Jordan folded her arms across her chest, her chin pointed outward in spite. "Your mom invited me. I'm not going anywhere."

"Nobody wants you here, Jordan. You only got invited because your mom totally made my mom feel sorry for you," Whitney said. "You're even more pathetic than I thought, you ho bag."

Jordan clapped. "Congratulations on using big words. Did you get a dictionary for your birthday?"

"Shut up, you loser."

"Seriously, is that the best you've got?" Jordan asked, laughing. "One year older and still no brains."

By now, a small crowd had started to form in a semi-circle around the girls, their heads swiveling between them like spectators at a tennis match.

Whitney squared her shoulders back. "At least my mom doesn't have to go around begging people to invite me to their parties. Honestly, how embarrassing." She looked over at Peyton. "I mean, honestly, if your mom said, 'Hey, invite my loser daughter to your birthday party because nobody will give her the time of day,' would you go?"

Peyton pursed her lips and shook her head rapidly, seemingly afraid to open her mouth. It was all the encouragement Whitney needed, because she threw her head back and laughed. "Poor pathetic Jordan who can't even get anyone to eat lunch with her, who looks like a straight-up clown, who needs her mommy to plan her playdates for her—"

"Please, your mom probably paid everyone to be here."

"Oh, no, Jordan, that would be your mom. I know that's why you didn't have a Sweet Sixteen, because who would come without Daddy's big fat checkbook?"

"Keep it up, Whitney. Keep. It. Up."

"You can't come in here and ruin this for me. This is my night. Mine!"

"You should have thought about that before you came after me," Jordan sneered. "I am going to make you wish you never met me."

Whitney narrowed her eyes. "Trust me, I wish that every day. Know that."

"Same here, you stupid little—"

Jordan didn't finish the sentence before Whitney wrenched Peyton's Whit-tini from her hand and threw it into a stunned Jordan's face, the red liquid cascading down the front of her dress. Whitney held up the empty glass and let it drop to the floor, smug triumph smeared across her face.

Jordan stared down at her dress, her mouth a dumbfounded 'O.' Her head flipped up as she threw daggers at Whitney.

"You fucking bitch," Jordan screamed, her nostrils flaring, her face red. "You're going to pay for this—"

"I'm not paying for anything—"

"I swear to God, Whitney, I will fuck your shit up," Jordan

shouted. "You just wait, because I'm going to tell everyone what you did, you nasty lying bitch—"

Once again, Jordan didn't finish the sentence as Whitney leapt toward her, tackling her to the ground, shrieking, tearing at her pony-tail, her dress, anything she could get her hands on. Everyone screamed and phones were immediately whipped out to film the melee as Whitney and Jordan rolled around on the floor, yelling and pulling at each other's clothes and hair. Carly wanted to jump in, defend Whit-ney, get Jordan away from her. Except she was paralyzed. All she could do was stand there, alternating between staring at the tangled mess in front of her and frantically looking around for someone—anyone—to parachute in and bust up the fight.

Finally, Whitney's dad, two of the servers, and the bartender jumped in to pull the brawling girls apart. Whitney and Jordan continued shouting and kicking as they attempted to hold on to each other, each with smeared lip gloss and mascara, hair flying out in a million crazy directions, and blood. Whitney's mouth was puffy, her cheeks scratched, while the lobe of one of Jordan's ears was split in two, blood dripping from the tear, one of her earrings missing. The DJ finally stopped playing, as the chants and horrified screams of the crowd, comingled with Whitney and Jordan's shrieks, filled the room.

"I hate you!" Whitney shrieked as her father finally managed to extricate her from Jordan's frenzied grasp. "I hate your fucking guts!"

"I hope you die! I hope you fucking die!" Jordan raged as she scratched and clawed against the servers trying desperately to control her.

Finally, Jordan was dragged outside, while Whitney's dad pinned her in a corner by the bar. She was crying hysterically, tracks of black mascara running down her face, her hair a broken nest of extensions and hairspray. Whitney's mom rushed over, her own tears running down her face as she tried to soothe her frenetic daughter. Carly wrung her hands for a few seconds, not sure what to do, before running over to a hyperventilating Whitney and her parents.

"Why did you have to let her in?" Whitney sobbed to her mother, who was rubbing her daughter's shoulder. "Why did you have to invite her? This is all your fault."

"Whitney, sweetie, calm down, calm down."

"Do you want some water, Whitney?" Carly offered.

"Go away!" Whitney screeched, and Carly blanched.

"Some water would be nice," Mrs. Dean said to Carly. "Thank you."

Carly ran to the bar and grabbed a bottle of water. Everyone was still standing around and staring before the event planner pointed frantically to the DJ, indicating he should start playing. The music scratched back to life, though the dance floor remained empty.

Mrs. Dean whispered something to Mr. Dean and he nodded as she lifted up a still sobbing Whitney and took her in the direction of the bathroom. Whitney's dad ran outside and through the doorway, Carly could see him talking to whoever had dragged Jordan from the dance floor. She was hunched over on a curb, holding her bleeding ear and rocking back and forth. He bent down to talk to her, placing a hand on her shoulder as she too continued bawling.

Carly bit her lip and fought her way to the bathroom. People were still standing around, everyone's face buried in their phones as they replayed the fight over and over again.

She opened the door to find Mrs. Dean dabbing Whitney's face with wet paper towels. Whitney had calmed down, but was still crying.

"I brought the water," she said as she held out the bottle in their direction.

"Thanks, Carly," Mrs. Dean said, taking it from her. "You're very sweet."

"Do you need anything else?" Carly asked. "What can I do?"

"Whitney, honey, how about we go out there and cut the cake, huh? That'll take everyone's mind off everything." Mrs. Dean stroked her daughter's hair, smiling.

"I want to go home," she sobbed.

"But sweetie, it's strawberry with lemon buttercream filling, your favorite—"

"I said I want to go home!" Whitney screamed as she burst into a fresh wave of tears and shoved past Carly, flinging open the bathroom door. Mrs. Dean ran after her, Carly following. The party had reignited, with quite a few kids back on the dance floor. As Whitney sprinted toward the front door, it was like the music screeched into silence as everyone stopped and stared at her.

Carly couldn't see Jordan anywhere and Whitney was pleading with her father to take her home. He nodded, looking at his wife, who kept trying to talk to a weeping Whitney. Mr. Dean said something to Mrs. Dean and she sighed and nodded, her head hung down in defeat as Mr. Dean took Whitney over to his car and put her inside. Carly walked over to Mrs. Dean, who stood staring after Whitney and Mr. Dean, her face lined with worry.

"Whitney's just too upset to go on so I think the party's over," she said.

"I'm so sorry, Mrs. Dean," Carly said.

"Oh, sweetie, that's nice of you to say, but you didn't do anything," she said, stroking Carly's shoulder.

"Do you want some help cleaning up everything?" Carly asked.

"Oh, no, honey, I'll—the event planner will make sure that gets taken care of. It's her job."

"Really, I don't mind," Carly said, following behind Mrs. Dean as she made her way back inside. "I mean it, I'm happy to help."

"I appreciate the offer, really I do, but I think you should give your mom a call, have her come and pick you up." Mrs. Dean grabbed Carly's hand and squeezed it. "Thanks again for coming."

She smiled one last time before heading inside, leaving Carly to stand there, fear and anger welling up inside her. Damn Jordan for ruining everything.

Carly hated her.

18

ERICA

Erica held up her hand to knock on Jordan's bedroom door, hesitating for a moment. She was still reeling from the shock of getting a teary, hysterical call last night from Jordan that she was too upset to drive home and needed a ride then pulling up and seeing her sobbing, bloody daughter huddled in her car, rocking back and forth, her dress in shreds, her earlobe torn in two.

A glum-sounding Jordan told her to come in. She was curled up on the bed, her laptop on the pillow on her lap, the stitches in her ear the ER doctor had sewn in at two this morning hiding beneath a thick white bandage.

Erica sat down on the king-sized bed. Jordan made no moves, her eyes glued to the laptop. "Jordan, we need to talk."

"I don't feel like it."

Erica slammed the lid of the laptop down, startling her daughter. She shot up, her eyes ready for a rumble, but Erica was not having it today. "Tell me what happened last night."

Her daughter sank against the pillows, scowling. "I told you, Whitney and I got into it."

"Why?"

"Because she's a bitch, that's why—"

"Jordan, I'm warning you."

Her daughter shrank back, seeming to rethink her defiance. "She got mad that I came to the party before she threw a drink on me and then we got into it." She touched the bandage on her ear and winced. "That's when my earring came out."

Erica ran her tongue across her teeth. "Did you say something to her?"

Hesitation. "No."

"Don't lie to me, Jordan."

She continued to sulk and Erica crossed her arms, waiting.

"Okay, I might have called her a nasty, lying bitch. And then she screamed at me to leave."

Erica closed her eyes and rubbed the bridge of her nose. "Oh, Jordan." She sat still for a moment. "You didn't go there to be the bigger person. You went there so you could start something with her, didn't you?"

Hesitation again. "No."

"Jordan."

Her daughter sighed, tears welling up in her eyes. "All right, I might have been mad at the way she's been acting and I wanted to mess with her a little bit."

Erica frowned. "How's she been acting? Is it something specific?"

Jordan heaved a big sigh and punched her pillow, dragging it across her stomach. "She's just a horrible person. Everyone thinks she's so sweet and innocent. But you have no idea how awful she is. No one does."

"So, she didn't do anything specific, you've just decided you think she's a horrible person and because of that, you went to her party to antagonize her and basically ruin her night." Erica pursed her lips. "Do I have it right?"

The girl said nothing as tears rolled down her face. She wiped them away with the sleeve of her faded blue hoodie.

Erica stood up, grabbing the laptop. "Give me your car keys."

"What?"

"Your car keys, now," she said, holding her hand out.

"Are you grounding me?" Jordan asked, surprisingly incredulous.

"For starters."

"You can't do that."

"Oh, I can and I am. Car keys. Now."

Jordan sobbed and jumped off the bed, stomping over to her purse crumpled on the floor and digging out the key, handing it to her.

"Phone too," Erica said.

"What?"

"Now, Jordan."

Sobbing, the girl handed over the phone and flopped down on the bed. "This is so unfair."

Erica shoved the phone and car key into the pocket of her skinny black pants. "You should have thought about that before you went storming over to Whitney's party to cause trouble."

"I can't believe you're doing this."

"You're grounded until further notice, so no car, no phone, no social media, no laptop—"

"Mom, I need my laptop for school!"

"They have a computer lab. Better yet, use the computers at the public library."

"You're being so ridicu—"

"Keep it up," Erica said as she scooped up the Mac Book from the bed and stood up. "I can go all day."

"Oh my God—"

"Actions have consequences," Erica said as she slammed the door behind her.

19

WHITNEY

Whitney winced as she turned over in bed. She had a cut lip, scratches up and down her arms, an ugly purple bruise on her thigh, one broken acrylic, ripped extensions, and a ruined party dress. Not that she ever planned to wear it again, but looking at it now at the foot of her bed, the silver tatters taunting her, she'd have to throw it in the trash because she damn sure never wanted to look at it again. Even her parents waking her up to present her with the brand-new Range Rover wrapped in a huge red bow that she was supposed to get last night hadn't been enough to make her feel better.

Twitter and Instagram were lit up with hundreds of videos of her and Jordan going at it. What kind of bullshit was that? Nobody jumped in to help her. Not one person. Even Carly, who was always saying she had her back, that she was a hundred percent ride or die for Whitney, just stood there acting as helpless as a baby.

She scrolled through the comments, her eyes tearing up at how everyone thought it was the most lit thing they'd seen all year. It was going to go viral. She just knew it.

Disgusting.

There was a knock on her door and she said to come in, knowing it was her mom.

"Are you feeling any better, honey?" her mother asked softly from the doorway.

"No."

Her mom sighed and came over to sit next to her on the bed. She gathered her in her arms and despite herself, Whitney started bawling all over again.

"It's okay, sweetie, it's okay," her mom said, rocking her gently.

"Jordan totally ruined my birthday," Whitney sobbed into her mother's arms. "She ruins everything."

"Oh, honey, I'm so sorry."

"You should be," Whitney said. "This is your fault too. I told you I didn't want Jordan at the party, and you invited her anyway—"

"Whitney—"

"God, at least apologize—"

"I—all right—I apologize, okay? I'm sorrier than you could possibly know. I shouldn't have invited her. Okay? I'm really, really sorry."

Her breath slowed a little, though her ears still pounded with the anger. She flopped back onto her pillows. "Thank you."

Her mom reached out again to hug her, not saying anything for several minutes. It actually felt good to have her mother hold her like she used to when she was a little girl.

"Whit, I need to ask you something," she finally said.

"What?"

Her mom was quiet for a few moments, just kept stroking her hair. "What did Jordan mean when she said she was going to tell everyone about what you did? What was she talking about?"

Whitney's heart did a somersault. "Huh?"

"Honey, your dad's trying to get these videos pulled down, but we both heard Jordan say she was going to tell everyone about you. Did —" Her mom pulled back to look at her. "Is there something you want —need to tell me?"

Whitney blinked back her tears. It would be so easy to tell her mom everything, all the stuff that Jordan was taunting her with. It might even feel good.

Instead, she shook her head. "I have no idea what she's talking about."

"Are you sure? Because, you know, whatever it is, you can tell me. Daddy and I will love and support you no matter what. I hope you know that."

She held her breath. The words were right there on her tongue. All she had to do was open her mouth and let them fall out.

Except, she couldn't do it.

"Jordan Mitchell is a liar," she said instead. "She makes stuff up all the time."

Her mother narrowed her eyes and pursed her lips as she looked at her, almost like she was deciding whether or not to push her. Finally, she clicked her tongue against her teeth. "Okay, honey."

"I want to be alone for a little while," Whitney said.

The doorbell sounded from downstairs. Her mom rolled her eyes. "Oh, jeez, who could that be?"

Her dad's voice raced up the stairs, letting them know it was Carly. Whitney wrinkled her nose and shook her head. "I don't want to see her, Mom."

"Come on, Whitney, Carly's your friend. A good friend. You know last night, she offered to help me clean up everything. She brought you some water. I'm sure she just wants to see how you're doing."

"Mom, no—"

"Just for a minute," her mom whispered. "Let her check on you, then tell her you're not feeling well, but thank her for coming by."

"Fine," Whitney said, groaning as she slid off the bed. "Just for a second."

She stomped downstairs to see a pale, fidgety Carly making awkward small talk with her father.

"Hey, Whit," she said, seeming relief spreading across her face. "I've been texting you all day. How are you?"

Whitney folded her arms across her chest. "Fine."

"We'll leave you two girls alone to talk," her mom said. "Thanks for coming by, Carly."

Her parents both smiled then crept out to the kitchen. Whitney waited until she knew they were out of range before whirling around.

"What the hell, Carly?"

"What?" She blanched.

"I thought you had my back. I thought you were ride or die."

"I—I am, Whitney, I am—"

"Jordan was beating the shit out of me and you just stood there. You didn't do anything," Whitney hissed. "I can't believe you didn't do anything, not one thing to help me. What about having my back? Huh? What about that?"

Carly grabbed at Whitney's arms, tears sliding down her cheeks. "Whitney, you know I would do anything for you. You know that."

"Well, then why didn't you do anything?"

"I, I just—I was—"

"So weak. So pathetic."

"Whit, please, please don't say that. You know how much I love you."

Whitney stomped over to her front door and flung it open. "You know what? Get the hell out of my house."

Carly shook her head, the tears streaming faster down her face. "Whit, no, please."

"No, seriously, get out and don't come back. Don't talk to me, don't text me, don't do anything. Just leave me alone."

"Don't do this, please, don't."

Whitney lowered her voice and leaned down. "If you don't get away from me, I'm going to tell everyone you're a total wackjob. Like, a serious cuckoo clock."

"What?" Carly sobbed.

"You know, one of my dad's little sisters, my aunt, is seriously cracked in the head." Whitney sniffed. "You totally remind me of her. Complete fruit loop."

"But, you know that's not true, you know—"

Whitney's eyes grew wide, her face moving closer to Carly's. "You know she's in a mental hospital? Because she's batshit crazy. She walks around talking to herself all the time. And every time they let her out, she has another breakdown. Maybe that's where you belong, in a padded cell somewhere."

"Whitney, please, please don't say that—"

"You know, I thought you were going to be totally different than Jordan. I thought you were going to be a true friend. I thought you were one hundred."

"But I am, Whitney, I swear it." Carly sobbed. "You know I am—"

Whitney rattled the doorknob in her hand. "I am so fucking serious right now. Get the hell out."

"But, Whitney please you're—you're my best friend. I love you—"

"Call your Uber or whatever from outside. Just get the hell away from me, you fucking crazy creeper."

Carly's face melted in anguish as she raced outside, and Whitney slammed the door behind her.

20

AVA

Ava pulled the curly black strands of her hair into a ponytail as she examined her face in the mirror, frowning at the ugly black spiral of chin hair that had sprung up overnight. There weren't many things Ava was vain about, but the hair—*the hair!*—would drive her to drink if she didn't already. This was the third in as many weeks. At this rate, she was going to have to start shaving.

She winced as she plucked the protruding stubble, instant relief flooding through her at the release and the sight of the wily coil, a white bulb of root bulging at the end. She rubbed the stinging spot on her chin and dotted it with some peroxide before heading for the stairs, glancing hesitantly down the hall toward Carly's closed door.

It had been a miserable twenty-four hours, starting with Carly's frantic phone call last night for a ride home, coupled with agitated babblings that even a UN translator wouldn't have been able to decipher. Then today's drama of the traumatic visit with Whitney, followed by frenetic bawling about how her life was over because the most popular girl in school didn't want anything to do with her anymore. The girl had been locked in her room since she ran sobbing into the house after her fight with Whitney. She was probably cycling between sobbing uncontrollably and watching Lifetime movies.

She flipped through her own memories of sixteen, searching the pages of her mind for any over-the-top, end-of-the-world meltdowns with her girlfriends. The closest she could find was the vicious argument she and Tammy Butler had senior year over Calvin Swank. Even though he was two-timing them both, the girls traded nasty barbs until her brother, Frank, stepped in and told her to calm down because he knew for a fact the guy was a dog. Ava realized her brother was right and told Tammy she could have him. Turns out she didn't want him either and also kicked him to the curb. The whole thing lasted about three weeks and they kissed and made up by going to McDonald's for Shamrock Shakes. There'd been no tears, no hair pulling, no earring ripping.

Ava shuffled into the kitchen, mentally starting to make the grocery list for dinner tonight. Her eyes continually flipped skyward in the direction of Carly's room as she stood at the kitchen counter scribbling ingredients on her notepad. Her plan was to cook Carly's favorites in order to coax her downstairs for dinner. The squeak of the bedroom door pulled Ava's gaze up again as Carly emerged, plodding down the stairs, her face puffy with tears, eyes pink and swollen. Ava watched in silence as she headed straight for the fridge, extracting a tub of hummus and some string cheese.

Ava cocked her head to the side. "Carly."

"What?"

She gestured to the kitchen table, indicating Carly should sit. Carly shuffled over, her shoulders hunched, and plopped down in the chair, her eyes pinned to the table.

"What?" Carly repeated.

"Baby, this isn't going to last forever," Ava said, stroking her daughter's hair. "This whole thing will be forgotten in no time."

"Whitney doesn't forget things. Once she's done with you, she's done with you." Carly shifted in her chair, tears shimmering in her eyes. "Mom, she said she was going to tell the whole school that I was crazy and belonged in a mental hospital."

"And that was a totally unnecessary thing to say and I'm going to talk to her mother—"

Carly jumped out of her chair. "Don't you dare! Don't you dare say anything to her mom, to anyone—"

"All right, calm down, Carly, calm down." Ava sighed. "Baby, you —listen, you can't wrap up all your self-worth into Whitney Dean, or anyone."

"Don't make me go to school tomorrow. Besides, you're not even going to be here, so why do you care?"

"Excuse me?"

"Mom, please, don't make me go. I can't face it, I can't—"

"Listen, you can't hide from Whitney or anybody. You've got to go and hold your head up high. Don't let anyone push you around."

"This is all Jordan's fault. If she hadn't come to the party and started the fight, none of this would be happening. God, I hate her—"

"Jordan's mother can deal with her. Right now, I'm more concerned with you." Ava exhaled. "Look, you're going to school tomorrow. And don't worry about Whitney—"

"God, you just don't understand." Carly burst into a fresh round of tears as she bolted from the table and back upstairs. Ava wanted to run after her then thought better of it, sinking back into her chair and groaning, wondering if she should postpone her trip tomorrow. Kyle came in from the living room, frowning.

"What's all that, then?"

"She is having a complete meltdown about Whitney and wants to stay home from school tomorrow and I said no."

He joined her at the table. "Would that be so bad? Even a day or two?"

"Look, she's already got shaky self-esteem. If we let her curl up in a ball every time something bad happens or things don't go her way, she's never going to learn how to cope with life."

"She's just so sensitive," he said. "We don't want her to tip over the edge, right?"

Ava picked up her grocery list and gave it a quick scan. "Jesus, English, Carly will be fine. We shouldn't baby her."

"I guess you're right, Mate." He came over and kissed the back of her neck. "Oh, wait, you always are."

She scoffed. "Seriously, stop acting like you're new here."

21

CARLY

They were supposed to reminisce about the party Monday morning.

That had been the plan.

Monday morning, she and Whitney would meet up at her locker with the rest of the girls to relive the glory of Saturday night. They would talk about the food, the searchlights with Whitney's name. Whitney's dress. All the songs they danced to. The cake being wheeled out. Mr. and Mrs. Dean presenting Whitney with a brand-new car.

Instead, everything had completely and totally gone wrong and now, Carly was down at the other end of the hallway peeking around the corner at Whitney's locker, hiding.

She saw Peyton, Lexi, and Madison pass by Whitney's locker, the confused swivel of their heads at not finding her there and eventual shrug as they scattered to their own first periods. Seconds later, she saw that miserable skank Jordan wander down the hall with the huge, hard-to-miss white bandage plastered over her right ear. Like Carly, today Jordan had traded her standard jeans and flowy tops for a drab hoodie and baggy sweats, her hair pulled back in a messy ponytail. She ducked into class and Carly licked her lips, wondering if maybe Whitney's mom, unlike her own, had been cool enough to let her stay home today.

She looked at her watch. If she hurried, she'd make it into class just before the bell.

Then again, she could just skip altogether.

Carly took a deep breath, fighting the urge to run out of the building. In the end, her good girl tendencies told her to sprint down the hall to class. She arrived breathless, her butt in the seat just as the bell rang. One second later, Whitney strolled in.

It felt like the entire class held its breath as Whitney scanned the room for a seat.

Carly's heart dropped at the sight of the still fresh bruises and scratches on her skin, though the simple short-sleeved black dress that flared out around her knees meant Whitney had put in a little more effort than either Carly or Jordan. And she wasn't afraid to show the evidence of the brawl.

Whitney flicked a scowl at Carly and rolled her eyes at Jordan. Carly sank down in her seat, tears burning in her eyes at the humiliation, the rejection. Did everybody see? Did they all know?

"You're late, Miss Dean," Mr. Byrne said.

"Sorry," she mumbled as she took a seat in a far corner of the room, a bank of windows on one side of her, Perry Hoffman, the string bean of a student with thick glasses and blotchy acne who nobody sat next to if they could help it, on the other.

Carly's gaze scurried around the room as Mr. Byrne started the lesson by pulling out a tattered copy of *The Scarlet Letter*. She could see everyone staring at her, Whitney, and Jordan. Trish Sellers whispered something to Rachel Clark, who turned to look at Whitney, who stared straight ahead at the board, while Carly locked eyes with Trish before glancing away, ashamed because she knew what Trish was thinking.

Why wasn't she sitting with Whitney?

"All right guys, today we're going to be diving deeper into *The Scarlet Letter*." Mr. Byrne cleared his throat and wrote the book's title on the board and the word, 'outcast' underneath. "As we've seen in the book so far, Hester is an eternal outcast in puritanical society. So, here's my question for you. Should the sin of one be the sin of the entire community?"

A few uncomfortable coughs broke the silence and some shifted in their seats, as though they were afraid to speak. The shuffling hiss of papers and click and hum of the air conditioner kicking on filled the room. Carly looked down at her notebook, while Whitney scoffed and shook her head and Jordan stayed hunched over her notebook, staring, doing nothing.

Trish Sellers's hand shot up in the air. Carly could see Mr. Byrne's eyes skip over her in search of someone else to answer the question.

"Miss Dean," he said, causing the girl's head to flip up. "What do you think? Did Hester deserve to be an eternal outcast or were her sins forgivable?"

She rapidly tapped her pen against her desk before clearing her throat and crossing her legs as she straightened up in her chair.

"I say if you're an outcast ..." She rolled the tip of her tongue across her front teeth. "You probably deserve it."

He nodded slowly as the rest of the room tittered uncomfortably. "Okay. Could you elaborate some more on that?"

Whitney's words triggered a flood of metallic saliva in Carly's mouth and churning in her stomach. Whitney meant that for her. She wanted Carly to know she was done. She was icing her out. Her days as number one companion to the queen were through.

She was going to be sick.

"Mr. Byrne?" Carly feebly held up her hand, her voice weak.

"Is there something you'd like to add, Miss Ewing?"

"I need to go to the nurse."

"Why?"

She clutched her stomach, afraid to open her mouth, afraid of what would come out. "I think—"

Her fears were well founded, because she spewed all over Jessie Tate's head as Patty Ford, Roberto Gimenez, and China Maxwell jumped out of the way of the splatter. The entire class gasped, one student yelping, someone else yelling out, "Yo, that is fucked up."

Whitney wrinkled her nose and Jordan snickered even as she hunched even further into her desk.

"I'm sorry," Carly sobbed as she dragged the sleeve of her sweatshirt across her mouth, feeling the rank wetness slide across her chin. "I'm sorry."

"It's okay. You're excused to go to the nurse," Mr. Byrne said as he rushed to open the classroom door.

Carly grabbed her books, carefully stepping around the pool of vomit spreading across the floor, and ran toward the door.

"I'm sorry," she repeated as she rushed past him, tears streaming down her face as she bolted for the hallway. "I'm so sorry."

22

ERICA

The house shook with thunder and the lights blinked off for a millisecond before blazing back to life. Erica winced as she wiped down her kitchen counters and finished loading the breakfast dishes before hitting start on the dishwasher. It had been one week since the birthday brawl, as she'd come to think of it. Video of Jordan and Whitney yanking extensions and screaming profanities at each other briefly went viral before Steve Dean had them all yanked off social media, threatening a bevy of lawsuits. If he hadn't, she was prepared to have Jay step in. Jordan spent her time locked and sullen in her room, going to school and coming straight home. Erica had left several apologetic voicemails for Lauren this week, but the woman had yet to call her back. She'd put it on her to-do list to call her again. Maybe she'd just show up at Lauren's house with a bottle of wine or something to smooth the way. Always have a plan.

Jordan galloped down the stairs, her book bag slung over her shoulder. "Where's Dad?"

Erica snapped open the trash bag she'd taken from the pantry to line the garbage can. "Upstairs."

Jordan slumped down into a chair. "When can I get my car back?"

"I want you to apologize to Whitney."

"No way."

"All right then." Erica shrugged. "I guess I keep the car keys, phone, and laptop for an extra week."

"This is so stupid."

"Jordan, you have to take responsibility for your actions." Erica leaned against the counter. "Now, after the library, you're going to walk to the Zindels' to babysit and then Mr. Zindel will bring you home, right?"

Jordan picked at an imaginary piece of lint on her pants. "Yeah."

"So, what time should we expect you?"

"I don't know, nine-thirty, ten."

Jay came bounding down the stairs in his seven-days-a-week uniform of Chuck Taylors, khakis, and long-sleeved button-down, the top two buttons undone to reveal a white t-shirt underneath. He kissed Erica's forehead before glancing at Jordan. "You ready to go?"

She pushed back from the table, the bottom legs of the chair scraping across the marble. "So ridiculous."

"Keep it up." Erica washed and dried her hands on a kitchen towel. "Every day that you stomp around here is another day of no privileges."

In defiance, as if to prove her point, her daughter stomped outside to the car while Jay looked after her, exasperated. "Don't worry, I'll deal with her."

"Oh, she'll get tired of this eventually and get it together."

"I'm going to drop her off at the library, run some errands, then I'll be in that meeting with Charlotte Morgan in Lake Bluff for a few hours." Jay stopped short. "We should have her and her husband, Rex, over some time."

"Sure, darling, you tell me when. Just not tonight."

"Hmm. No, not tonight. Okay, anyway, I'll be home around six-thirty."

"Sounds good." She curled into him, running her hand up the length of his arm. "Since Kennedy has a sleepover tonight and Jordan will be babysitting, why don't we meet in the hot tub for a little time alone?"

They laughed the naughty, knowing laugh of a couple who can't wait to be alone together. "You bring the burritos."

They kissed before he headed out to the car. Within seconds, she heard him and Jordan pull out of the driveway, her shoulders loosening somewhat at having the house to herself for the day. It would give her a chance to get a jump start on a few upcoming projects.

Another bang of thunder slammed into the house and the lights flickered once again as Erica ambled into her office. She frowned as she flipped open her laptop, perturbed that the Wi-Fi seemed to be as intermittent as the electricity. For the next hour, she kept resetting the router, knowing it was futile, but unable to stop herself from at least trying. Finally, she sighed, looking forlornly around her office. Maybe this was the day to run a few errands she'd been putting off throughout the week, since it didn't appear she would be getting any work done today. She sighed again and headed into the kitchen for her purse and keys.

23

LAUREN

Lauren's cheeks burned with her realtor smile, plastered across her face since she'd raced out of the house at eight that morning for a grueling day of back-to-back showings from Highland Park to Evanston and every suburb in between. Saturdays during the buying season were always punishing and today was no exception. Fortunately, the season was ending soon, and though it had been exceedingly lucrative—one of her best ever—Lauren was ready for the slowdown so she could catch her breath.

Her stomach growled as she showed them the kitchen, the hasty pack of peanut butter crackers at two that afternoon a distant memory. Despite the insistent rain pelting the picture windows and the electricity falling victim to the storm, she ran through her spiel about natural light, open kitchens perfect for entertaining, spacious closets, and stunning views for the young couple looking to upgrade from their condo in the city in anticipation of starting a family soon, reminding her of when she and Steve had made that leap. He'd been perfectly happy for them to continue living in the Lincoln Park condo he'd bought a year before they met (at a bar on St. Patrick's Day, of all the ridiculous things), with his ten-minute commute and favorite pub around the corner. She'd been desperate for the status of the North

Shore and what it represented, spurred by the lingering scar of a child-hood with skinflint parents.

In addition to giving up his city life, Steve worried about the cost of living in the high-rent North Shore. Despite his best efforts, he hadn't made it to the NFL, though fortunately, he'd majored in architecture and had that to fall back on when the pros didn't throw themselves at his feet. Despite the success he was having with his burgeoning career, he still felt they needed to be more settled, have more zeros in their bank account. He inexplicably worried that living in the suburbs meant they'd have to give up their weekly Mary Jane habit, which Lauren found especially funny. Who did he think was lighting up every chance they got?

His hesitancy stimulated her determination and after a series of dead-end office jobs, she got her license at the suggestion of a former co-worker from one of those nowhere office jobs. It took a little while, but in due time, the money was gushing into her bank account like a tsunami, effectively obliterating his objections. Getting pregnant with Whitney bolstered her cause and off they went to Lake Forest. There'd been times she'd made more money than him, but it didn't bother her—it wasn't like he sat on his ass all day while she hustled for the bacon. And it certainly didn't seem to irritate him to have a wife who out-earned him on occasion. They were both workaholics, reflected in every aspect of their luxurious, nothing-off-limits life-style. As far as the money was concerned, it was theirs, not his, not hers. Not that she didn't do what she damn well pleased with hers when she wanted to.

Lauren's phone vibrated inside her purse with an incoming call. She ignored it as she answered the husband's question about commuting downtown via the Metra, then fielded the wife's query about schools, as the phone rang four more times in quick succession. She apologized as she dug into her purse, agitated to see Steve's face. She encouraged them to explore the upstairs further while she took the call.

"Steve, I'm busy—"

"Jay Mitchell just called me. He's having one of his last-minute dinner parties tonight and wants us to come. And you know, when Jay says come, you come."

Lauren's hand smacked against the counter in frustration. The absolute last place on Earth she wanted to be was trapped with Jay and Erica at their house. For one, she was exhausted. Spending an evening with him and Erica was as tempting to Lauren as peeling off her fingernails with pliers, one by agonizing one. Especially after last week's fiasco with Whitney's birthday party, her stomach still churning at the memory. However, as Steve said, when Jay Mitchell said come to dinner, dropped however casually, however jovially, however last-minute, you went to dinner.

She rubbed a hand over her eyes, everything humming inside her to say no, but knowing she had to agree to it.

"All right," she finally said. "Fine. Fine."

They coordinated a few details and Lauren rushed to get off the phone, taking a few deep breaths and plastering on a smile to get back into the right headspace. Just as she started to feel centered, her feet pointed in the direction of the stairs so she could find the couple, her phone buzzed again, alternating with a series of pinging texts. This time, her son Parker's name flashed urgently across her screen.

"What's wrong, buddy?" she asked.

"Whitney's not home to take me to Matt's," he said.

"Well, did you call her or text her?"

"Like ten times. It keeps going to voicemail." He paused. "Her car's here, though."

"Oh, for—" Lauren sighed, plunking her hand down onto the granite countertop in exasperation. "All right, I—I'll come home and take you to Matt's. I'll text you when I'm a few minutes away, so be packed, downstairs, and ready to go when I pull up, all right?"

"Okay, Mom. See ya," he said, before ending the call.

Fury at everyone named Mitchell and irritation with her daughter burned beneath Lauren's skin as she dropped her phone on the counter and took another round of deep breaths to calm her jangled nerves. She'd explicitly told the girl this morning she was in showings all day and wouldn't have time to take Parker to his sleepover. Her snotty attitude was particularly galling after Lauren spent almost two hundred thousand dollars for both a brand-new Range Rover and the Sweet Sixteen to end all Sweet Sixteens. Granted, everything had gone south, but wasn't it the effort that counted? A modicum of gratitude and honoring the occasional errand wasn't too much to ask.

Lauren snatched up her phone to fire off a terse text, which Whitney was far more likely to respond to than a phone call.

You need to call me. Now.

Silence.

"Damn it," Lauren muttered to herself as she ascended the stairs to find the prospective buyers, as she thought about how she'd like to wring Whitney's neck.

24

AVA

Ava stood in front of the dry cleaners, watching through the brick archway as the ferocious wind rippled across the slanted sheets of the early October rain, the plastic bags containing her husband's suits battering her legs. Her SUV waited for her at the far end of the jammed parking lot, but it may as well have been across a moat, perched on a mountaintop, teetering on the head of a pin. Her umbrella was, of course, on the floor behind the driver's side seat. Of course.

Fucking Kyle. He was always doing this: waiting until the last minute to beg her to help him with some domestic crisis that only she could solve. Today was please, please, please, pick up his suits, because he didn't have any more and they closed at five and he was stuck in Lisle with a client and he owed her one.

Then again, she was always saving his bacon, so she was as much to blame as he was.

At least she had her book club to look forward to later that evening, even if they had to endure discussing Sami Benson's pick, the latest in her long line of pseudo-intellectual selections that allowed her to parrot moronic talking points she found on the Internet, thinking she was fooling everyone with her superior grasp of the material. Rolling their eyes at Sami and taking a drink every time she uttered some variation of, "The intellectual prowess of the book really spoke to me," had become sport.

Carly intruded on her thoughts, their conversation earlier that morning flickering across her mind like a broken film reel. Ava had stopped the girl as she rushed to leave the house, impatiently insisting she had to spend the day volunteering at the animal shelter, and that the volunteer coordinator had insisted Carly absolutely had to be the one to work the two four-hour shifts. The anxious jumble of words surging from Carly's mouth had made Ava feel ... *unsettled*. She didn't think the girl was lying to her necessarily, but it also felt as though she was doing a bit of a tap dance. *Up to something*. Maybe that was more apt. She couldn't put her finger on it, but something was off with the girl. Dodgy, as Kyle would say.

Not to mention, she'd been beyond pissed that Kyle let her stay home from school all week while Ava had been first in New York, then routed to Denver the rest of the week at the last minute. And had gifted her with the birthday BMW to cheer her up, as he'd so feebly put it. Had she been home, there definitely would have been no car and she would have marched the girl to school every day herself. Of course, he was such a pushover, all Carly had to do was whimper about cramps and Kyle would melt like a popsicle in the sun.

She'd deal with Carly tomorrow. Right now, she wanted to get out of this rain and finish reading the last few pages for book club. Ava squared her shoulders, took a deep breath and darted toward her car, rain pelting her like hot needles as she cursed the puddles of water seeping into her loafers.

However, it was the one pothole heaving with rainwater, just steps from her car, that she would curse the longest and the loudest for years to come. The one that conspired with gravity to reach up and slam her to the ground with the force of a two-ton house, directly onto the delicate bones of her left wrist.

As she wailed in pain, howling even louder at her first glance at the mangled mess dangling from the end of her arm, Ava saved her most ferocious ire for Kyle, a part of her secretly glad the suits had flown out of her hand and landed in a puddle of their own.

25

LAUREN

"We really should have made up an excuse not to go tonight."

"You think anybody ever tells Jay Mitchell 'No'?"

"Just because he's the richest guy in town doesn't mean he's got the biggest dick and that we all have to come running every time he swings it around," Lauren said as she pulled up to a stop light.

Steve side-eyed her. "Babe, I think you know who has the biggest dick in Lake Forest."

"You're such a jackass."

"That's not what you said last night." He winked.

"That might be what I'm saying in a few hours." She glanced out the driver's side window. "Did Jay say who these people are?"

"Something about somebody I should meet, great opportunity, blah, blah, blah. You know, the usual with Jay."

"Well, the last three pieces of business he threw your way worked out all right, so I guess for you I can put on a happy face and ignore how fucking exhausted I am." Lauren sighed. "And deal with Erica to boot."

"Just drink a lot."

"You know she's going to be gushing all over me with all that fake, phony … tears and all that shit, and the next thing you know,

I'll be apologizing to her." Lauren shook her head. "Fucking ridiculous."

Steve scratched his scalp through the close-cropped waves of his low-cut fade, the outline of his still rippling football player muscles straining against his button-down shirt. "You can suck it up for a few hours."

"And what if Jordan is there? I have to deal with her now too?" Lauren rolled her eyes. "Yeah, this is the fun Saturday night I had planned."

"Listen, babe, like you said, I may walk out of here with some business. Hell, knowing Jay, you might, too, so just roll with it."

Lauren groaned because he was right, of course. "I know, I know."

"That's a good wife," Steve said.

"You're not funny."

"You sure about that?"

"What do you want to bet Jay was the president of his frat in college?"

"I was thinking Beer Chair," Steve said as she turned down the Mitchell's street.

They looked at each other and laughed as Lauren focused her attention back to the dark, winding road, illuminated with only the bouncing white beams of her headlights and shadows of tree branches crawling across the pavement. When she'd left that morning, she'd anticipated crawling into a bubble bath, a few edibles, and a bottle of wine at the end of the night. Not being summoned to the Mitchells for one of Jay's infamous last-minute dinner parties. The dread of having to make nice with Jay and Erica wasn't her only concern. Whitney still hadn't answered any of her texts, a stunt she sometimes liked to pull when she was being pissy about something. Lauren would need to pull rank in order to elicit a change in attitude.

Her SUV wailed as it came to a stop behind a silver Porsche parked in the circular driveway of the Mitchell's. Lauren gathered up the bottle of wine from the backseat, a sparkly red bow tied around its neck. She shivered a little in the damp, cool air, the day's pounding rain having stopped only briefly.

"Here we go," Steve murmured as they linked hands, her tiny hand lost in his paw, and made their way up the front walk.

As soon as Steve rang the bell, the door swung open to reveal a hulking Jay, as big and jovial as ever. Jay, the bulky, red-faced giant, bird legs holding up the barrel of his body. Who told stories at the volume of loud and louder, dominating conversations with blaring opinions, tasteless jokes, and adolescent pontifications. Who'd turned rumpled khakis, Chuck Taylors, and untucked dress shirts into his own version of the black turtleneck and jeans. He'd always struck Lauren as more of an overgrown frat boy than a wunderkind who'd built and sold three multibillion-dollar software firms in the last twenty-five years.

"Deans!" Jay bellowed through the bullhorn of his mouth, as he swallowed them both into bear hugs before ushering them inside and offering them drinks.

Erica was in the living room talking to a slightly older couple, both with silver hair and tanned, well-etched faces, who Jay introduced as Lance and Gabby Adams as Erica came over to offer Steve and Lauren double cheek kisses.

"Wonderful to see you," Erica said as she took their coats and handed them to a server hired for the evening, who whisked them away to some unseen corner of the house. "So glad you could make it tonight, especially on such short notice."

"Our pleasure," Lauren said with as much stiff graciousness as she could muster, as she handed Erica the bottle of red she'd skidded into the wine shop for twenty minutes ago just as they were closing. "Everything smells lovely."

"Oh, yes, well, thank goodness for catering companies. I wasn't even home when Jay called wanting to do this so last-minute." She laughed. "I barely got here ahead of the caterers."

"Hey, Lance, this is the man you want to talk to about your project," Jay said, slapping Steve on the shoulder. "Best architect in the city." Lauren and Steve snuck a knowing smile at each other. Jay could always be counted on to be Jay.

The three men immediately fell into conversation, the wife, Gabby, joining in their small talk as Erica tapped Lauren on the shoulder.

"Can we speak for a few minutes?" she asked.

Lauren nodded, her realtor smile sliding across her face, freezing into place. "Sure." She steeled herself to brace for impact as Erica signaled for her to join her in a dimly lit corner removed from the excited chatter happening across the room.

"I just wanted to say how sorry I am for what happened at Whitney's party last weekend," she said, her voice hushed and plaintive as she planted a bony hand against her equally bony collarbone, the ubiquitous gold Tiffany bracelet sliding the length of her bony wrist. "I am absolutely … mortified."

"I appreciate you saying that," Lauren said, her heart speeding up a little, her eyes searching over the woman's shoulder for Steve to rescue her, he instead seemingly mesmerized by whatever Lance was saying.

"I truly thought if Jordan came, she and Whitney would kiss and make up and get back to being friends. I had no idea it would fall apart the way it did."

"I understand, Erica," Lauren said, her skin itching with heat, threatening to ignite with an army of fiery red hives that tended to rear their scratchy, angry little heads when she was nervous.

"I grounded Jordan," Erica continued, her voice a whisper. "I mean, I let her go babysitting tonight, so she's not home, so you don't have to worry about her or Kennedy either, because I sent her to a sleepover—well, anyway, as Jay would say, the point of departure is, she has to understand that actions have consequences. In fact, we'd like to take both of you to lunch so that Jordan can apologize properly to you and Whitney."

"It's really not necessary." Lauren swallowed. Her thigh burned, an indication at least one hive had made its entrance. "But I do appreciate the sentiment."

Erica placed a hand on Lauren's arm. "Really. I want to. *We* want to."

Lauren forced yet another tight smile. Saying yes was easier. "Okay. Thank you."

Erica lit up like the proverbial Christmas tree. "Wonderful. We can figure out all the details on getting together later. Come. Let's have a good time tonight."

Like the flick of a switch, Lauren's temperature receded, the itch of her thigh settling down to sleep. She'd expected a ten-minute drone, mild histrionics, haughty disbelief. Even a tear or two. This was surprisingly brief. Restrained. This was getting off easy.

Mostly. There was still an uncomfortable lunch to get through.

She quickly checked her phone, perturbed to see there was still no word from Whitney. She tried to catch Steve's eye as the men broke off to continue their business discussion and a server appeared to freshen Gabby's wine.

"So, how do you and Erica know each other?" Gabby asked, her silver arrow earrings batting against her neck as she turned toward Lauren.

"Our girls are in the same class," Lauren said.

Erica sipped her wine. "They've been best friends since ballet class, what twelve, thirteen years?"

"Right," Lauren said. "LoMastro. Jordan was the star of the class."

"You're so sweet to say that," Erica said. "Whitney, though—she's a phenomenal dancer. Then and now."

"It's wonderful you all have this history," Gabby said. "That your girls are still friends after all these years."

Lauren let the comment slide, Jordan and Whitney's friendship beyond repair in her eyes. Instead, she smiled. "It has been a long time."

"Hard to believe how long ago that was." Erica shook her head. "I honestly don't know where the time has gone."

"Well, you really do blink and miss it, don't you?" Gabby said. "Both my girls are in their late twenties now and I swear just yesterday they were twelve with braces and pimples."

"I'd rather deal with zits and crooked teeth," Erica said, about to set her glass down when a server appeared with a fresh drink. "Now they have to deal with social media and the Internet and all of that. We had it so much easier."

"God, I'd never want to do sixteen again. Twenty-two maybe, but not sixteen," Gabby said, laughing.

"Oh, I would." Erica smiled. "Parties every weekend, cheering at football games, dances, class ski trips. It was a blast."

Lauren took a sip of wine, remembering Erica's forty-fifth birthday party from a few years ago, and the blown-up yearbook pictures plastered around the room featuring Erica in all her high school glory. She hadn't quite been able to reconcile the image of Erica as a queen bee that all the girls in school buzzed around with the haughty people pleaser who used her status as the wife of one of the richest men in the world as a cudgel to beat people into submission. Then again, those same arrogant tendencies were probably why she'd been so popular in high school.

"No wonder you loved high school," was all Lauren said.

Jay smacked his hands together loudly and announced dinner was ready. Lauren checked her phone again and saw Whitney was still playing hide and seek. She fired off another terse message commanding the girl to call her immediately before checking her doorbell video, only to see it was still out because of the storm. She signaled to Steve as they all moved toward the dining room.

"Whitney's still not responding to my texts," she murmured.

"I'm sure she's fine," he said. "We can deal with it when we get home."

"Well, you better back me up, because she is going to be punished."

"Maybe her phone died."

She cocked her head. "Are you kidding?"

"Okay, okay, you're right. She never lets that happen." He shrugged. "I'm sure there's an explanation."

"There better be," Lauren muttered as they joined the group at the table. "Otherwise, I'm going to kill her."

26

RON

He needed an alibi.

Ron pounded his steering wheel, the heat of his stupidity racing through him like a missile.

He'd spent the rainy afternoon lesson planning for the coming week, jotting down notes as he thumbed through *The Scarlet Letter* while huddled on his saggy brown couch from college—as what to do about dinner that night seized his attention. A pepperoni pizza, a six pack, and rewatching *Sense 8* from the beginning.

The perfect quiet evening at home.

Then, his door had exploded with a rapid series of knocks, intensifying to a relentless banging. He'd edged over to the door and pressed his eye against the peephole.

Her. Right outside his door.

He thought about leaving her out there, if it hadn't been for his car in the parking lot, which she'd likely seen, as well as the faded lamplight from his window.

He'd hustled her inside, hoping no one had seen them, before slamming the door behind him.

That had been his first mistake.

She'd taken an Uber as a preventative measure. Flung herself at him, swarming his senses with Bubblemint gum and strawberry shampoo. Her wild black hair. Her tight jeans. The shimmering pink quiver of her bottom lip. The drowsy, half-slits of her dark eyes. He'd allowed that tight, lithe body to squirm against him. Let her climb him like a tree.

He grabbed her, slammed her against the wall, ready. So, so ready. *Who cared, who cared, who cared.* Just throw her down and bang her until the sun came up. Melt into those silky legs. Bury himself in all that soft, sweet, savage hair. God, how bad did he want that.

Instead, he snapped himself back to reality, reluctantly tore himself away from those raw, greedy kisses tinged with mint. He suggested they go somewhere and talk. He made it sound like a date. Normal. Romantic. A nice, quiet meal, then come back to his house afterward.

And that had been his second mistake.

And then, they left together, heading out to his car in all that pounding, persistent rain.

Which had been mistake number three.

27

AVA

Ava's eyes fluttered open as she allowed the scene around her to come into focus and she remembered where she was. Doctors and nurses buzzed around in hushed, syncopated movement, accompanied by beeping monitors while dizzying streams of medical jargon soared from their lips. Despite floating on a cloud of pain meds, the sensation of slamming to the ground as her wrist shattered continued to ripple through her body. She winced as she looked down at the temporary splint holding her wrist in place until someone came to set it in a cast, whenever that was.

She had a fleeting thought of searching for her phone, both for the time and to update Kyle that she had no update. However, her bladder intruded as she realized she couldn't remember the last time she'd gone to the bathroom.

A harried nurse flew past and Ava called out, stopping the woman in her tracks.

"Yeah?"

"Bathroom," Ava mouthed.

The nurse nodded curtly and helped Ava out of bed and pointed her to the right place, before rushing off in the direction of her previous destination. She shuffled into the tiny room and quickly relieved herself, grateful that the faucet and soap dispenser only required a wave of her good hand for satisfaction. As she trudged back toward her bed, the doors to the ER slid open followed by the clatter of a gurney shouting over the low rumble of thunder and spatter of rain. She turned to see a team of paramedics zoom toward her and flattened herself against a wall as a doctor in pale green scrubs whizzed by her in pursuit of the gurney. The glimpse of an oxygen mask and strings of wet black hair splayed against the gurney's white sheet flew past in a dizzying blur.

"What have we got?" the doctor boomed as she strapped on a pair of latex gloves.

"Minor female with multiple stab wounds. Non-responsive. Airway looks clear. Pulse ox eighty-one."

"All right, let's get her into curtain one, spin a crit, and start a central line."

Ava frowned as the gurney clattered past her. Lake Forest was one of those charmed, tree-lined utopias where violent crime was trapped behind a TV or movie screen. A distant, gritty echo that plagued their neighbor to the south. Residents of Lake Forest woefully shook their heads at shootings and stabbings as they snuggled deeper into the cocoon of grand old mansions, high-tech security systems, and imposing metal gates at the end of the driveway.

Bad things just didn't happen here.

A set of metal swinging doors swallowed the gurney and a distraught, sobbing woman, silver threads running through her wet brown hair, the front of her lightweight cream sweater soaked with blood, attempted to run after it, only to be stopped by the slight, balding security guard who gently told her to have a seat in the waiting room so the doctors could work. The woman sank into a chair, tears continuing to gush from her eyes, prompting the same nurse who'd shown Ava the bathroom to sit down next to her with a clipboard and questions. Ava had to admit, what Kyle called her nosiness, and what she termed as healthy curiosity, spurred her to edge closer in an attempt to eavesdrop, but she was only able to glean from the woman's distressed, staccato answers that she wasn't a relative. Within moments, a man, probably the woman's husband, came bustling through the admit doors followed by two police officers, who pulled them to a secluded corner just out of Ava's earshot, presumably to question them about how they came to bring this young stabbing victim into the ER on a rainy Saturday night.

She waited a few seconds before surreptitiously moving to tuck herself into a nearby nook, her eyes boring into the cops and the couple as she managed to pick up snatches of conversation about what they knew.

"Ma'am?"

Ava's eyes shot up into the warm, questioning gaze of an older nurse. "What?" she asked, irritated.

"Did you need some help back to your bed?"

Ava grunted to herself in frustration. She wanted to know what was going on, but clearly that wasn't going to happen.

She hoisted herself up and shook her head. "No, I can find my way back."

The nurse did that weird thing where she hovered behind Ava, her arm encircling empty space in order to invisibly guide her back to her bed. Still, she couldn't help but glance back a few times, hoping the girl would be okay.

28

JORDAN

A t the library until around five researching her American history project. Due in two weeks. Civil Rights Act of 1964. Lots of books, microfiche, and old magazines on the subject. Yeah, the library is great. A quick stop at Left Bank for a Walking Taco and a pop. Walked the six blocks to the Zindels' to babysit. Wasn't really raining by that time. Anyway, she'd thought to throw an umbrella into her bag that morning. Why was she a mess? Tripped on her shoelace, fell to the ground. Fed the kids macaroni and hot dogs. Yeah, they sure can be a handful, but it was fun. Watched a movie. *Frozen*. Played tickle monster. Mr. Zindel brought her home.

Jordan bit her lip as she continued rehearsing what she was going to say when grilled by her mother about her day. She wished she had one of those distracted mothers who would be fine with getting only a few little details before murmuring 'how nice' as she went back to tapping out emoji-laden texts on her phone or posting her vacation photos to Instagram for her twelve followers. No, her mother would require the exact titles of the books she used for her research, how many pieces of ground beef were in the taco, and a detailed rundown of every scene from *Frozen* start to finish.

But it was okay, because she knew what to expect. Sixteen years of practice. She was ready. Her parents hadn't talked to the Zindels for at least six months and the last four times she'd babysat for them, her mom hadn't called Mr. or Mrs. Zindel pretending like she wanted to know how everything had gone, when really, she was checking up on Jordan. It was safe to use them as cover.

Her story was good. She just had to stick with it. Put in enough details to make it sound real, but not so many that she'd sound suspicious.

Believe in a lie deeply enough and you could easily sell it as truth.

Water splashed around her ankles as she walked up the dark, quiet road toward her house, the only one on Lenox Circle, wistful thoughts swirling through her head about her car sitting cold and alone in the garage, the keys clenched in her mother's fist as punishment for the fight at Whitney's party last week. She grasped the damp handle of her Longchamp bag, ready to face her mother. She came to an abrupt stop at the edge of her circular driveway, jarred by the two cars sitting on either side of the fountain. She didn't recognize the silver Porsche, but she knew Mrs. Dean's cream-colored Escalade, a mirror image of the one her mother drove. Jordan's heart sped up as she continued staring at the car, her mouth dry. She must be here for one of the last-minute dinners her dad was famous for throwing. Tonight, of all nights. She hadn't planned on this—couldn't have planned on this. Mrs. Dean. Here. Now. The guilt seized her insides. She couldn't face her.

Jordan took a faltering step backward, her head whipping left then right in search of a nonexistent answer.

She didn't have a choice. She had to go inside.

And pretend like everything was fine.

29

LAUREN

Dinner proved as entertaining as always with Jay at the helm. The wine flowed freely as did his boisterous jokes and nutty stories, each one louder than the last. He could be forgiven though, as he kept them all doubled over with tears of laughter. She momentarily forgot her fatigue and anger at Whitney, who continued to be radio silent despite Lauren's repeated text messages and occasional surreptitious phone calls away from the table, which kept going to voicemail. Even Erica, with her sly glances of adoration in her husband's direction and overall gracious demeanor, put Lauren at ease. The tenderloin fell off the bone, the scalloped potatoes melted, the asparagus firm and tender all at once. Not that Erica ate any of it, instead consuming a lonely salad overflowing with multicolored strips of lettuce and other salad-y things. Steve and Lance set up a meeting for the coming week to discuss potentially working together on the latter's project. Gabby was witty and charming and Lauren supplied her own card upon request.

As Lauren stepped out of the powder room on the first floor, the front door swung open and Jordan stumbled in, a sheepish look on her face. An involuntary gasp escaped Lauren's lips, as much for the girl's shifty, disheveled appearance—dirt and scraps of leaves clinging to the drab hoodie and baggy jeans she wore, a dried river of stain trailing down the front, her messy ponytail—as the shock of seeing her for the first time since the fight last Saturday. A week later, her earlobe still sported a thick white bandage, stitches no doubt trapped beneath the gauze. Seeing the girl stirred Lauren's hives, as they contemplated if they should come out to wreak havoc.

The two stood in an uncomfortable standoff for a few moments. Jordan's gaze pinned to the floor, her lips pressed into a thin line. Lauren, her mouth slightly agape as she ransacked her brain for what to say. Finally, she cleared her throat.

"Hello, Jordan," she said, her voice stiff and cautious.

"Hi, Mrs. Dean," Jordan responded, still staring at the floor.

Lauren couldn't help it; as much as she wanted to scratch the girl's eyes out and bang her head into the ground, seeing her unkempt appearance gave her slight pause. The motherly instinct always kicked in whenever a child was in distress, even if it wasn't yours.

"Are you all right?" Lauren asked.

Finally, Jordan looked up, her chin trembling. "I tripped and fell in a puddle. I'll be okay."

Lauren nodded. "Oh. Okay. Good."

"Mrs. Dean—I—I wanted to say um, you know, about the party … sorry." The words rushed from Jordan's lips in an almost indiscernible mishmash, her cheeks flaming red.

Lauren understood this was the best she could expect. There was no need to push or demand for searing, tearful, pleading atonement. None would be coming. Sometimes, you had to accept what you got instead of mourning what you never would.

"I appreciate you saying that," she said quietly before pausing. "I think it would be nice if you called Whitney too."

"Lauren, Steve sent me—" Erica stopped short as she flew into the foyer and saw the state her daughter was in, gasping as she marched toward her.

"Jordan, what on Earth—are you—what happened? You're an absolute mess."

"I tripped over my shoelace earlier and fell in a puddle," Jordan repeated, flicking a quick, guilty gaze toward Lauren, then shifting her eyes downward just as fast.

"You went to the Zindel's looking like that?"

"Mom, they don't care what I look like—"

"When did you fall into the puddle?"

"I told you it was earlier—"

"Earlier when?"

"When I was walking to the Zindel's from the library—"

Erica's eyes narrowed. "What time did you walk over to their house from the library?"

Lauren scratched her arm, distressed to see a blueberry-sized welt had taken up residence. "Erica, I think Steve and I—"

"Jordan," Erica plowed on, oblivious to Lauren. "What time—"

"I left the library around three then went to Left Bank because I wanted a Walking Taco—" Jordan started.

"How long were you—?"

Lauren cleared her throat. "Erica, Steve and I really need to get going. We haven't heard from Whitney all day and—"

Erica gasped as Jordan took advantage of the distraction and bolted for the stairs, sending her mother running after her, shouting questions at the girl's back.

"What the hell's going on?" Jay's voice boomed over Lauren's shoulder as he walked up behind her.

"Jordan just got home and—Steve and I should really get going."

"Oh, yeah, of course," Jay muttered, distracted, before screaming upstairs for his wife.

Lauren scurried to the dining room to grab Steve as they exchanged stiff, knowing glances with the clearly embarrassed Lance and Gabby. The sound of a slamming door echoed throughout the house followed by Erica huffing down the stairs, long honey blond tendrils flying away from her red face.

"What the fuck was that all about?" Jay asked, his own face scrunched in a cross of confusion and irritation.

"Steve, Lauren, thank you so much for coming tonight," Erica said, sidestepping the question. "It was so lovely to have you. Lauren, let's get together later in the week for a drink, talk about that lunch with the girls."

Lauren groaned inwardly. A semi-impromptu dinner party with Steve as cover, Jay directing the proceedings, and two other guests as a buffer was one thing. Hell, even an uncomfortable lunch with their two warring daughters would be something else. However, just the two of them spinning niceties over cocktails for the better part of an hour was more than Lauren could manage.

"Sure," she said instead, already calculating what excuse she could come up with to get out of it. "Text me."

The protracted goodbyes commenced and finally they were on their way. The confrontation between Erica and Jordan, fraught with snarling teenage girl irritation and bewildered mother frustration, had further stoked her already squirming anxiety over the inevitable show-down with her own daughter. As she and Steve made their way home through the dark, twisty roads sodden with rain, she tried to decide what punishment the girl had coming.

30

AVA

The doctor finished setting the cast around her wrist then leaned back, satisfied with her work.

"Are we done?" Ava asked, the shock and buzz of such a freak accident having long ago worn off, her senses snapped back to life. "Can I go home?"

The loud crack of the doctor removing her rubber gloves echoed throughout the tiny exam space where she'd been sitting since one o'clock this afternoon.

"All done," the doctor, Dr. White, said with a slight lisp as she scribbled something in her chart. "We'll have you come back in about a month for a checkup, but it will probably be about six to eight weeks before the cast comes off. Tonight, rest, and I've given you a prescription for ibuprofen to get you through the next few days. Who's driving you home?"

"Oh. I drove myself here."

Dr. White winced. "Whoa. Wow. Okay, uh, well, since we gave you pain meds, you can't drive yourself. Especially not in this weather. You'll need to have someone pick you up or call a cab or Uber."

"I'll text my husband."

"Good." She slapped the medical chart shut, the ends of her ash blond hair blanching backward in response. "Any questions for me?"

Ava shook her head. "Just ready to get out of here."

"Of course. I'll let you get dressed, then meet you at the admit desk."

Dr. White left and Ava sat in bed for a few moments before slowly pulling on her snug black tee and wrestling with her jeans. As her father would say, she felt as tired as a mosquito after a picnic. Before a final sweep to make sure she had everything she came in with, Ava sent a voice text to Kyle to come and pick her up. She trudged out to the admit desk for her discharge, ready to crawl into bed and put this miserable day behind her.

The couple who had brought in the girl earlier flashed across her mind and she scanned the waiting room for them, wondering if they were still there. She spotted them in a corner, the wife's head resting against the wall behind her, her eyes closed, the garish slash of blood still streaked across her sweater. The husband stared at the floor, his legs crossed at the ankles, the salt and pepper curls slicked back from his pale face, which was pinched in thought. Ava bit her lip and contemplated sidling up next to them and chatting them up to glean the details of what had happened.

Just as she started to edge toward them, the metal doors swung open with a *whoosh* to spit out the doctor who'd run past her earlier, now removing her latex gloves, eyes skimming the room for the couple. They looked up, hope smeared across their faces as the cops headed the doctor off, no doubt to let her know the couple wasn't next of kin. Not far behind, another nurse emerged from the doors to hand over what looked to be a bloody wristlet purse to the police as the doctor sighed and shook her head, her shoulders slumped, the message clear.

The girl was dead.

31

CARLY

S he ran.

Her feet splashed into craters overflowing with rain as she dashed toward her car. Her socks, white and fresh from the dryer this morning, now waterlogged, squished insistently inside her sneakers, themselves gray with water, as she bolted for the safety of her car. The rain had stopped momentarily, leaving the air fresh and clean, her skin slimy and raw, the itch for a hot shower and the toasty warmth of her favorite plaid green pajama pants, slouchy blue socks, and oversized Northwestern hoodie propelling her forward.

Carly dove into the car and slammed the door shut, the silence and sudden stillness engulfing her, ringing in her ears, prickling across her skin. She gripped the steering wheel, her breath coming in heavy, gasping spurts, the dots of rain on her windshield splashing shadows of oversized circles against the interior. She squeezed the hard plastic tighter, unable to start the car, fear keeping her hands glued in position.

Fucking Jordan. This was all her fault. Why did she have to come to Whitney's party last week and ruin everything? If she'd just stayed home and minded her own damn business, there never would have been a fight and Whitney never would have gotten mad at Carly for not jumping in the middle of everything to defend her. Carly hadn't proved to be the good little soldier after all and Whitney had let it be known she was a total failure and she was icing her out.

Which had left Carly no choice.

She closed her eyes, whispering commands to herself while simultaneously trying the deep breathing her meditation app was always preaching, but that Carly could never quite seem to master. She squeezed her face in even harder concentration, willing her finger to put the fob in the ignition, press start, and drive herself home.

A flash of lightening followed by rapid pops of thunder, like fireworks detonating all at once, jerked her eyes open. It was time to go home. Carly sniffed back the line of mucous threatening to crawl out of her nose and started the car, flipping on the wipers, hitting the lights, scrunching up her toes inside her wet socks as she put the car in gear and pressed the accelerator.

A fresh wave of rain spit against her windows, before a wallop of water pounded the glass. Her wipers squealed in protest as she turned them up two settings to wash away the rain.

Her phone trilled beside her, the screen lighting up with her dad's face. Carly ignored it. Whatever he wanted, it could wait.

Carly inched across the rain-swollen streets of Lake Forest, desperate to get home. Finally, she turned down her street, her anxiety swelling like a balloon the closer she got to what she was sure was her empty house. It was times like these that she missed her brother, Jimmy, away at Berkley for his freshman year of college. On a lonely, rainy Saturday night when their parents were out and neither of them had plans with friends, they'd watch movies, or play cards or video games, though Jimmy was way better than her at both. Between their crazy busy jobs and hobbies that stretched from book clubs to poker nights, her parents weren't really homebodies, so there was every chance they wouldn't be home on Saturday night. Probably what her dad was calling to tell her. Like it mattered.

As expected, Carly's driveway was empty as she pulled up. Saying a silent prayer, she came to a frantic, haphazard stop, the car jutting out at a crazy angle. Thinking better of it, Carly repositioned it before she ran into her dark, empty house—it not occurring to her until later that

Alexa was supposed to have turned on some of the lights an hour ago —then she flew up the stairs to her room, slamming the door behind her. She collapsed against the floor, bells ringing in the muffled hollows of her ears, her heart pounding fast and furious against her ribcage. Outside, the rain beat against the windowpanes.

The rain.

She glanced down at her hands, distressed to see the rain hadn't washed away the blood.

32

LAUREN

"I agree, we need to ground her. At least a week."

"Two weeks," Lauren said. "No phone, no car." She looked down at her own phone again, her rage rising like mercury, dangerously close to the boiling point. "I'm now officially beyond pissed."

Steve pulled into the driveway and Lauren frowned. Whitney's car was still there, just like it had been when she'd come home earlier to pick up Parker for his sleepover. The electricity appeared to be restored from the storm and the timers for the outside lights and living room were on, the windows upstairs dark.

"What the hell?" Lauren said, more to herself than Steve at the sight of Whitney's car. If she'd been home, why wasn't she answering any of Lauren's texts or calls? They glanced at each other and she knew he was just as confused as she was.

"Maybe she was out earlier and came home and fell asleep," Steve said. "And Parker didn't think to look in her room."

"Steve, she hasn't answered her phone all day," Lauren said, her heart pounding, her spine now tingling with the heat of fear, the mother's intuition that *something was wrong*. "And Parker said he did look in her room and she wasn't there."

He exhaled. "Come on. Let's go inside, find out what's going on."

They entered the house, shadows receding from the gray and silver wallpaper, the glass coffee tables and slate gray couch and matching chairs as they flipped on more lights. As Steve checked the alarm, Lauren called out for Whitney as she poked her head into each room. She tried to tamp down her growing panic as she went upstairs to Whitney's room, turning on the light to find what she suspected.

An empty bed.

Lauren ran downstairs. She'd call Peyton's mother, Regina. Maybe her phone had died. Maybe it was broken or lost. Maybe Peyton had come to pick her up—because as a new driver, Whitney was nervous about driving in the rain—and the girls were huddled up at her house, watching Netflix and taking selfies. She had no choice but to wrap herself in these increasingly improbable scenarios, anything to avoid confronting the painfully glaring obvious.

Something was wrong.

She grabbed her phone from her purse, ignoring the trembling of her fingers as she located the number, how hard her heart was beating.

"Lauren, hi, how are—"

"Regina, I need to talk to Whitney."

"Whitney? She's not here."

"You're sure?"

"Lauren—I—I wouldn't say she wasn't here if she was."

She rubbed her forehead as she paced across her living room. "Can you put Peyton on the phone?"

"What's going on?"

"Just put her on the phone. Please."

"All right," Regina said, sounding flummoxed before she called out to Peyton, who came to the phone after a few seconds.

"Hi, Mrs. Dean."

"Where's Whitney?" she asked, hoping the hysteria didn't creep into her words.

"I don't know. I haven't talked to her since this afternoon."

"What time was that?"

"Um … maybe around one-fifteen, one-thirty? Hold on, let me check. No, yeah, it was one-thirty."

"What did she say? What did you talk about?"

"We were going to meet up at the mall, but then she texted me back and said she had something else to do instead and would call me later."

Steve stood in the threshold between the living room and foyer, concern crinkling his face. She shook her head to indicate she still didn't have any answers.

"Did she say what she had to do?"

The girl hesitated and Lauren could picture her twirling her hair as she tried to avoid looking at her mother, who was no doubt standing over her, a mixture of concern and confusion clouding her face.

"Peyton?" Lauren repeated.

"No."

"Honey, you're not in trouble, but I need you to tell me, right now, where Whitney is."

Lauren could hear Regina in the background asking what was wrong, and finally the girl sighed. "She just said she had something to take care of and she'd call me back. I swear that was all, Mrs. Dean."

"Take care of what?"

"I don't know, I—"

Lauren knocked her fist against her forehead. "Did she tell you where she was going? Was she meeting someone?"

"I don't know, Mrs. Dean, I swear to you." The girl sounded on the verge of tears and it was obvious to Lauren she really didn't know where Whitney was.

"Okay." She sighed. "If you hear from Whitney, you tell her to call me right away."

"Sure, Mrs. De—"

Lauren didn't give the girl a chance to finish, ending the call, shaking her head.

"What happened?" Steve asked.

Lauren paused, her finger already on the nine. "She said they were going to meet up at the mall, then Whit texted that she had something to take care of instead and would call her later."

"What are you doing?"

"Calling the police."

"Do you … do you really think that's necessary?"

"Do I—what? Are you joking? Our daughter could have been kidnapped or in an accident or, who knows what—"

"I just meant maybe there's a really simple explanation."

"Don't you dare tell me I'm overreacting." The 911 operator came on the line and Lauren held up her finger to indicate her husband should stop talking. "Yes, my daughter is missing."

"Okay, ma'am, you say your daughter is missing?"

"Yes, I—" The doorbell rang and Lauren's heart lurched. Whitney. She must have forgotten her keys or lost them somewhere. She was fine. Her baby was fine.

"Ma'am?"

"My doorbell, I think—"

Her face fell as Steve opened the door to two uniformed police officers and the glare of red and blue lights flashing from her driveway. She shook her head, knowing they were there to tell her something horrible about her daughter, some awful thing about her daughter.

Sorrow and shock closed around her as she heard one of the officers ask if he was Steve Dean and if his daughter's name was Whitney.

Which was when Lauren knew her daughter was dead.

33

AVA

S till numb with disbelief, Ava stared at the morning paper splayed out on the table, Whitney Dean's smiling face staring up at her.

When the news about Whitney Dean being stabbed to death flashed across her phone shortly before one this morning, waking her out of a fitful sleep, it had rocked Ava to realize she'd practically been standing next to the girl as she lay dying on a hospital gurney. It made the pain of her fractured wrist seem less than trivial. Her first thought was to call Lauren. The next snowball of emotions was shock, then horror, then relief, then guilt because her own daughter was slumbering down the hall, safe and sound. Then came the cavalcade of text messages from friends, everyone stupefied that pretty, popular, charmed *Whitney Dean* had been murdered in their safe, quiet little suburb, the kind of place where the police would do a vacation home watch for you if you left town for more than five days. It was so unbearably trite, but things like that didn't happen here. Nothing bad happened here. Unlike Chicago, the police department of this affluent community was exceedingly underworked, so much so, Ava didn't have a lot of faith they'd even solve this—not without some outside help. She'd read a newspaper article last year that the chances of being the victim of a violent crime in Lake Forest was one in one hundred and fifty.

Because nothing bad ever happened here.

And yet, something bad *had* happened.

She glanced up at the ceiling in the direction of Carly's room. Ava wasn't ashamed to admit she'd snuck into the girl's room and swiped her phone from the nightstand, not wanting to risk her waking up in the middle of the night to the news. Carly's back had been to her, muffled snores fluttering from her mouth as Ava stared down at her, tears pricking her eyes with equal parts guilt and gratitude.

Kyle shuffled into the kitchen, the crust of a good night's sleep clinging to his eyes, his plaid boxers and beat-up navy blue t-shirt still clinging to his lanky runner's body. "How's the nub, then, Mate?" he asked as he ran his hand across his tight black waves and beelined for the coffee.

"Like shit."

"Right," Kyle said as he took his first sip. "Still can't believe someone pinched my suits."

Ava smacked her good hand against the table, rolling her eyes. "Seriously? This again?"

"I guess I have to take PTO tomorrow and go buy some more," he mused more to himself than Ava.

"Oh, cry me a fucking river," she said as she picked up her coffee mug, grimacing at the iciness of the liquid inside. "Look, we need to talk to Carly."

"Huh? What? Right now? Should we go and roust her?"

"Yes. No. Hell, I don't know." Ava exhaled as she pushed back from the table. "Where's the handbook for this one?"

"I still can't believe it," Kyle said, grabbing a banana out of the bowl of fruit on the counter. "Whitney Dean. Of all people. Here, of all places."

"You aren't safe anywhere," Ava murmured as she dumped her coffee and poured herself a fresh one. "Even here."

"I guess not. That's bonkers that you actually saw Whitney last night in the ER." He shook his head. "Bloody insane."

"I didn't know it was her. Trust me, I still can't believe it myself. I wonder if I should call Lauren or wait a few days," Ava murmured as she stirred cream and sugar into her mug.

"I'd give it a few days. I'm sure things are crazy over there."

"Yeah. Probably. Anyway, back to Carly. We should be the ones to tell her."

"Tell me what?"

Ava and Kyle whipped around to see a pale, withdrawn Carly, sunken dark circles pulling at her eyes. She stood at the threshold of the kitchen, a mixture of curiosity and fear clouding her face. They glanced at each other, the pleading look of who could come up with a game plan faster passing between them.

"Hey, honey. How'd you sleep?" Ava asked as a way of stalling.

"Did you take my phone?" Carly asked as she headed in the direction of the kitchen table, and more specifically, the morning paper, Whitney's picture splashed across the front.

"Carly—" Ava dashed over to snatch up the newspaper, but Carly beat her to it. First, she frowned, then her face collapsed as she realized what her mother hadn't wanted her to see.

"Is this—is this true? About Whitney?" she asked, her voice trembling. "She's dead?"

"Honey—" Ava said.

"Come on, Lamb, why don't you sit down?" Kyle interjected, attempting to guide her to a kitchen chair.

"That can't—that can't be true." Carly shuddered as though she were standing outside in the pouring rain of yesterday. "She can't be, she can't be, I—I didn't think that would happen—that's not what was supposed to happen. She wasn't supposed to die—"

Carly's eyes rolled into the back of her head right as her knees buckled, and Ava thanked God Kyle was there to catch her.

34

RON

Ron took a tentative sip of his coffee, hoping his trembling hands wouldn't betray him and send all that black liquid running down his worn white work shirt as he watched Mrs. Perkins, one of the geometry teachers, gab furiously with American history teacher Mr. Staub about Whitney Dean's brutal murder, the talk of the teacher's lounge.

In truth, it was the talk of Lake Forest. The lead story on every newscast, her smiling pom squad picture splattered across all the local papers. The disbelief had rumbled across Coffee City during the hour he spent there yesterday morning. His trip to the grocery store last night revealed clerks and customers chattering nonstop, in a tailspin that someone would murder *such a lovely girl* in their wealthy, sheltered community where bad things didn't happen. All night, his phone pinged with text messages from friends and family asking if he knew Whitney. He'd only responded with a terse, "yes" each time and that he was too in shock to talk about it.

Driving into school this morning, TV cameras, photographers, and eagle-eyed, anxious-looking reporters rimmed the edges of campus, shouting questions at students and teachers alike as they fought their way past the crowds. The superintendent had instructed all staff and faculty via a concise email late last night to say nothing, to give no interviews and to refer any and all direct inquiries to the district's PR director. Students had no such compunction about talking to the media, as he'd seen several standing on the sidewalk across from school being interviewed as he made his way inside.

"It's just so awful," Mrs. Perkins said as she poured caramel creamer into her coffee and took a sip, leaving behind a bright pink lipstick print on the white mug. "I wonder if it was someone she knew."

"Why do you think that?" Mr. Staub asked, the shine of his bald head matching the high sheen of his brown Oxfords, which were propped up on one of the hard plastic orange chairs, like he was hanging out at home, not at work.

"I just have a hard time believing someone is going around knocking off teenage girls in Lake Forest." Mrs. Perkins scoffed as she played with one of her gold hoop earrings. "An earthquake would sooner happen here than that."

"Anything can happen," Ms. Probst said, a tall gangly chemistry teacher with a huge gap between her yellow smoker's teeth. "Even here."

"Maybe it was a boyfriend. Lover's quarrel," Mrs. Perkins said.

"Could have been a friend." Ms. Probst paused. "Could have been another student."

A gasp went up around the lounge, the possibility of a fellow student murdering another student too terrible to contemplate. Everyone fell silent, the only sounds in the room the occasional slurp of coffee, rustle of papers, the awkward clearing of throats.

"I wonder how long it will be before we're all questioned," Mr. Staub said, breaking the silence.

Ron's heart jumped at the query. It probably *was* a matter of time before all of Whitney's teachers were rounded up by police. Of course they would be. He'd been stupid to think they wouldn't. First the questions would come, then the poking into their personal lives. He bit his bottom lip. Everything would come out.

Everything.

"They'll probably only interview any of us who had her in class." Mrs. Perkins looked around. "So? Who did?"

Ron smoothed down his tie, his stomach in knots, as some of the teachers raised their hands. He cleared his throat and added his to the group. Mrs. Perkins gave a careless wave and scoffed again.

"Well, we know none of us did it," she said, laughing uncomfortably. "Like I said, it was probably a boyfriend, someone none of us knows."

Ron knocked the mug of coffee over, causing the three people sitting at his table to jump back. Heat inched up his neck, burning his cheeks.

"Sorry, sorry about that." He ran over to the sink to grab a roll of paper towels to sop up the mess.

"Well, all I know is that I'll sleep much better at night once whoever did this is behind bars," Mr. Staub said. "I don't care if this is Lake Forest or Lake Titicaca. This is some scary shit."

The conversation floated to the all-school assembly planned for third period as Ron continued wiping up his mess, the prospect of the police banging down his door making his bowels churn, his same dilemma from Saturday night continuing to plague him.

He needed an alibi.

Ron glanced at his watch. Fifteen minutes before the bell would sound, signaling the official start of his day. His hand closed around his phone in his pocket as he edged toward the door of the teacher's lounge to slip out into the hallway, only to collide with the school secretary.

"*Hola*," she said, smiling as she shifted the stack of papers in her hands to wave at him expectantly.

Normally, he would have flashed what he'd been told was a killer smile, chatted her up in Spanish for a few minutes, and told her for the tenth time that yes, he'd love to get her tamale recipe.

But he didn't have time for genial chitchat right now.

He hopped from one foot to the other. "Baño," he whispered, smiling sheepishly.

She nodded knowingly and sent him off with a giggle and another wave as she entered the teachers' lounge. He raced toward one of the exits, sequestering himself around the side of the building before tapping the ICE name in his contact list.

"Hey," his brother, Brandon, said from Michigan. "I'm at work so I really can't talk long—"

"I need a favor."

An audible, exasperated sigh on the other end of the phone. "What?"

"If anyone asks, you and I were on the phone Saturday night. From seven thirty to about nine. And I was at home when you called me."

Brandon paused. "Excuse me?"

Ron peered over his shoulder. "B … I need you to do this. Please."

"What the hell is going on?"

A trickle of sweat dripped down the side of his face. "Okay, don't be mad, but I saw her Saturday night, and—"

"You what?" Brandon exploded. "Are you kidding me?"

"I know, I—listen, nobody can know I was with her and I just need you to back me up—"

"Jesus, for someone so smart, you sure do have shit for brains sometimes."

"Please, Brandon. Please. I'm begging you."

Ron could hear his brother's hostile exhale from Michigan as he waited. Birds chirped happily in the trees and the muted sounds of cars from nearby Green Bay Road floated over his head. Ron looked up at the cloudless blue sky, his terrified breath rattling in his chest.

"Fine," Brandon finally said. "I'll tell whoever asks that you and I were on the phone Saturday night."

Relief gushed through Ron. "Brandon, man, you have no idea how much this means to me—"

"Save it, all right?"

"I just wanted to say thank you." Ron pursed his lips. "For every-thing. Again. Always."

"I have to get back to work." The line went dead.

Ron palmed his phone and shoved it back into his pocket, his distress easing slightly at knowing his big brother would have his back once again, a remnant of childhood that might not ever dissipate. He checked his watch as he rushed back into the school building and raced down the hall toward his classroom, his mind slipping into teacher mode, wondering how to comfort his students today in the wake of Whitney Dean's murder.

35

ERICA

C oncentrating on her workout and to-do list distracted Erica from thinking about Whitney, how they'd been laughing at Jay's frat boy stories, toasting to a good night and a good life, while that girl was being murdered. Shock had rippled through her when her phone dinged early Sunday morning with the news and had continued to reverberate when she read the story in the paper, the stark black headline, 'LAKE FOREST GIRL STABBED TO DEATH,' jumping off the page and running over her like a freight train.

There had been times when Whitney felt like her own, given how close she and Jordan had been since their days at LoMastro. They'd both been stars and it wasn't long before they became best friends, sisters, inseparable, thick as thieves, joined at the hip—all the insufferable, maudlin clichés used to describe exceptionally close friendships. Pom-pom squad, skating and swimming parties, sleepovers, breathless messaging, texting, and social media posting kept Whitney and Jordan willingly tethered to each other for years.

She quickly finished her cool-down before heading to the locker room, her focus on taking sips from her water bottle, not seeing the solid wall of woman she collided with.

"Excuse me—" she smiled. "Oh, Regina. Hello."

Erica involuntarily wrinkled her nose at being forced into proximity with Regina Knowles, mother to Jordan's former pom teammate, Peyton. Loud, obnoxious, militant helicopter mom Regina. At least Jay's megaphone mouth was entertaining. Charming, even. Regina was just loud and boring. The woman ran around town in long, shapeless, oversized t-shirts draped over the mountainous domes of her breasts, biker shorts hugging her muscular, tree trunk thighs, a visor plunked atop her straggly brown mop of hair, and of course—of course!—a fanny pack. Peyton was so pretty and graceful that it had crossed Erica's mind more than once that the girl must be adopted. At one time, Regina had been a big shot at a financial services firm, enabling her to retire at forty, leaving every minute of her day free to be perpetually outraged about any and everything: street signs tilted at the wrong angle, grocery stores not stocking her favorite brand of keto bread, Coffee City spelling her name wrong on her cup. Erica wondered how the woman made it through the day without having a heart attack.

"How are you, E?" Regina said as she slapped Erica on the shoulder, her voice blasting across the already noisy room, causing more than one person to cast glances their way.

Erica stiffened, her shoulders hitching upward in aggravation, both at the bombast of Regina's tone and the casual greeting. How many times had she told Regina to call her by her name? She'd let it slide today.

"Well. Trying to get over the shock," she said instead as she took another swig of water.

Regina nodded soberly as she fanned the red splotches of her doughy face with her hand. "I still can't believe it."

"That something like that would happen here," Erica said. "So hard to fathom."

"And to Whitney Dean of all people. Whitney Dean! What the hell is this world coming to?"

"It's beyond nerve-wracking. I hope the police make an arrest soon."

Regina snorted. "Don't count on it."

"How's Peyton?"

"Crying nonstop. This whole thing just infuriates me. It's horrible. Absolutely horrible."

"I know," Erica said. "Horrendous."

"Douglas and I were talking about it last night and I'm telling you, I think it's someone from the high school."

"Oh, no, you don't really think that."

"I would bet every dollar I have it was someone who was jealous of Whitney. A classmate. I mean, she was the most popular girl at East Lake Forest." Regina clicked her tongue knowingly. "That's what my gut is telling me and my gut is never wrong."

"God. I don't know what's worse. The thought that it could be someone Whitney knew or a complete stranger," Erica said, shaking her head. "Inconceivable—appalling—any way you think about it."

"They better tighten up at that school, because nobody better be coming after my kid, I'll tell you that right now. I will yank her out so fast."

"Oh, well, since it didn't happen on school grounds, I don't think we have anything to worry about," Erica said.

"Well, we'll see about that." Regina glanced over both shoulders before leaning down conspiratorially, lowering her voice, the unsettling scent of grape jelly emanating from her pores, causing Erica to clench. "You know I talked to Lauren that night."

"Saturday?"

"She called me around nine-forty-five or so, and she was going nuts. Got Peyton on the phone to grill her about whether she knew where Whitney was."

"Well, Jay and I actually had them over for dinner that night."

"Lauren and Steve?" Regina gasped. "Oh, man."

"When I think about how we were laughing and joking, having a lovely time, while that poor girl—I feel just terrible about it."

"Have you talked to Lauren since Saturday?" Regina asked.

"I texted her, but haven't heard back," Erica said. "Understandable, though. I thought I might bring her a casserole."

"I hadn't thought of that. Maybe I'll do that, too, bring her a casserole." Regina clicked her tongue against her teeth. "Dougie is just crushed. You know he and Whitney dated last year."

"I don't think I knew that."

"It wasn't any great romance or anything like that. A month if that. You can guess how much Peyton loved her brother dating one of her best friends." Regina looked at her Fitbit. "I have to run. My class is starting soon."

Erica hoped her relief at being released didn't show as the women said their goodbyes, sharing another semi-awkward dual kiss, Erica trying not to breathe in the woman's weird jelly scent.

As she grabbed her bag from the locker room and headed out to her car, her phone trilled and she smiled when she saw Jay's goofy grin staring up at her. "Hello, darling," she said, switching to Bluetooth as she signaled left out of the gym's parking lot. "What would you like for dinner tonight?"

"Whatever. I'm not feeling picky."

"Well, then I'll surprise you. Speaking of surprises, I bought a new car today," Erica said.

"You—what?"

"Bought a new car. Black Range Rover."

"Oh. What brought that on? It's not like you to go car shopping on a whim like that. You usually plan these things out like a year in advance."

"I guess for once I wanted to do something spontaneous."

"How is it?"

"Absolutely love it. Drives like a dream."

"Well, I can't wait to see it."

"I just ran into Regina Knowles at the gym. She told me after Steve and Lauren left on Saturday, Lauren had actually called her looking for Whitney."

"I still can't believe it."

Erica rubbed at her eye, stinging beneath her sunglasses. "I don't know. It's horrible. Almost made me forget how angry I was because I will tell you, I don't believe for one second she was babysitting for the Zindels on Saturday night."

"I wouldn't make too big a deal out of it," he said.

"So you think it's okay for her to lie to us?"

"I didn't say that—"

"Well, what are you saying?"

Jay sighed. "I'm saying, our daughter came home Saturday night. Lauren and Steve's didn't."

She shook her head, letting the silence fill the empty, uncomfortable space between them. "Anyway," she said breezily, haughtily, by way of changing the subject. "I'm going to stop at the store, pick up a few things. I thought I'd make a casserole for Lauren, take it over within the next day or two."

"You're joking."

"Oh, stop it. You know I can cook."

"I remember so well that lemon chicken and scalloped potatoes. I had just renewed my Blockbuster membership and all the cool kids were dialing up AOL."

"Oh," Erica tsked. "Enough."

"Okay, look, the really important thing here is, what am *I* getting for dinner?"

"Whatever you want, my love."

"Well, then I'll just put in my usual order."

They both laughed, the mood lightened, the unpleasantness wiped away, however momentarily, before exchanging "I love yous" and ending the call.

She pulled into the grocery store parking lot and grabbed her phone and purse, mentally scrolling through the list of ingredients for a potato gratin. Simple, delicious, quick.

Her thoughts floated back to Jordan and her disheveled appearance Saturday night and her certainty the girl was lying about where she was. If there was one thing she couldn't stand, it was being lied to. She walked past the newsstand for the local community paper, Whitney's smiling class photo staring out at her from beneath the thick pane of scratched, dirty glass. She stopped and stared at it, mesmerized.

Almost without thinking, she looked down at her phone and went in search of Ted Zindel's office number. Ted's second wife was an airhead who Erica had little patience for and she was in no mood to dumb down her inquiries.

Ted's voicemail filled her ear.

"Hi, Ted, it's Erica Mitchell and I was wondering if you could give me a quick call." She paused, a shiver snaking down her spine as she looked at Whitney's picture again. "It's about Jordan."

36

AVA

Ava glanced down the hallway toward Carly's closed bedroom door as she moved between her closet and bathroom while she got ready for work, an unsettling question looping in her mind since Sunday morning when her daughter saw that Whitney was dead.

What did Carly mean when she said Whitney wasn't supposed to die? Ava slid a simple silver hoop into her earlobe with her good hand as she turned the odd statement over in her head like a coin she was about to toss, puzzling over the words, which no matter how many times she repeated them, she couldn't make any of it make sense.

Adding to her unease had been Carly's demeanor the past few days, vacillating between moodiness—flinching at the slightest noise, ready to dissolve into tears if you so much as glanced at her—to wandering around the house in a daze, staring off into space, unintelligible whispers slipping past her lips.

The details of what happened to Whitney were still scant, though sinister theories abounded, if the torrent of social media posts she'd seen were any indication. Whitney had been kidnapped from her house by a sex offender who'd murdered her after assaulting her. She'd willingly gone off with someone she knew, probably a secret boyfriend who snapped and killed her. Some had even speculated it was a jealous classmate. Around town, pink fliers with screams of a reward had started to fill up community boards in search of tips on the murder. The school had sent a few verging-on-hysteria emails about increasing police patrols and beefing up internal security around campus, measures Ava didn't quite understand, since the murder didn't take place on school grounds. Of course, if someone was knocking off East Lake Forest students, perhaps the moves did make sense.

The only certain thing was that Whitney Dean had been savagely murdered, found face down in a patch of black-eyed Susans in Middle-fork Preserve.

And the murderer was still out there.

She'd finally settled on sending Lauren a hasty text on Sunday night, followed by a lengthy, heartfelt condolence card and the requisite flowers. She'd dropped by the house yesterday, bearing a candle, as she had never been a casserole person. She'd decided not to share that she'd been in the ER when Whitney was brought in, that she'd been mere feet from Lauren's dying daughter. Ava couldn't see what solace the information would have brought the woman, who was indeed inconsolable, wavering between spontaneous crying jags and stony, distracted silence. Ava spent a half hour sitting with her friend, but she doubted Lauren remembered much about that day or any span of time since her daughter's murder.

Ava snapped her watch around her good wrist, groaning as the skin trapped beneath her cast exploded in fire. She grabbed a pair of scissors from the bathroom, carefully inserting the metal blades into the opening between the cast and her hand, moaning as she was able to scratch the itch. As she returned the scissors to the drawer, she looked down the hallway again. Carly should have been up for school by now and she hadn't heard a peep out of her all morning. Maybe she thought she could call in sick, something Kyle would let her get away with but that Ava wouldn't tolerate. She bit her lip and made the march down the hallway to plant her ear against the door. No sounds. No crying. No vomiting. No nothing. Ava raised her hand and knocked firmly against the door, calling out Carly's name. She waited a few seconds before repeating.

"What?" came the barely perceptible reply from the other side.

Ava took that as an invitation to open the door. Carly was dressed for school, slowly filling her book bag, her back turned to Ava.

"You okay?" Ava asked.

"I'm fine."

"I didn't hear you get up this morning."

Carly turned slowly, a 'duh' look on her face. "I'm up."

"Right." She inhaled slowly. "Did you eat breakfast?"

"I had a yogurt."

"Oh. Okay." Ava chewed on her bottom lip. This may not have been the perfect time to ask Carly what she meant on Sunday, but she was seized with a sudden need to because she couldn't hold it in any longer. "Carly—"

"I told Lexi and Peyton I'd meet them this morning," Carly said, brushing past her. "I'm going to be late."

"Do you have pom practice after school?"

"Yeah, why?"

"I was thinking maybe we could go to Sweet's today. Just the two of us."

"You won't be home that early."

She winced inwardly at the truth of that statement. "Well, maybe you and I could grab dinner and go to Sweet's afterward for some ice cream."

Carly's phone sounded with a text and she looked down at the screen, deftly responding to the message with one hand. "I really have to go, Mom," she said as she rushed out, leaving Ava standing in her room.

Ava wrinkled her nose as she navigated around a mound of clothes on the floor. "Carly—"

The girl was out the door, slamming it behind her, shaking the whole house.

"Damn it." Ava kneaded her forehead. When the hell had she lost control? If she was being honest, that had probably happened years ago and obviously, when she wasn't looking. She sighed as she looked at her watch, tripping over another pile of clothes as she did so.

"For the love of—" She sighed and bent down to move the mound, most of which crawled under the bed. Ava wrinkled her nose as she gathered up the pile so she could throw it down the laundry chute next door to Carly's room. With so little of her dirty clothes making it down the chute on a regular basis, one would think she actually had to carry them downstairs.

A pair of pants and two shirts broke free and Ava bent down to scoop them back up, causing a few items from the top to tumble to the ground in solidarity. She groaned and snatched everything back up into a big ball.

And that's when she saw it.

Ava dropped the jumble as she picked up the sweatshirt she remembered seeing Carly in last Saturday.

Blood.

Caked and red and unmistakable.

She gasped, momentarily paralyzed. Whose blood was this?

Carly's?

Or Whitney's?

Ava's knees buckled and her head floated to the ceiling. She sank to the bed, staring at this blood, running her fingers over it hypnotically, memorizing the pattern, the stiffness.

The front door slammed shut and Kyle called upstairs. She'd forgotten he was working from home today and had made a coffee run. Without thinking, she kicked all the other clothes back under the bed, balled the shirt up in her good hand and hid it behind her back. She raced out of the room just as Kyle reached the top of the stairs.

"Morning, Mate," he said kissing her lightly on the lips.

"Hey."

"Right, what's all that huffing and puffing, then?" he asked.

"Oh—um," she sputtered as she searched for something plausible to say. "I was just—"

Kyle's phone rang and she exhaled as he went digging in his pocket for it, quickly becoming preoccupied with whoever was on the other end. Ava turned and ran to their room, not wanting him to see her with the bloody shirt in her hand. She slammed the door and fell against it, her heart pounding as she closed her eyes.

Kyle would be coming in soon.

She needed to hide this until she figured out what to do.

Beads of sweat popped up across her forehead as she stood in the middle of the room, turning and turning in search of a good hiding place.

Ava licked her lips and ran into her closet in search of the wide shoe box for the pumps she'd bought two weeks ago and just hadn't gotten around to tossing yet. She grunted and the fingers of her good hand trembled as she pulled the box down from the top shelf and removed the lid, shoving the shirt inside. Just as she slammed the lid back down, Kyle opened the bedroom door. She hurriedly threw the box back on the top shelf as he poked his head around the closet door.

"What are you doing? Why'd you slam the door?"

"Did I?" she asked.

"Yeah, Mate." He laughed. "You don't remember, then?"

"You know what? I'm late," she said before she kissed his cheek, hoping he wouldn't feel her quivering or notice how warm she was. She quickly gathered up her purse and briefcase and raced downstairs, trying not to think about the shoe box and what was inside.

37

JORDAN

Jordan pulled at the collar of her sweater, the fabric itchy and blistering against her neck. It was one of those weird days when it was too hot for a sweater but not cold enough for a coat or jacket. Getting comfortable was impossible.

Not that she'd worried about her clothes this morning when she got dressed.

A pall continued to hang dark and heavy over the student body, even now, five days after the murder. During the all-school assembly on Monday, Principal Bain prattled on about Whitney and how much she meant to the East Lake Forest community, rattling off her résumé of bests and firsts and mosts like a proud grandmother at a family reunion. The principal had repeatedly gestured to all of the school guidance counselors sitting behind her with the appropriate looks of concern and distress that they were all ready, willing, and able to provide counsel to any student who wanted to talk about how they felt. Students were discouraged from granting media interviews, but from what Jordan had seen all week, it didn't stop anyone. That bigmouth Dionne Cruise was the worst of all, spouting fake tears and hysterics for the cameras any chance she got, totally exaggerating her connection to the most popular girl in school.

Like she knew Whitney. Like any of them did.

School itself had been like swimming through a lightning storm with her eyes closed. Torture. Not just because the hallways and classrooms buzzed incessantly with the disbelief over Whitney's murder, but also, due to the slyly pointed fingers, laser beam gazes burning holes into her, barely concealed whispers containing her own name.

Jordan Mitchell, suspect number one.

The late afternoon sun pelted her face as she made her way off campus. Since her mother took her car, she was stuck with the school bus, which she'd missed because she got busy in the library last period. She now had to walk the mile plus to the Pace bus stop and wait for another forty-five minutes to an hour or call her mother. She'd rather deal with the long walk. Despite apologizing to Mrs. Dean about Whitney's party, Jordan remained grounded. It felt weird to think this way but to Jordan, it didn't seem to matter anymore, apologizing. Whitney was gone.

As she started to make her way in the direction of the stop, a police car slow-rolled beyond the perimeter of campus. She'd seen two this morning when her mom dropped her off. An increased police presence around the school wasn't the only security measure, as the district had also hired additional safety and security guards, urging students to buddy up with each other outside of school hours, to never walk around campus alone.

Music blasted from the direction of the practice field where she knew the pom squad was rehearsing. Jordan stopped and turned, lulled by the beat of the music and her memories. She walked toward the field, ducking beneath the dark, cool bleachers, where she knew no one would see her peeking through the open spaces between the metal steps, rays of sun shooting through the slats. As she watched the girls twist, twirl, and smile, she felt a tug of remorse. She was so mad at Whitney for the bullshit she'd pulled on her over the summer, she just wanted to get as far away from her as she could. So, she quit, stunning pretty much everyone, herself included.

She'd never tell her mother—she'd never tell anyone—but, if she was being honest, she missed it.

Jordan watched Coach K on the sidelines, the strands of her blond Dutch boy haircut blowing in the breeze, her compact gymnast's body swathed in an oversized multicolored track suit. She slowly stalked the field, her clipboard affixed to her hand, looking up every few seconds to observe the girls' moves as she scribbled notes. Her Wrong Notes, as she and Whitney used to call them. Coach K would always have everyone do the routine through once while she took notes about what each girl needed to do to improve, before making them practice it over and over until their arms were limp as spaghetti, their legs jelly, their faces crimson, bodies soaked in salty sweat.

Jordan and Whitney never got Wrong Notes. Well, almost never. It'd be stupid stuff like hold a turn a little longer or kick a little higher. She always thought Coach K just did that so the other girls wouldn't think she favored them or something. Even though she did. Everyone knew she did. Jordan and Whitney were the stars of the team. A spectacular pair. They would have ruled the team this year, no question about it. They would have been co-captains and there would have been no animosity about having to share, either. They made each other better. Stronger. There would have been no stopping the team with Jordan and Whitney at the helm.

They were both nearly letter perfect each and every time.

The song they were practicing to ended and Coach K clapped her hands to get everyone's attention. She ran through her notes, calling out Madison for, as usual, not straightening out her arms enough and Peyton for forgetting to smile when she came out of her turns. Every time.

"All right, girls, a change of plans. I know we've been working on the Cake routine, but after a lot of careful thought, I've decided to pull it in favor of Hotline."

They all looked at each other, and it was clear that unease and confusion were pressing against them. Jordan knew why.

Lexi raised her hand. "Coach K?"

"Yeah, Lexi?"

Lexi chewed on her lip and looked around at all the girls. "Like, totally not to step on your toes or anything, but shouldn't we keep practicing the Cake routine? I mean, we've been working on it for a while now."

"I think under the circumstances, it's best if we pick back up with the Hotline routine."

Lexi raised her hand again. "Okay, but I think it would be a really cool tribute to Whitney if we kept on with her routine. I totally think she would want us to."

A murmur of approval tittered through the crowd and Jordan fought to keep the sting of tears behind her eyes from bursting forth.

This was harder than she thought.

"Girls—"

"Well, let's ask Whitney's best friend," Peyton said.

Jordan's heart skipped a beat. Could they see her under the bleachers? She braced for all eyes to turn to her.

Instead, they swiveled to Carly Ewing.

"Don't you think we should do the routine as a tribute to Whitney?" Madison asked, looking at Carly.

Carly looked from girl to girl, before she nodded. "I think Whitney would totally love that."

Coach K sighed and nodded. Jordan couldn't tell if she was smiling or frowning. "All right, let's just keep practicing the routine then." She looked at all the girls. "For Whitney."

Jordan wiped away a tear. This was too much. She had to get out of here.

She gripped the handle of her book bag on her shoulder as she inched her way out from beneath the bleachers. Jordan gasped as she ran smack into Dionne.

"What are you doing here?" Dionne asked in her usual snotty tone, snapping her gum, before she flung her hair over her shoulder. "I thought you quit."

Jordan put her hand on her hip, her eyes flicking up and down the length of Dionne's body. "Here for pom practice, Dionne? Oh, wait, you never made the team. How many times did you tryout again?"

Red humiliation bloomed across Dionne's cheeks. Jordan had watched the girl audition for pom since eighth grade and no matter how many private dance lessons her mother shelled out money for, she would never make the squad. No rhythm, no flair, no coordination. The girl was one long Wrong Note.

"Whatever," was the best Dionne could come back with. She cracked her gum again. "Maybe you're looking for your next victim?"

Jordan's heart fluttered. "Excuse me?"

"Where were you that day, Jordan? Huh?" Dionne hissed. "Where were you on Saturday?"

"What?"

"Where were you when Whitney was being stabbed to death?"

Jordan scoffed and went to step around Dionne, who blocked her. "Leave me alone, you freak show."

"I'll bet the police are coming for you right now."

Jordan's mouth went dry. "Get out of my way, Dionne."

"When they question me, I'm going to make sure they know they should talk to you. That you totally betrayed your best friend. That you probably killed her."

"I didn't do it," Jordan said, her voice pitching upward.

"Look at how you acted at her party. Totally ruined everything. Whitney said you couldn't be trusted. You totally killed her, because you're nothing but a jealous ho bag who nobody likes."

She backed away, Dionne's words slicing into her like a million, pointed little blades. "I didn't do it," she repeated.

Dionne rolled her eyes. "Yeah, right."

Because she couldn't think of what else to do, Jordan turned and ran, hoping Dionne hadn't noticed how badly her fingers trembled.

38

ERICA

Erica ripped back the foil cover of her fresh pack of contacts, carefully extracting the tiny oval and fitting it onto her cornea, repeating the process with her other eye, blinking them into place. She swept the empty foil and plastic packets into the wastebasket next to her before knotting up the garbage bag to carry downstairs and take outside.

She checked the timer on the potato gratin she'd made for Lauren, an attempt at busy work, since the pursuit of her actual work had been an exercise in futility. Try as she might, she couldn't stop thinking about Whitney.

Or Jordan.

She hated to admit there was another uncomfortable thought biting into her, which was Jordan's whereabouts on Saturday night. The notion had wrestled with her since the girl came blowing through the door, a complete mess, and shifty-looking to boot. Despite pushing down her unease, she needed to know if her daughter was telling the truth, hence why she'd called Ted Zindel, hoping he could allay her growing unease.

Her phone rang from the pocket of her pants. She grimaced when she saw Ted Zindel's name flashing urgently across her screen, alternately scared and hopeful at what he might tell her.

"Ted, hi, how are you?" she asked brightly as she stepped outside to drop the trash bag into one of the bins out back.

"Fine, thank you. Sorry I didn't get back to you right away. I'm just getting home from several back-to-back business trips."

She closed the kitchen door behind her and slowly paced the length of the island in the middle of the cavernous room. "Quite all right. I appreciate you getting back to me."

"Tell Jay I'm looking forward to our next golf game."

Erica rolled her eyes, scoffing to herself. "I definitely will."

"What can I do for you? You mentioned something in your voice-mail about Jordan?"

She paused. "Yes. About her babysitting for you the other night—"

"Baby—did you say babysitting?"

"Yes, that's right."

"Erica, Jordan didn't babysit for us, not the other night, not for a year, at least."

The twin lumps of fear and fury clamped her throat shut. "You're sure?" she croaked. "Absolutely sure?"

"Yes, I'm sure. Trini has asked, a few times in fact, but Jordan has always been busy, so we've used someone else."

She wanted to scream. Throw the phone. Kick something. This girl had deliberately lied to her about where she was on Saturday.

"Why do you ask?" Ted asked, interrupting her ruminations.

"What?"

"Why are you asking about—"

"I apologize, Ted, I must have misunderstood. I'm sorry to have bothered you."

"Sure. Tell Jay—"

"Yes. Golf. I'll tell him. Goodbye, Ted."

She hung up on his sputtering, red rage dancing in front of her eyes, unable to focus on anything else except *Saturday*.

The front door slammed open. Jordan. Home from school. Erica smoothed her hair down, her mission sliding into focus. Jordan huffed into the kitchen and beelined for the refrigerator for her customary after-school snack of blueberry Greek yogurt, mumbling a monotone greeting.

Erica folded her arms across her chest and leaned against the kitchen island, watching her daughter rifle through the silverware drawer for a spoon.

"You, know, Jordan, you never told me how babysitting was the other night." She kept her voice steady and calm as she edged around the kitchen island to come face-to-face with her daughter. She ran her tongue across her bottom lip. "For the Zindels. The night Whitney was killed."

The girl's eyes flicked down briefly, so briefly, no one else would have known. Except Erica did.

She shrugged. "It was fine. You know."

"It's just you haven't babysat for them in a while. Over a year." Erica rubbed her collarbone, her heart pounding furiously against her fingertips. "I thought maybe you were a little rusty. Especially since those girls are somewhat of a handful."

Jordan fingered the yogurt lid. "Um, yeah, it was pretty low-key. I gave them some macaroni and hot dogs and then we watched a movie. Played a little tickle monster. Like I said, pretty basic."

"What movie did you watch?" she continued on, her nerves, her anger, her disbelief over being lied to propelling her to *keep digging.* "With the kids."

Jordan dunked her spoon into the yogurt, mixing the fruit on the bottom, the purple eventually obscuring the white. "*Frozen*, for like, the hundredth time." She chuckled. "That's all they ever want to watch."

"Oh." She folded her arms across her chest. "*Frozen*."

Jordan nodded. "Yeah."

"Okay. *Frozen*." Erica pursed her lips. "*Frozen*. What's it about?"

"You know. Princess Elsa and her sister. 'Let it Go.'"

"What do you mean 'let it go'? I'm asking you a question, a simple question. Why can't you answer it?"

Jordan rolled her eyes. "Oh, my God. Mom. It's a song. In the movie. 'Let It Go.' Elsa sings it."

Erica shifted her feet at the flush of heat racing through her, angry at herself for Jordan momentarily besting her. *You have the upper hand.* "Oh. I didn't realize. A song."

"Jesus Christ, Mom, Kennedy's blasted it probably a million times."

"You still didn't tell me what it's about. The movie, I mean."

"Mom, come on, you took Kennedy to see it when it came out. She played the song on repeat every day for like a year." Jordan rolled her eyes. "Seriously."

"I guess I hadn't really paid attention," Erica said, chewing her bottom lip.

Jordan rolled her eyes. "Elsa's trying to find her sister, Anna, who's trapped in some ice somewhere."

Erica's heart continued its slow, agonizing sink to the bottom of her stomach. How had she never realized what an accomplished liar her daughter was? What else had she lied to her about over the years? "And what about your paper?"

"What about it?"

"You were at the library working on your paper. That same Saturday." Erica paused. "Except I don't remember you telling me what it was about."

"The Civil Rights Act of 1964."

"Something specific or about the act in general?"

"We just had to write about some of the different things that happened that led to it." Jordan spooned a glob of yogurt into her mouth. "The library was a really good resource. I used a lot of microfiche and old magazines and stuff for research."

"I see." Erica unfolded her arms and tapped a nail against the kitchen island, the sharp, tinny sound echoing across the room. "I can't wait to read it."

"I mean, it might be a while. Mr. Staub kind of takes a long time to grade stuff."

"I see," Erica repeated. "And what library were you at again?"

"In Lake Forest. Remember? Dad dropped me off?"

Erica made a face. "Of course I remember."

"Then why are you asking me?"

"Jordan," Erica's voice held an unmistakable warning.

"What?" Jordan asked, exasperated.

"Tell me more about your paper. What you learned about the Civil Rights Act."

"Can we do this later? I've got a lot of homework," Jordan said as she slung her book bag over her shoulder and turned in the direction of the stairs.

"Jordan."

Her daughter sighed and turned around wearily. "Yeah?"

"How are you feeling? About Whitney?"

The color drained from her face as she stepped back a bit. "I—I don't know."

Erica's eyes narrowed as she studied Jordan. "Are you sad?"

"Yeah. I mean of course, I'm sad. Of course." Jordan sighed as she looked away, tears teetering on the edge of her eyes. "It's just really complicated," she whispered.

"What's complicated, sweetheart?" Erica asked softly, afraid, on some level, of the answer.

A single tear drifted down her cheek and her bottom lip trembled. Erica held out her arms and Jordan rushed into them, sobbing quietly. She stroked the girl's hair. "You know how much I love you, right? You know that I would do anything to protect you. Anything."

"I know."

"And you know you can tell me anything," Erica continued. "No matter what it is."

Erica felt Jordan tense in her arms, heard her breathing still as the girl stayed silent. "Is there anything you want to tell me? Anything at all?"

"No." The utterance was small. Plaintive. As though whatever she wanted to confess might be hovering on the tip of her tongue.

"I promise, whatever it is, just tell me and I won't get mad. We'll figure it out. Together."

"I'm really tired, Mom." Jordan breathed out the words in a sad, slow stream.

She was at a loss. Should she push her? Plead with her? Threaten her? The wilderness of dealing with a teenage girl was treacherous and unrelenting. Bewildering. One false move, one wrong declaration could send the whole expedition swirling down into quicksand in a millisecond.

Except Erica knew her daughter was lying about where she was on Saturday night. It shook her to her core to realize that her daughter could lie so casually, so easily.

She pulled back and cupped Jordan's face in her hands. "Why don't you go up and lie down for a little while before you start your homework?"

Relief seemed to fill Jordan's face at having been released. She nodded like a grateful mouse before she darted upstairs and quietly closed her bedroom door. Erica did a slow, deliberate stroll around her kitchen, lost in thought over what to do, how to proceed. Could Jay shake the truth out of the girl? Or would she just lie and lie and lie some more?

She jumped when the oven timer beeped, indicating it was time to take the casserole out of the oven. As Erica slid the glass dish from the rack, steam rising from the center, the cheesy top bubbling and crisp all at once, two thoughts ping-ponged relentlessly across her brain.

Find out the truth.

Protect Jordan.

39

LAUREN

Lauren stared at the ceiling in her living room, the soft hum of a daytime talk show droning on in the background. The topic something that caused the audience to erupt into wild applause every few minutes.

She burrowed deeper into the cushions of the slate gray couch, vaguely aware she'd been cocooned inside of her bathrobe the past few days, that she needed to use the bathroom, maybe drink a glass of water, as her mouth was gummy, her lips dry.

Except she was afraid.

She'd been afraid since Saturday night when the doorbell rang and for a split second, she thought it was Whitney, her anger at the girl for being MIA all day temporarily muted by the relief that her daughter was home, but must have forgotten her key. Instead, two police officers were on the other side of her door, their lips asking if they were Steve and Lauren Dean and did they have a daughter named Whitney. Saying they were sorry to inform them Whitney had suffered multiple stab wounds and had died from her injuries. That they were sorry for their loss.

That her daughter was dead.

Dead.

Lauren had actually laughed when they said it. Because it had to be a joke. Told them they were kidding. It was asinine, Whitney dead. Whitney wasn't dead. She was sixteen years old. She couldn't be dead. Lauren and Steve were supposed to die first. Whitney had her whole life ahead of her. There were colleges to choose, a fiancé to meet, a wedding to plan, grandchildren to spoil.

Those were the hopes and dreams a mother had for her teenaged daughter.

It wasn't until they went to the hospital and some official-looking person peeled back the gray-ish white sheet draped over a body on a metal slab to reveal the closed eyes, the still, quiet, pale face, that Lauren realized those police hadn't been joking, they hadn't been kidding.

Whitney was gone.

The realization sent her plummeting to the cold concrete beneath her, as the comprehension smashed against her that there would be no colleges to choose, no fiancé to meet, no wedding to plan, no grand-children to spoil.

Lauren didn't have any other memories after that. There were blurry, fragmented images of Steve trying to console her, of Parker crying uncontrollably, the woman who'd brought Whitney to the hospital attempting to offer teary condolences. The flimsy gauze of her brain held faint, faraway recollections of faint, faraway phone calls and texts from friends and family. She vaguely remembered agreeing to a private family-only burial followed by a public memorial service at a later date.

Mostly, though, everything past Saturday night and her dead daughter was a blank. A giant white spot.

The doorbell rang and Lauren blinked as she looked in the direction of the door, trying to fix the image in her head. Steve had taken Parker out for breakfast and would be back soon. At least that's what she thought he said. The past few days, it felt as though all her conversa-tions took place underwater. Distorted blobs emitting sound with no real meaning.

The bell sounded again as Lauren continued staring at the door. She winced as she pushed herself upright and sat for a few seconds, as though she'd forgotten what she was doing. The bell sounded a third time. Lauren took a deep breath and launched herself off the couch and shuffled to the door, slowly turning the knob to open it.

Two women she didn't know. Cops. At least, that's what she thought cops looked like according to TV. One short. One tall. Both with ill-fitting pants, bulky belts housing guns, walkie talkies and who knew what other equipment. Bad hair, no makeup. Plain.

"Mrs. Dean?" the tall one asked.

Lauren continued staring at the women and their inquisitive faces, pinched with concern and authority all at once. She tilted her head to the side, not entirely sure what to say.

"Mrs. Dean, I'm Detective Prentiss and this is my partner, Detective Diehl. We have a few questions we'd like to ask you. May we come in?"

Silently, Lauren moved to the side to allow them in. She didn't offer them anything to drink, no have a seat, please, pleasantries. Instead, she trudged behind them, her feet feeling as though they were trapped in sludge as she sank back down on the sofa like a pebble tossed into the ocean, exhausted by the whole effort.

"We spoke with your husband at length the other day, but we did want to ask you some questions," the short one—Detective Diehl—said as they lowered themselves down onto the sectional.

"When was the last time you saw your daughter?" the tall one—Detective Prentiss—asked as she retrieved a tiny spiral bound notebook and a pen from her jacket pocket, shooting an inquisitive look Lauren's way.

"Saturday morning, around eight," Lauren said, her voice suddenly foreign to her. Gravelly. Deep.

"Here at the house?"

Lauren cleared her throat, the phlegm caught in her larynx, necessitating a few hacking coughs to liberate it. She patted her chest. "Yes. I had showings all day and I asked her to take her brother to his sleepover that evening."

"Did you talk to her at all during the day? Exchange text messages?"

Lauren shook her head, the tears welling in her eyes at the memory of not speaking to Whitney the whole day, now knowing—

"Mrs. Dean?"

She focused in on their faces again. Still etched with concern and authority. "No," she said. "We didn't talk or text at all that day."

"Your husband said you had to come home to pick up your son for his sleepover because you were unable to reach Whitney, is that right?"

"Yeah, uh, Parker, my son, he called and said he'd been calling and texting her, but she wasn't picking up, but that her car was here."

"Was that unusual? For her car to be here, but not her?"

"She, uh … the car was a Sweet Sixteen present. She'd only had it a week." Lauren sighed, fatigue pulling at her, her brain not wanting to think about this. Any of this. "I assumed that because it was raining so hard that day, that she might have been nervous to drive and had one of her girlfriends pick her up instead."

"I see. What time did you and your husband arrive home?"

Lauren rubbed her forehead, weary. "I don't know. Maybe around ten-thirty."

Prentiss nodded as she scribbled this down. "Okay. And how did she seem to you on Saturday morning?"

"Fine. Normal."

Both detectives nodded before glancing at each other. Diehl put her notebook down and fixed a stare on Lauren.

"Mrs. Dean, can you think of anyone who would have wanted to hurt Whitney?"

A pea-sized lump in her throat swelled to a grapefruit as tears stung her eyes. "No," she croaked. "My daughter, she was the most popular girl in school."

"What about Jordan Mitchell?"

Her head snapped up. "What about her?"

"The fight at your daughter's birthday party?"

"It was nothing, just stupid teenage girl stuff."

"Didn't look like nothing in the videos," Prentiss pressed. "Any idea what prompted it?"

Lauren dropped her face into her palms. That stupid fucking video. Steve had gotten it taken down, but the damage was done. The memory of her daughter's Sweet Sixteen would only ever be about a thirty-second brawl.

She sighed as she lifted her eyes to meet their gaze. "Whitney didn't want to invite Jordan, but I went ahead and invited her and … what does any of this have to do with finding the person who murdered my daughter?"

"We're just trying to cover all our bases," Diehl said.

Lauren rubbed her temples. "Just teenage girls being overdramatic. Nothing to kill anyone over."

"What about boyfriends?"

"Um … no, not recently. There were a few boys she dated last year, but nothing major."

"Their names?" Prentiss asked, her pen poised over her notebook.

Lauren's lips flapped. "Dougie Knowles was one. I can't remember the others."

Prentiss nodded as she scribbled in her notebook. "Mrs. Dean, we weren't able to find Whitney's phone on her. Could that be why you didn't hear from her at all on Saturday?"

"She never goes—" Lauren stopped herself, closing her eyes briefly. "My daughter never went anywhere without that phone."

"Okay." Diehl scrawled a note in her notebook. "Who would be able to tell us about any boyfriends your daughter may have had?"

Lauren rubbed her temples. This was too much. Just too fucking much. "Peyton, probably. Peyton Knowles. And Carly Ewing."

Another scribble in the notebook before both women stood. "Okay," Prentiss said. "That's all for now. We'll let you know if we have additional questions."

"Do you think … maybe the person who did this might have it?" Lauren ventured. "The phone, I mean. Can you trace it, find out where it is?"

"We already tried that and didn't get a signal," Diehl said.

Lauren's face fell at the dashed hope. "Oh."

"We're pursuing all leads right now, Mrs. Dean," Prentiss said. "Like I said, we'll be in touch."

They all stood and ambled over to the front door. She watched them get in their car as a black Range Rover pulled up. A woman got out. A woman holding something shiny and square in her hands. Walking over to her right now, an uncertain smile on her face.

"Lauren."

Lauren blinked as she stared at the exceedingly thin woman, mentally rearranging her features until they fell neatly into place to reveal Erica standing in front of her, the glint of foil shining in her hands. A casserole, no doubt. She had a vague recollection of casseroles streaming through her front door, accompanied by the mushy, insufferable platitudes of well-meaning friends and neighbors. If potatoes, peas, and carrots smothered in cheese sauce and topped with buttery brown breadcrumbs didn't ease your pain, nothing would.

"Erica," Lauren said firmly, proud she was able to croak out the woman's name.

"I hope this is an okay time." Erica glanced over her shoulder. "I saw you just had some visitors."

"It was the police."

"Oh. Dear. You must be drained."

"Yes. I'm very tired." Lauren's eyes fluttered to the black Range Rover in the driveway. "Is that your car?"

"Hmm? Oh, yes, I bought it a few days ago."

Lauren continued staring at the hulking, gleaming behemoth. "We bought Whitney a Range Rover. It's blue."

"Of course. For her birthday."

She glanced down at the dish in Erica's hands. For some reason, the sight of the casserole plucked a string of malevolence in Lauren. She didn't want well-wishes, casseroles, people awkwardly standing on her front walk, their gums flapping with useless words and fake tears. What she wanted was her daughter. What she wanted was to have not been sitting at Erica's table laughing at Jay's jokes, guzzling wine, or slurping down tenderloin. She should have been out looking for Whitney. Her attention should have been on her daughter. She should have paid attention to the guttural, distressing instinct that something was wrong.

She should have, she should have, she should have.

"I wanted to bring this by for you." She shook her head. "I can't imagine what you're going through."

"No." Lauren said, her voice far away. "You can't."

Erica's smile faltered. "Of course." She held the foil-covered dish out in front of her. "Please. It's just a little something for your family."

"My family." The tears stabbed her eyes like pricks from a needle. Her family would never be the same.

"Oh, Lauren. You'll … you'll get through this. You will."

Lauren swiped at her face, her hands now slippery and salty with tears. "That's very sweet, Erica," she said, her voice stoic.

"You can put it in the fridge, heat it up for later. You don't have to eat it now."

"Thank you."

"Okay." Erica pressed her lips together and nodded. "I don't want to keep you—"

"I should have been home that night," Lauren whispered, more to herself than to the woman standing in front of her offering commiserations in a glass dish. "I knew something was wrong. I just knew it. Why didn't I come home—?"

"Lauren. Oh, Lauren," Erica said, her own tears glistening against her cheeks.

"And now, she's gone." Lauren choked back a sob. "Gone forever."

"It's—it's too horrible to even think about, I know. But please, if there is anything I can do, anything you need—"

"I don't mean to be rude, Erica, but I'm really tired and I think I need to lie down."

"Of course. Of course." She looked down at the foil-covered whatever before thrusting it toward her. "Please. Please accept this."

Lauren's jaw cranked as she looked down at the dish in Erica's hands. She took it, the casserole heavy as a barbell in her hands.

"Thank you," Lauren repeated.

"Remember, please don't hesitate to call me for anything, anything at all. Any calls you need made. Anything."

Lauren could only nod as Erica turned and headed toward her car. She stood in the doorway for a few seconds before slowly closing the door and plodding into her kitchen, the warm glass bottom of the casserole dish stinging her palm. She sat at the kitchen table and placed the casserole dish in front of her, staring for several minutes at the shiny foil top. Without thinking, Lauren pressed the tip of her index finger against the side of the glass dish and slowly pushed until it sailed over the edge of the table and slammed onto the floor.

40

AVA

Ava looked at the clock on her nightstand. Seven. Kyle would be getting up for his Saturday morning run soon and she'd lain in bed for the past two hours watching dawn slink into the room, waiting. He stirred beside her and she slammed her eyes shut and went statue-still. Sometimes, he liked a quickie before a run, and normally, she was all about it.

Today, though, she couldn't concentrate on anything but Carly.

The faint ping from Kyle's phone woke him up and Ava continued to play possum, barely even breathing as he stretched, sniffed, and coughed for a few minutes before finally rousting himself out of bed and heading toward the bathroom to throw on his running clothes. Ava released her breath, but stayed in her same position.

She still needed to decide what to do about Carly's sweatshirt.

Part of her wanted to slip it back into the pile of clothes it sprung from and pretend as though she'd never seen it.

Part of her wanted to ask Carly whose blood was on the shirt.

The bathroom door opened and Kyle came out, the soles of his running shoes thudding lightly against the Indian print area rug. The bedroom door squealed as he opened and closed it, eliciting another sigh of relief from Ava.

She looked toward her closet, the image of the bloodied shirt floating through her mind as she finally got up and went in search of the box. She stood on tiptoe, brushing her fingers against the slick cardboard before tipping the box toward her. Her fingers shook as she held the box, the sweaty palm print from her good hand visible on the glossy black top. She ripped the lid off, almost hoping there was no shirt, no blood.

Both were still there, undisturbed.

She only had one option: confront her daughter. She'd tell Kyle and the two of them would sit Carly down together to get to the bottom of this. In the meantime, she'd ask Carly to spend the day with her. Pedicures, lunch, maybe a movie. Keep things light and breezy while keeping an eye on her.

She only had to fake it for a day.

Feeling better that she had a plan, Ava quickly brushed her teeth, showered, and washed her face before sticking her letter opener down into the space between her cast and skin, groaning at the relief the scratching brought her. Sated, she grabbed her phone and headed for the door, gasping when she found a pale, anxious-looking Carly on the other side, about to knock.

"Honey, you scared me," Ava said, clutching her chest. "What's going on?"

"Have you seen my Northwestern sweatshirt?" Carly asked, her eyes darting around like loose marbles as she fidgeted with her fingers. "The gray one?"

She licked her lips, trying to stall. Carly knew she had the shirt. She had to.

Confront Carly now or wait?

Wait. Wait and lie about it tomorrow. Lying for the greater good was her parental prerogative.

"Have you checked the laundry?" Ava asked as she ran her tongue across her bottom lip, watching to see what her daughter's response would be.

"You're sure you haven't seen it?" Carly asked again. "Like when you were in my room the other day before school?"

Ava shook her head slowly, her heart booming, afraid to breathe. "No, Carly. I haven't seen it." She cocked her head. "Why?"

Carly's face fell as she shook her head rapidly. "Nothing, no reason, I just—I can't find it and I wanted to make sure you haven't seen it. I mean, you really haven't seen it?"

"Sorry, honey," she said, her voice cracking a little with the lie.

"Never mind," Carly muttered to herself as she swiped her hands through her hair and turned toward her room.

"Hey, honey, I was thinking, why don't we spend the day together? Like a girl's day."

"I don't feel like it."

"Come on, it'll be fun."

"I said I don't feel like it!" Carly screamed and darted back into her bedroom, slamming the door.

"Shit." Ava shook her head and marched down the hall, knocking on Carly's door before opening it, finding the girl sobbing face down on the bed. She sighed and went to sit on the corner, hugging the girl's back, drawn tight as a drum.

"Mom, just leave me alone, please."

"Carly, what's—?"

The girl curled further away from her. "Mom, I said I want to be alone."

Ava closed her eyes. "Okay," she said. "But you have to leave the door open."

Shuddering sigh. "Fine. Whatever."

Her phone pinged in her hand as she left the room and Ava groaned inwardly. An email from her boss, Psycho Kitty, needing her to do a quick overnight to Atlanta, leaving first thing in the morning, back Monday afternoon.

"Damn it," she whispered as she shook her head and replied that she'd email her when she landed.

Confronting Carly would have to wait.

41

CARLY

W *here was that sweatshirt?*
          She tuned out Mr. Byrne's droning on about Hester
Prynne as she replayed for the hundredth time the scene from that
Saturday night. She'd come home, run upstairs and taken it off, certain
she'd wedged it under her bed for safekeeping until she could wash it
without her mom knowing what she was up to.

Instead, it was nowhere.

How did a sweatshirt just vanish? Admittedly, she'd gotten
distracted, with Whitney and everything and now, it was gone. She was
sure her mom must have found it, but she would have said something
about it, because if there was one thing Carly knew, Ava Ewing wasn't
someone who would let a bloody sweatshirt go unanswered. But she'd
denied having or even seeing it and now, Carly didn't know what to do.

A knock on the classroom door interrupted Mr. Byrne's praise of
Trish Sellers for her analysis of Hester Prynne's needlepoint. It was
Principal Bain, who motioned for Mr. Byrne to step out into the hall.
Moments later, he came back in, distress wrinkling his face.

"Carly Ewing? You need to go with Principal Bain to the office."

Everyone turned to look at her, mouths hanging open. Her bowels
cranked inside her as heat flushed across her face. She cleared her

throat and gathered up her books, pulling the sleeve of her turtleneck over her wrist as she tried to ignore the stares as she made the slow, agonizing walk across the classroom.

"What's going on?" she asked as Principal Bain turned in the direction of the office.

"The police would like to ask you some questions about Whitney," Principal Bain said as she rushed down the hall, her sensible beige pumps striking hard and fast against the shiny tiles, Carly's timid flats hissing silently as they fought to keep pace.

The flat statement sunk like an anchor inside of Carly. The police wanted to talk to her? Why not Jordan? She should have been the one to get hauled out of class for questioning, not her.

"Why?"

"They're talking to everyone who was friends with Whitney," Principal Bain said as she opened the door of the main office and allowed Carly to go ahead of her. She hesitated at the edge of the principal's office, gaping at the sight of the two women she assumed were the police. One was tall and husky, the other short and thin. Both looked tired and maybe slightly poor, given the cheap-looking khakis and boxy, ill-fitting blazers they wore. It would surprise her if they lived in Lake Forest.

"Carly, this is Detective Diehl and Detective Prentiss," Principal Bain said as she smoothed back a stray silver hair of her tight bun. "As I mentioned, they want to ask you some questions about Whitney."

Carly yanked her sleeve over her wrist again as she took a seat and looked around the office. She'd never been called into the principal for anything. Ever. She was one of those good girls who never got into trouble.

The short thin one took the seat next to Carly and smiled. "How are you today, Carly?"

"Fine."

"So, I understand you and Whitney were good friends."

"Yeah."

"When was the last time you saw her?"

Carly squirmed in her seat. "The Monday before..." She cleared her throat, embarrassed.

"Monday before what?"

"Before she was ... we have English class together, but then I was sick all week and stayed home."

"Where were you Saturday, Carly?" Diehl wanted to know.

"Volunteering."

Prentiss nodded and jotted this down in a tiny spiral notebook. "Where? What time?"

"The Forest Animal Shelter from about ten until seven thirty."

"So, Carly, is there anyone who you could think of that would want to hurt Whitney?" Diehl asked.

She squirmed in her chair again. "Like kill her, you mean?"

The detective cocked her head, still staring at her. "Anyone at all?"

This was her chance. She might not get another one. She had to take it. She cleared her throat. "I guess Jordan Mitchell."

The two detectives glanced at each other. "Jordan Mitchell. She's also on the cheerleading squad with you and Whitney?"

"Pom-pom. Cheer is totally different. We dance. They do tumbling and cartwheels and stuff. And Jordan's not on the team anymore. She quit."

"Sorry. Pom-pom," Diehl said. "So why do you think Jordan would want to hurt Whitney?"

"They used to be best friends and then they weren't."

"Any idea why?"

"No."

"So then why do you think she would want to hurt Whitney?" Prentiss asked.

Carly took a deep breath. "Probably because of all the stuff on Twitter. And the party."

"What stuff on Twitter?"

"A few weeks ago. Everyone on Twitter was calling Jordan names and Jordan blamed Whitney for it."

Diehl tilted her head. "What kind of names?"

Carly gulped and glanced nervously at Principal Bain. "Um, you know. Not nice names."

"Like what?" the detective pressed.

"Oh, uh … like slut. Stuff like that." The words rushed out of her mouth and she wondered how red her face was.

"Okay." Prentiss nodded and scribbled in her notebook. "So, you're saying Jordan believed Whitney started this social media campaign against her and it made her mad enough to kill her?"

"I mean, I don't know if she killed her, I'm just saying Jordan hated Whitney. She ruined her birthday party and was saying all kinds of stuff about her."

"Right. The videos. You were there that night, the night of the party?"

"Yes."

"Tell us what happened."

"Whitney wanted Jordan to leave and she wouldn't and they got into it. Then Jordan said she was going to tell everyone what Whitney did."

"What did she mean by that?"

Carly shrugged. "I don't know." She bit her lip. "I heard Jordan say something like that before. To Whitney."

"When was this?"

"The Friday before the party. We were outside of American lit and they got into it and Jordan said, she would fuck Whitney up." Carly covered her mouth, embarrassed. "Sorry," she said, looking again at Principal Bain. "I'm just saying what Jordan said."

"Did anyone else hear this?"

"A lot of people. A whole bunch of people."

The detectives nodded and Prentiss flipped her notebook closed. "Thank you, Carly, for your time today. You've been very helpful."

"Do I have to go back to class?" Carly asked.

"Since the period's almost over, I'll give you a pass to the library," Principal Bain said, pulling a small green notepad from her desk drawer and scribbling across it, before tearing off the square of paper and handing it to Carly.

She slid out of the chair, her heart racing as she opened the door, clutching the pass on her way to the library. She didn't feel bad about what she'd said about Jordan. She'd get arrested and they'd throw her in jail.

Better her than Carly.

42

RON

Had his fear been obvious? Had anyone seen the way he twitched when the principal knocked on the door, asking to speak with Carly Ewing?

Could they smell his terror?

As had been the chatter of the teacher's lounge, it was a matter of time before the police got around to questioning Whitney's teachers. What was she like in class? How did she get along with her fellow classmates?

How did *you* get along with her?

His brain oscillated between his choices like an unmanned water hose, dancing wildly across the terrain of his mind. Stay and let the police question him, hoping—*hoping*—the questions would stay mundane, that he wouldn't raise their suspicions.

That they wouldn't want to know where he was that night.

Who he was with.

What he was doing.

Or he could leave town. Disappear into the ether where they wouldn't be able to poke at him with their questions.

That wouldn't work either. He had few places to go. His brother's in Ann Arbor, the small house heaving with a wife who didn't much care for her pseudo-intellectual brother-in-law, a barking dog, and a squawking, red-faced toddler. His parents had moved to Ireland last year. There were a handful of couches he could crash on. A hotel for a night or two.

There was no such thing as a vacation in the middle of the school year. Calling in sick was frowned upon. You pretty much had to be dying. Or dead.

He was stuck here. Stuck with the ever-increasing dread that they were coming for him.

Poke, poke, poke.

Worst of all was how suspicious it would look if he fled.

But that may be the only choice he had.

43

JORDAN

Jordan swiped the hairbrush through her hair one last time before binding the slippery strands into a ponytail. From downstairs, the doorbell rang. She frowned and looked at the clock on her nightstand. Who would be ringing the doorbell this early?

She shoved her feet into her flats and grabbed her book bag before she bounded down the stairs, stopping in her tracks at the two women in really bad suits talking to her mother. She wondered if this had anything to do with Carly getting pulled out of class yesterday. Or worse, Dionne threatening to point the cops in her direction. There wasn't anyone she could ask about what had happened, so she'd had to rely on creeping around online. There wasn't anything on any of the local news sites except the usual that police were investigating. Trish Sellers had posted on Twitter about Carly, trying to make it sound all sinister and conspiratorial, when fifteen other people chimed in that they'd been questioned too, so it all died down pretty quickly.

And now they were here for her.

"Mom?" she asked as she reached the bottom of the stairs.

Her mother whirled around, a startled expression on her face. "Oh, honey, these two detectives would like to ask you some questions about Whitney. And they promise to make it quick, since you have school. Right, detectives?"

"Um," Jordan said, wondering if they heard the tremor in her voice. "You talked to Carly Ewing yesterday, right? And you're just talking to everybody, like on *Law and Order*?"

The tall one smiled. "Something like that."

"This isn't going to take long, right?" her mother repeated.

"No, Mrs. Mitchell, this shouldn't take long," the short thin one— Detective Diehl—said.

Her mother motioned for her to sit and she lowered herself onto the ottoman for her father's favorite wingback chair while the two detectives perched on the couch. Her mother remained standing, arms folded across her chest.

"Jordan, we're just talking to all of Whitney's friends and we wanted to ask you a few questions," Prentiss said.

"Okay," she said as she ran her hand through the slick of her ponytail.

"How long were you and Whitney friends?" she asked.

"Since we were three."

"Best friends, right?"

"Yeah, best friends."

"But you hadn't been getting along lately, right?" Diehl asked.

Heat flamed across her cheeks. She cleared her throat. "No, not really."

Diehl pulled her phone from her suit jacket pocket and swiped across the screen, which blazed to life with the fight from the party. From the corner of her eye, her mother sighed and closed her eyes, rubbing her temple with her fingers.

"What happened the night of the birthday party?" Diehl asked.

Jordan chewed on her bottom lip and looked down at her skirt. "We just both got a little heated, that's all."

"Huh." Diehl scratched her chin before swiping some more across the phone's screen. "Did it have something to do with these tweets about you?"

"Tweets?" her mom asked, straightening up. "What tweets?"

"It's nothing, Mom."

"It seems a few weeks ago there were some not-so-nice things said about your daughter online," Diehl said.

"What? Are you serious?" her mom asked, looking at her. "Why didn't you say anything?"

"Mom, give it a rest."

"What things?" her mom demanded. "What were they saying?"

"Jordan, did you think Whitney had something to do with the tweets?" Prentiss asked, ignoring her mother.

"Whitney was totally behind it."

"We also had some witnesses say that the Friday morning before the party, you threatened to 'fuck Whitney up'." Diehl put her notebook down as her mother gasped. "What did you mean by that?"

Jordan's heart dropped to her shoes and for a moment, the only sound she heard was the blood pounding in her ears.

"I didn't mean anything by it," she finally said. "Just talking, that's all."

"The night of the party, you said to Whitney, 'I will tell everyone what you did'." Diehl narrowed her eyes. "What were you going to tell everyone about Whitney?"

Damn. They'd heard that?

Jordan's mouth went dry and from the corner of her eye, she could see her mother's jaw drop open as she stared at her.

"It was just a stupid fight."

One of Diehl's eyebrows went up as she stared at Jordan for a few minutes, allowing the silence to stretch between them like silly putty. "Okay," she finally said. "And where were you on Saturday?"

Her breath quickened. She went to swipe her hands through her hair then plopped them back down in her lap. "At the library."

"Anybody that can verify that?"

"I mean, I don't know if anyone saw me, but I was gone all day," Jordan said.

Prentiss clicked her pen. "What time?"

She pursed her lips. "My dad dropped me off around ten that morning and I came home about nine-thirty."

"Why so late?"

"Well, I was babysitting."

"Who'd you babysit for?" Prentiss asked, her pen hovering over her notepad.

"Detectives, my daughter really needs to get to school," her mom said.

"Jordan?" Prentiss looked at her, her eyes two slits of skepticism. "The name of the family you were babysitting for that Saturday night?"

Jordan's throat closed, her head heavy as a bowling ball. Why did her mother have to be sitting here? With her mom sitting here, she had to keep to her story about babysitting. That meant they would call the Zindels and they would tell them Jordan hadn't been babysitting for them that night, or any other night in the last six months.

She was screwed. So, so screwed.

Her mother's phone blared. She looked down at it and groaned. "Client emergency." Without saying anything else, her mother jumped up and ran out of the room, phone glued to her ear.

It was the break Jordan needed.

"Listen, I don't want my mom to know where I was on Saturday," she whispered. "I told her I went babysitting after the library, but really, I was at this coffee house, club kind of thing in Evanston, and if I tell her that's where I was, she'll freak."

"What's the name?" Prentiss asked.

"It's called Click's. It's—they do like slam poetry and stuff like that. She hates that kind of thing."

"Did you go with anyone? Anyone that can vouch for you?" Diehl asked.

"No, I—I took the train, the Metra. It was a last-minute thing."

"Do you still have your ticket?"

"It was on my phone. It's gone now." She glanced over her shoulder at the approaching sound of her mom's voice. "Please? Don't say anything?"

Her mom came back in before either of the detectives answered and Jordan was left to cast them nervous, pleading glances, hoping they didn't press her anymore about Saturday night.

"My goodness, it's always something with clients." Her mother exhaled as she regarded the detectives. "I really do have to cut this short. Jordan has school—"

"We just had one more question," Diehl said. "What else were you and Whitney fighting about?"

Jordan pressed her lips together, partially grateful for the detour, even if it still wasn't a question she wanted to answer. "I told you, it was just a stupid fight. It doesn't matter anymore."

"Detectives—"

"God, Mom, stop—"

"This is really the time to tell us everything going on between you and Whitney," Diehl said.

"It was over a guy, okay?" she said, her voice scratchy with irritation before she remembered she was trying to stay on their good side. "She said some stuff to him about me and I was pissed—"

"Jordan!"

"Mom, please—! I was pis—upset about it and we stopped being friends. That's it. I swear."

Diehl ran her tongue across her bottom lip. "What was this boy's name?"

"Alex. He was … he was just this guy we met at a party. It was no big deal and whatever, I was almost over it."

Diehl nodded, her pen scribbling. "Alex what?"

"I don't know his last name. We only met him like a few times. I don't know anything about him."

"You have a phone number, an email address for him?" Diehl asked.

"No, I deleted everything."

Diehl frowned. "What about the people at the party?"

"They were Whitney's friends. I didn't know them."

Diehl rapidly tapped her pen against the metal spirals of her notebook before flipping it closed. "Thanks for your time. We'll be back in touch."

Without a word, Erica showed them out, while Jordan sat hunched over on the ottoman, trembling.

Her mother came and stood in front of her, hands on her hips. "Are you okay?" she finally asked.

"I'm fine," Jordan said, surprised. She expected another interrogation. Maybe that was coming later. She stood up, slinging her book bag over her shoulder and brushing past her mother. "I'm going to miss the bus."

"So you and Whitney were fighting about a boy. That's what this whole thing was about, the whole reason why the two of you stopped talking?"

"Mom, please, just stop." She looked at her phone. "I'm going to be late."

Her mother's phone pealed again. She scoffed. "I have to take this. Jordan, we're not done with this conversation—"

Jordan didn't say a word as she stormed out of the house and sprinted toward the bus stop, barely making it. She flopped back against her seat, her head swimming from the impromptu interrogation.

She had lied. About everything. Where she was on Saturday, the imaginary boy named Alex. All of it.

She wasn't worried about her mother. She'd just boo hoo a little and suck up to her and her mom would get out of her face.

The cops were a whole different thing, though. But honestly … could they really figure out she was lying?

No. Probably not. Everything she said was so vague.

Besides, Whitney was dead, so she wasn't talking.

And just like Whitney, she'd take her secrets to the grave.

44

AVA

S he needed Carly out of the house.

Her quick overnight had turned into a week and now here she was in almost the exact same spot she'd been in last Saturday as she steeled herself to confront her daughter about the bloody sweatshirt she'd found. However, the trip had given her plenty of time to think and she concluded that if there was a bloody sweatshirt, it reasoned there was more evidence possibly tying her to Whitney's murder. Which meant she needed to search the girl's room and her car.

Because she needed to know.

She hadn't yet worked out what she would actually do if she found anything. Crossing bridges when she got to them, she supposed. Right now, she just needed the girl gone so she could do her searching in solitude.

Carly was upstairs, her face likely buried in her phone or watching one of her Lifetime movies, or probably both. Ava sipped her coffee as she drummed rapid, agitated fingers against the side of her coffee mug.

"Hey, Mate, I'm off to the hardware store and the bank," Kyle said as he bounded down the stairs. "You need anything?"

Her head swiveled around at the sound of his voice, the moment seizing her. "Take Carly with you."

"What?"

Ava pursed her lips in an attempt to force herself to stay and appear calm. "What I meant was, I was just thinking maybe you could take her to lunch or for ice cream or even a movie. You guys used to do that all the time."

"Right, in case you missed it, she doesn't much care to roll with the old man anymore."

"Just—I think it would be good for her to spend some time with you. With us. Maybe tonight we'll order in a pizza and watch movies. You know, like we used to when the kids were little."

Kyle stared at her, his face scrunched together in confusion. "Have you gone mad?"

Ava dumped the dregs of her coffee into the sink. "We should just spend more time together as a family, that's all."

"Some of us were going over to Joe's tonight to watch the American football match."

"Okay, it's a football game, and … I'm sure Lauren and Steve wished they could spend more time with Whitney."

"Right." Kyle exhaled. "Okay, I'll stop by the bank, skip the hardware store and take her to The Lantern for a burger and walk over to Sweet's after for ice cream."

Ava did a quick calculation. Two hours and some change at least. Plenty of time to search Carly's room and car.

"Perfect. I'll come up with some movie ideas for tonight."

He pecked her cheek before calling upstairs for Carly, who didn't respond, so he went up to her room to relay the Saturday plan. Ava paced the kitchen for a few moments, keeping her ear cocked for whines of dissent. A few minutes later, she heard them descend the stairs and she made a big show of rinsing her coffee mug and putting it in the dishwasher before wiping down her clean counters to keep herself busy. Carly pouted as she pulled on her coat, while Kyle seemed to beam at the prospect of spending some time with his daughter.

"You guys heading out?" she asked innocently.

"Yeah, we'll be back in a few hours," Kyle said as he ruffled Carly's hair. "Come on, Lamb."

"Dad, stop."

"Have fun," Ava said to their retreating backs.

She listened for the sound of Kyle pulling out of the driveway then edged over to the front window to watch them drive off down the street. As soon as they were out of her sight, she bolted upstairs to Carly's bedroom. The door was closed and she flung it open, not sure what mess to tackle first, before beelining for her dresser, carefully opening the drawers to rifle through the contents, mindful not to disturb things too much, lest she raise suspicion.

Ava continued her tour around the room, searching Carly's closet, pawing through the stacks of clothes, skimming through the books and papers scattered across her desk and checking under the bed. Unlike her own sixteen-year-old self, her daughter didn't keep a diary. Maybe girls didn't do that anymore.

A sliver of sweat ran down the side of her face as she flopped down on the bed, satisfied she'd unearthed every secret the room held. She looked at her watch. She'd been in here about forty-five minutes, leaving her plenty of time to search the car. She ran down the hall to her bedroom for the spare key before flying down the stairs and outside, shivering as she threw the door open, her thin sweater no match for the crisp fall breeze. She quickly deactivated the alarm, preparing to jump inside.

"Ava, hi!"

She stopped cold, whipping around at the sound of her next-door neighbor, Jaime, all five feet of her waving excitedly to Ava over the hood of her own car, her strawberry blond ponytail swaying behind her.

"Jamie, hi," she said meekly.

The woman held up her wrist, tapping it. "How much longer?"

Ava looked down at her cast. "Oh. A few more weeks, I think."

"Ugh. I'll bet it's itching something awful, isn't it?"

"A little, yeah."

"I remember when Tobias broke his wrist when we were first

dating. Oh, and actually, you knew Spatz fractured his wrist last year, right?"

"I remember that, yes."

Jaime took a deep breath and rolled her eyes and Ava groaned inwardly, because she knew the woman was gearing up to drop a story on her. She'd never met a woman with more stories, all of them long and boring.

Not today, not today, not today. Dear God, not today.

"My gosh, we are having to do so much travel for Spatz's swimming. Meet after meet, every weekend. It's exhausting. Thank goodness we're getting this weekend off."

"Yeah, I remember going through that with Jimmy."

"Oh, my gosh, let me tell you about the trip from last weekend— actually, how is Jimmy? Coming home for Christmas?"

Ava glanced at Carly's car, then down the street, irrational panic that she and Kyle would be ambling toward the house any minute surging through her. Logically, she knew there was plenty of time before they got back, but frittering it away with a bunch of BS chitchat would eat into it.

"Yeah, he's planning on it. It'll be good to have him home." She racked her brain for an excuse to get out of prolonging this conversation. She could just get in the car and go somewhere, but she didn't want to chance it.

"That's great. Anyway, this trip last weekend—" Jaime's Fitbit sounded and she jumped before a nervous, sputtering giggle burst from her lips. "Oh, gosh, I said I was going to the gym for a class today since I had the time. I guess I better scoot. See you soon," she said breezily as she got into her car.

Ava didn't bother waving goodbye as the woman backed out of the driveway before she pounced and opened the car door, patting the seats and floor and ransacking the armrest, relief flooding through her with each non-discovery. All that was left to check was the glove compartment and the trunk and she'd be home free.

There's nothing here, there's nothing here.

She yelped when she accidentally banged her cast against the door handle, but kept going, determined to get this done in one shot. She yanked the glove compartment open in order to rummage through the contents. Car manual, registration, insurance card, a flashlight, Kleenex, and protein bars.

And shoved way in the back, the last thing on earth Ava wanted to see, much less lay her hands on.

She gasped when she saw it, shock and fear pushing tears to the rims of her eyes. With the sleeve of her shirt wrapped over her trembling fingers, she reached in and dislodged the bloody X-ACTO utility knife from inside the glove box, it's thick black handle still smeared with brownish-red streaks. Ava could only stare at it, the awful possibilities blazing to life in stunning, inescapable color.

"Oh, God. Carly. What did you do?"

45

ERICA

E rica took a slow sip of her coffee as she stared out the kitchen window, the waves of Lake Michigan churning gently. She kept her ear cocked for the sound of Jordan clomping down the stairs. It was Saturday. Jay had left early for the office and she'd already dropped Kennedy off at gymnastics earlier that morning. She glanced at the clock. Any minute now.

On cue, Jordan clattered into the kitchen. Erica couldn't help but frown at the oversized hoodie and jeans, hair hanging limp and frizzy at her shoulders, not even a stich of makeup. Her daughter was usually so stylish, so attuned to wearing the latest fashions. These days, she looked like she crawled out of the garbage can.

Instead of spitting out the retort simmering on her lips, she simply smiled. "Good morning."

"Hi," Jordan said, going into the refrigerator for one of her Greek yogurts.

"Jordan."

"What?" she responded as she slammed the door shut, shaking the kitchen.

"I've decided to give you your car and phone back."

"You—seriously?"

"I think you've learned your lesson about your behavior the night of Whitney's party." Erica turned her attention back to the window, the tops of the trees blowing slightly. "Somehow, it all seems so trivial now."

She rubbed her now stitch-free ear. "Yeah. I guess."

"So," Erica said as she reached into her pocket for the phone and car keys, placing them on the counter. "Here you are."

Jordan frowned as she looked at the phone. "You got me a new phone?"

"You were due for an upgrade, so I went ahead and took care of that."

"Oh. Wow. Thanks."

Erica held out her arms. "You're welcome, darling," she said as Jordan ran around the table to embrace her, the freesia shampoo and Juicy Couture perfume igniting a kaleidoscope of memories, mostly joy and wonder.

"So, what do you have planned today?" Erica asked, stroking the girl's hair.

"Well, now that I have my car back, I think I'll go to the mall. I need some new gym shoes. Maybe go to Coffee City for a little bit."

"All right, well, be home in time for dinner."

"Sure. Thanks, Mom." Jordan scooped up the keys and phone, smiling as she turned on her heel to leave.

"Jordan?"

"Yeah?"

"I love you."

"I love you too, Mom."

"Have fun today." Erica kissed Jordan's cheek and watched the girl skitter out the front door, the muffled sounds of her liberated car pulling out of the driveway.

Erica drained her coffee, then picked up her own phone and tapped the app connected to the tracker she put on Jordan's car yesterday afternoon. The little red car zoomed along the route to the mall and the app tracking her texts remained silent, putting her instantly at ease.

Always have a plan.

46

AVA

Ava lifted the chicken out of the marinade with her good hand before dunking it into the bright orange sauce again and swishing it around the bowl. She narrowed her eyes as she watched Carly methodically chop stalks of broccoli for dinner. Both the bloody sweatshirt and the bloody X-ACTO knife were now locked in a drawer in her home office. She'd take them to work with her in the morning, though she knew the geographical change would still plague all of Ava's waking and sleeping moments. After finding the X-ACTO knife yesterday, darkness had closed in around her as she struggled to come to grips with the discovery. Her daughter, a murderer. Her *daughter*. All last night, she'd watched Carly as she munched on pizza and laughed at Reese Witherspoon sashaying her way through Harvard, searching for some sign, some clue about just who her daughter was.

Each day that passed with no arrest in Whitney's murder made Ava that much more nervous. She knew she wasn't the only one chewing her fingernails, anxiously watching the news for a ripple of movement. The private Lake Forest Facebook page swelled by the hour with more anger and bewilderment over the lack of any real progress toward an arrest. Leading the charge of course was that loudmouth wannabe activist Regina Knowles, who slapped up seething posts about the ineptitude of the police department seemingly every fifteen minutes. When she wasn't staging ill-advised protests to get stupid ordinances passed, she was a chronic petition starter, many of which went nowhere. The woman reveled in hopped-up indignation.

The story had all but fallen out of favor with the local media, having moved on to other tragedies, other calamities. But the stain remained on their community, becoming more stubbornly entrenched each day, threatening to become a permanent, unbreakable thread in their fabric.

"Mom?"

The sound of her daughter's voice jerked Ava back to the present. She looked down at her hand still submerged inside the bowl of marinade.

Her head snapped up. "What?"

"The broccoli?"

"What about it?"

"What do you want me to do with it?"

"Oh, um, just add some olive oil and salt and pepper then mix it around with your hands, then put them on the sheet pan to roast," Ava said as she pulled her own hand out of the marinade and quickly ran it under the tap.

"Wait, what?"

Ava reiterated how to season the vegetables, then watched as Carly doused them in olive oil and spices then tossed everything together, the suspicions, the uncertainty, the *fucking terror* around the possibility that her daughter was a murderer squeezed against her like a vise. What could possibly drive her daughter—or anyone—to such a heinous and horrific act? What could be so bad as to elicit that kind of response?

A weird, unsettling jolt of memory pulsed beneath her skin as the ghost of an incident when Ava was in junior high swarmed around the kitchen. During the middle of her seventh-grade year, a new girl transferred into the eighth-grade class. Laney. A girl whose last name she didn't know at the time and couldn't remember now. They weren't friends, Ava only seeing her in the halls on occasion. In their predominantly middle to upper middle-class school, Laney was hard to miss. Her family obviously struggled, given the stained, ripped, ill-fitting clothes Laney repeatedly wore week after week. Worse, Laney never wore bras. She kept her books pressed against her overdeveloped breasts to keep them from jiggling when she walked down the hall, head bowed in shame as she plodded from class to class.

She couldn't hide behind books in the girls' locker room while changing for gym class, though. Teased and tittered about mercilessly by malicious, immature junior high girls, awkward, timid Laney lugged around a hefty bullseye from day one. Her street clothes stolen from her locker one time forced her to spend the rest of the school day in her gym shorts and t-shirt. Nasty scrawls in the restrooms about what Laney would do for blowjobs. Slam book pages shoved through the vents of her locker, the vitriolic jabs decrying everything from the ratty state of her generic, dollar store sneakers and near-tattered clothing, to her lopsided, homemade haircut, the vicious sneers written in loopy, girlish swirls of purples, pinks, greens, and blues.

Laney took the blows in silence. Never fought back. Never said one word. Not even one tear shed.

Until one day, when she calmly walked up to the ringleader of her bullies in the cafeteria and smashed an empty Coke bottle into the girl's face.

Laney was expelled. Her tormentor lost an eye.

Ava never knew what happened to either girl, as neither came back to school. There had been a rumor during junior year that Laney overdosed on a bottle of pills and died, but that's all it was, a rumor.

She snuck a glance at Carly again. Which one was her daughter?

The tormentor or the tormented?

"Mom? Did you hear me?"

For the second time that evening, she was jolted back to the disquieting reality of the here and now.

"What did you say?"

"I asked if you wanted me to set the table?"

"Oh. Sure. Yeah, thanks."

Carly nodded and Ava bit her bottom lip as she watched her

daughter silently take down placemats and plates for the table. "Carly?"

"Yeah?"

"Have you been volunteering lately? At the shelter?"

A noticeable stiffening of the back as she straightened up awkwardly. "Why?"

"It's just that I haven't heard you talk about volunteering since … since the day of Whitney's murder."

"I—I've just been busy, with school and pom and stuff."

"Did something happen?"

"No."

"You sure?"

Carly dropped the handful of forks in her hand on the table and whirled around, her dark eyes blazing with irritation and the shimmer of tears. "God, Mom, why are you asking me all these questions?"

Ava decided to come right out with it, stop dancing around the elephant. "Where were you that day, Carly?" she asked calmly.

"I already told you, I was volunteering with the shelter."

"The whole day?"

"Yes, the whole day."

Ava took a deep shuddering breath as she narrowed her eyes. "Did something happen to you that day?"

Carly fidgeted with the edge of her sweater sleeve, yanking it over her wrist. "Like what?"

Ava edged closer and put her hand on the girl's shoulder. "Did you get into trouble that day?" she whispered.

Mother and daughter stood locked in suspended animation, Carly seemingly on the verge of spilling her guts about *something*. Ava's breath still and heavy in her chest as she waited. Behind her, the hot oven groaned quietly as it too waited.

"Mom, I—"

"Hey, what smells so good?"

The bang of Kyle's entirely unwelcome entrance into the room shattered the fragile moment. Carly retreated away from Ava, whose chin plummeted to her chest at being so close to extracting *something*.

"Chicken," she said flatly as she returned to the counter and slapped the bird on the stovetop grill, both hissing in angry response.

"Hey, Lamb, how are you?" Kyle asked, kissing Carly's forehead, totally oblivious to what he'd just ruined.

"Fine," she said. "Everything's fine."

Ava and Carly both glanced at each other, Carly's eyes the first to flit away as she finished setting the table. Father and daughter continued chatting about the sort of nothing stuff people chat about at the end of the day until dinner was on the table.

Meanwhile, Ava alternated between genuine worry and silent fuming at being so close to getting to the bottom of what was going on with her daughter.

And one way or another, she would.

47

RON

R on closed the door of his classroom and collapsed into his desk chair, spent. It seemed like every period today was fraught with students who either didn't care that they hadn't bothered to read the material for class or who were so terrified of being called out for not knowing anything, talking in wild, preposterous loops instead.

Corralling dispassionate students only made the knife edge he was teetering on that much sharper. Everywhere he went around town, Whitney's smiling face stared out at him, courtesy of the fliers dangling with the carrot of a reward courtesy of a band of concerned parents. The pink pages were posted on seemingly every community bulletin board, beseeching the public to share any information they may have had about the killer. Adding to his anxiety was the late after-noon buzz across seventh period that Whitney's public memorial was at the end of the week, her family apparently having had a private cere-mony in the days immediately following her death. He'd be expected to go, of course, as one of her teachers.

But he couldn't possibly go, images of his bowels loosening and betraying him in the middle of all that mourning and wailing floating across his brain like flotsam. No way.

He jumped as his phone pinged with a voicemail. He licked his lips as he took note of the blocked number, his heart racing as he tapped the voicemail icon on his phone.

"Mr. Byrne, it's Detective Diehl with the Lake Forest PD. Was calling again because I wanted to ask you a few questions about Whitney Dean, who I understand was in your class. Please call me—"

Ron deleted the message and dropped the phone on the desk. She was persistent, he'd give her that. This was the fourth time she'd called him and Ron knew she was a step away from paying him a visit. He just couldn't face that, knowing he'd never withstand the pressing interrogation, hard-nosed stares, or psyops tactics designed to pry words from his lips. As his ruddy, hard-bitten father had always been fond of telling him all throughout his childhood, he was a sensitive type, disdainfully declaring he was too much like his mother, a woman gleefully free of guile or subterfuge of any kind. All the detectives would have to do was ask him the right questions and he'd spill like a kicked over garbage can.

And he just couldn't do that.

He jumped as his phone blared again, the sonic boom of his heart reverberating through his body. His stomach plummeted to the floor as he realized this was a call he had to answer.

He said a quick prayer.

"Hello?" he said, his voice shaky, wondering just how cool he could play it.

"Byrne."

"Yes. Speaking. Who's calling?"

"Stop pretending you don't know who this is."

Ron cleared his throat. "I'm sorry, sir. I didn't recognize your voice right away."

"Did you know this girl who was murdered, this cheerleader?"

Straight to the chase as always. "Um, yes, sir, she was in one of my classes."

A long heavy pause. "Because that's how it always starts with you."

"Sir, I swear I had nothing to do—"

"I hope you're telling the truth, that you didn't have anything to do with this."

Blisters of sweat exploded across his forehead. "No, sir, no, I promise you, I didn't."

"Because I promise *you*, there won't be any more cushy jobs at East Lake Forest courtesy of my good friend Jay Mitchell."

"No, sir, I know, I know—"

"You fuck up one more time, I will personally put your balls in a vise and squash them like grapes."

Ron winced and forced back a strained yelp. "I understand, sir."

"I thought you might."

The phone went dead and Ron sat in his chair for a good five minutes, his entire body clenched tight as a fist, sopping wet with flop sweat. Slowly, he allowed each body part to release themselves one by one from the grip of the not-idle threat. He gently placed the phone on his desk, a strangled exhale seeping from his lips.

If what happened that Saturday night came out, what he did—

Ron slammed his hand against the desk shaking his head. He didn't want to have to do this, but the choice seemed crystal now. He had to leave.

His brother would whine and put up a fuss, but he'd let him stay at his place, at least for a few days. The flash of an old college buddy up in Toronto raced across his memory. That would be even better. Just get in the car and go.

Whatever it took to save himself.

48

AVA

"Ava?"

Her head flipped up. "Huh? What?"

Kyle put his after-dinner coffee down on the table and frowned. "You okay, Mate?"

She ran her tongue across her bottom lip. "Fine."

He gave her a knowing look. "Seriously?"

Ava inhaled sharply. Days had passed since finding the X-ACTO knife in Carly's car and she still hadn't figured out how to tell him that their daughter had potentially stabbed another girl to death. Every day that ticked by and she kept this horrible secret locked inside her, it made things worse not only for Carly, but for their marriage.

"Nothing. It's nothing."

"Mate, come on, tell me what's on your mind."

She sighed softly. Dear God, she couldn't put this off any longer. "Kyle—"

"Ewings!"

Ava flinched at the thunder of Jay Mitchell's voice behind her as she swiveled around to find him and Erica approaching their table. Kyle stood up and did a bro back slap and handshake with Jay, while Ava hesitated a second before rising to do a dual cheek kiss with Erica.

"Well, isn't this funny? I was just telling Jay that you and I have been trying to get together for a drink for a little while now," Erica said, pointing her gaze in Ava's direction.

"I can't keep up with this one myself, Erica," Kyle said as he took his seat. "I might have to put one of those tracking devices on her."

"It's been a busy time," Ava said weakly. "Always on a plane to somewhere."

"Kyle, I've been meaning to call you. I've got a potential business opportunity for you," Jay said.

Her husband's eyes lit up like winning slot machines. Anytime Jay Mitchell dangled the possibility of anything in front of you, jumping like a dog after a treat was a standard response.

"Well, that sounds absolutely brilliant," Kyle said. "I'd love to hear more."

"Darling, why don't we kill two birds with one stone and have Kyle and Ava over for a nightcap?" Erica asked. "Ava and I can have our glass of wine while you two discuss business."

Jay slapped his hands together and murmured his agreement while Ava panicked in silence. She'd finally worked up the nerve to open the door to the conversation about Carly with Kyle and now she'd have to wait, because there was no way Jay or her husband were going to let her wiggle off this hook.

Kyle gave Ava the expected look and she plastered on a fake smile. "Sure, since it's early, that sounds great."

"All right!" Jay bellowed. "We'll meet you back at the house in about twenty minutes?"

A ripple of agreement went up around the group and Ava sank back down into her chair, the waves of nausea rising once more.

"I STILL CAN'T BELIEVE the police haven't made any progress with Whitney's murder," Erica said as she took another sip of wine.

"Are you serious?" Jay snorted. "They don't get anything more dangerous than parking tickets around here."

"They'll have to call in some outside help, then, right?" Kyle asked. "If they haven't already."

Ava drained her wineglass, hoping she wouldn't be expected to contribute anything to the conversation. They'd been here an hour already and between Jay's eleven-decibel stories, Erica's chattering about Ava wasn't even sure what because she'd tuned it out, and now, the perpetual hot topic of conversation around town, her head was about to split open like a cracked nut.

"You're going to the memorial service tomorrow, aren't you?" Erica asked.

Ava flicked her head up. "That's tomorrow?"

"Eleven," Erica said. "Regina told me they had a private service for the family some weeks ago. I guess they just weren't up for planning anything publicly before now."

"Jesus, I forgot," Ava shook her head in stunned disbelief. The conversation with Kyle would now have to wait until tomorrow night.

"You all see what I mean then, right?" Kyle asked. "Busy bird, this one."

"Ava, when does the cast come off?" Erica asked.

She looked down at the dingy plaster on her wrist. "Maybe another week or so. Can't come soon enough."

"I broke mine years ago playing tennis. Sucked ass, man," Jay said. "What happened with you?"

"Tripped and fell." A bead of sweat inched its way down her back. "And yes, it does suck ass."

Everyone laughed and Ava took the distraction to excuse herself to the powder room. On her way back to the living room, the cascade of family photos spilling across the wall above the staircase caught her eye. She wandered over, a melancholy smile tugging at one corner of her lips as memories of a gap-toothed Jordan in her tutu and tight ballerina bun came flooding back. The Mitchells were an unusual-looking family. Jordan wasn't what could be called pretty or beautiful—cute, even—but attractive in an arresting sort of way. Little Kennedy had Jay stamped all over her and it was true that sometimes, little girls could look too much like their fathers. Jay was hard to ignore of course, as much for his quivering size as the perpetual smile. Jovial had Jay in mind when it was deciding to be a word. And Erica—

Ava frowned, her eyes scanning the rows of frames and glass in search of a photo of Erica.

Not a single one.

In the countless times she'd been over here through the years, how had she never noticed that?

A lifetime of pictures splashed across the wall. The two girls. Jay.

Erica nowhere to be found.

"Ava?"

She spun around, gasping when she saw Erica standing in front of her, puzzled.

"Oh, gosh, sorry, I just … I got caught up in looking at your family photos." She tapped the glass of Jordan dressed as a genie from a dance recital. "I remember this. So cute."

"You were gone so long, I told Kyle I'd come check on you, make sure you were okay." Erica fiddled with the lone heart charm on her gold Tiffany bracelet as she stepped forward for a closer look. "She hates that I keep this up."

"You know, Erica, I just realized, you aren't in any of the pictures." She crossed her arms. "In fact, I don't think I've ever seen you in a picture. Never in your Christmas cards, not on Facebook, not on anything."

She scrunched up her nose and shook her head. "I hate, absolutely hate having my picture taken. I cannot stand the way I look in photos."

"Really?" Ava scratched her neck. "Those pictures from your yearbook that Jay did for that collage at your birthday were great. I mean you were in so many. Homecoming queen and cheerleading."

"Oh. Those. God, Jay badgered me so much about that. I literally threw the book at him and told him to use whatever. I couldn't even look at the thing and made him throw it out the next day."

"Well, your pictures looked better than most. You should be proud."

A peal of Jay's raucous laughter followed by some gibberish from Kyle rang out from the dining room. Erica smiled. "We'd better get back in there." She beckoned for Ava to follow her. "I guess we'll have to walk down memory lane another time."

Ava smiled and followed Erica back to the dining room, but not before taking one last glance over her shoulder at the wall of smiling photos.

49

ERICA

The memorial service for Whitney Victoria Dean almost a month after she was murdered was standing room only. Hundreds of weeping, tear-stained faces crowded into First Presbyterian Church, snug against each other in the pews, lining the hallways, watching the closed caption feed in the Sunday school rooms.

Erica studied Whitney's picture looming over the altar, the smiling perfection of her sophomore yearbook photo forever freezing her in time.

Sixteen forever.

All these weeks later, the shock of Whitney's murder still rattled her, memories ricocheting across her brain like flashes of lightening. Dance recitals, pool parties. All the sleepovers the girls had. Once, during a slumber party for Jordan's tenth birthday, Whitney convinced the girls they needed to raid Erica's makeup so they could make a music video. She should have been furious, but watching them lip-synch to some silly song, their faces slathered with every shade of purple, pink, red, and blue they could find, as they recorded themselves with Whitney's phone, ridiculous and adorable all at once, it was hard to stay mad. A tear pricked Erica's eye. That was Whitney.

Ahead of her by eight rows, Lauren Dean sat in the front pew, flanked by her husband and son, her stepdaughter to Steve's right. Predictably, she wore a prim black Chanel suit, her eyes obscured by large sunglasses, even inside, though they did nothing to hide the tears, the shaking shoulders, or the muffled wails that occasionally escaped from her tiny frame.

Erica's gaze wandered around the sanctuary, the faces of her friends and neighbors sliding across her vision in a blur. Some of Jordan's teachers, the principal, and the superintendent had taken up residence near the back, their faces wavering between distress and shock. Eventually she landed on Ava Ewing staring straight ahead, a glassy vacant look in her eye, her husband Kyle engrossed in the program. Erica was surprised at how wrecked Ava looked today. She hadn't had *that* much to drink. This definitely seemed like more than just grief or the residue of one too many glasses from last night. She tried to catch Ava's eye to no avail. Erica put it on her mental to-do list to check in with Ava later in the week, see if she could unearth what was troubling her friend, which was probably a touch too familiar a way of describing their relationship. Granted, she didn't spend a lot of time with Ava, as she had always been a little cool to her. Friendly enough, but never chummy, not like she was with Lauren or the passel of girlfriends (from work, high school, college?) she saw her in photos with whenever she creeped her Facebook page. But surely last night was the start of something, wasn't it?

Erica frowned to herself, wondering where Carly was, knowing she had to be here somewhere since her name was listed in the program, given the task of reading a poem. Erica had been unable to compel Jordan into paying her respects. She couldn't even get Jay to intervene, as he was of the mindset to let Jordan be, to allow her to grieve in her own way, whatever the hell that meant. *She* was of the mindset that there was a proper and fitting way of doing things and that even if Jordan didn't want to be here, she should have been. She pulled her phone from her purse to check that Jordan's car and phone were still at home. In fact, her daughter had been quite dutiful—and truthful— about where she was spending her time. School, the library, Coffee City. Old Orchard on occasion. There had been nary a blip to her routine since Erica had installed the trackers on the phone and car. She'd consider keeping them on for a little bit longer. Just to be sure.

The organ's groan rumbling through the sanctuary stopped Erica's musings, snapping all of them to attention. Carly emerged from a cluster of the pom squad teammates stuffed next to each other across one pew to give her reading. In spite of herself, the pang of not seeing Jordan among the pom girls snapped against Erica. Whitney's half-sister, Janine, delivered the eulogy, a missive on fighting over hair-brushes, jeans, and shampoo, followed by teary remembrances of the sweet, funny sister who she was happy to have had for sixteen years and devastated because she would never know what the future held.

Erica managed to keep her composure throughout the teary, emotional service, electing to hold in her feelings, as she was wont to do. Just the way she trained herself for so many years.

"That was good," Jay whispered as the service drew to a close and he grabbed her hand with his bear paw, giving it a hearty squeeze. "Really nice."

"Yes. Quite nice."

"I guess we should start making our way to the reception," Jay said.

Erica nodded as they edged into the clogged aisle, keeping her focus on the light of the vestibule, her mild claustrophobia nudging against her. She unfurled the crumpled program in her hand to fan her face, relieved when they finally reached the threshold, fresh, cool air mere steps away.

A scream erupted from outside. Through the crowd, she could see Madison hyperventilating as she looked down at her phone.

"What the hell is going on?" Jay muttered.

Erica's confused look matched the rest of the crowd as she spotted Carly running to Madison's side just as Lexi snatched her phone away and gasped at the screen.

"What is it? What's wrong?" Peyton screamed.

"They just arrested Mr. Byrne for Whitney's murder!" Lexi yelled.

50

RON

Technically, yes, he'd been arrested.

Not for Whitney's murder, though. A stupid fucking traffic ticket. It was just an excuse to get him in here. Their last resort, he supposed.

The plan had been to flee to his brother's in Detroit for a few days and lay low in the vain, preposterous hope the police would get tired of bugging him to come down to the station for questioning because they'd moved on to someone else. As soon as he opened his door, duffel bag in hand, there they were.

Of course they were.

As he sat here now in the interrogation room, parked at a battered metal table, glued to a metal chair, the sickly yellow walls burning his eyes, he wondered what on earth he'd been thinking.

He hadn't been thinking. That was the problem. That's how this whole mess started.

Ron smoothed down his shirt, his fingers trembling, his tongue sticking to the roof of his mouth, both crying out for water. All sorts of awful possibilities ran through his head on a loop about how this little sit-down would go.

He didn't see it ending well.

The door swung open and the detective who had shown up just as he was fleeing to Detroit came into the room. Ron straightened up involuntarily and smoothed his hair back.

"Can I go now?" he asked.

"No." The detective went quiet, thumbing through a manila folder in front of her, the rustle of the papers filling the room.

"Did you have to haul me out of my apartment like that, for all my neighbors to see?"

"Mr. Byrne, we've left you several messages, which you haven't returned." She ran her tongue across her teeth. "Guess you should have paid that speeding ticket."

He squirmed in his seat under the pointed accusation.

The detective—he couldn't remember what she said her name was—leaned back in her chair, which squealed with delight, and smiled at him, which made him even more of a wreck, because he knew what was coming.

"Mr. Byrne, how long have you been a teacher?"

"Seven years."

"And how many of those years at East Lake Forest High School?"

"This is my first full year."

"I see. And where were you prior?"

Sweat flooded his underarms and he was grateful for his windbreaker hiding the moons of sweat he knew were soaking his shirt.

"I was with CPS right out of college."

"That's a pretty big leap from CPS to Lake Forest. Why'd you leave?"

His bowels pinged and pressed against him. If he moved even an inch, he was likely to shit all over this interrogation room. Why was the detective bothering with the pretense? They knew the story. Why didn't they just come out and say it?

Ron sighed. "Listen, we both know why I left."

The detective hunched over the manila folder and pulled out a piece of paper from beneath the stack. "An inappropriate relationship with a student."

"She was a former student—"

"What was your relationship with Whitney Dean?"

"What?"

The detective pulled another piece of paper from her magic hat. "We had several witnesses tell us that you often kept Miss Dean after class."

"Listen, I had nothing to do with her murder—"

"I'll ask you again, what was the nature of your relationship with Whitney Dean?"

Tears pricked the backs of his eyes. "I didn't have a relationship with Whitney—Miss Dean. She was my student, that was it."

"Why'd you keep her after school so often?"

"Because she…" He let out a frustrated sigh. "She had a bad attitude in class and I was trying to nip it in the bud. That was it. There was nothing going on between us other than student and teacher."

"Isn't that how things started with you and Miss—" The detective checked her notes. "Anthony? Keeping her after class?"

"No."

The detective raised an eyebrow. "No?"

Mr. Byrne leaned back in his chair, his fingers trembling as he held them to his mouth. "Liane Anthony was in my American lit class as a junior and the only time I saw her after that was in the hallways at school. She graduated and as far as I knew, went to college out of state."

"So how did your affair start?"

He gulped again, still afraid to move. "I was out with some friends one night and ran into her and that's how it started. She was twenty, okay? By the time I ran into her again, she was twenty years old. She wasn't my student anymore, she wasn't a minor. Look, it didn't last very long, but then her father, who's very protective and not all that reasonable, found out and because I'd been her teacher, he assumed … anyway, he threatened to ruin me if I didn't cut ties with his daughter. He's chummy with Jay Mitchell and here I am. That's what happened. That's the story."

"When's the last time you saw Miss Anthony?"

He hesitated, then sighed. His life was on the line. There was no sense in holding the dam back anymore. "The Saturday that Whitney Dean was murdered."

The detective raised an eyebrow. "That so?"

"She—she found out where I lived and showed up at my apartment."

The detective tapped her pen against the table. "Go on."

"I was at home, grading papers and she just showed up."

"What'd you do?"

Ron closed his eyes and shook his head. "I—we went to dinner. I mean, we were about to go to dinner. I mean, we got in my car to go to dinner and we—"

"Had dessert first?" Diehl asked, smirking.

"That's really crass."

She rolled her eyes. "My apologies for offending your delicate sensibilities."

"Yes, we had an … encounter, in my car and then we grabbed a burger at Chief's. I sent her home in an Uber and haven't seen her since."

"Why were you leaving town?"

"I … I was trying to avoid this."

"'This?'"

Ron ran his hands across his head and sighed. "Because of my past. I didn't want it to get out to the school and lose my job. I just wanted to lay low. Let it blow over."

"Hmm." The detective nodded her head as though she were contemplating this. She dropped her pen and gathered up the manila folder. "I have to step out. Make yourself comfortable."

Ron bent over the table, his head dropping into the cradle of his hands. This was bad. Really bad.

A seeming eternity passed before the detective swung the door open, causing him to jump. "We're exercising our right to hold you for forty-eight hours, while we check out your alibi."

He slumped in his chair. They were going to talk to Liane, and her father would find out, because he had a knack for uncovering things that didn't want to be found. As usual, he was out of his depth. He needed help.

"You know what? I want my phone call. I want a lawyer."

"You'll get your phone call soon," she said as she led him out of the squad room to a holding cell.

51

JORDAN

Jordan took a shaky sip of her latte as she played with the ends of her hoodie string and watched her phone for updates on Mr. Byrne.

Nothing.

It had been two days since Whitney's memorial service, two days since he'd been hauled out of his apartment building. Two days since they'd found out he had sex with students, that he may have been having sex with Whitney.

That he may have killed her.

All weekend, the only thought that had burned through Jordan's mind was that if the police thought Mr. Byrne did it, they would leave her alone, wouldn't be asking her anymore questions about what she was doing that day. She didn't know anything about Whitney and Mr. Byrne, but it wouldn't have surprised her. Whitney was into older guys and was all about playing games and doing shit she wasn't supposed to. Everyone thought she was so special and so perfect.

Jordan knew all too well what a viper her best friend was.

Her eyes flicked over to the community bulletin board next to the front door, one of those pervasive pink fliers with Whitney's face asking people to come forward with any information about her murder still tacked prominently to the crowded cork. Now that Mr. Byrne had been arrested, she wondered how long it would be before those pink pieces of paper disappeared.

The bell dinged over the door of the busy café and Jordan groaned when she saw Dionne and Carly. They were so gross. Two wannabees in a pod.

Carly and Dionne stopped chatting as soon as they spotted Jordan across the room and scowled at each other. Jordan looked back down at her phone, determined to ignore them, until a shadow fell over her table, forcing her to lock eyes with the girls. Dionne looked defiant, her hand on her hip, gum snapping and popping, while Carly fidgeted with the buttons of her shirt, her eyes darting around the café.

"I'll bet you're glad the police arrested Mr. Byrne instead of you," Dionne said.

"Go away, Dionne."

"Maybe you helped him," she continued. "Maybe he was sleeping with you too and you both killed Whitney."

"You're pathetic," Jordan said.

"You're pathetic," Dionne shot back. She ribbed Carly. "Have you ever seen anything more pathetic?"

Carly cleared her throat and shook her head. "She's disgusting. No wonder Whitney hated her."

Jordan plunked her coffee cup down on the table and gathered up her book bag. "Don't you have a broom waiting somewhere to fly you around?" She looked them up and down. "A two-seater?"

Dionne scoffed. "Oh, my God. So original."

"Yeah, Jordan, like come up with something else," Carly chimed in.

Over Dionne's shoulder, Mr. Byrne's face flashed across the café's TV and someone at the counter yelled for the barista to turn up the sound on the afternoon news. All three girls turned their attention to the screen. An older woman in a red suit, a large spider pin affixed to the lapel, wiry strands of white woven through her wavy dark hair, rushed Mr. Byrne past the frenzied media throng and toward a black SUV idling nearby. She hustled him into the back seat and got in behind him, before the car inched away from the curb and the shouted questions from the pack of reporters.

"After being held for questioning in the murder of East Lake Forest High School junior, Whitney Dean, Ron Byrne was released today, the police citing his alibi for the night of the murder. Byrne's attorney, Gail Emmets, emailed this statement to us earlier today, saying, in effect, there were a trough of false and egregious statements made with regard to Mr. Byrne and his teaching career and that he would 'have his day' in order to set the record straight. Although she did not indicate what that meant, we can safely assume this will mean an interview of some sort in the near future. Until then, Byrne has been released and police have not indicated they have any additional suspects or persons of interest at this time. Reporting live in Lake Forest, Wendy Sheridan, Channel 4 News."

An audible gasp had gone around the café at the news of Mr. Byrne's release and the barista quickly turned the sound back down on the TV, the void filled with the churn and whir of coffee machines and resumption of alt-rock crooning softly from the overhead sound system.

Dionne whirled around, her eyes hard and cold on Jordan. "Too bad, so sad for you. They're coming for you."

"Yeah." Carly cleared her throat again as her voice cracked. "You'd better be careful."

Jordan's shoulders tightened and she felt her legs lock into place. They were right. The police *would* be back now, pressing her all over again about where she was that Saturday.

Now she was in trouble.

She gulped and forced her legs to move, bumping against Dionne and Carly as she rushed out of Coffee City, trembling all over now, the sounds of the weather man presenting tomorrow's forecast of partly cloudy with a chance of rain fading behind her.

52

AVA

"Didn't I read that they'd arrested someone? A teacher or something," Ava's brother, Frank, said as he handed her a glass of white wine. He grunted a little as he settled onto one of Ava's barstools, his beer gut drooping over the top of his baggy jeans, his metal studded bracelet knocking against the counter.

Ava's stomach seized, an all-too-familiar sensation these days. Selfishly, she'd been elated when Ron Byrne had been arrested. If he did it, that meant Carly hadn't, though it still didn't tell her why Carly had a bloody sweatshirt and an X-ACTO knife.

But for a moment, a glorious moment, her daughter was innocent of murder.

Except now that he'd been released, she had to confront the question of her daughter's possible guilt all over again.

And now, it was the thick of the holiday season. There had been Thanksgiving at her parents in Minneapolis and now Christmas at her house. Her son, Jimmy, had arrived a few days ago from college, taller, it seemed, more handsome, if that was possible. Her older brother and his fiancée, Melody, had flown in last night and her parents would blow in on Christmas morning. Between shopping, decorating, hosting, and cooking, Ava convinced herself that she would just get through the holidays and then, she and Kyle would sit down with Carly and extract a confession from their daughter. They'd take her to the police station then blow their world apart.

"He had an alibi for that night," she responded to her brother's question. "They had to let him go."

"And they don't have any other suspects?" he asked.

Guilt and fear hammered her insides as she quickly gulped her wine. "I'm not sure."

"Was Carly friends with her?" Melody asked as she fluffed her hands through her wiry dark waves, her modest engagement ring flashing in the kitchen light, her accent a mash-up of her Texas upbringing and summers spent in Mexico with her extended family.

"Yeah, they uh ... they were on the pom squad together, so she and Whitney were pretty close."

"Melody was telling me earlier a girl she went to high school with was murdered too," Frank said, pointing his wineglass toward his fiancée.

"Oh. Wow. Really?" Ava said as she rolled around her recently liberated wrist, still getting used to the freedom.

Melody quickly swallowed her wine. "It was my senior year. The girl who was killed was a year behind me. They both were."

"What do you mean 'both'?" Ava asked.

"It was another student."

Fear surged through Ava. "Another student?" she asked, her voice raspy.

"I can't remember all the details, it's been so long, but Ruthie stabbed her. Shannon. Ruthie stabbed Shannon to death."

Ava gripped the kitchen counter, her bowels cranking, her mouth dry and gummy. She whirled around toward the refrigerator to fill her wineglass with ice and to keep her brother and future sister-in-law from seeing her distress.

"Wow," she repeated, hoping she sounded appropriately horrified as she watched the ice chunks shoot into her glass. "How awful."

"It never made any sense," Melody said. "Shannon was one of

those pretty, popular girls. You know, varsity tennis, pom-pom squad, drama club—"

Ava bit her bottom lip. "Sounds just like Whitney."

"Were they friends and got into a fight or what?" Frank asked.

Melody shook her head. "No, they weren't friends. I think they may have had a few classes together, but that was about it. There wasn't a trial, so Ruthie didn't have to testify and she never did any interviews, never wrote a book, so we never really knew why. A lot of people thought maybe Ruthie was jealous of Shannon or something and that's why she did it, but that didn't make any sense either."

"Whatever it was, it sounds like some crazy shit," Frank said.

"My sister got interviewed a couple of times since she and Ruthie were sort of friendly." Melody ran her finger along the rim of her wineglass. "April always said she was the last person you'd ever suspect."

"She still in jail?" Frank asked, scratching the bottom of one bushy sideburn, which stopped just below his jaw.

"Nope. Because she was a minor, she only got ten years." Melody sipped her wine. "Don't know what happened to her after that."

"Ten years? For killing someone? That's bogus," Frank mumbled as he opened another bottle of wine.

"Yeah. Gosh. How awful," Ava said, her voice croaking.

"I heard later Shannon's mother died. Heart attack, I think. My mother always said it was really a broken heart. Her father remarried, had a couple of kids with his new wife." Melody took a sip of wine. "Life goes on."

"Jeez. No kidding," Frank said as he poured more wine into Ava's glass. "Well, sis, I hope they catch your murderer here before too long."

Ava's arms prickled with goosebumps and she nodded feebly. "Yeah, me too."

53

LAUREN

Lauren fingered the red top of the storage bin, 'Whitney' scrawled across it in black Magic Marker. Whitney's box of Christmas decorations. She'd always given the kids their own set of decorations, adding to it each year with the little crafts they made in school, or ornaments they saw in the stores each holiday that would leave them incomplete if they didn't get them right that minute: singing Nutcrackers, jingling bells, blinking reindeers. Mostly though, she'd been the one to make the deposits into their boxes, sometimes choosing a theme such as Swarovski-encrusted snowmen and snowflakes, or ornaments from around the world like bagpipe-playing Santas or Fabergé egg replicas. There were always too many, the tightfisted Christmases of her childhood—filled with pathetic disintegrating Charlie Brown Christmas trees wrapped in cheap red and green yarn, cylinders of tube socks underneath—never far from her mind.

Once upon a time, despite her misgivings, she used to invite her parents over for Christmas every year. Her parents hadn't approved of her marrying a Black man and having brown babies, didn't like her clothes, her big house, or the luxury cars she upgraded every few years. Still, despite their condemnation of every aspect of her life, she was their only child, so Lauren felt she had to try.

So, every year, she extended the invitation. And every year, it was a disaster. Her mother brought half-eaten vegetable platters pilfered from her office holiday parties. Her father brought boxes of old, tangled tinsel, dusty strings of Christmas lights pocked with burned-out bulbs, and mangy stockings reeking of mothballs, always hurt when she refused to put any of it anywhere near her tree or her kids. Her mother criticized the poofy velvet dresses with stiff crinoline slips she dressed Whitney and her stepdaughter, Janine, in, while her father unplugged the tree every time her back was turned.

And never any presents for their biological granddaughter. Definitely nothing for Janine, whose existence Lauren learned about when she was nine months pregnant with Whitney. Her mother, a woman whose name Steve probably never knew and definitely didn't even remember from a bachelor party fling he was subsequently forced to fess up to, showed up on Lauren's doorstep one day with two-year-old Janine and said she couldn't do it anymore.

Instead of even something benign as nice sweaters for the girls, her parents passed out pamphlets on starving children in Africa with a note clipped inside declaring that what they would have spent on presents was used to donate to the cause in Whitney and Janine's names. The year Whitney was seven, Janine nine, Parker a newborn, Lauren bought gifts for them from Grandma and Grandpa. Her parents flipped, shredding the cashmere sweaters, ripping the Barbie dolls from Whitney's hands, her mother throwing them in the trash, her father berating her for her "irresponsible stunt," while the kids howled with terror, both her parents fuming they wouldn't be made to reimburse her for her gross excess.

That was the last straw. She stopped inviting them to any family gatherings at all. Inexplicably, they were shocked at the exclusions. It was the end of any formal relationship, their interactions limited to Lauren sending the family Christmas card and exchanging terse, uncomfortable phone calls for birthdays. She was shocked they came to Whitney's service. Apparently, even they had limits to their heartlessness.

Lauren looked down at the box, running her palm against the hard plastic. What was the protocol for celebrating Christmas when your child had been brutally murdered? Did you put on a happy face and spout platitudes about gratitude and tradition? Did you ignore it, the guilt of celebration and reveling in good cheer threatening to swallow you from the inside? Did you trim the tree with one ornament honoring your dead child?

She pushed the box away, tears pricking her eyes. Lauren hoisted herself up from the floor of the basement and went upstairs, the sanctuary of her bedroom calling her. She stumbled toward the bed, flopping into it and letting the tears flow. From inside the pocket of her jeans, her phone dinged. She blew her nose into a Kleenex before digging the squawking device from her pocket.

At first, she tilted her head to the side, not sure what she was seeing.

Then she got angry.

A news alert previewing an interview that Ron Byrne would give in the New Year, sharing his side of the story regarding what his lawyer called his false arrest for the murder of Whitney Dean.

Rage ripped through Lauren like a hot spear. Tell his story? Why should he get to tell his story? What about Whitney's story? What about her child?

Her fingers trembled as she dialed Steve's number, pacing the room as she waited for him to pick up. The call went to voicemail and she tried four more times, getting the same result. She ran downstairs in search of her purse, specifically the card of that reporter who was on Channel 4 every night. Wendy something. Lauren should be the one telling stories about Whitney. Not these cable news talking heads, these pedophile teachers who got away with murder.

The card poked out of the inside pocket of her purse and she plucked it out with two fingers, slamming it down on the kitchen counter and dialing. She sniffed and waited, irritated when the call went to voicemail.

"Hi, Miss Sheridan, this is Lauren Dean, Whitney's mother. I'm ready to talk about my daughter."

54

AVA

The air hummed with the jingle of Salvation Army bells and a small band of carolers in full Dickensian garb stood in front of the fountain at the head of Market Square, their breath billowing out in song, sporadic bits of snow swirling around them like confetti. Behind them, the bell of an approaching Metra train jangled. Strings of sparkling white lights, garlands, and wreaths blanketed the tiny shops, while ice sculptures of snowmen with carrots for noses, and real-life Nutcrackers filled the courtyard. Some weary shoppers clutching coffee cups parked themselves on the black metal benches and at the wrought iron tables that ringed the lawn as they listened to the carolers.

"Hard to believe by this time next year, I'll be married," Melody said, pulling her coat closer around her small frame as she and Ava stepped out of the bookstore and strolled in the direction of Coffee City, glittery red, gold, green, and silver shopping bags swinging from their arms. Getting swept up in the revelry of the holiday had loosened Ava's shoulders considerably as she shoved her hot, gnawing guilt about Carly down into the farthest cavern she could find in her soul. *Get through the holidays* had become her persistent mantra.

"It's hard to believe someone is about to get my brother down the aisle for the first time. Ever," Ava said. "Woman, you are a saint."

"Only a little," Melody said, and the two women giggled.

Erica stepped out of Coffee City, a handful of shopping bags adorning her wrists, a large coffee cup in one hand, the bottom fringe of her black wool poncho fluttering against the top of her tall black leather boots.

"Oh, no," Ava groaned, as she weakly returned Erica's excited wave. Another happy hour invitation was coming, she just knew it.

"What's wrong?" Melody asked.

"I'll tell you later," she murmured before forcing the corners of her lips into a pained smile. "Happy holidays," Ava said brightly as the three women came together.

"Happy holidays to you, too," Erica said as she pulled Ava toward her, who allowed for the dual cheek kiss ritual to boot. Erica glanced at Melody and smiled uncertainly.

"Erica, this is my sister—well soon-to-be sister-in-law, Melody. She and my brother are visiting for the holidays. Melody, this is Erica Mitchell."

"Erica." Melody paused before slowly grasping Erica's extended hand.

"Looks like you're getting in some last-minute shopping as well," Erica said, quickly dropping Melody's hand and gesturing to Ava's bags.

"Yes, and thankfully, this is the last of it," Ava said. "I'm officially done and if I don't have it by now, it'll have to wait until next Christmas. Are you all done?"

"I'm heading into the bookstore to grab a book for Jay and then that's it, thank goodness," Erica said. "How's Carly? Jimmy?"

Ava ignored the pang of panic piercing her chest. "Carly's okay. It's been great having Jimmy home, of course."

"How was his first semester?"

Ava smiled in spite of herself. "Dean's List."

"Well congratulations, Mom," Erica said. "Sounds like he's off to a great start."

"So far, so good. How about you, how are things?"

"Busy as ever. Business is going really well, and Jay's heading into yet another acquisition, which makes him crazy, which means I'm crazy. Makes the holidays look like a cakewalk."

"And Jordan?"

"Oh, you know, like Carly, okay. Day to day."

"Have you seen Lauren at all?"

Erica shook her head. "Not since Whitney's memorial, and even then it was for a few seconds. I've called her a couple of times, sent a few text messages, but no response."

"First Christmas," Ava said. "Can't say I blame her for hiding out."

"I know. Terrible." Erica looked at her watch. "Oh, listen, hon, I've got to run, but maybe we can have drinks in the New Year, get caught up?"

Ava winced inside, wondering how soon to beg off from that little get-together. "Sure, sounds great. Let me look at my schedule."

"Wonderful." She smiled at Melody. "Nice to meet you. Enjoy the rest of your trip."

"Thank you." Melody paused. "Erica."

Erica rushed off and Ava and Melody ambled down the sidewalk toward the coffee shop. Melody frowned as she looked back over her shoulder in Erica's direction.

"What's wrong?" Ava asked.

"I—" She shook her head. "I'm probably just imagining things."

"What?" Ava repeated.

Melody rolled her eyes and shook her head. "This is probably because I was talking about it the other night, but you remember I was telling you about the murder that happened when I was in high school, how the one girl stabbed the other girl?"

"Yeah, what about it?"

"It's—God, this is going to sound crazy."

"What?"

"Your friend, Erica. She looks like Ruthie Stowers."

Ava frowned. "Who?"

"I mean, she's thinner—way thinner—and the teeth and the nose are different. Not as pale. The eyes, but…" Melody nodded and looked over her shoulder again. "I would almost swear on it."

"Wait, who do you think she looks like?" Ava repeated, still confused.

"Ruthie. The girl I was telling you about the other night. The girl who went to jail for murdering another girl."

Ava grabbed Melody's arm, bringing them both to a stop. "Wait a minute. Wait a minute! You think *Erica* stabbed someone? Murdered a girl?"

"Like I said, it's crazy, but..." Melody shook her head. "She looks just like Ruthie—different, like I said, but yeah, I would swear it's her. It's Ruthie."

"You're from Texas, right? Houston?"

"Yeah."

Ava laughed. "Oh. Well, Erica's from Ohio so..."

"Oh," Melody said, clearly stunned, shrinking back a little before she shrugged. "Okay. Obviously, I got it wrong. My bad."

"They say everyone has a twin, right?" Ava pointed in the direction of Le Colonial across the street. "Come on. Let's ditch the coffee, grab a glass of wine instead."

"Sure, yeah. Sounds good," Melody said, throwing one last glance over her shoulder in Erica's direction.

55

ERICA

Erica slammed the front door behind her, her bags sliding out of her hands and crashing to the floor in an explosion of paper and plastic. Blood thrummed in her ears.

Melody Gonzalez.

What in the hell was she doing here?

She couldn't even remember the last time she'd seen her. High school, obviously. A lifetime ago. She didn't even know Melody all that well. More in passing, really. She knew her sister, April, better, since they had a few classes together. She and April had been friendly, but not friends.

Of course, Erica's face—her old face—was seared into the memories of most—if not all, of the three million—at the time—residents of Houston, Texas, the 10,456 who'd lived in Willow Branch in particular. They'd never forget who she was. She would forever have the honor of being one of its most notorious residents.

It didn't mean any of them would recognize her, though. It didn't mean *Melody* would recognize her. It just wasn't possible. She looked so different now. *Completely* different.

Maybe she'd have a faint tickle of familiarity and think Erica looked like someone she used to know, but would brush it off because it couldn't possibly be *her.* What would be the odds?

What would be the odds, indeed.

Still, it seemed like Melody looked at her a little too long, a little too closely, a little too carefully. If she saw her again, she just might start to put it together.

And Erica couldn't let that happen. She'd just avoid Ava over the next few weeks or so. Melody couldn't be in town that much longer.

Erica bent down to retrieve the groceries from the floor, pushing her former classmate's face to the background, concentrating on gathering her lettuce, tomatoes, olives, and cucumbers, her mind groping ahead to what she should pick up for dinner. Maybe she'd just order a pizza. Pepperoni. They all liked pepperoni. Her mouth watered at the thought of the spicy, greasy disc of meat, the buttery, crunchy crust, and creamy, salty cheese. The last time she remembered having a piece of pepperoni pizza was that night at the kitchen table with her mom. After. A lifetime ago. It had been so long since she'd had anything really good and greasy or buttery, or sweet, or food with any kind of taste. But like an addict, those tastes hovered on her tongue every day, never far from memory.

She couldn't relapse, though. She would order a pizza for everyone else and stick with her salad, her plain boring salad and flavored waters that kept her rail thin. There couldn't be any drastic changes to her routine, nothing that she did differently. Calm and steady until she was certain Melody was long gone.

Her hands trembled as she carefully put away her groceries, stuffing Melody's face and voice as far down away from her as she possibly could.

Erica poured herself a glass of water, draining it in a few gulps before slipping into her study and locking the door behind her, even though no one was home. The last thing she needed was Jay sneaking up on her or one of the girls bursting in with some dire request about a missing sock or hangnail. She unlocked the bottom drawer of her desk and pulled out her second laptop, the one she used to order the colored contacts she had sent to a P.O. box in Glenview five times a year and for occasional clandestine missions like this. One she'd destroy if it ever came down to it.

Her fingers hovered over the keyboard before typing the name she despised into the incognito window of her preferred search engine.

Ruthie Stowers.

The same stories filled the screen as had always popped up over the years. Links to old articles, obsessed, bargain basement, homemade crime blogs with pedestrian cartoon graphics detailing every last gruesome detail of what happened between her and Shannon. Speculation over the contents of the last conversation between the two girls, on what, exactly, had sparked her own explosive actions. The same musings over her whereabouts, opinions on her crimes. Pictures of her. Pictures of both of them. Forever intertwined.

But no stories outing her. No fiery exposés on where she was now. Several bloggers had tried to unearth her identity, scouring the Earth in fruitless searches, apparently, but none had any luck, of course. She'd covered her tracks so carefully. No social media, no websites, no blogs, no headshots. No pictures at Christmas parties, PTA meetings, or charity functions. No trace to be found.

She was safe.

Erica wiped her browser history of the search and returned the laptop to its locked drawer before folding her hands in front of her, her eyes sliding shut, the blood thundering in her ears, the pressure crowding her organs, pressing everything to near bursting.

"Nobody knows that you're Ruthie Stowers," she whispered. "Nobody knows that you're Ruthie Stowers."

She repeated the mantra over and over, driving the words into her brain, manifesting this divine truth until the universe believed it and made it so. Ask, believe, receive.

Nobody knew she was Ruthie Stowers.

And nobody ever would.

56

RUTHIE

Every day, she watched her float down the hallway on Pepsodent smiles and frosted pink lipstick, her permed, blue-black curls crunchy with mousse in the back, bangs at half-staff in the front. Her daily glide through the corridors of Willow Branch High School were typically accompanied by GUESS? jeans miniskirts, Dooney & Burke purses, suede booties, and United Colors of Benetton sweaters, all generously spritzed with Liz Claiborne or Bonne Bell. She never wore the same outfit twice and Ruthie was convinced she threw her clothes out after a single wear. A gold Tiffany heart charm bracelet always swung carelessly from her slender wrist, though her bottomless jewelry box provided an endless supply of earrings, necklaces, and sparkly, oversized rhinestone brooches. Their lockers were close to each other, so every day, Ruthie Stowers pressed herself against the glass to witness the magic that was Shannon Kendall.

Every single time, every single day, everyone stopped and stared at her: the jocks, the cheerleaders, theater geeks, class officers, the pretty girls, the hot guys. They were all, each and every one of them, thunderstruck by all that bubbly perfection, grateful and envious all at once in its presence, clawing to be next to her, vying for a hello or even a glance in their direction. Boys swooped in on her, swallowing her into bear hugs or casually slinging arms over the perfection of her glossy golden shoulders. Girls solicited her opinions on everything from lip gloss to albums to hairspray brand, wanting to drool over Don Johnson or catch up on what happened on *All My Children* the day before. She bet Shannon's family could afford a VCR—several probably—to record the show every day, unlike her, who had to rely on the recaps in the Saturday paper, sick days, and summer vacation to keep up with Pine Valley.

Shannon wasn't beautiful, though she would probably earn that honorific in the school yearbook at the end of the year. She was pretty. Fresh-scrubbed pretty, even under the thick, glittery varnish of blush, foundation, and eyeshadow she painted on each day. Her dimples, straight white teeth, sparkling eyes, and airbrushed skin were seemingly ordered straight out of the pages of *Seventeen* and *YM*. Always full of hugs, smiles, laughter, and squeals. A lover of life.

And who wouldn't love her life? She lived in a big house with a swimming pool which the cool kids crowded around all summer long. She zipped around in a pink Karmann Ghia convertible, just like Molly Ringwald in *Pretty in Pink*. She had her own private line in her room, where she spent hours gabbing on the pink Princess phone with those lucky enough to be granted those seven precious little numbers. Her father was a handsome ER doctor, her mother, a shellacked news anchor on the local television station, deftly alternated between stories on deadly fires and newborn baby pandas at the zoo every night at ten with polish and aplomb. Sports and academics were putty in this girl's hands, as she easily excelled at both. And friends. So many friends, spilling from every corner of her charmed life.

And what Ruthie wouldn't have given to trade places with Shannon Kendall for a day. An hour. Five minutes, even.

Not that it would be a fair trade. Shannon would most definitely be getting the raw end of the deal. Ruthie wasn't boiling over with fizzy fun. Sure, there were some name brands in her closet, bought with hard-earned babysitting money, but they would cower next to what was in Shannon's. She didn't have a mouthful of gleaming white teeth to blind the masses with every time she smiled. She couldn't even tan right, turning lobster red instead of golden brown. Boys' eyes didn't glint with lust when they looked at her, a plain, splotchy, pudgy girl who couldn't make those stubborn pounds drop no matter how many carrot sticks she ate for dinner or miles she jogged. There were no breathless, desperate queries from girls about whether she swabbed her lips with Perfect Pink or Peachy Keen.

She wasn't an outcast or anything. People liked her okay. No one tripped her in the hall, called her names, or made fun of her. She had a small group of equally nondescript friends to eat her bagged lunch of PB&J, chips, and cookies with in the cafeteria each day. She was in the art club. Played flute in the band. She wasn't poor, her mother a nurse, her father a mid-level manager at an insurance company with incremental raises each year. They had a nice house with two cars in the driveway. There was money every summer for family vacations to Galveston or South Padre. They'd been to Disney World and Disney Land once each, and she and her sisters pooled their allowance and went to AstroWorld every July. They could afford dinners at Red Lobster or Fuddruckers a few times a month, a family night out at the movies—popcorn and SnoCaps included—every once in a while. Mrs. Stowers was a whiz with the sewing machine, able to duplicate every outfit you could possibly want, from The Limited, Express, Esprit, and just about every mall staple in between. With four children, there wasn't a lot to go around, but none of the Stowers kids would ever say they were poor or struggling. They had a roof over their heads, meat and fresh vegetables in the refrigerator, shoes and clothes free from holes. All the Stowers children were considered nice kids who kept their noses clean, did what they were told, and led morally suitable lives.

But they weren't special. *Ruthie* wasn't special. Her life wasn't charmed. Her small house was modest, the furniture as old as she was, their cars, plain and boxy, kept for transport, not luxury. Her clothes, no matter her mother's artistry with the sewing machine, would never quite measure up. *She* would never measure up. She was just basic, boring Ruthie Stowers who no one gave much thought to. The girl no one really noticed.

Just once in her life, she wanted to be somebody.

She wanted to be special.

As she watched Shannon walk down the hall every day, greeting her admirers with kisses blown through frosted pink lips and pearly white smiles, the longing was almost too much to bear. It occurred to her one of those mornings, if she and Shannon were friends, she'd be somebody. If people saw them laughing and joking together, swooning over Don Johnson or how they'd bought Madonna's latest cassette at Sam Goody over the weekend before purchasing matching outfits at Wet Seal, maybe they'd think she was cool, too. Worthy.

Somebody.

And that was how Ruthie Stowers started her junior year.

Determined to make Shannon Kendall her best friend.

57

AVA

"I mean, she's thinner—way thinner—"

Ava stared up at the ceiling of her bedroom, Melody's words squirming through her brain like a worm in search of sunlight, Kyle's soft, wheezing snores filling the room as shadows from the moonlight danced across the walls. The blur of the holidays was over, the New Year ushered in, and the doom of knowing what she had to do next about Carly hovered over her like the sharp, shiny, unrelenting blade of a guillotine.

And yet, Melody's words had refused to dislodge themselves from her thoughts, swirling around her in moments of quiet and chaos. The odds, the insane odds that Melody had gone to high school with a convicted killer who, if her future sister-in-law were to be believed, bore a more than comfortable resemblance to Erica Mitchell? It was too … ridiculous. Absurd. Flat-out crazy.

And over thirty years later, a similar murder, in the vicinity of—again, if Melody were to be believed—the same woman? It was too much for her pea brain to process.

And yet, Ava couldn't release this vexing improbability, the fantasticalness of it.

Way thinner.

Over the years, she and some of the other moms had mused privately about whether Erica was a recovering anorexic. She flirted with being skeletal, though it seemed she managed to stay just this side of needing an intervention. Her painfully petite stature was all the more obvious anytime she stood next to Jay, given his almost comical girth and elevation.

The odd eating habits were another puzzle. She couldn't ever recall seeing Erica eat anything other than salad. Not a piece of fish, not a plate of pasta. Barely even a smoothie, like that day at the gym. At her big birthday party a few years ago, where cheeses, meats, sweets blanketed every table, Erica munched on a salad all night. She wouldn't even take a bite of her own birthday cake, flown in from New York for the occasion. Not even a swipe of frosting. God knows, avoiding carbs was a rite of passage to live in Lake Forest, but even Erica's discipline seemed extreme.

Way thinner.

Ava glanced over at Kyle, dead to the world. She pushed the heavy duvet back, her joints snapping like crickets as she headed toward the bedroom door. The banister was cool beneath her palm as she padded down the staircase toward the kitchen, her stomach grumbling despite the late, heavy date night meal she and Kyle had at their favorite restaurant, neither of them embracing the mantra of healthy eating in the New Year. She flipped on the light and poured herself a glass of almond milk, before slipping onto the bar stool, staring out the windows at the dark night.

Way thinner.

Her head snapped up as she plunked the half-full glass down onto the counter.

The party invitation.

She hopped out of the chair and rushed toward her office, beelining for her desk. She flicked on the small desk lamp as she opened the bottom desk drawer to rummage through the files. The tab for 'Past Parties,' poked up through the sea of hard plastic tabs attached to the army green hanging files. She pulled out the file, slapping it on the desk, sifting through the mountain of invitations. She'd hung onto

Erica's because she liked the design, thinking she might use it as inspiration for her fiftieth in a few years.

The hot pink square was at the bottom of the pile. The morass of cardstock and envelopes cascaded out of Ava's hands, thudding to the desk, as she seized on the invitation. Her desk chair squealed as she leaned over, studying the picture of Erica on the front.

Erica the homecoming queen smiled at her from inside the symmetrical square announcing a party to celebrate her forty-fifth birthday. Though the black and white picture of Erica and her king standing beneath their crowns, loaded down with sashes, corsages, and bouquets was grainy, there was no mistaking it was her. Her shoulders were visible beneath the mounds of celebration paraphernalia and the sweetheart neckline of her form-fitting dress showed a thin girl with a hint of curves, not terribly different than how she appeared now. Hardly dumpy. Hardly plump. Hardly a girl who would need to be *way thinner*.

"This is crazy," she muttered, as she shoved the invitations back into the drawer and turned off the desk lamp. She stopped in the kitchen to rinse out her cup and put it in the dishwasher before climbing the stairs, her mind drifting toward sleep.

"Way thinner."

Ava stood on her landing, not realizing she'd said the words out loud. They rattled through her brain like stones skipping down an empty well.

The sound was too much for her to ignore.

Ava whirled around to rush back into the study to retrieve the invitation, getting lost in the picture, the streams of moonlight through the window illuminating the smiling queen in all her glory.

58

RUTHIE

W illow Branch was one of those Houston communities that felt less like a neighborhood in a booming metropolis and more like a small town with its own mores and traditions.

Like any small town, it had haves and have nots, but mostly haves. Great wealth and privilege dominated Willow Branch, with a smattering of middle-class or affordable homes, and of course the 'apartment people.' Its neighborhoods were ones that families from less desirable pockets of Houston clamored to get into because of that all-consuming elixir of 'good schools.' The self-imposed mandate of the city council to incorporate affordable housing put the dream of life in a nice, safe community in the reach of the middle class, the chance to slot their children in alongside the sons and daughters of lawyers and doctors and businessmen. The achievers. The strivers.

Ruthie and her family were fortunate enough not to be apartment people. That white-hot yearning for good schools and boundless opportunity for the four Stowers children had propelled the family from its scratching-to-be middle-class neighborhood on the other side of town the summer Ruthie turned twelve, to the peaceful, tree-lined streets of Willow Branch. Though their house was small and ordinary, particularly by Willow Branch standards, Bob and Grace Stowers were happy and proud they had the ability to give their children the chance to do better than they had, and this community afforded them the opportunity.

Ruthie crossed paths with Shannon Kendall the first day of her new junior high, catching a glimpse of her as she glided into the classroom across the hall from hers while gabbing excitedly with another girl (Lyz Cox). Ruthie was mesmerized by Shannon and her long, blue-black curls and smooth skin, the oversized print sweater cinched at her waist with a giant white leather belt, suede purple boots hugging her knees. Like she lived in the pages of *YM* or *Teen*.

She was the coolest girl Ruthie had ever seen.

As she sat in the cafeteria next to a girl in her social studies class who'd invited her to lunch, Ruthie stole glances at Shannon, holding court at a crowded table across the room. She wasn't eating crap from the cafeteria line, or lame bagged lunches like she did. She brought gourmet salads from home in a special pink Tupperware container. Girls hung on her every word and it was clear this beautiful, bubbly mystery girl was the queen bee of Willow Branch Junior High.

In three years, they'd never had any classes together, never had a locker near each other, but it didn't matter. Everyone knew pretty, popular Shannon, the apple of all eyes, envy of all girls, desire of all boys. In junior high, when the PTA held its annual Valentine's Day carnation fundraiser, every year, Shannon continually broke her own record for most flowers received. Not only from her cabal of girl-friends, of which there were many—but every boy in school, from the expected jocks, to the invisible boys who knew they never had a shot with Shannon Kendall but were so bowled over by her that secretly gifting her with carnations she'd never acknowledge was enough for them.

For Ruthie, there was no jealousy. Just pure, longing admiration. A careless ponytail looked like the chicest of hairdos. Gobs of spinach never wedged themselves between her two front teeth. She didn't trip, fall, stutter, or flounder.

Even in junior high, she'd been perfect.

Ruthie had no real plan for how she would get Shannon to be her friend. At first, she worked up the nerve to cast a shy smile at Shannon one morning as she passed her locker. She didn't see her, of course. She'd breezed right by Ruthie, squealing as she made a beeline for the group of Skip Lane (star tight end, first baseman, CEO father, homemaker mother), Mikey Gold (star receiver, star shooting guard, lawyer mother, CFO father), Sharla Ritter (pom-pom, varsity swim team, student council, doctor mother, doctor father), Lyz with a 'y' Cox (cheerleader, varsity volleyball, VP of marketing mother, managing partner father), and Chad Warner (star quarterback, track, star pitcher, mother owned a chain of successful aerobics studios, stockbroker father) at his locker. She watched Shannon throw her arms around Sharla and Liz, while Mikey, leaning against the row of lockers, bit his lip and smiled, just watching her.

Ruthie knew if she wanted to be Shannon's friend, she'd have to be more proactive than weird, quiet smiles. Her options were few, however. She didn't play tennis, so going out for the team wasn't going to work. Not to mention, Shannon was varsity. She'd be laughed off the court before she even picked up a racket. Ruthie couldn't fathom running track, which left pom-pom squad. Tryouts wouldn't be held until the spring and her chances of making that were less than tennis and track. Not that she wasn't a good dancer—she was actually pretty coordinated. The problem was, she didn't have the personality for it. Too shy, too self-conscious.

She'd have to come up with something else.

Fate intervened a few weeks after school started. She'd lucked out by being given the assignment to work in the administrative office at the start of junior year, which gave her the opportunity to sneak a peek at Shannon's schedule. That year, they were finally inputting all of the paper schedules into the new IBM computer the school had purchased over the summer. Mrs. McKenzie, the ancient secretary in charge of maintaining students' schedules, had no idea how to operate the bulky morass of plastic, metal, and wires and entrusted her quiet, hard-working assistant to help her keep it all straight. And just like that, Ruthie magically inserted herself into four of Shannon's classes: American lit, American history, chemistry, and French. She couldn't do anything about her calculus or Shannon's algebra or her second period gym or Shannon's eighth period gym, which was really tennis practice.

Four out of seven periods was good, though. Really good.

It would give her a chance to get closer to Shannon.

Which was all she ever wanted.

59

RON

Ron ran his hands over the six-day stubble as his eyes flicked to the frosty window next to the front door of his apartment. He'd been trapped in the tiny one-bedroom apartment for days, the tip of his nose icy cold and red from keeping the heat turned down, the bland white walls seeming to close in on him with each passing minute until he was short of breath. His lawyer, a steely, no-nonsense, yet somehow kind and nurturing woman, had ordered him to stay inside and talk to no one until the interview she'd negotiated aired tomorrow night. She wouldn't even let him go to his brother's for the holidays, insisting he spend it with her family, all so she could keep an eye on him. In less than twenty-four hours, he would officially go on the record with the truth about his stupid affair with Amber to hopefully quiet the chants about him being a predatory child molester. He'd made one dumb mistake with the wrong twenty-year-old girl who just happened to be a former student.

When you said it out loud, it sounded stupid and simple all at once.

It was clear that he would have to leave Lake Forest. It was even clearer his teaching career was probably over. He'd been placed on administrative leave without pay and he doubted they would have him back. It didn't matter that he was innocent of all he'd been accused of.

The stain was embedded and no school district would want to be tainted by it.

So, what the hell was he supposed to do now? What was he going to do with the rest of his life?

At the moment, he wanted to eat. Ron wandered into his kitchen, already knowing the answer to the question, but somehow unable to resist believing things had changed since his trip in here two hours ago to scrounge the last of some club cracker packages from a long-ago trip to a salad bar. His cupboards still revealed two cans of minestrone, a bag of peanuts down to the dusty skins, a near empty box of Cheerios —not even enough for a bowl—and a handful of ketchup, hot mustard, and salt and pepper packets huddled in one corner. The refrigerator offered an even sadder commentary with its half loaf of bread, shriveled up slice of bologna because he forgot to seal the package shut, and swallow of orange juice. Somehow the prospect of a ketchup and hot mustard sandwich and bowl of minestrone was about as appealing as a ketchup and hot mustard sandwich and bowl of minestrone.

The TV behind him hummed with a commercial from one of those fast-casual restaurants that promised the best night of your life with your five best buddies, complete with a plate of nachos for the table, frothy goblets of sickly-sweet cocktails, and a sizzling platter of fajitas for your entrée. Finished off, of course, with something chocolate and molten. Or strawberry and creamy. Imagining the smell of a hot, freshly cooked cheeseburger and salty, crispy fries made his mouth water.

He glanced at the clock on his cable box. Nine-fifteen on a Sunday night. Who would possibly be out at this hour? Parents were at home dreading the work week, kids wondering what mystery ailment they could conjure up between now and the alarm clock in the morning.

He knew just where to go. A little bar over in Libertyville that was open until three. Dark, anonymous, out of the way.

Perfect.

Ron rushed into his bedroom to throw on a clean-ish pair of jeans resting on the lid of his hamper and a blue cotton sweater hanging in his closet. He shrugged into his coat before grabbing his keys and wallet from the shelf next to the front door, feeling happier than he had in days at the prospect of this clandestine jaunt. Cheeseburgers and fries were always a good cause.

The bitter crush of cold January air rattled through his body as he blew into his cupped hands. The only sounds were the soft shudders of cold breath pushing past his lips, the jingle of his keys as he shook them in his trembling hands, and the squish of his gym shoes gripping the salt-stained pavement as he made his way toward his car, parked in a far corner of the lot.

Ron's first indication something was wrong was the sound. The growling rev of an engine from across the lot caused him to turn his head, first out of curiosity, then fear as he realized the hulking SUV was barreling toward him. He gasped, his feet momentarily glued to the pavement, the high beams piercing his eyes.

As the roar of the engine grew louder, he commanded the concrete of his feet to move out of the path of the monster, now dangerously close to making contact with him.

Except, he'd made the demand of his feet too late. The SUV plowed into him, mowing him down in a single batter-ramming wallop. Ron wasn't even sure if he screamed. Just that his torso bent around the hood of the car for mere seconds before he snapped back and thudded to the pavement.

The last thing he remembered before his lids fluttered shut, besides the screech of tires and bright red eyes of the retreating taillights as the car sped away, was that he wasn't going to get his cheeseburger.

60

ERICA

"Christ, I always knew Regina Knowles was a nutjob, just not enough to try and kill somebody." Jay threw the morning paper down on the breakfast table in disgust and resumed eating the dense yellow oval of his hard-boiled egg, some of the hard pieces dribbling down the front of his shirt. "Fucking lunatic."

"Well, she thought she was doing the right thing," Erica said, scraping the last of her strawberry yogurt out of the carton, spooning it into her mouth. "Protecting her child."

"She's been all over Facebook railing against this guy. I mean, you should see some of her posts. She's fucking unhinged."

"At least Mr. Byrne is okay. That's all that matters."

"It wasn't even her kid that got killed!" Jay said, disbelieving laughter escaping his lips. "What, does she think she's the caped crusader of Lake Forest or something? Jesus. Let the police do their fucking jobs."

"How'd they know it was her?"

"Surveillance at his apartment complex. Apparently, she'd been staking out his place, just waiting for her shot. Too much fucking time on her hands." Jay scooted back from the table, leaving his breakfast dishes. "Like I said, lunatic."

"Do you think he'll press charges?"

"I would, then I'd sue her for every penny she's got." Jay poured himself another cup of coffee. "You just can't go around trying to kill people because you got mad about something. That's not how the world works."

"Like I said, I'm sure she thought she was doing the right thing," Erica said, carrying Jay's dishes to the sink.

"Now you sound like you're defending her."

"What? Oh, no, I'm not, no. All I'm saying is, I'm sure she thought she was doing the right thing."

Jay scoffed and they both looked up as Jordan thudded down the stairs, beelining for the fridge and her own cup of yogurt, before flipping the hood of her sweatshirt over her head. Erica gawked silently, unable to believe her daughter planned to go to school looking like that.

"Jordan—"

"What?"

Erica sighed and plastered on a smile. *Bite your tongue.* "I ran into Coach K at the grocery store yesterday."

"So?"

"Well, we got to talking about pom, and she said you can come back anytime and in fact the squad could really use your leadership right now—"

"You know what, Mom, since you're so obsessed with pom, why don't you join?"

"Jordan." Though he didn't have to say much, Jay merely uttering the girl's name caused her to shrink back a little, her eyes pinned to the floor.

"I'm going to be late," she mumbled, pulling her car keys from her pocket before she quietly closed the front door.

"Babe, give the pom thing a rest," Jay said. "She obviously doesn't want to do it anymore."

"But I just can't understand why. She's so good at it. And with Whitney—" She stopped herself. "What I meant to say was, I think it would be good for her."

"Maybe it's because of Whitney that she doesn't want to do it anymore," Jay said. "Might bring back too many memories, since, you know, that was kind of their thing."

"I hadn't thought of it that way."

He kissed her cheek. "You know what, just … stop pushing, all right?"

"Fine, fine. I'll leave it alone. For now."

He winked at her then yelled for Kennedy to finish brushing her teeth so he could take her to school. The pair bounded out of the house and Erica busied herself with finishing the breakfast dishes. Her eye fell on the newspaper still on the table. She picked it up and stared at Regina Knowles's picture, clicking her tongue against her teeth.

61

AVA

R*uthie Stowers.*

Ava stared at her computer screen, the words of the report she was supposed to be working on all seemed to morph into that name.

Her brain had traded *way thinner* for *Ruthie Stowers* as she woke up this morning, showered, muddled through the breakfast routine with Kyle and Carly. It tugged at her all during her commute, three conference calls, and her lunch meeting. Those four words nagged and teased and Ava couldn't shake the feeling that something—*something*—about those four words fit together in some alarming sequence she couldn't quite grasp.

She felt further spurred to action by the lunacy perpetuated by avenging angel Regina Knowles. How she thought running down Ron Byrne was the answer to whatever ridiculous question was propelling her was astounding to Ava.

It was all too much to fathom. She had to do something.

Ava placed her fingers on the keyboard, a sheen of sweat moist against her upper lip, her underarms burning. The keys rattled against the pads of her quivering fingers and she closed her eyes and typed the name into Google.

Erica. Mitchell.

A LinkedIn profile was the first entry. Ava double-checked that she'd set her LinkedIn searches to anonymous before clicking on Erica's profile, which featured a grayed-out avatar offering the years her graphic design company had been in business, along with the year she graduated from design school. Glowing recommendations from clients. Not even connected to Jay, whose profile featured a professional headshot and a raft of job titles, companies, connections, and endorsements.

That was it. No other information existed for the woman she'd known for all these years. No other social media profiles. Not a single photograph. Nothing. A plethora of other Erica Mitchells across the country spanning teenager to grandmother filled her screen.

But nothing on *her* Erica Mitchell.

How was it possible to be a ghost in the twenty-first century?

She scoured her memory in search of a maiden name for Erica, thinking she could type that in, but found nothing for her trouble.

Ava sighed and rubbed a hand over her face, her heart pounding, as she knew the words she had to type next, but terrified to do so. She took a deep breath, her fingers assuming the position on her laptop.

Ruthie. Stowers.

Images of two young girls flooded her computer screen alongside words like, 'horrific murder,' 'brutal stabbing,' and 'vicious attack.' Ava leaned closer to the screen to study the two grainy pictures attached to each other. The girl on the right was undeniably gorgeous. Megawatt, movie star smile, jet-black hair teased out of the frame, dark smoldering eyes, sunken dimples, a pound of glittery makeup, detectable even in an ancient black and white photo. There was no denying this girl was stunning.

Ava's eyes flicked over to the other girl, scared of the story it would tell.

The girl was cute. Plainly so. Round, chubby face. Tentative smile. Her hair also teased high and mighty. Minimal make up. A perfectly nice-looking girl who probably would disappear in proximity to Shannon Kendall, superstar. A girl who would fade into the wallpaper.

Ava blew up the picture, searching for remnants of Erica Mitchell, and finding none. No straight white teeth, plump lips, button nose. No hazel eyes. Not to mention, the ages were wrong. Erica Mitchell was forty-seven. If Ruthie Stowers was sixteen in 1986, she'd be over fifty now.

Except Melody had seen something in Erica that plucked the chord of Ruthie Stowers.

That had to mean Erica was buried in there somewhere.

Didn't it?

There was a mountain of stories, her eyes skimming over the details of one humid night in the late spring of 1986 in the wealthy Houston, Texas neighborhood of Bellaire when sixteen-year-old Ruthie Stowers stabbed her sixteen-year-old classmate, Shannon Kendall, to death with a pair of scissors.

In every picture of Ruthie following her arrest, her chin was tucked into her chest, hiding from the cameras, shunning the glare of the spotlight. As though she wanted to fold into herself and disappear.

Just like Erica.

Ava jammed the print icon on her laptop repeatedly, the printer spitting out pages as fast as she could print them. After an hour of skim and print, she gathered up the sheaf of papers and secured them with a thick rubber band, shoving the bundle into her briefcase to read when she got home.

Find Erica.

No. Scratch that.

Find Ruthie.

62

RON

He winced as he limped over to the dresser, a lightning bolt of agony shooting across his right ankle. The doctor told him he'd probably always feel prickles of pain, but it was nothing serious. Ron had scoffed. Nothing serious. Like it was no big deal getting hit by a car.

Truthfully, he knew he was lucky, managing to sustain only a broken ankle and a broken finger. It could have been so much worse.

Still, he wondered how many years it would take not to wince at the roar of an engine, or not feel the impact of a car slamming into his body.

Years, likely.

And frankly, the fading bruises had played well during the follow-up TV interview that had run last night. Finally being able to unburden himself and explain it all had been like sawing a shackle from his ankle. Confession had been so very good for his soul, because for the first time in years, freedom tickled at his ears. No more hiding. No more lying. If social media was any indication, the whole thing had gone exceedingly well. So many came out expressing sympathy for his being falsely accused and mowed down for his trouble, expressing remorse for flinging the manure of 'child molester' and 'pedophile' in his face. There were, of course, still some who were convinced the police had bungled the case, letting Whitney Dean's murderer get off, free to roam the streets to defile and brutalize yet another pretty teenager. For the most part though, despite his initial reluctance, he was glad he'd done the interview. At least he'd gotten his side out there. He knew until Whitney's actual murderer was caught, he'd have to live with the stigma of accusation.

He hoped whoever had really killed that girl was rotting in hell.

They deserved nothing less.

Ron threw a pile of his sweaters into his suitcase before zipping it shut. He looked around the room. His lawyer was springing for movers to pack up his meager Ikea bookshelves and Target couch and coffee table and put them into a storage unit she owned for a few months. The apartment manager would let his lawyer's assistant in tomorrow and they would supervise what was likely to be a quick transaction. For now, he was getting the hell out of dodge, his brother, Brandon, albeit reluctantly, letting him crash in his spare room in Ann Arbor. He'd tried to impress upon his brother that his lawyer was banking on him getting a hefty times two settlement from the Knowles family, which meant he could be set for life. They wouldn't have to put up with each other for long.

His teaching career was toast. The district provided him with a meager severance and wished him well. The death of his career saddened him. He loved teaching and was good at it. There'd be plenty of time in that small, pleasant guest room in Ann Arbor to mourn it. Maybe he'd tap out that novel English teachers always said they wanted to write, but could never find the time for.

God knows he had plenty of it now.

He hoisted his suitcase off the bed and limped over to turn off the light before hobbling through the living room, past the few boxes of odds and ends he'd packed up for when the movers came tomorrow. He grunted as he bent down to pick up the shopping bag of books he was taking with him, his essentials, as he thought of them: *Madame Bovary, Dante's Inferno, Of Mice and Men, To Kill a Mockingbird, Brave New World, Lord of the Flies, The Scarlet Letter.*

Crime and Punishment.

Ron sighed, wondering how long the relatively short drive to Ann Arbor would take with his hobbled ankle. He'd just have to do the best he could.

He opened the front door, squinting at the blinding winter sun, shining white and intense in the periwinkle blue sky. A beautiful, sunny day. A bright new beginning.

He rolled his suitcase outside and locked the door behind him.

63

CARLY

C arly puckered in the mirror glued to her locker door as she blended a glob of Gold Glow with the Pink Pow already on her lips.

Whitney's favorites.

Just as she threw the lip gloss back into her purse, Lexi and Madison waved to her from a few lockers away as they made their way toward her. She smiled and waved back as she grabbed her copy of *The Crucible* along with her English notebook.

"What up, girly," Lexi said as she and Carly locked pinkies and winked at each other.

"What up?" Carly responded.

"That dress is super fierce," Madison said.

"Thanks, girl." Carly beamed. "It's new."

"So sick," Lexi agreed. "Here, let's post it."

All three girls immediately went to their phones and took individual selfies then a group one, each posting to Instagram, dotting them with emojis and smearing them with filters before falling into chatter about homework, pom, TV shows, music, and boys.

This had become the new morning routine, meeting at Carly's locker before first period. It made her woozy, how fast she zoomed up the social ladder. Even her spewing in class had been forgotten. Now, girls clamored to sit next to her at lunch. Coach K was letting her choreograph not one but two routines for pom and there were even rumblings that captain was hers next year. Lexi and Madison sought her advice on clothes and shoes and lip gloss. They both loved Lifetime movies just as much as she did and they spent hours goofing on how awesome they were. When she walked through the halls, boys called out her name. Girls looked at her with longing, wishing they were her. Carly strutted down the hallways like she owned them, no longer worried about saying the wrong thing or stressing out if her clothes were good enough.

For Carly Ewing was the new queen bee of East Lake Forest High.

And Whitney's death made it all possible.

She was so confident in her new status, she'd stopped worrying about the sweatshirt. Well, that wasn't entirely true. Sometimes, late at night when she couldn't sleep, she would think about it. She'd searched her house up and down, even sneaking into her mom's home office when she was out of town one time and it wasn't there. Eventually, Carly convinced herself that she must have thrown it out and just couldn't remember.

That had to be it.

Didn't it?

From the corner of her eye, Carly saw Jordan duck into the girls' room down the hall. She smiled to herself.

"I've got to make a run to the bathroom. Who's coming with me?" she asked.

Lexi and Madison both eagerly agreed as Carly slammed her locker shut and sauntered down the hall. She could see Jordan's boots still pointing from beneath the stall. She flipped her hair back and set her books down on the ledge of the radiator.

"Has anyone talked to Peyton lately?" Carly asked.

"We texted last night," Lexi said. "She's pretty sure she'll be back to school next week. We totally have to stand with her, let everyone know she's still cool."

"I still can't believe her mom tried to kill Mr. Byrne," Carly said. "I mean, if she wanted to go after the person who killed Whitney, she should have been trying to run Jordan over."

"So embarrassing," Madison said. "I would literally die if my mom tried to kill somebody."

"How long do you think it will take for the police to do something about Jordan?" Carly pressed, taking a quick glance toward the stall. "I mean it's been months. Obviously, Mr. Byrne didn't do it. Who else could have killed Whitney?"

The door to the stall swung open, clanging against the wall as a seething Jordan stepped out and rushed over to Carly.

"Shut your fucking mouth," she said, face pinched, teeth clenched.

"Make me," Carly said, hand resting on one hip.

"Weren't you a neek like six months ago? What, now you think you're somebody?" Jordan narrowed her eyes. "You're that same pathetic baby you've always been."

Carly flinched at the arrow, which hit her right between the eyes.

"Oh, my God, ignore her." Madison jumped to Carly's defense. "After all, *she's* still the same skank she's always been. And now, she's a murderer."

"What, are you going to kill me too?" Carly asked, her confidence back at knowing Madison was her ride or die. "Like you did Whitney?"

Jordan drew up. "I didn't kill her."

"Oh, please, we all know you did," Madison said, rolling her eyes. "When are you going to confess?"

"Shut up."

"Whitney knew what a loser you were," Carly said. "I'll bet that's why you did it, huh? I'll bet that's why you killed her."

"We already know you're trash," Lexi said.

"Yeah," Madison chimed in. "Total trash."

"God, I hope when they arrest you, you get your fucking brains bashed in, you nasty, trashy bitch—"

Carly didn't see the shove coming until she was flying across the bathroom. Lexi and Madison screamed and rushed to push Jordan back from delivering another blow. Madison bent down to help Carly to her feet.

"You fucking bitch!" Carly screamed.

Tears spilled from Jordan's eyes. "Don't come for me, Carly—"

"Did you hear that?" Carly laughed. "Oh, my God, if I wind up stabbed to death in the woods somewhere, you know who had the knife."

The warning bell sounded for first period. Jordan ran out of the bathroom, sobbing, while Lexi and Madison rubbed Carly's back and offered soothing words about how awful Jordan was.

"You should totally report her to Principal Bain," Lexi said. "She's like, completely out of control."

Carly smoothed down her hair and reapplied her lip gloss, her hands shaking. "I'm not worried about her."

"Come on, we should get to class," Madison said as the girls gathered their books.

Lexi and Madison ran down the opposite hall from Carly, who floated into first period American lit as though nothing had happened. She couldn't help but be a little relieved when she saw Jordan was nowhere to be found.

64

LAUREN

W hitney's bedroom door stared back at Lauren as she stood in the hallway. She hadn't been in there since she'd gone in to choose a dress for her daughter to be buried in. Pink. Of course.

The door was adorned with the paraphernalia of teenage girls. Sparkly holographic letters spelling out 'Whitney' across the top. The fluttering first place ribbons announcing her as the best in dance competitions, the champion of champions. A stark black and white, 'Keep Calm and Beyonce' sign. A pink and white metal parking sign nailed to the door, embossed with 'My World, My Rules.' Her varsity pom letter.

Her interview was scheduled for tomorrow and Wendy Sheridan had suggested it might be nice to have something of Whitney's to show on camera. A memento, a favorite photo—something to make Whitney real to the millions of people who would be gawking over her grief.

Lauren took a deep breath, heat washing over her skin, her under-arms tingling. All she had to do was open the door, something she'd done a million times.

But never like this.

She reached her hand toward the knob, her fingers quaking as they brushed the metal. Her hand sprang back as though she'd been burned.

Lauren pursed her lips and closed her eyes, giving herself one last pep talk to just do it.

The door creaked as she slowly opened it. She was startled not to see Whitney sprawled across the bed, watching *Black Mirror*, an obsession Lauren didn't quite understand, or seated at her desk, her Spotify playlist droning on in the background, snapping selfies or texting, or reading the countless women-in-jeopardy mystery novels she tore through like fire burning into wood.

Instead, the room was quiet. Still. The red and white striped Styrofoam cup from a stop at Portillo's sitting on the desk, likely holding the watery, moldy remnants of Dr Pepper, the bent red straw stamped with her teeth marks, sticking up out of the lid. The king-sized bed draped in the hot pink polka dot duvet, the hot pink sheets still wrinkled from her last sleep. The hot pink and white striped walls adorned with glossy photo collages, posters of Beyonce and Lady Gaga. The lacquered white bookshelf crammed with her crumbling ancient paperbacks she'd easily had since elementary school. She didn't like reading on her phone like Lauren did. She always said she liked the feel of a book in her hand. The pile of shoes that hadn't made it into the closet. Her pom gear, the shimmering pom-poms tossed in a corner like forgotten rag dolls, spiral-bound notebooks filled with what Lauren knew were choreography notes and song ideas. Her uniform wrapped around a puffy satin hanger, the handle on a hook over the top of the bedroom door.

Exactly as she'd left it.

Lauren crept over to the bed, running her hand across the soft, cool cotton of the duvet and the wrinkled form of her daughter. She picked up one of the pillows and buried her face in it, tears pricking her eyes at the lingering ribbon of peach shampoo woven into the fabric.

Her beautiful daughter.

Lauren laid down on the bed, snuggling into the coolness of the sheets and the memories, coming at her like fastballs now: discovering she was pregnant, bringing her home, the first lost tooth, twirling around the house in a tutu and nothing else. A little clutch purse fastened in one hand, a book in the other. Always. The tears that would ensue if she didn't have her little purse and a book. Rushing through the front door, bursting with excitement over having made pom squad.

Tears soaked the pillow and for a moment, Lauren panicked. Having to wash anything would be devastating. She didn't want to lose her girl's scent.

Sniffing, woefully trying to hold the tears and snot in, Lauren ambled over to the box of Kleenex sheathed beneath a pink Plexiglass container on Whitney's desk. As she pulled a clump of tissues from the box, her eye fell on Whitney's diary. Lauren lowered the tissues as she stared at the book, her heart pounding. She'd never wanted to violate her kids' privacy, disdainful of being one of those snooping moms like she suspected Erica probably was.

Still, Whitney was gone and this was a last link to what her daughter thought, felt, wanted, needed.

Lauren bit her bottom lip as she impulsively picked up the book, surprised it didn't have any type of lock or impediment. She couldn't help but smile. That was how much trust they had between them. Whitney knew she'd never go tiptoeing through those pages, so a lock hadn't been necessary.

She lowered herself down onto the bed, flipping through the lined pages as she scanned the looped, girlish script. There didn't seem to be anything earth-shattering. Complaints about teachers, petty squabbles with girlfriends, ruminations on the hopelessly entangled politics of pom squad. Some boys she liked. Lauren continued to turn the pages, skimming the words, hesitant to read them deeply now, determining she would soak them up later.

Jordan's name jumped out from one of the pages toward the end. She frowned as she opened the book wider and held it closer to her face, squinting a little. The twenty-third. About a week before the party.

That bitch Jordan keeps threatening me, that I better watch my back and I better be careful—

Lauren slammed the book shut, rage bubbling inside her like hot lava.

Jordan.

Did Whitney say Jordan was *threatening* her?

Threatening her little girl? Her baby? Was Jordan the one who took that knife and—?

"Oh, God," Lauren whispered as she bolted down the hallway to her own room. She grabbed her purse and keys, the diary wedged beneath her arm as she shoved her bare feet into her Uggs and haphazardly stuffed her arms into her coat, before she flew down the stairs and out of the house, one thought pounding against her brain the whole time.

That bitch Jordan.

65

JORDAN

There had been nowhere to run to after Carly's assault in the bathroom. Going to class was out. So was sitting in her car all day.

Instead, she left. Jordan got in her car and escaped, sobbing uncontrollably as she drove aimlessly out of campus wondering where she should go. In the end, she decided on the mall, sitting in the food court picking at a stale, cold pretzel from the pretzel place and nursing a mammoth Diet Coke. Occasionally, tears ran down her face as she remembered Carly's accusatory finger and Lexi and Madison, who she'd never had a problem with—ever—chiming in.

It was humiliating.

And it hurt.

Jordan hit her blinker to turn down her street, dreading the confrontation with her mother about why she'd missed school today. The automated texts notifying parents of an unexcused school absence usually went out by late afternoon.

She pulled into the driveway and glumly slung her book bag over her shoulder as she trudged toward the house, opening the door to quiet, which didn't mean anything. Her mother was probably in her office, working as always. Jordan tiptoed over to the stairs, ready to throw herself into bed and forget this day ever happened.

"Jordan."

She rolled her eyes at the sound of her mother's voice at her back. She slowly turned around to find her mother standing at the base of the stairs, her arms crossed, frowning.

"Yeah?"

"I know you didn't go to school today."

A surge of tears welled up inside of her, which she bit back. "I just wasn't feeling well, that's all."

"Well, what's the matter?"

"Mom, I'm just … can I just go and lie down? Please?" she asked, her voice jittery, her insides crumbling.

Her mother opened her mouth like she was going to say something, but nodded instead. "Okay. I'll come to check on you later."

Relief ran through her at being let off the hook and not subjected to a round of a hundred questions. Jordan plodded upstairs to her room and dropped her book bag to the ground as she kicked off her shoes, just wanting to snuggle into the cool comfort of her bed and wipe out Carly, Lexi, Madison—Whitney.

All of them.

As her head hit the pillow, a series of wallops against the front door sent her bolting upright, certain it was the police.

66

ERICA

No sooner than Erica had heard the soft click of Jordan's bedroom door did the front door explode in a manic series of short, angry slaps, rattling the vase on a glass table in the foyer and echoing throughout the house.

"Jesus," she muttered as she looked at her phone and saw Lauren Dean battering away like a mad woman. She opened the door and Lauren pushed past her into the house, her hair jutting away from her face in wild spikes, her red-rimmed eyes bright and savage with hysteria.

"Lauren, what's—?"

"Where is she?"

"Who?"

"Jordan. I know she's here, I saw her car."

"Lauren, Jordan—Jordan's not feeling well—"

"Yeah, well, my daughter's dead, how's that for not feeling well?"

Erica blanched. "I think you need to leave."

The woman ignored her, beelining for the stairs, wielding the pink book she held in front of her like a weapon as she screamed for Jordan to come downstairs. Erica took a few deep breaths, willing herself not to grab the woman and throw her out of the house. She was grieving after all. Instead, she touched Lauren's elbow, which ignited her into whirling around, her eyes popping out of their sockets, her lips twisted into a snarl.

"You go up there and bring that girl down here or so help me—"

"Mrs. Dean?"

Her and Lauren's heads both flicked up at the meek squeak of Jordan's voice at the top of the stairs. Lauren scrambled around Erica, waving that pink book in the air as she dashed up the stairs toward her daughter.

"What did you do?" she demanded of Jordan, who looked help-lessly at Erica as she trailed Lauren on the stairs.

"Lauren, what's going on?"

She whirled around and pointed that book at her. "Whitney wrote in her diary that Jordan was threatening her and I want to know what in the hell your daughter did to my daughter." Lauren pivoted back to Jordan. "I'm going to ask you again, what did you do?"

"Lauren, you need to calm down, please—" Erica tried again.

"I will not calm down," Lauren hissed. "Your daughter was threat-ening my daughter and now my daughter is dead. For the last time, I want to know what the hell Jordan did." She turned on Jordan once more. "You killed her, didn't you?"

Tears streamed down Jordan's face as she stumbled backward. "Mrs. Dean, I would never do something like that. Whitney was my best friend—"

"A best friend who's Sweet Sixteen you ruined with your ghetto trash antics—"

"Lauren, I can call Steve or call the police," Erica said, her own temper ratcheting up a few notches. "Your choice."

"I'm going to ask you one more time before *I* call the police and have them come here and arrest you and throw you in jail for the rest of your life," Lauren screamed, ignoring Erica. "Confess. Confess right now that you stabbed my daughter, that you murdered Whitney."

"Okay, that's it, I'm calling the police." Erica put her finger on the nine. "You can't come over here harassing my daughter—"

Lauren licked her lips, ignoring Erica. "Why did she say you were threatening her? We all know you're nothing but a jealous bitch—"

"Mom—?"

"—who could never, ever be as good as my daughter. Second best Jordan. That's what you'll always be. Second best. You couldn't touch, Whitney. You could never, ever be as smart, or as beautiful or as special—"

"Do you want to know what your special *daughter* did to me?" Jordan screamed.

Erica lowered the phone, her senses on high alert. She gulped, watching tears gush from her daughter's red, twisted face.

"What are you talking about?" Lauren asked in a pained whisper.

Jordan's jaw cranked beneath her skin as she seemingly weighed whether to keep pushing forward. "Well—"

"I knew it. She didn't do anything," Lauren snapped. "You're just trying to get out of admitting what you did."

"Whitney put my picture on one of those sugar daddy websites."

Lauren's grip on Jordan's shoulders relaxed slightly. "She did what?"

Jordan closed her eyes and took several deep breaths. "There was —she had a crush on some guy, some guy we met at the mall who goes to U of C and she had a huge crush on him and was totally throwing herself at him, but he—" Jordan gulped. "He asked me out instead, but he was like a hundred and I thought it was gross, but she went nuts and to get back at me, even though I didn't do anything … she put my picture on one of those sites and planned to show it to him."

"No." Lauren shook her head frantically. "Whitney wouldn't do that."

"Mrs. Dean, she stole pictures of me off my phone and my private profiles and put them on a sugar daddy website. All because some guy liked me instead of her."

"That's not true."

"You wanna know how I found out?" Jordan spat. "Huh?"

"How?" Lauren whispered, seemingly afraid of the answer.

Jordan glanced at Erica before continuing. "My dad was having one of his last-minute dinner parties and one of the guys … he saw my picture and then when he saw me here at the house … I told him I didn't know what he was talking about and then, he showed me. I knew right away that it was Whitney."

"Oh, God." Lauren's face plummeted into her hands, tears gushing into her palms.

"When was this?" Erica asked quietly.

Jordan wiped her nose with the back of her hand. "Last summer. When Dad had all those guys that did that travel app over here. The guy was like sixty and he got all excited when he saw me and I finally had to threaten to tell Dad if he didn't calm down. That was the only reason he did."

"It could have been anyone else that put your pictures on that site, any one of those girls," Lauren said, weak defiance lacing her words.

"I confronted her and she owned up to it. Showed me all the fake profiles she'd created, the accounts. She thought it was funny. She actually laughed about it. She thought it was one big joke."

Lauren seemed to wilt at this information as she faltered backward and leaned against the banister. Erica fumed as Jordan continued crying softly, though her hysteria had subsided.

"Jordan, why didn't you tell anyone about this? Me? Your father?"

"I just wanted to forget the whole thing. She didn't even apologize. She told me it was no big deal, to 'chill out,'" Jordan said, making air quotes with her fingers. "She didn't care that some guy could have done I don't even know what to me."

"So, Whitney did all this and you threatened to tell everyone about it," Erica said. "That's why you stopped talking. That's what you meant when you said you were going to tell everyone what she did."

Jordan fidgeted as her gaze dropped to the floor. "I didn't even want to look at her face, I was so angry. So, I quit pom, unfollowed her, just totally disconnected from her. I couldn't believe my best friend would do that to me."

"And that's why you came to the party, isn't it?" Lauren had reared back up, seeming to find a new angle to her ire. "You wanted to ruin her, you—"

Jordan's eyes filled with tears again. "I should never have gone to the party, Mrs. Dean. I'm so sorry—"

"And when that wasn't enough—"

"Okay, Lauren, that's it," Erica said. "Please leave."

"This isn't over," Lauren hissed, pointing a finger at Jordan. "I'm going to make sure you pay for what you did, for lying, for slandering my daughter—"

"You know, Jay's going to be furious when he hears about this," Erica warned.

Lauren's eyes grew wide with seeming disbelief. "Excuse me?"

"I'm just saying, your daughter put my daughter in danger and my husband, her father, has really deep pockets." Erica leaned closer, lowering her voice. "You sure you want to go there?"

"Are you threatening me?"

Erica marched over to the front door and flung it open. "Goodbye, Lauren."

Lauren snorted before following the directive. "Get your daughter a good lawyer," she sneered as she slammed out of the house.

"Mom, is she going to send me to jail?" Jordan asked, bursting into tears all over again. Erica rushed over, gathering her in her arms, rocking her as she stroked her hair.

"Oh, sweetie, it doesn't work that way. She's—she's upset about Whitney. She's not thinking straight."

"But she said—"

Erica pulled back, cradling her daughter's face in her hands, eye to eye. "Jordan, honey. You're not going to jail."

Jordan threw herself against her and Erica wrapped her arms tight, rocking her back and forth in an attempt to soothe her girl.

Jay could deal with Lauren. He relished fights like this, the chance to swing his dollars around in order to bring a rival to their knees, crush them beyond all comprehension. Let him have his fun.

After Lauren's embarrassing little tirade and Jordan's reveal, any doubts she'd had were scrubbed clean now.

She'd done the right thing.

67

RUTHIE

Midterms came and went and Ruthie was no closer to Shannon than she'd been at the beginning of the school year. Though they had four classes together, all the seating was alphabetical, so she couldn't even finagle a seat next to her. If Shannon noticed she and Ruthie had so many classes together, she never acknowledged it.

Since the class thing wasn't working out, Ruthie tried to be strategic in her approach. She applied for a position at the country club where Shannon played tennis every Saturday with Abby Franklin (pom squad, varsity tennis, varsity basketball, banker father, university professor mother), but didn't get the job.

Shannon signed up to go on the class trip to Galveston at the end of January and so did she, babysitting every weekend to subsidize the hundred dollars her parents gave her. Ruthie had visions of her and Shannon sharing a room and bonding over virgin piña coladas and inside jokes borne of the weekend. Except, of course, Shannon shared a room with Lyz, Sharla, and Abby, while she got stuck with Peggy Dubin, Autumn Frayzen, and Lori Tifton. Every time she turned around, Shannon and her cabal were off doing their own thing, usually with Skip, Chad, and Tyler Abbott (star point guard, track and field, realtor father, newspaper publisher mother) trailing after them.

Nothing was working. She and Shannon weren't best friends. Not even close.

She still wasn't special.

And then finally—*finally*—the opportunity presented itself in February.

That year, the drama department's spring musical was *Bye Bye Birdie*. Auditions were open, so anyone could try out.

It was only a lucky coincidence that Ruthie even knew Shannon had signed up. She was coming out of her art club meeting when she saw Shannon, Abby, Lyz, and Sharla outside of Ms. Grazoli's office, giggling and pointing to the piece of paper tacked to the wall. She lingered in the classroom until the girls sauntered off down the hall before wandering up to see what they'd found so fascinating.

Shannon Kendall's name in looped and swirling script, announcing her intention to audition for the school play.

And so would she.

As Ruthie painstakingly printed her name underneath Shannon's, her hands trembling, her heart racing, she knew—*she knew!*—this was going to change everything. This is how she was going to get close to Shannon. It didn't matter that the other members of her gaggle had also signed up to audition. One way or another, by the time it was all over, Shannon was going to notice her. They were going to be friends.

She'd make sure of it.

She and Shannon, along with Lyz and Sharla and about a hundred other girls, took their shot at the lead. Not that Ruthie had a prayer of being cast as Kim MacAfee. How could she? She couldn't sing, her dance moves confined to rhythmic bopping. She wasn't much of an actress. She definitely wasn't pretty enough. She could see Ms. Grazoli trying to stifle her quiet shock that Ruthie Stowers would deign to audition for something so prestigious, so high profile. They didn't understand. No one would ever understand. It was enough to know she and Shannon were in proximity for the same thing, working for the same goal. It wasn't a shock at all when Shannon got the lead. Not only was she a good actress—and pretty, of course—she had a beautiful singing voice. The drama teacher took pity on Ruthie and cast her as one of the four nonspeaking teenagers.

It was enough. More than enough.

Sharla and Lyz, both awarded bit parts, dropped out after the first rehearsal. But Shannon stayed, meaning Ruthie had her all to herself. Those girls were disloyal. Not like her. For the first time, they were part of the same team. *Really* on the same team. She and Shannon would share scenes together. Shannon might even need her help to run lines. They'd go to costume fittings together. They'd spend every afternoon together for the next six weeks. Shannon had to notice her.

And she did. She made a point of saying hi to everyone every afternoon before rehearsal and asked how they were doing and wished everyone a good night at the conclusion of rehearsal. She'd even waved to Ruthie the next day during her morning glide through the hallway, the tiny gesture stunting the dismay over the C+ she'd gotten on her chemistry exam earlier that week.

And then came the day—*the* day—Shannon spoke directly to her for the first time. Ruthie was standing next to one of the prop records she'd left backstage and Shannon asked if she'd mind grabbing it for her. Her hand shook as she passed it over, exploding with happiness when Shannon smiled and said thank you.

Ruthie thought she'd died.

As she watched Shannon during those weeks of rehearsal, she continued to be awed by her singular talent. It wasn't just the purity of her voice, the limbs seemingly made of rubber, or her comic timing easily interspersed with dramatic talent. She sparkled, throwing a wink and a smile at the end of a rousing dance number, or knowing how long to hold a dramatic beat.

She was a superstar.

Opening night was coming soon and Ruthie knew she had to do something to move the needle on their friendship. Her chance came after a long rehearsal that saw them run through the complete show twice. Shannon was flawless, of course. Ruthie had dawdled after rehearsal, taking extra time to help put away props, carefully watching as Shannon bid everyone good night before floating down the hall to the restroom. She quickly followed her, making sure no one saw her, timing it so she made it in just as she did, waiting to exit the stall only seconds after Shannon.

"Hi," she said, her voice squeaking as Shannon looked over from the sink where she was washing her hands, her voice echoing around the room.

"Hey." She snapped her fingers. "Wait, tell me your name again?"

"Ruthie. Ruthie Stowers."

"Right. Oh, my God, Ruthie." She laughed and took a handful of paper towels out of the battered and rusty white metal dispenser. "I am soooo bad at names. Like so bad."

"That's okay." Ruthie dried her own hands. "You were so good today. I mean, you're good every day, but today you were like, amazing. Seriously, you're like a star."

"Awww." Shannon's face melted into puppy dog cuteness, Ruthie's insides right along with it. "That is so sweet."

"I'm just being honest. You could seriously win an Oscar one day or something."

Shannon laughed again, reaching into her purse for a mint green tube of Estée Lauder lipstick. "I totally tried out for fun. My girlfriends were like 'you should do it, you should it' and 'let's all do it' and then I got it and I could not believe it." She puckered her lips a few times then smiled at Ruthie. "What do you think? Does this color look okay?"

"It's great. Really, that color looks so good on you."

Shannon threw the tube back into her purse. "I'm going with pink for spring. You know, totally lighten it up." She turned to Ruthie. "I'm thinking of getting blond highlights for the summer. Do you think they'd look good on me?"

"Oh, yeah." Ruthie nodded. "You should totally do that."

Ruthie jumped when the pink Swatch watch on Shannon's wrist sounded. "Ugh. I have to get home, take my medication," she said, turning on her heel toward the bathroom door. Ruthie ran to catch up with her, afraid to let this moment slip through her fingers.

"Your medication?" she asked, panicked by this casually dropped tidbit. Was Shannon sick? Was she dying?

"For my diabetes," she said nonchalantly.

"Wow. Really?" Ruthie asked, working to keep pace with Shannon. Her own heart pounded at the nearness of her. The sharp scent of Aqua Net, the Liz Claiborne perfume, sparkling white Keds, GUESS? jeans mini, and oversized black and white Esprit jacket she herself had coveted at Palais Royal just a few weeks ago.

"I was diagnosed when I was seven. I keep it totally under control. Take my insulin, get lots of rest, play tennis, swim. I'm in super good shape."

"I'm so sorry," Ruthie said, sobered by this chink in Shannon's armor. "I had no idea."

Shannon shrugged. "It's no big deal. It's not like I'm dying or anything."

"No, it's just … I thought only old people got diabetes." Ruthie felt a flush of heat across her face. "Oh, my God. That sounded so stupid."

"Don't worry about it." Shannon smiled. "Lots of kids get it, they don't know why."

"So, are you nervous about opening night?" Ruthie asked, desperate to steer the subject away from this grim discovery about Shannon's not-so-perfect life.

"Huh? Oh, I don't know. Maybe a little, I guess. I probably won't think about it until it's here, you know?"

"Sure, yeah, that makes sense."

Shannon grabbed her car keys from her purse. "Well, I'll see you tomorrow. Have a good night."

Ruthie's heart plummeted to her feet, crashing as it hit the bottom. "Yeah, sure, have a good night," she said, turning slightly away.

"Where are you parked?"

"Oh, I walk home. It's not far."

"Hey, I can totally give you a ride," Shannon said.

"It's okay, you said you had to get home—"

"Seriously, it's no big deal. You said you live close, right?"

"Glenora Lane?"

"So close." Shannon gestured for Ruthie to follow her. "Come on. I'll take you."

Ruthie clutched at her heart through her blouse as she walked lock step with Shannon toward her gleaming hot pink Karmann Ghia. Shannon Kendall—*the* Shannon Kendall—was giving her, Ruthie Stowers, a ride in her car. Had insisted on it! She was no longer pressed up against the glass of Shannon's life. She was *in* Shannon's life. The adrenaline rushing through her almost made it difficult to open the door, relishing the soft hiss of her bottom sliding across the supple white leather.

Shannon cranked up Power 104, squealing just as Culture Club's new song came on. "I love this song. Don't you love this song?"

"Such a good song," Ruthie agreed, even though she really didn't like it all that much.

Shannon sang along with the radio, tapping Ruthie's arm, encouraging her to join in. For those magical few minutes on the way to Ruthie's house the girls sang together as though this was their normal Wednesday afternoon routine, as though they'd been doing it forever. Once Shannon turned down her street, Ruthie reluctantly directed her toward her house. Why couldn't she go home with Shannon? Why did she have to be deposited back into her dreary life?

"Thanks for the ride," Ruthie said, hoping Shannon didn't detect the warble of sadness in her words. "I guess I'll see you tomorrow in class."

"What?"

Ruthie tucked a hunk of hair behind her ear. "I'm in your American lit class. And history, physics. Social studies."

"Really? Do you sit in the back?"

"Yes."

"I guess that's why I haven't seen you before...?" Shannon's eyes searched her face, grasping for her name.

"Ruthie."

Shannon snapped her fingers. "Right. Ruthie. I told you, I'm so bad with names."

"It's okay. It's kind of a forgettable name."

"No, it's cool. Kind of old-fashioned. Okay, I totally have to run. See you tomorrow. Ruthie," she said, giggling.

As Shannon backed out of her driveway, Ruthie floated through her front door on a cloud, a knowing secret smile on her face all through dinner, as she and her sisters cleaned the kitchen while her brother played Nintendo. For the first time in her life, her drab little house didn't bother her, her father yelling at the boxing match on TV didn't bother her. Her mother's sensible white hospital shoes stacked neatly next to the front door alongside the canvas tote that would carry her Tupperware lunch of tuna salad sandwich, carrot sticks, and an apple when she left for work in the morning at five, didn't bother her. As she doodled Shannon's name in her journal that night, nothing but the wonder of Shannon Kendall consumed her.

She knew they'd be friends forever.

That knowledge was solidified the next morning when Shannon waved to her across the room as she came into American lit and said hi, followed by her name. She could feel the eyes fall on her, envious eyes. Shannon Kendall knew her name. Her. Ruthie Stowers. She smiled shyly and waved back, the same secret, knowing smile tugging at the corners of her lips.

Ruthie didn't know it wouldn't last forever.

Nothing good ever does.

68

AVA

A va rubbed her eyes and looked at the clock on her home computer. Quarter of six. She'd been at this for five hours, becoming a pseudo expert on Ruthie Stowers and Shannon Kendall in the process. Stacks of paper obliterated her desk, alongside her scribbled notes and endless pictures. Thanks to the rabbit hole of YouTube, she'd also watched countless documentaries online about the case, almost able to recite the facts by rote with each new show she found.

Ruthie and Shannon were in drama club together, though as far as Ava could tell, their membership primarily consisted of a one-time appearance in their high school's production of *Bye Bye Birdie*, Ruthie's name lumped into the program with three other girls as nonspeaking teens, Shannon receiving star billing as the female lead. The girls also shared some classes, but no one who was interviewed—not a student, not a teacher—said the two were close. One student remembered the girls attending the class trip to Galveston for spring break, though no one could recall any interactions between the two. Some drama club members commented Shannon had given Ruthie a ride home after rehearsals a few times.

But Ruthie was not part of Shannon's circle of friends. There were no trips to the mall on Saturdays, no sharing makeup tips or marathon phone sessions. Ruthie did not score invites to Shannon's pool parties, or rate mentions in her diaries. She was not asked to sit at Shannon's table during lunch. Mrs. Kendall told the police she'd never heard Ruthie's name until her arrest.

Ruthie was nobody to Shannon Kendall.

Until that Saturday night when Ruthie murdered Shannon.

Despite extensive interrogation from the police, the only thing Ruthie would ever admit to was stabbing her classmate. And then, after serving her ten-year sentence, she vanished into thin air, never to be heard from again.

In general, the similarities between Whitney and Shannon were more than a little eye-opening for Ava, a little too uncomfortable. Both pretty, both popular, both on the pom-pom squad, both hailing from prosperous families in desirable communities.

Both savagely stabbed to death.

One could say it was all a coincidence.

Or history repeating itself.

She hoped to God it was the former.

Ava picked up a sheet of paper from atop one of the piles, examining Ruthie's picture for about the hundredth time, scouring the girl's face for even a glimmer of connection between her and Erica and continuing to find none.

It didn't seem possible that Erica and Ruthie were the same person.

Yet, she still wasn't convinced they weren't.

She needed an irrefutable link, a concrete anchor between the two to definitely say they were one and the same.

Her eye fell on the invitation from Erica's birthday party. She picked it up, mesmerized by the photo of a teenaged Erica.

Maybe it was time to roll the dice.

Ava bit her bottom lip and shook her head before she picked up her phone on the desk next to her, scrolling through her contacts for Erica's number. She hit the phone icon and waited.

"Ava. Hi," Erica answered. She could hear the genuine surprise in Erica's voice. "How are you?"

"Well, I was calling because we've been saying for a while now that we need to get together for a drink and I wanted to see if you were free this week."

"Oh. Um … Jordan and I just had a run-in with Lauren and she's really upset. I don't feel good about leaving her tonight."

"What happened?"

Erica sighed. "She came storming over here accusing Jordan of murdering Whitney and—"

Ava's heart lurched. "What?"

"Yes, I don't—I don't really want to go into it," Erica said. "The whole thing is disgusting."

"What about tomorrow?" Ava asked, hoping she didn't sound like the eager puppy scrapping around her human's ankles. "You can tell me all about it. If you want to, I mean."

"Actually, tomorrow would be perfect. I'll probably have calmed down by then," Erica said. "Why don't you come to the house? We can sit out by the firepit."

Fear burst inside her, blood hammering in her ears. No way in hell did she want to be trapped in Erica's house, just the two of them.

She licked her lips, the soft, salty sheen of nervous perspiration catching the tip of her tongue. "Why don't we go to The Gallery? I haven't been there in ages." Ava chuckled nervously. "Let someone else do the work."

"Well, I can't argue with that."

"I'm working from home tomorrow, so how about five?"

Erica agreed and the two women said their goodbyes. She leaned back in her chair, telling herself this little tête-à-tête would ease her discomfort, that Melody got it all wrong and Erica Mitchell was no more Ruthie Stowers than Ava was. She'd surreptitiously ask her some questions about her background, compare it to the bits and pieces she'd gleaned about the woman over the years, looking for any discrepancies and put the confetti swirl of theories to rest. People had always told her she had a way of extracting information and she'd do it tomorrow night.

Even as she told herself this, the twang of uncertainty snapped inside of her.

She rolled her head around to relieve the cricks in her neck, her hand dropping down atop one of the fresh stacks she'd printed off earlier as she sighed, too tired to plow through the printouts. Without thinking, she plucked a sheet off the top to skim it, vowing to read it more thoroughly tomorrow. A brief article about Ruthie's parole hearing. Granted four to one.

The last line of the story jolted Ava straight up, her leather office chair squealing like a pig.

The lone dissenting member of the parole board explaining why she voted to deny Ruthie early release.

Ruthie has a hair trigger temper that she has a difficult time controlling. The last time she lost control, it resulted in the brutal murder of an innocent young girl. I'm convinced there will be a next time with Ruthie. I'm convinced she'll do it again.

69

JORDAN

Jordan took a deep breath, glancing toward the door, then at her phone, and back again. She'd been sitting in the interrogation room for twenty minutes already. Flop sweat stung her underarms and paste lined the inside of her mouth. She finally folded her arms over the dusty metal table and nestled her face inside, her breath deep and ominous inside the dark cocoon of her hoodie. Detective Diehl had called her yesterday and asked her to come down to the station to answer some questions. She hadn't told her mom, deciding to risk it all on her own. Her mom would totally take over and be super obnoxious. At least when her dad was obnoxious, he was blunt, which made people snap to attention. Her mom just looked like a fool and was annoying.

The door swung open, flooding the room momentarily with ringing phones and the low murmur of voices. Jordan shot up and smoothed her hair down, fear racing through her once again. The detective smiled as she closed the door behind her before taking a seat across from Jordan, a manila folder and a tablet in her hand.

"How are you today, Jordan?" she asked, folding her hands on the table in front of her.

"Fine."

"Thanks for coming down this afternoon. I really appreciate it."

She didn't say anything, squirming in her chair as she watched the detective flip open the folder and shuffle some of the papers inside.

Diehl stopped and looked up at Jordan, smiling. "As I mentioned on the phone, we're still trying to clear up some things around the day Whitney was murdered and I was hoping you could help us by answering a few questions."

"Okay."

"So, I need you to tell me again what you did on the day of the murder."

Jordan gulped, her heart hammering against her chest. "What do you want to know?"

"Just what you did that day. Walk me through what you did from the time you got up until you went to bed that night."

She pursed her lips and alternated between picking at her cuticles and stretching her ponytail holder. "What, you mean like what I had for breakfast?"

Diehl chuckled. "Why don't we start with what time you got up that morning."

"About eight."

"What did you do when you got up?"

"I mean, I took a shower, came downstairs and grabbed a yogurt, talked to my mom while I waited for my dad to take me to the library, since my mom took my car keys and my phone."

"Okay. And what time did you and your dad leave for the library?"

"I guess about nine-thirty."

"All right, so you got to the library and then what?"

She shrugged noncommittally. "I did my research for my paper and then I went to that club. I told you."

"Right. And what time was that?"

"I guess about three. Maybe four. Definitely in the afternoon."

"What was your paper on?"

"The Civil Rights Act of 1964."

"Anything in particular?"

Jordan winced. It was exactly the kind of question her mother would ask. "We just had to write about some of the different things that happened that led to it," she said, repeating almost verbatim what she'd told her mother when grilled. "There was a lot of microfiche and old magazines that I looked at."

"What did you get on the paper?"

"An A."

"Sounds like all that research paid off," Diehl said. "I was a terrible student, so I'm impressed."

Jordan stared at her, waiting.

"And how did you get to Evanston? Since you said your mom took your car keys."

"I took the Metra. The station is across the street from the library. I told you. Remember?"

Diehl clicked her tongue against her teeth and nodded as she contemplated this. "And remind me, what time did you get home that night?"

"About nine-thirty."

"Just to make sure I have it right, you got up that Saturday around eight, came downstairs, talked to your mom, waited for your dad, who took you to the library around nine-thirty. You got there, stayed for a couple of hours, then took the Metra into Evanston to hang out for a few hours at Click's?"

"Yeah."

Diehl nodded. "Okay."

A soft hiss of relief escaped Jordan's lips and she leaned against her chair and crossed her legs, confidence creeping up her spine like the slow rising mercury of a thermometer.

The detective leaned over, her eyes glittering. "Except, the thing is Jordan, we have a little problem."

Jordan's heart plummeted and her stomach gurgled, the sliver of relief evaporating. She twisted the ponytail holder around her index finger until the tip turned purple, the painful pressure of the stunted blood supply oddly comforting. "What do you mean?"

"For starters, no one remembers seeing you at the library that day."

"So?" Jordan sniffed. "I don't remember everyone I see every day."

"And we checked the surveillance of the Metra station for that Saturday and you weren't in any of the footage."

Jordan pushed her fingernails into her palm. "I mean, I—"

The detective picked up the slender black tablet in front of her and swiped across the screen. "I'm going to show you something, Jordan, and I want you to tell me what you think about it."

She waited, her breath still as the detective swiped and tapped some more before pushing her chair back and walking around the table until she was standing over Jordan's shoulder. She leaned down, placing the tablet on the table. Surprisingly clear surveillance footage in color flickered across the screen as her dad's white Jaguar came into the frame.

Jordan's heart slammed against her chest. It was over. It was so over.

"There's your dad's car and there you are getting out," Diehl narrated. "He rolls down the window, says something to you, and you turn around just a second to respond to him before you go inside."

The blood pounded in her ears. She knew what was next.

"Not five minutes later, you come out of the library," Diehl continued. "That hardly looks like a day spent researching a history paper to me."

Jordan sat in stony silence, her lips pressed together, aware of how loud her breath had become.

"And you don't go in the direction of the Metra." She tapped some more and there was Jordan, walking down the street and getting into a waiting car, which disappeared from the view of the camera. Diehl walked back over to her seat, placing the tablet quietly on the table, and looked at Jordan. "Now. Do you want to tell me where you really were that day?"

"Please don't say anything to my parents."

"Where were you that day, Jordan?" she repeated.

She sniffed, swiping her arm across the line of mucous from her nose as she grasped for breath. Diehl continued staring, her face blank.

"I can't help you unless you tell me where you were that day," she said, her voice softening.

"All right," she finally said. "I'll tell you where I was that Saturday."

70

LAUREN

"Are you okay?"

"You have to stop asking me that. I'm fine."

"Lauren…"

She raised her hand to rub her eyes before remembering they were rimmed in thick black eyeliner, taupe eye shadow, and false lashes coated with three swipes of the black mascara brush, the most makeup she'd worn in months. Lauren scratched an imaginary itch on her cheek instead and no sooner than she'd lowered her hand did a makeup fairy appear to flick her face with a blush brush. Unconsciously, she smoothed down the front of the Chanel suit, feeling oddly uncomfortable wearing something that was once a second skin, longing suddenly for her sweats and ponytail.

Steve grabbed her hand and squeezed it and in spite of her irritation at his repeated inquiries as to her state of mind, she squeezed back. Even though he didn't agree with this little sit-down, he was supporting her need to do so.

Someone had to speak for Whitney.

Wendy Sheridan sashayed onto the set, absorbed by the pile of oversized notecards in her hand, ignoring the makeup fairy struggling to keep up with her. Lauren had never thought of Wendy as especially attractive anytime she saw her on the air. She had a gap between her two front teeth, her nose was weird, her dark eyes beady. But there was something magnetic and compulsively watchable about her all the same and was part of the reason she'd chosen Wendy to do the interview. They wanted to do this at their house, but Lauren didn't want the intrusion, so instead, they were sitting in a shivering studio with a hideous blue couch, an ugly vase bursting with dusty fake flowers, and oversized books ranging from Chicago architecture to sports stacked atop a small wooden coffee table. Wendy glanced up and saw the Deans, her demeanor softening as she lowered the notecards and held one hand out to Lauren.

"Mrs. Dean." She smiled and shook Lauren's hand. "Thank you so much for agreeing to talk to me."

"Thank you for the opportunity."

"When is this going to air?" Steve asked.

"We'll do a quick edit after we talk and do some teases tonight, then it will run in its entirety tomorrow morning."

"Seems pretty fast," Steve said.

"There's so much interest in this story and so many people want to hear from Whitney's family," Wendy said. "This could even help provide a clue to police."

Steve frowned. "Like what?"

"Who knows?" Wendy shrugged. "Someone might be watching who saw something, remembers or knows something, and they might be compelled to come forward with new information." She turned to Lauren. "Are you ready?"

"Yes." She nodded. "Let's do this."

They were seated on the couch as the makeup fairies continued to float around, their magical brushes filled with magic dust, while someone miked them and asked them to say "testing, testing," three times. Lauren worried the glare of the lights would cause sheets of sweat to cascade down the inside of her suit, or worse, send all that makeup sliding down her face. Doubtful the makeup fairies could fix that.

Wendy flashed her high wattage smile one final time before a woman with a mike attached to her headphones called for quiet before counting them down.

The questions were all as Lauren expected. Tell her about Whitney. What she was like. What things she liked. Her favorite memory. A funny story. What did she want people watching at home to know about her daughter. She'd chosen to have Whitney's old teddy bear, Sniffles, in her lap as the personal memento Wendy had suggested. Steve teared up discussing his grief, how their son was coping. About Mr. Byrne. About the day of the murder. Please, Lauren, Steve, relive that horrible night for our viewers.

She'd answered every question carefully. Measured. Tears quivering in her voice, even when she smiled at an anecdote. Her guilt about how irritated she'd been with Whitney that day.

And then the question Lauren had been waiting for.

Her shot, as it were.

"Lauren, Steve," Wendy asked with breathy sincerity, her head tilted in sympathy. "Can either of you think of anyone who would want to hurt Whitney?"

Next to her, she saw Steve take a breath, prepared with his pat answer of, "No, of course not. Everybody loved Whitney." A tired banality she'd heard him utter over and over again.

He wouldn't get that chance today.

"I do have an idea," she said, cutting him off. From the corner of her eye, Steve's head swiveled toward her, and though she couldn't see the expression on his face, Lauren knew confusion—maybe even a little shock, a little irritation—was smeared across it.

Wendy, however, perked up, as she leaned closer. Lauren had to give it to her. The woman was no dummy.

"You're saying you think you know who murdered your daughter?"

"Whitney was a stunningly beautiful girl, perfect in just about every way. She was kind. Funny. Smart. She had the world on a string and I have no doubt she would have made a positive and indelible impact on the world. In sixteen years, she already had."

Wendy leaned even closer, almost as if she knew Lauren was about to drop a bomb, that she should simply keep quiet and let Lauren pull the pin.

"The person who murdered my daughter was jealous of all her gifts. This is someone who would never measure up to my daughter and hated her for it. Someone who was second best." Lauren looked directly at the camera. "A classmate. A classmate who is well aware of what they've done."

"You believe a classmate murdered Whitney?" Wendy asked. "Another student?"

"Yes."

"Do you have a name that you could give us?" Wendy asked, panting practically, like a child grasping for a forbidden cookie just out of its reach.

"The only thing I can tell you is that I expect the police to do their jobs. They know. They know who murdered my daughter."

The air in the room hung still and heavy. Someone coughed. The cameramen all stole glances at each other, one of them shaking their head in disbelief. She knew Steve was fuming silently and would rip into her when they were locked in the confines of their bedroom.

"Well." Wendy leaned back, obviously disappointed she wasn't getting the true scoop of the century. "We can all hope the police will do just that. Thank you for your time today, Mr. and Mrs. Dean."

The stagehand called cut. Wendy shuffled her notecards while Steve and Lauren were unmiked. They all stood.

"Lauren, I hope you'll call me when the police make an arrest," Wendy said. "We'd love to do a follow-up."

"You'll be the first person I call," she said.

Wendy smiled stiffly and shook their hands, thanking Steve a little more profusely before she summoned her producer and they exited the set. Lauren grabbed her purse and Sniffles as Steve clutched her hand under the guise of supporting her. No one knew his hand was a vise around hers, cutting off her circulation, crushing the bones of her fingers.

The stiff pleasantries continued, though no one would look at her directly. Finally, they were outside and in their car.

"Steve—"

"Be quiet."

"Look, I know I should have told you what I was planning, but—"

"I said be quiet."

Lauren folded her arms across her chest, as she stared out the front window, Steve peeling out of the parking lot. Well, it was done. There was no snatching the words back from the ether.

Jordan Mitchell had murdered her daughter and tomorrow morning, the whole world would know it.

71

RUTHIE

For the next few weeks, every day after rehearsal, Shannon gave Ruthie a ride home. They sang songs on the radio, talked about the play, and riffed on Mr. Ford, their fat, sweaty English teacher with the creeping crud around his neck. Shannon waved hello to her in the halls when she saw her in between class. She hadn't invited Ruthie to sit with her at lunch yet, but she could be patient. With each new interaction, Ruthie was certain it was a matter of time before she usurped Lyz and Sharla and Abby as Shannon Kendall's sole best friend.

It was a thrilling thought, the imminence of it taking Ruthie's breath away.

Then there was the day she scored an invite to Shannon's house. Ruthie hadn't even been angling for one. It had just ... happened.

They were in the restroom after rehearsal. Ruthie leaned against the sink and stared in longing admiration as she always did while Shannon expertly swabbed her lips with gloss.

"That's such a pretty color on you," Ruthie said.

Shannon smiled. "That is so sweet. You always say the nicest things." She smacked her lips together a few times. "How come you never wear any makeup?"

"Oh." Ruthie shrugged. "My mom said not 'til senior year."

"God. I would die. Absolutely die." Shannon teased her bangs in the mirror with her fingers. "My mom let me when I was thirteen."

"I know," Ruthie murmured.

"What?"

"Where'd you get that lip gloss?" Ruthie said, hoping she'd adequately covered her slip. "Maybe I'll get it as a birthday gift to myself."

Shannon gasped and turned to Ruthie, her eyes wide as saucers. "Oh, my God, I have a spare. Come to my house and I'll give it to you."

Ruthie was sure she hadn't heard right. Had Shannon Kendall—*the* Shannon Kendall just invited *her*—Ruthie Stowers to her house?

She had. She really had.

"Uh, yeah, uh, sure," Ruthie stammered. "That sounds great."

"I mean … you don't have to be home or anything, do you?"

Ruthie shook her head. "No, no, I'm totally free."

"Awesome. We can listen to the new Pet Shop Boys cassette, too. I got it this weekend."

Blood rushed to Ruthie's head and she had to grab the sink to steady herself before she hurried out of the bathroom to catch up with Shannon, who jabbered on about her father having a fit when she bought a new boom box along with a bunch of new cassette tapes. Ruthie barely heard any of what Shannon said, her mind racing, images of Shannon's house cramming into her head at a dizzying, wonderful, breakneck speed.

Ruthie continued to smile faintly as they reached Shannon's car and sang along to "What Have You Done for Me Lately" on the radio. They drove past Ruthie's street and crossed Lessner Lane, the dividing line between small, comfortable homes like the Stowers's and grand, luxurious homes like the Kendall's, winding their way through the spaghetti bowl of serene, curvy streets shrouded in lush, imposing trees. Ruthie had never been back here and it was hard to believe these quiet, stately homes with pillars out front and swimming pools out back shared pieces of her zip code.

Shannon expertly navigated her car up a long driveway, stomping on the brake as she shut off the ignition, not bothering to turn off the radio. "Home sweet home."

Ruthie tried to act cool as Shannon grabbed her purse and book bag, slamming the door shut as she bounded up the brick walkway and two short steps, keys jingling in her hand. She unlocked the front door and a whoosh of cool, flowery-smelling air flooded out of the house.

"Come on in, make yourself at home," Shannon said nonchalantly as she threw her keys into a brass bowl on a table in the entryway and dropped her purse and book bag on the floor.

"Hola, Miss Shannon," a cheerful Spanish accent called out from somewhere in the house.

"Who's that?" Ruthie asked as she quietly closed the front door behind her.

"Our housekeeper, Yolanda," Shannon whispered in response. "Como estás, Yoyo?" she yelled out.

Yolanda responded in Spanish, but Ruthie barely heard her, and further, didn't care about the woman. As she crept further into the house, barely able to drink in the details spinning around her like a carousel whirling off its axis, she kept pinching herself that she was *here*. Her presence inside Shannon Kendall's house was a surreal, wonderous reality. The glass wall that had separated them was forever shattered, because Ruthie was *here*.

And *here* was a fairytale. Beautiful deep blue velvet couches, vases of fresh flowers she didn't know the names of, antique lamps, the shimmering blue of the backyard pool peeking through French doors leading to a patio, Oriental rugs, oil paintings on the walls, ornately carved coffee and side tables, wallpaper—*wallpaper!* She didn't know anyone who had actual wallpaper. And glinting with tiny lines of gold on top of that. There wasn't even a TV in the living room—they probably had a room just for that.

She bet their garbage didn't even stink.

Ruthie followed Shannon into the kitchen, another dazzling room full of all white appliances, one wide countertop housing a glass bowl of green apples too shiny to be real, and gleaming white floors. A petite Mexican woman was emptying the dishwasher, a fast-paced song in

Spanish humming softly from the small clock radio on the counter. She came over and kissed Shannon's cheeks before waving to Ruthie, greeting her with a cheery, "Hola."

"Yoyo, this is my friend, Ruthie," Shannon said, turning to her. "Want something to drink?"

Friend? Did Shannon Kendall just say Ruthie was her friend? The blood rushed to her head in a giddy stream.

"Ruthie?"

"Huh, what?"

"Did you want something to drink?" Shannon opened the refrigerator, the wood door painted white to match the rest of the kitchen. The bottom shelf was a sea of green Perrier bottles, while clear, neatly labeled containers filled the remaining clean shelves. Not like the misshapen, foil-covered Tupperware that populated the Stowers's refrigerator.

Ruthie gulped. "Sure. Whatever you have is fine."

"We have juice, sparkling water. You can have one of my mom's Diet Cokes if you want."

"A Diet Coke sounds good," she managed, her breath quickening.

Shannon smiled and took one out of a bottom drawer filled with the silver and red cans and set it on the counter. "You want it in a glass with some ice?" she asked.

"Out of the can is fine," Ruthie said, popping the top after Shannon handed it to her. "Thanks."

Shannon grabbed a Perrier for herself and an apple out of the bowl. "Come on, let's go upstairs."

"Goodbye, Miss Shannon, goodbye Miss Ruthie." Yolanda waved to the girls as they departed the kitchen.

Ruthie didn't respond to the woman, still on a cloud as she obediently followed Shannon, who slung her purse and book bag over her shoulder before heading up the stairs, each step covered in plush beige carpet. Shannon Kendall had called her a friend. It was too much to handle.

The walls leading up to the second floor were filled with pictures of the Kendall family through the years, adorned in beautiful, dust-free frames behind streak-free glass. The Stowers's had a handful of school photos hung crookedly and displayed haphazardly around the house in cheap plastic frames. Most of their photos and negatives lived in big, dusty blue plastic bins in their garage that her mother swore every year she'd put into a photo album and get frames for, but never did.

Ruthie took several deep breaths, inhaling the scent of all those fresh flowers and lemon polish, and another smell she couldn't quite place, but couldn't get enough of nonetheless. She counted six closed doors upstairs and Ruthie's heart beat a little faster at the thought of running over to one and turning the knob, just to see what it looked like inside.

Shannon walked into the only upstairs room with an open door and Ruthie's heart stopped as she crossed the threshold. The bedroom was even more magnificent than in Ruthie's dreams. A striped pink canopy over a brass bed, a window seat, gauzy white sheers barely hiding the view of the pool below. Outsized posters of Madonna, Prince, and Janet Jackson sprung from every corner, and a huge framed replica of Duran Duran's Rio album cover dominated one rosy pink wall. Her makeup table was crowded with lipsticks, powders, eye shadows, perfume bottles, and cans of hairspray. Dried mums from dances past were bunched together alongside the mirror, the faded ribbons brushing against the wood frame. Smiling photos of Shannon, Lyz, Abby, and Sharla were everywhere and showed them everywhere—AstroWorld, South Padre, the River Walk, school dances, football games, slumber parties.

"Wow," Ruthie said, doing a slow spin around the room, about the size of three bedrooms in her own house. "Your room's huge."

Shannon shrugged. "I guess." She walked over to her brand-new boom box and flipped it on, "Manic Monday," blasting out of the speakers. She mouthed the words and danced in place for a few seconds.

"Doesn't your mom get mad for the music being up so loud?"

"She won't be home until late. Eleven at least. So ... no."

"You have the house to yourself?" Ruthie asked, a tinge of jealousy lacing her words. There was usually always somebody at her house.

"Yeah, except for the days Yolanda is here. Sometimes, my dad is here and we cook dinner together and watch my mom's shows. Otherwise, Sharla, or Lyz or Abby are here, or I go to their house. Actually tonight, my dad and I are going to Strawberry Patch for dinner." She clicked her tongue and took a swig of her Perrier. "Every Thursday."

"Wow. I never go to dinner with just my dad. I think he's scared to go anywhere with just us and not my mom."

Shannon laughed. "Oh, my God. That's *sooooo* funny. My Dad and I are super close. My mom, too. We go shopping or to the movies and lunch on Sundays after church, just the two of us. Daddy and I play tennis every Saturday morning. The rest of the time, he plays golf." She plucked the promised tube of lip gloss from the drawer of her makeup table and handed it to Ruthie. "Here you go. Happy Birthday," she said, winking.

"That's so nice of you, Shannon. Thank you."

"So not a big deal. I'd already gotten one the last time I was at Town & Country and totally forgot and got another one when I was at The Galleria a few weeks later." Her watch beeped. "Ooops. I gotta check my insulin, then page my dad. Need anything?"

Ruthie shook her head and Shannon bopped into the bathroom next to her closet, still singing to herself. Ruthie sipped her Diet Coke and took another survey of the room, imprinting the details into every crack and crevice of her memory, not wanting to forget a fiber of carpet or a bump on the wall.

Shannon's pink Princess phone trilled from the bed stand next to Ruthie and she jumped, fizzy Diet Coke jerking out of the can and spilling down her chin. Shannon came flying out of the bathroom past Ruthie to grab it, slightly out of breath when she answered.

"Oh, my God, are you serious?" Shannon asked whoever was on the other end. "Really? Like seriously. Holy shit. Okay, okay, no, I'm coming. Seriously, I'm coming. Okay. Okay, yeah. Okay, bye."

Shannon slammed down the phone and squealed.

"Everything okay?" Ruthie asked.

"Sharla just called and said she and Lyz are hanging out and now

Chad is coming over and that he's bringing Mikey and I have to get over there."

"Mikey Gold?"

"He's seriously, the hottest guy in school." She slapped her hands against her thighs. "Ugh. I look gross. I need to change." Shannon ran over to the closet and disappeared. Ruthie frowned that she didn't hear hangers swooshing across metal poles. She stood up and followed, gasping when she realized Shannon hadn't just gone into a closet, but into an adjoining bedroom designed to look like a closet. Racks of dresses, shirts, and pants lined the walls alongside shelves of sweaters and shoes. It was like stepping into a department store.

"This—is this your closet?" Ruthie asked, stunned.

"You should see my mom's." Shannon held up a blue jean skirt and oversized turquoise pocket T. "What about this? With a belt over the t-shirt?"

"It's cu—"

"No, no, it's terrible. It sucks. I can't wear that," Shannon said before she discarded it along with six other outfits, before settling on a pair of Paris Blues, sky blue Coca Cola rugby shirt, and silver flats.

"Totally cute, right?" Shannon said as she modeled for herself in the mirror. "Cute, but not trying too hard, cute."

"Yeah, totally," Ruthie said, her heart hammering, a new thought occurring to her. Would she be going to Sharla's, too?

"Okay, I'm gonna drop you off then speed like hell to get to Sharla's. I can't stand it. Seriously, I've been trying to get Mikey Gold forever. I'm hoping he'll ask me to junior prom."

Ruthie's heart dropped to her shoes, the bubble bursting. She wasn't good enough to tag along with Shannon to hang out with the cool kids. She was just Shannon's dirty little secret.

Shannon squealed again as she ran past Ruthie back into her room, draining her Perrier and sticking her apple in her mouth as she grabbed her purse, but not before spritzing herself with perfume from the red plastic triangle of Liz Claiborne and dusting her cheeks with powder, mumbling to herself she'd put on lipstick once she got to Sharla's. Ruthie glumly followed Shannon downstairs, who was oblivious to her misery as she chattered on about how she'd had a crush on Mikey since freshman year, but it seemed like he always went for blondes instead of brunettes. It was finally her turn.

Shannon grabbed her keys from the bowl, muttering to herself again, this time about calling her father from Sharla's that she'd just meet him at Strawberry Patch instead of picking her up at home.

"Okay, girl, come on, let's go," Shannon said, flinging open the front door, running to her car, a shattered Ruthie following suit.

Shannon had all but kicked her out of the car before peeling off to pursue Mikey Gold at Sharla's. She'd barely even said goodbye. Ruthie had brooded about it all night and even the next day at school when she spotted Sharla and Shannon with their heads together in the hallway. There was no rehearsal that night since it was Friday, and with the play just a week away, the leads were asked to put in extra time, so Ruthie walked home those days.

The night of the play was madness and Shannon didn't have time for her. There were too many people fluttering around her, pulling at her, wanting her attention. Even though Ruthie missed those brief snatches of time with Shannon, was depressed about being thrown over for Mikey Gold, she still wanted the play to be a huge success. Wanted Shannon to be a huge success.

And they were. Everyone loved Shannon. They threw roses at her, demanding multiple encores, their cries of happiness not possibly rivaling Ruthie's own tears of joy at her friend's triumph. All sins were forgiven. Her victory was so great, Ms. Grazoli invited Shannon to permanently join the drama club next year. Ruthie overheard her tell Mrs. Kendall that Shannon should seriously consider a four-week summer program at a drama camp she knew of in North Dakota.

It was a magical night.

As the fervor over the play died down and life returned to normal, it seemed as though Shannon drifted out of Ruthie's life almost as instantaneously as she'd drifted in. With the play over, there were no more rides home and inexplicably, Shannon gave her the same fake waves and smiles she gave everyone in the hallway every morning. It was as though that lip gloss she'd given her didn't matter, that she hadn't offered her one of Mrs. Kendall's Diet Cokes, hadn't asked for her opinion about which of her five Coca Cola rugby shirts she should wear to impress Mikey Gold. Shannon's enthusiasm for her dimmed swiftly and to Ruthie, brutally, as the school year began its inevitable race toward summer vacation, her interests seemed to lie elsewhere.

Ruthie panicked.

She couldn't let Shannon slide through her fingers.

They were on the cusp of being real and true friends. She knew they were. Ruthie couldn't give her up.

If she could just get her alone.

And then the plan came to her. So simple.

Ruthie would win Shannon back.

All it took was a phone call to Mrs. Kendall.

72

AVA

Ava checked her phone for the tenth time, making sure it was set up correctly as she took another sip of wine. She'd already done the run-through numerous times before she left the house, but she was nervous about accidentally swiping the wrong thing and screwing it all up. She'd managed to snag one of the more secluded tables at The Gallery, a quiet nook dominated by a mix of oversized and miniature paintings adorning the olive-green walls. The soft clink of forks and knives accompanied the muted peals of laughter that rang out from the tables of friends, families, and couples scattered throughout the rest of the space, as servers maneuvered around the strategically placed art exhibits, trays of drinks in their hands.

She looked up to see Erica making her way over and she waved, her heart thumping as she drew closer.

"How are you?" Ava asked as Erica leaned in for a hug before sitting opposite her.

"I've been better," Erica said, hooking her bag onto the back of the chair. "I guess I'm still shaken up about Lauren."

"What happened, exactly?"

Erica sighed and relayed Lauren's accusations and Whitney's sugar daddy scheme. It all made Ava's head spin. Is that what teenage girls did now?

"God, and the social media, the tweeting." Erica shook her head. "Teenage girls can be so vicious."

"What are you going to do?" Ava asked, taking another sip of her wine, her eyes flicking down to her phone on the table in front of her.

"Oh, Jay is out for blood. He said if Lauren keeps up this vendetta, he'll drag her name through the mud."

"Well, maybe the police will make an arrest soon," Ava said, rubbing her formerly shattered wrist. "Then we could all sleep easier."

"Yes. It would be good if we could all just move on." Erica smiled brightly, an indication she wanted to change the subject. "So ... how are things with you?"

Ava took a deep breath. The exact opening she'd hoped for.

"Good. Just getting ready for my brother's wedding this summer."

"Oh, right, yes. I met the fiancée. What was her name again?"

"Melody." Ava bit her bottom lip, searching Erica's face for any hint of recognition or even worry.

"That's right. Melody." Erica held up her glass. "Let's make a toast to your brother."

"Oh, thank you. We're all so excited. Melody's fantastic." Ava chuckled as she clinked glasses with Erica. "Of course, we're not excited about a wedding in Texas in July." Ava held her breath, looking for a flicker or shadow from Erica.

Nothing.

Erica laughed. "Can't say I blame you. Why are they getting married in Texas, anyway?"

"That's where Melody's from. Houston, actually."

A complete blank. Not even a twitch.

"Gosh, I don't know how people live somewhere so hot. I couldn't do it," Erica said. "Give me the seasons."

"I'm looking forward to getting to know Melody's family better. She keeps raving about her sister, April, so I can't wait to meet her."

Melody had said April and Ruthie were friends. Surely that would elicit a wide-eyed blink, a faltering of some kind.

Still nothing.

"I'm sure you'll have a wonderful time, despite the heat." She took a sip of her wine. "Make sure to wear lots of sunscreen. And drink lots of water."

Ava laughed and nodded. "I'm also trying to figure out a time to visit my mom back in Minneapolis before the wedding."

"Oh, you're from there, right?"

"Yup, born and raised. I went to Minnesota State then got a job in Minneapolis, then got transferred down here a million years ago. I don't get back home nearly enough." Ava paused. "What about you? How often do you get home?"

Erica smiled ruefully. "Oh, I haven't been back home in a long time. You know my parents died in a fire right before I graduated from high school."

"That's right. I'm sorry. I forgot about that." Ava took a sip of wine. "What happened? I mean, if you don't mind me asking."

"They said it was faulty wiring or something like that. I was having a sleepover at a girlfriend's house. It was awful, her mom waking me up in the middle of the night to tell me." Erica shuddered. "Anyway, as I said, haven't been back since."

"And that was in Ohio, right?"

"Small little town outside of Cleveland. No place you would have heard of."

"Is the rest of your family still there?"

"No, you know it was just me and my parents. I was an only child and both of my parents were, too, so, basically, Jay's family is my family."

"Ah." Ava pursed her lips. "And he's from Naperville."

"That's right. I got a ton of in-laws and nephews and nieces and everything in between in exchange for marrying into the Mitchell family." She laughed. "Just imagine a whole family of Jays. Each one louder than the next."

"I'll bet your holidays are insane."

"Are you kidding? I should own stock in an earplug company. It's only taken twenty years to get used to it."

"That's great you've got Jay's family." Ava cocked her head. "Still, that must make you sad. About your own family. That they never got to meet Jay or the girls."

"Sure. Of course. I can't change it though." She shrugged. "It is what it is."

"Hmm." Ava nodded. "Of course. So, did you go to school here? Is that how you wound up in Chicago?"

"I went to a small design academy in Ohio and after I got out, got a job with an ad agency here and quickly realized I didn't like working for anyone, so after about a year, I decided to go freelance."

Ava's nerves hummed. She needed to get on with part one of her mission. She cleared her throat and picked up her phone, swiping and tapping until she got the screen she wanted. "Sorry, Kyle's texting me. He's supposed to take Carly out for pizza tonight."

"Speaking of, I need to figure out what I'm going to pick up for everyone tonight."

Ava angled her phone and continued hitting her screen until she was satisfied she had what she needed. She set the phone down and tucked a chunk of hair behind her ear.

One down, one to go.

"You know," she said. "I don't think I know how you and Jay met."

"Actually, he was a client. My third one to be exact."

"No kidding."

Erica chuckled as she signaled their server she wanted another glass of wine. Ava surveyed her own glass. She could drink, no question about it, but her nerves were so taut, she was terrified of overdoing it. Of course, it would look suspicious if she didn't chug-a-lug. She decided to risk it and tapped her own glass, determining she would sip it slowly.

"It was his first company and he needed someone to design some signage for a conference. I thought he was the nicest, sweetest guy I'd ever met and then he asked if he could take me to dinner and six months later, we got married."

"God, it took me years to get Kyle off the pot. We met in college and I thought a ring was going to be my graduation gift. It was three more years before he finally popped the question." Ava licked her lips, ready to go for broke. "I used to joke with my girlfriends the real reason I wanted to marry him was so I could take his name, since it was so much better than mine."

"Why, what was your maiden name?"

"Zajaczkowski. I mean people were always mangling it. Zakowski, Zowsky, Sacajawea … you name it."

"Yikes," Erica said, giggling. "I mean, it is kind of a mouthful."

"Actually, growing up, people always called me Zach, you know, as a nickname. Even today, every time I go home, it's always, 'Hey, Zach, what's up?' 'How's life, Zach?'" Ava laughed her fake-sincere laugh. "What about you? Was Mitchell a trade-up?"

"Oh, I was lucky. My maiden name was Dane, so Mitchell was fine. I considered keeping it Dane or hyphenating, but it was important to Jay, so I became Mitchell."

Giddiness flooded through Ava and she fought to keep her smile from being too broad.

A name. She had a name.

"Erica Dane. That's beautiful. Sounds like a movie star."

"Oh, you're so sweet. Thank you." Erica smiled. "Like I said, lucky."

The two women chattered on for another hour, Ava's itch to get home so she could search out Erica Dane growing with each nonsensical word that came out of her mouth.

Still, she had a role to play.

"Listen, like I was saying, Kyle's taking Carly out for pizza tonight. Should we grab some apps to share?"

"Ah, I wish I could. I need to pick up dinner."

"Next time, then," Ava said, relief warming through her at not having to be subjected to Erica one minute more.

"Definitely." Erica looked at her watch. "In fact, I should get going."

"Oh, go ahead. I'm just going to finish my wine and head out myself. And I'll take care of the check."

"I'll get it the next time."

"Looking forward to it."

"This was fun," Erica said, getting out of her chair to hug and dual kiss Ava. "We should do this more often."

"Absolutely."

"I'll text you to set up something," Erica said.

"Sounds good. Have a great rest of the evening."

Erica waved and headed outside. Ava waited until she saw her car pull away from the curb, safely on her way. She picked up her phone and tapped on her camera as she swirled the last of her wine around in her glass. She scrolled through the clandestine pictures she'd snapped of Erica as she sat across from her, having made sure to turn off the flash and mute the phone beforehand so no clicks were audible.

She had pictures.

A name.

And now, it was time to unravel the mystery of Erica Dane.

73

ERICA

Erica found herself smiling as she tapped the steering wheel, warmth spreading through her at the memory of the happy hour with Ava. She didn't even mind that the car smelled of grease and salt, courtesy of the bags of hamburgers and French fries she'd picked up for Jay and Kennedy. Jordan, predictably, hadn't wanted anything, declaring she planned to broil a piece of salmon paired with rice and some kind of vegetable. Erica had merely shrugged, feeling, as she often did, that more mothers should commit to her non-cooking stance. She was actually a pretty good cook, having learned from her grandmother during summers spent in Louisiana, mastering fried chicken, shrimp and grits, and macaroni and cheese by the time she was twelve. She was an even better baker, her apple pie and cherry chocolate chunk cookies in particular being popular items at the holidays.

Despite her skill in the kitchen, Erica had no desire to stress herself out over the triviality of what to make for dinner every night. She'd watched her mother rush through the door every night from her days as a nurse, distraught about what to cook, fueled in part by her insecurity about her culinary abilities. Her mother was a passable cook, able to accomplish the basics, but no more. There were no gourmet tricks up her sleeve, no Julia Child moments of awe to behold. She had her staples of baked chicken, a hit-or-miss meatloaf, a reliable tuna casserole, and a middling beef stew. She could open canned soups and vegetables with the best of them and bake a potato like nobody's business. Store-bought cake mixes lived in the pantry, always at the ready for somebody's birthday or last-minute bake sale. Cooking every night was an obligatory imposition, something Grace Stowers was told she had to do, so she did.

Except she found no joy in the kitchen. It filled her with anxiety, these frantic attempts to please everyone, the constant worry the chicken was overdone, the rice underdone. There was the year Erica's sister, Alice, stopped eating anything green, or when her brother would only eat meat or chicken—no potatoes, no rice, just meat or chicken. Or when her other sister, Patricia, ate a bowl of Wheaties every night for six months. Her father was always easy, eating whatever his wife put in front of him. So was she for that matter. There was her mother, though, bending over backward to avoid putting broccoli or green beans on Alice's plate, or trying to come up with new ways to cook chicken and steak for her brother, and just plain old giving up on wacky Patricia with her cereal fetish. Even when she offered to cook for her mother so she could relax when she got home from work every night, she was politely rejected. Erica finally decided it was because she was afraid her daughter would upstage her. She would have, no doubt, but Erica wasn't sure why it mattered.

Watching her mother panic over how to meet the nonsensical whims of weird, occasionally snotty children convinced Erica cooking dinner for your family every night was dumb. Why shouldn't everyone get to eat whatever they wanted? So, she'd vowed, when she grew up and had a family, that's exactly what she would do.

Jay was thrilled not to have a wife clucking over him to diet or watch his salt intake. Fast food practically every night satisfied his frat boy tendencies. And Kennedy was a slender, healthy little girl, as Erica made sure she got regular exercise and gave her fruit and veggie smoothies for breakfast alongside her cereal, lots of vitamins, plenty of water, and a salad with grilled chicken from The Lantern at least twice a week. Jordan was the only one who complained, which baffled her.

She would have been thrilled if her mother had declared she could eat whatever she wanted for dinner.

Her phone pinged with a text from Ava saying she had a great time, eliciting another smile from Erica. She'd been so surprised and thrilled to hear from Ava about meeting for happy hour, the occurrence being so rare. Ask, believe, and receive.

Mostly, she was especially proud of herself for not even flinching when Ava mentioned her brother's upcoming wedding to Melody. She thought it was a nice touch of making a point of asking for Melody's name as though she'd forgotten it and showing zero emotion when Ava mentioned April. Even throwing in that mild dig about how could anyone ever live in Houston's oppressive heat was inspired. If Melody had said anything to Ava about Ruthie, she would have heard something by now, she was sure of it. And what were the chances of Melody and April talking about her at a wedding? They were going to be more than a little preoccupied that day. It's not like Ava or Melody had a picture of her that they could show to April to see if she bore even a little resemblance to Ruthie. Even if she did, she barely looked the way she used to, so it was all for nothing.

"Nobody knows you're Ruthie," she said out loud.

Ask, believe, receive.

Erica pulled into the driveway and grabbed the greasy brown paper bags, humming to herself, even looking forward to the sad little salad she'd make for her own dinner.

"Hello," she called out when she opened the door, delighting as always at the scent of lemons and lavender, with the faintest hint of bergamot, the mystery exotic scent it had taken her years to uncover.

Just like Shannon's house.

She called out again and shrugged when no one answered, heading to the kitchen to deposit the bags onto the counter where she found Jordan bent over the oven, poking at something inside. Probably her salmon.

"Hi, sweetheart," she said coming over to kiss her daughter's warm, damp cheek. "How are you?"

"Fine."

"And how was school?"

"Fine."

"Where's Dad? Where's your sister?"

Jordan slammed the oven door shut and picked up a box of rice from the counter, skimming the back. "Dad's in his office."

"And your sister?"

"Who cares?"

Erica sighed. "Jordan."

"What?"

"Will you track her down, please, then tell her to wash up for dinner."

Jordan didn't respond, instead screaming up the back stairs for Kennedy, who screamed back that she was in the bathroom. Erica scoffed and went down the hall in search of Jay. She knocked on the door, then waited for his muffled voice to invite her in.

"Hey," he said, his voice sounding distracted as he frowned, his gaze focused on the huge computer monitor in front of him.

"Well, hello, darling." Erica slid her arms around his beefy neck and kissed him on the cheek. "How are you?"

He leaned back, letting out a heavy breath. "I just got an alert and apparently, Steve and Lauren did an interview with Wendy Sheridan. It's going to air tomorrow morning."

Erica shrank back, her arms loosening. "What?"

"I'm not worried about Steve, but Lauren..." Jay clicked his tongue against his teeth and shook his head. "She's not thinking straight."

"Well, what should we do?"

"We'll just have to wait, see what she says." He kissed Erica's palm. "If she even whispers Jordan's name, I'll sue her for every penny she has and even the ones she hasn't made."

74

AVA

E rica Dane didn't exist.

At least, that's what the Internet told Ava. She'd stayed up late after happy hour scouring the Internet for something—*anything*—about an Erica Dane from Ohio. She searched for news stories about this mythical house fire that had killed her parents.

Nothing.

She'd searched every yearbook or alumni site she could plug Erica Dane's name into.

Nothing.

She'd Googled and Binged and Yahooed long into the wee hours.

Nothing.

Ava made a face as she Googled Jay's name, quickly scanning the mountain of articles for a sliver of information about Erica in the profiles about him. Over and over, the most she turned up was that Jay Mitchell and his wife lived in Lake Forest with their two daughters. Unlike her contemporaries, the other wives of software titans, there were no lavish spreads featuring Erica's palatial home, no articles lauding the woman's philanthropic efforts for curing pediatric cancer or building water irrigation systems in Africa. No beaming photos from society galas.

A blank.

The tug of sleep finally pushed her to shuffle off to bed, though the frustration of continually coming up empty—and why—scratched at her brain through a fitful sleep as Kyle snored softly beside her.

There had to be another way.

Ava sighed and looked at her phone on the nightstand. Four a.m. Sleep was a farce at this point.

She pushed the duvet back and quietly shut the door behind her as she padded downstairs to make coffee, yawning as she scrolled through her emails, rolling her eyes at the missives from her boss, fired off at one-thirty, two-fifteen, and three-ten.

Ava dumped cream and sugar into her mug when it hit her.

Ruthie's family.

Look for Ruthie's family.

Renewed vigor tore through her as she grabbed her phone and coffee and raced back into her office. She set her mug down on a metal coaster on the desk and opened her laptop, her eyes skimming across the room at the Ruthie piles as she'd started to call them, trying to remember which ones contained articles mentioning her parents and siblings.

Her phone pinged and she picked it up, frowning at the alert that popped up on her screen.

A news interview happening this morning with Steve and Lauren discussing Whitney's murder, the headlines promising bombshells.

Ava's hand flew to her mouth as she watched some of the snippets of video featuring Lauren talking about Whitney, her eyes sinking shut at the grieving mother's salvos.

"This person is well aware of what they've done."

She was pointing the finger at Jordan.

Ava ran a shaky hand through her curls, visions of Mr. Byrne being arrested and mowed down by Regina Knowles playing on a loop in her head. The police had gotten it wrong. Now Lauren was hurling accusations at Jordan. What pound of flesh would misguided, outraged zealots try to extract from this teenage girl based on the veiled insinuations of a grieving mother?

It could be any of them with the finger pointed at her.

And her daughter could be next.

Ava dropped the phone, feeling clear in her mission, her heart pounding as she frantically pawed through stacks of paper, skimming the tiny newsprint from ancient articles for any mention of the names of the Stowers family. A trickle of sweat crawled down her spine as she ignored her bladder filling from the coffee. After forty-five minutes and two massive paper cuts, she extracted an article featuring a granular photo of the parents surrounded by three of their four children coming out of the courthouse after Ruthie's sentencing.

A cry of triumph escaped her lips as she slapped the page onto the desk and hunched over it, taking note of the names.

Ruthie's mother, Grace.

Her father, Edgar.

Her brother, Edwin.

Her sister, Alice.

Her sister, Patricia.

She scooted closer to her laptop, her fingers shaking as she typed 'Edwin Stowers' into her search engine, deciding to skip her parents and go right to the siblings. The thought of reaching out to elderly people with sketchy questions about their daughter the convicted murderer felt like a line Ava couldn't cross.

A LinkedIn page popped up indicating an Edwin Stowers who worked for a cable company in Dallas. Another one who worked in pharmaceutical sales in Iowa. Another who appeared to be retired law enforcement from Wyoming. No Facebook pages, no other social media presence.

Ava bit her bottom lip and searched for the names of Ruthie's sisters, Patricia and Alice. Patricia Stowers returned nothing, while Alice Stowers spit out a Facebook page filled with inspirational quotes and pictures of flowers, the most recent update from two years ago.

Ava drummed her fingers across the desk, flummoxed about what to do next.

Roll the dice.

She hunted down emails for all three of the Edwin Stowers,

mentally composing and rejecting messages in her head that she hoped didn't make her sound like too much of a lunatic.

Her fingers hovered over the keyboard of her laptop as she continued turning words over in her head about what to say, starting and deleting numerous versions, unsure of what would provoke a response. In the end, she decided to keep it simple:

Dear Mr. Stowers,

I'm working on a project about Ruthie Stowers and wondered if you might have fifteen or twenty minutes to talk with me via phone. Thank you for your time.

Ava Ewing.

She frowned and hit the backspace key against her last name, replacing it with her maiden name instead. Just in case.

She debated about sending a Facebook DM to Alice Stowers, but decided to see if her emails got a response. Ava refreshed her email a few times, which she knew was silly. It was barely five in the morning. She was the only nutjob sending emails at the crack of dawn. Well, her and Psycho Kitty.

Ava jumped when her email dinged from her phone. She held her breath as she pulled up the message.

I don't wish to talk about Ruthie. Please don't contact me again.

Her heart sank as she read and reread the message from Edwin Stowers, who worked for a cable company in Dallas. She sighed, disheartened. It had been a long shot, of course, but she'd held out hope that not only would it be the right Edwin Stowers, he'd be eager to spill what he knew about Ruthie. She sighed and closed her eyes.

Back to the drawing board.

75

JORDAN

"*This person is well aware of what they've done.*"

Jordan had watched the clip of Mrs. Dean's interview from this morning on her phone about a dozen times. Her mother had the TV on in the background during breakfast before shutting it off when the first promo came on. Even though Mrs. Dean hadn't said her name, Jordan knew she was talking about her. Everyone would know she was talking about her.

Her dad had gone completely berserk, screaming about how they would sue Mr. and Mrs. Dean for every fucking penny they had. Her mom, surprisingly, stayed chill. Unbothered, almost, and said they'd do whatever they had to do. Her own stomach churned and boiled and she begged to stay home from school. Her mother said yes, but her father overruled her, saying Jordan had to put on her big girl pants, hold her head high.

Easy for him to say. He'd clearly forgotten what a cesspool high school could be.

Mrs. Dean was so angry that day she came to the house with Whitney's diary, Jordan was sure the cops would be banging on the door before too long, despite telling Detective Diehl the actual truth about where she was that Saturday, which she said she would check out thoroughly.

Lots of innocent people were in jail.

Jordan's heart flip-flopped as her phone flashed eight-ten. Why was she even here? Especially after the way Carly, Lexi, and Madison had come after her the other day. What was stopping her from skipping, driving to the city and taking the day off like that kid in that movie her dad made them watch every year on his birthday?

She took a deep breath and opened her car door, reluctantly exiting the warmth from the blasts of heat coming out of the vents. She pulled her coat close around her and gathered her book bag and purse while taking glances over her shoulder. She'd parked in a far corner of the student lot and the school building loomed large and sinister in front of her as she made the long walk.

No one made eye contact with her on that long walk. They glanced at her briefly before huddling back together in furtive whispers and averted stares. She wouldn't have the cover of her hoodie and sunglasses once inside the building, as they weren't allowed. Her own eyes darted across the steps where kids usually gathered in the morning before class, watching as the whispers continued. They parted when they saw her coming, nobody wanting to get even a little close to her.

Jordan pushed open the heavy door of the front of the building, grudgingly removing her sunglasses and lowering her hoodie. The reception inside was just as chilly outside. She shoved her hands into the pocket of her sweatshirt and looked down, concentrating on her boots walking quickly across the glossy tiles toward her locker. As she got closer, she sped up, feeling the daggers puncture her back, the whispers stab her ears.

Relief flooded through her at the sight of her locker. She fingered the strap of her book bag, her other hand reaching for the lock when a hand slammed against the metal, causing her to jump back.

"Why are you here?"

Carly stood in front of her, snarling, her hand still affixed to her locker, stopping her from opening it. Lexi, Madison, and Dionne surrounded her, all sneers and angry gum-chewing, like a pack of wild, salivating dogs, all backing up Carly in Operation Get Jordan. It was unbelievable that *Carly* of all fucking people had the nerve to stand in front of her like she was queen of the court. Quiet, simpering little Carly. Just last year, you could have passed right by her in the hall and never looked at her once, much less twice. And now, with Whitney being gone, she decided she ruled the universe.

"Excuse me," Jordan squeaked, upset at the unnatural sound. She cleared her throat and tried again. "Move."

"I can't believe you have the nerve to show your face around here," Carly said. "I mean, shouldn't you be in a cell or something?"

"You should be ashamed of yourself. We all know it was you. Whitney's mom said so," Madison said, even more emboldened than she'd been the other day.

Jordan's heart exploded in fear and heat prickled across her skin. "The last time I checked, Whitney's mom wasn't the police. And neither are you."

"I'll bet the police will be coming to arrest you today," Carly sneered. "Better get ready."

"Yeah, how do you like the color orange?" Dionne laughed.

"God, you're all even more pathetic than I realized," Jordan said, squaring her shoulders. She looked at Carly. "And you're Queen Pathetic."

Carly laughed. "When she gets arrested, we'll be in court every day. Front. Row."

Jordan slammed her locker shut. "Leave me the hell alone you busted ass bitch."

"You're going to pay for what you did to Whitney." Carly held up her hands, balled up in fists and clinked her wrists together twice. "Clank, clank."

Madison and Dionne dissolved into laughter as Jordan opened her mouth, ready to annihilate Carly when Lexi hissed, "Murderer." She swiveled her head around, ready to yank the girl's two-dollar extensions clean out of her head.

Except everyone joined in with a buzz of, "Murderer," the chant growing louder. Tears hovered on the edge of Jordan's eyes as she scanned the crowd of snarled, furious faces, spitting out that word in her direction.

Murderer.

Jordan blinked back the tears, determined they wouldn't see her cry, determined she would do what her father said and hold her head high.

"What's going on here?" a teacher—she didn't know who—boomed, breaking the circle, her face falling a bit when she spotted Jordan.

Wow. Even the teachers.

"All right, break it up, break it up, get to class," the teacher said, clapping her hands. The crowd scattered.

Carly leaned down to Jordan, getting close to her ear. "You're going to get what's coming to you. Murderer."

A single tear managed to escape, sliding down her cheek. She turned and wiped it away with the sleeve of her hoodie. The teacher looked at Jordan and she realized it was Mrs. Finch, Mr. Byrne's no-nonsense replacement. The woman's usual concrete line etched into her pale face looked like it might have been twitching in sympathy. Or disgust.

"Miss Mitchell," she said. "Perhaps you'd better go to the principal's office."

"For what? I didn't do anything," Jordan said in disbelief. She was being blamed for this too?

"What I meant was perhaps Principal Bain could excuse you for the day. It seems your presence is … distracting."

Jordan's head spun and her knees oozed jelly. Now, she was distracting. Carly picks a fight with her—the second one in a week—and she was the distracting one.

She drew up, gripping the strap of her book bag even tighter. "Yeah, fine, whatever."

The final bell rang and Mrs. Finch gave her a tight, quick nod, before she click-clacked down the hallway to the same classroom where Jordan was supposed to be learning about *The Crucible* and what it felt like to be an outcast.

Instead, she turned on her heel and went to the principal's office.

76

AVA

"Mate."

She flicked her eyes toward Kyle, who sat across the table staring at her, an exasperated look on his face.

"What?"

He sighed and put his fork down and looked at the creamy swirls of truffle pasta on the plate in front of him.

"Bloody hell. You didn't hear a word I said, did you?"

She tucked a chunk of hair behind her ear. "I heard you."

He narrowed his eyes. "What'd I say?"

Ava licked her lips, scouring her brain for the last sliver of what he had said, relieved when she locked onto it. "You said you're signing a contract tomorrow for a new project in Philly, that things are moving full steam ahead."

He rolled his tongue around the inside of his mouth. "Lucky guess."

"English, really, I'm listening. Now, tell me what your next steps are to get started?"

He cleared his throat and took two silent mouthfuls of pasta before resuming a cautious recitation of the deal he was working on as she slowly retreated into her own thoughts, yet making sure to tune back in for bits and pieces and uttering appropriate attentive murmurs.

She'd hunted high and low for an email address for Alice Stowers, but found nothing, instead taking a chance and sending her a DM through Facebook in the vain hope she'd see it.

That had been two days ago and so far, nothing.

Like everyone else, Lauren's interview had also been preoccupying her thoughts. Her Facebook feed continued to be lit up with posts reacting to it, about half cheering her on for putting some pressure on the police, half dismayed she'd fingered Jordan, albeit cryptically. Ava fell in the camp of dismay, well aware of where that finger could really be pointed.

From across the table, Kyle heaved another big sigh. "All right, Mate, what is going on with you?"

Ava blinked and focused on a perturbed Kyle, his head cocked and face scrunched up in irritation.

"What do you mean?"

"These past few weeks. You've been distracted and holed up in your office way more than usual, all hours of the night and morning. And I hear the printer constantly running. What the hell have you got up to?"

Ava hesitated, not ready to tell Kyle her suspicions about Erica. Her fears about Carly. She licked her lips and shrugged. "It's nothing. Psycho Kitty has me on a huge project. It's just taking up a lot of time, that's all."

"That's all?"

"Yeah."

"How long is it going to take, then?"

Ava pursed her lips. "I don't know."

Kyle wiped his mouth with his napkin and leveled his gaze at her. "You'd tell me if it was something else, right, Mate? Something serious?"

"Like what?"

He shrugged. "I don't know. You're the one keeping secrets."

Ava's heart fluttered. It was tempting to spill it all. He'd think she was nuts, which these days, she wondered.

Instead, she reached across the table and grabbed his hand, kissing it. "English, just bear with me a little while."

The hard line of his lips melted into the sexy, lopsided grin that had first intoxicated her at the Lambda Chi party her roommate, Skyler, had dragged her to junior year. She'd always thought love at first sight was a crock until she met Kyle.

"Okay," he whispered and squeezed her hand. "But I'm serious Mate, if there's anything—"

"I know."

He winked and they gave each other knowing smiles and she asked him to finish telling her about his deal, deciding to listen in earnest this time.

And that's when the thought drifted into her head.

"Yearbooks," she whispered out loud.

Kyle squinted. "What?"

Ava threw down her napkin and grabbed her purse, afraid if she didn't act on this impulse right now, she'd lose it somehow, though the thought was now stamped onto her brain.

"I have to run to the restroom," she said as she scooted back from the table, dropping a quick kiss on his bewildered cheek as she ran to the back of the restaurant toward the restrooms. She groaned as she tried to decipher which was the ladies' room, thwarted by the cutesy, nearly indiscernible illustrations meant to stand in for gender. She hated that shit.

She figured out the right one and bolted inside while digging into her purse for her phone. Tremors surged through her fingers as she pulled up one of the yearbook sites she'd been fooling around with the other night and took a deep breath and typed Patricia Stowers into the search function, wondering why it took her so long to connect those dots.

"Yes," Ava whispered triumphantly, smiling as the name Patricia Davis, Stowers in parentheses, popped up. It had to be her.

She went back to Facebook and typed in Patricia's married name.

Her profile popped up instantly.

Ava gasped as she leaned closer to the screen to examine the smiling, euphoric image of Patricia Davis, an HR VP in Houston, Texas. Same chin. Same cheekbones. Same wide forehead. Practically the same nose, though the thin taper of Patricia's was a little closer to Erica's than Ruthie's flat, wide one and the yellow overbite of Patricia's smile was no match for Erica's pristine little white rows.

But there was no mistaking it—the two women were related.

Mesmerized, Ava scrolled through Patricia's timeline. Unlike her other sister, Patricia was an active and engaged Facebook user, constantly posting pictures of her kids' sports games, date nights with her husband, boozy tropical trips with her gang of girlfriends, funny memes, and silly videos. Her most recent update was late last night.

And she was online now.

Roll the dice.

Ava clicked on the messenger app and typed her spiel about doing a project on Ruthie.

The response came within seconds.

What do you want to know about my sister?

77

ERICA

"Mrs. Mitchell, what I'm saying is, East Lake Forest may no longer be the best environment for Jordan."

"No, what you're saying is, you're kicking my daughter out of school."

Principal Bain sighed and cocked her head as she looked at Erica, a mixture of pity and resolve on her face. She'd been summoned to the principal's office this morning after Jordan called her in tears yesterday to take her out of school. The principal had said something about discussing Jordan's future at East Lake Forest and that she wished to meet with her and Jay, who'd left town this morning to finalize his merger. Erica wished she didn't have to deal with this alone, as he would have blown in here, swung his dick around, and by the time he was done, Jordan would have been appointed principal.

"Whitney's murder ... it's been quite a blow to the student body. She was so beloved. Homecoming queen. Honor Society. Pom-pom. President of the French Club. Secretary for the Young Women's Club. She was quite respected and looked up to here. Very popular."

"Jordan is also very popular," Erica shot back.

Principal Bain nodded slowly. "Yes, Jordan has always been an admirable young lady. Pom-pom squad, Honor Society, class boards. Very admirable."

"I'm still not understanding what popularity has to do with you wanting to kick my daughter out of school."

"I'm afraid Mrs. Dean's interview has put an unfortunate focus on Jordan. A distracting focus."

"She didn't mention my daughter by name," Erica said. "Why is she being punished for innuendo?"

Principal Bain folded her hands together as she delivered one of those condescendingly warm smiles people gave you when they wanted you to bend to their will and didn't understand why you hadn't just given in already. A message Erica knew how to send all too well.

"I just feel that Jordan's continued presence here will be a disruption both for her and her fellow students, and it might be best if she were in an environment where she could just ... blend in as it were."

Erica flinched inwardly. How did everything go so wrong? With Whitney gone, things were supposed to turn around for Jordan. She could go back to pom squad free and clear, and definitely would have been named captain. Not co-captain. Captain. Homecoming queen, prom queen—the sky was the limit.

Instead, it was backfiring in spectacular fashion. Lauren accusing Jordan of murdering her precious, utterly awful, utterly vicious daughter. Her fellow classmates were turning against her. The principal wanted her gone.

This was not how this was supposed to go. None of it.

Erica gathered up her purse, her resentment cranking inside her like a furnace as she stood up, commanding her shoulders to snap back in haughtiness.

"I'm keeping Jordan out for the rest of the week and my husband and I will decide if we want her to come back."

"Mrs. Mitchell, I—"

"Goodbye," Erica said, huffing toward the door of the office and flinging it open before she slammed it shut.

78

AVA

E ven at this early hour of seven forty-five a.m., the dawning days of April, vapors of heat floated up from the asphalt as the white-hot sun beat down on the streets of Houston. Despite the frost of the AC billowing out of the vents in voluminous clouds, Ava's palms itched with sweat, leaving wet smears on the steering wheel of her rental SUV as she pulled up to the little coffee shop Patricia Davis had directed her to for their meeting. She took several deep breaths, but the action did little to quell the churning in her stomach over this impending get-together.

Ava had been so shocked by Patricia's quick—and agreeable—reply, she could only stare at her phone in a stupor for a few minutes before hastily responding that she was working on a book idea about the murder of Shannon Kendall. She didn't know why she said that, or how on earth she planned to back up the lie if the woman started firing questions at her about when the book was coming out, or who else she'd interviewed. To her relief, Patricia had merely replied she had some time that afternoon and asked when would be good for a phone conversation. She was about to write back when it occurred to Ava she could hop on a plane and talk to the woman in person. She had a stock-pile of PTO and despite Psycho Kitty's best efforts to run her ragged, was between projects, so being out of the office a couple of days wasn't going to bring her division to its knees. Patricia was open to it, saying she'd caught her at a good time, as she was headed out of town herself. Though he was used to these last-minute emergencies she sometimes had to tend to, Kyle was perturbed when she told him that night as they were going to bed, though he wearily told her to have a good trip. Carly had been unfazed, like Kyle, numb and accepting of these urgent, out-of-the-blue trips. She'd lied that she was going to Atlanta for a few days, not wanting to invite any additional questions. The less said, the better. She'd quickly made reservations using her deep stash of points and miles and hopped on a plane yesterday morning, smacking into a dense, impenetrable wall of heat and humidity when she stepped out of the airport, even in April.

After checking into her hotel, she'd beelined for the public library until it closed, holing up in various research rooms, on the hunt for articles she'd been unable to access online, poring over decades-old microfiche, yellowing newspapers, and ancient magazines, her unease swelling with each new uncovered article or tidbit. Unable to tamp down the growing horror that a killer was in their midst.

The clock on the dash ticked nine-fifteen. Now or never.

Ava gathered up her purse and large leather tote bulging with her research and headed inside. The whir of machines grinding beans and whipping up coffee drinks rammed into her ears as she walked inside, her eyes scanning the room for Patricia, seeing only an old man leafing through his newspaper and young woman hunched over a laptop, both with steaming cups of coffee on the tables in front of them, even in the stifling heat. The café featured an odd tropical theme with fish stenciled onto the water-blue walls and affixed to the beige floor tiles. Ava looked at her watch and wondered if she should chance an iced coffee. She was already so wired, the caffeine might shoot her through the roof like a rocket.

She chose a secluded table in the back and took the chair facing the door. She folded her hands in front of her and waited, her nerves twitching like they did before a big presentation, particularly when she knew she would eventually have all the mansplainers in the room cowering on their knees. The moment when everything would turn on a dime.

It was coming. She could feel it.

The tinkle of the bell over the door pulled her gaze up. Her breath quickened at the sight of the woman walking through the door, scanning the room in search of a stranger.

Erica.

Or more precisely, her sister.

Ava's mouth dropped open into a dumbfounded 'o' as Patricia spotted her and smiled. She strode over and held her hand out, the bright purple acrylics of her fingernails catching the morning sunlight.

"You must be Ava," she said, her throaty, Texas drawl snapping Ava out of her malaise and forcing her to her feet.

"I—yes, I am. I mean…" Ava stuttered as she took Patricia's hand, giving what she knew was a far cry from her typically vigorous handshake. *Pull your shit together.* She squared her shoulders. "Ava Ewing."

Patricia looked down at Ava still furiously pumping her hand. "Everything all right, Sweets? This heat scrambling your brain?"

Ava forced herself to let go of Patricia's hand, though she couldn't stop staring. The differences and similarities were jarring and expected all at once. Patricia was thin, like her sister—though more fit than skeletal—her orange print leggings stopping at her knees and orange tank top hugging an ample chest. Her thick black hair was pulled back into a high, tight ponytail, accentuating her round face and dark, wide-set eyes, the lids of which were rimmed in thick wedges of eyeliner. A spray of tiny black moles peppered one cheek, her pink frosted lips spitting out a husky Texas twang that rolled off her tongue with ease. How long had it taken Erica to erase her *y'all's* and *fixin' to's*? Patricia's wide-open warmth and direct demeanor stood in sharp contrast to Erica's cold, condescending manner and reinforced Ava's long-held belief that growing up in the same house was no guarantee of duplicate outcomes.

"What, uh … what can I get you to drink?" Ava asked, still mesmerized.

"Oh, Sweets, I got it," Patricia said as she headed toward the counter. "You just get yourself together."

Ava sank into her chair, her heart racing, all the questions she'd planned to ask now a hopeless word jumble in her brain. She could only sit and wait for Patricia to join her, still unsure of what she was going to say.

"Now." Patricia slid into the chair across from her, a sweaty plastic cup of iced tea in her hand. She fanned herself with the batch of napkins in her other hand before she flashed Ava another smile. "You get your brain working?"

Ava shook her head as though she was casting off cobwebs. "As my daughter would say, you've got me shook."

"Why's that, Sweets? Am I uglier in person?" Patricia winked, a husky laugh escaping her lips.

"Oh, no, it's—it's not that." Ava sighed, squirming under the woman's friendly, questioning gaze. "Patricia, I have to confess. I got you here under false pretenses."

"My favorite kind," Patricia said, taking a healthy slug of tea as she looked Ava up and down. "Don't look like you're gonna shoot me, not with that Tory Burch hanging off the back of your chair. Of course, maybe that's how you got it."

Ava laughed nervously. "No, nothing like that."

"All right, so what'd you get me out here for?"

"I—" Ava picked up her phone, scrolling through her surreptitious pictures of Erica before holding it out to Patricia. "Is this your sister?"

Patricia took the phone, squinting as she studied the shots of Erica, a small, wry smile tugging at her lips before she looked up and let out a long, genial laugh, drawing a look of irritation from the old man before he resumed reading his paper. "Sweets, now you know good and well by looking at the two of us that we couldn't be anything but related."

"So you do recognize her?"

"Do I recognize—of course I recognize her. That's Ruthie." Patricia looked down at the phone again, shaking her head before bursting into laughter once more. "Though, as Mr. Davis would say, got-dang she's had a lot of work done." She passed the phone back to

Ava. "Now, what's she calling herself these days, 'cause I know it's not Ruthie."

"She goes by the name of Erica Mitchell."

Patricia took a gulp of tea. "Erica, huh?"

"Do you know Melody Gonzalez?"

"I mean, I knew of Melody, but I didn't know her. What, she saying I stole her boyfriend back in the day or something?"

"Melody's engaged to my brother and we ran into Erica one day over the holidays and she recognized her. Told me about Ruthie. And Shannon."

Patricia frowned. "Wait, so you said you ran into Ruthie—Erica—whatever she's calling herself—does that mean you know her, like you're friends with her?"

"I wouldn't say we're friends. Social acquaintances, really, but yes, I have known her, gosh, twelve, thirteen years," Ava said. "Our daughters used to take dance class together, went to the same schools."

Patricia let out a low chuckle. "Well, got-dang. Things I didn't have on my bingo card sure is filling up fast sitting here talking to you."

Ava inhaled. There was no use in beating around the bush with Patricia. *Spit it out.*

"Listen, the reason why I wanted to talk to you is that there was a murder in our community and there's a connection to Erica. Ruthie."

Patricia let out a slow hiss of air. She closed her eyes for several moments, clicking her tongue against her teeth, nodding. Seeming to understand. She finally leveled her gaze at Ava. "A connection." The two words weren't a question, but rather, said flatly, matter-of-factly. Undisputed truth. "What's the connection? Exactly?"

"Erica's daughter, Jordan, was best friends with the girl who was murdered—Whitney. Whitney Dean. Right before Whitney's murder, the two got into a huge fight. A week later, Whitney was dead."

"How?"

"Multiple stab wounds."

"Lord, Jesus. Just like Shannon." She tilted her head staring at Ava for several moments. "And you think it was Ruthie's daughter—my—" The woman stopped, her gaze traveling up to the ceiling. "My niece?"

Ava hesitated. "There are a lot of similarities between the two murders, between Shannon and Whitney, and I think it warrants a closer look," she finally said.

"I'll ask you again. You're saying you think my sister's daughter murdered this girl. Just like Ruthie murdered Shannon when she was sixteen?"

"I'm just following the evidence."

"And what's the evidence tell you?"

Ava looked down at her purse, the corner of the birthday party invitation peeking at her. She plucked the invitation from her purse, holding it to her chest. "Was Ruthie homecoming queen at her high school?"

Patricia stared at her for a few seconds before that bawdy, unbridled laughter erupted from her once more. A tear slid down her cheek and she dabbed at it with one of the recycled napkins she'd used earlier to fan herself. "That what she told you?"

Ava slid the envelope across the table. "This is from her forty-fifth birthday party a few years ago."

Patricia exhaled as she picked up the invitation and studied it. "You said forty-fifth birthday? Two years ago?"

"That's right."

The low rumble of Patricia's laugh lulled Ava in even more. "Ruthie was born in June 1970. She'll be fifty-two in a few months."

Ava clicked her tongue against her teeth. *Was anything about Erica true?*

Patricia looked at the invitation again. "She sure did go through a lot of trouble to put this little piece of nonsense together."

"She's a graphic designer, so I doubt something like this would be hard for her."

"Homecoming queen." Patricia scoffed as she dropped the invitation back on the table. "That's rich."

"Did your sister have her Sweet Sixteen birthday party at a country club?"

Patricia's eyes grew wide. "A country club?"

Ava clicked her tongue against her teeth. "She's also said she was a cheerleader in high school."

Once again, Patricia roared with laughter, drawing perturbed gazes from the barista. "First of all, I was the cheerleader, not Ruthie. And is she really saying she had her Sweet Sixteen at a country club?"

"Yes."

Patricia sighed and rubbed the bridge of her nose with her middle finger. "Oh, Lord deliver. Ma'am, I think I'm fixin' to have a heart attack."

"So, none of those things are true?"

"Not only no, but hell no," Patricia's voice boomed across the café. "I wish I could say any of this surprises me, but it doesn't. Vintage Ruthie."

"What do you mean?"

Patricia raised and lowered the straw of her iced tea, the resulting squeaking noise against the lid reverberating across the still nearly empty café. She sighed and released the straw. "She lied about stuff all the time."

Ava held her breath. "Like what?"

"One year, I guess she was thirteen, I was sixteen, Mama sent us to summer camp in Austin for a week and Ruthie told everybody there that Daddy was some rich lawyer and Mama used to be an actress and we lived in a big ol' mansion in River Oaks. Later on, that same summer, we were visiting our cousins in Louisiana and some of their friends had come over to hang out and I overheard her telling them she was a prima ballerina about to move to Paris to be in *Swan Lake*." She snorted. "She wasn't any more of a ballerina than the frogs we used to catch behind Granny's house every summer."

Ava pushed down the laugh threatening to escape her lips. She cleared her throat. "Go on."

"Let me tell you something. Mama was a nurse, Daddy was in insurance. Now, we had a small house, but it was a house. We had food on the table *every* night, clean clothes in the closet, and two cars in the driveway. Now they may not have been Cadillacs, but they were good, clean, reliable cars. Ruthie never took ballet lessons, never went to

Paris, and the closest we ever got to River Oaks was passing through on the way somewhere. But, we had a good life." Patricia sipped her drink. "It just wasn't good enough for her."

"So that's why she lied—because she was embarrassed?"

"Listen, she was a dreamer, my sister. She wanted to be popular and pretty, wanted people to like her. Desperate for people to like her. So, she made stuff up 'cause she thought that'd *make* people like her."

"What about Shannon?"

"Oh, Lord, Shannon." Patricia shook her head. "Beautiful girl. Just beautiful."

"Did you know her?"

"No, I didn't know her, since I was older, but you know her mama used to be on the news here every night and looked just like her. Anyway, Ruthie, she idolized this girl, and you know, that's dangerous."

Carly flashed across Ava's brain. "Idolized her how?"

Patricia sighed. "She talked about her constantly. How pretty she was. How nice she was. Special. Just yap, yap, yap all damn day long about Shannon. What did I think of her, where did I think she got her clothes from, how someone that pretty could be so nice, how she gave her a lip gloss or something silly. She even tried doing her hair like Shannon a few times, like curling it the same way? Didn't look anything like Shannon, of course, but I guess give her points for trying."

"Did she ever tell you why she did it? Killed Shannon, I mean."

"Never. Not one word. None of us could understand it."

"When was the last time you talked to Ruthie?"

Patricia rubbed her chin. "Right before she got sentenced so, over thirty-five years. Since it was a juvenile facility, they only let parents visit the prison, which was fine with me 'cause I didn't have any interest in going. Anyway, Mama went every week for the whole ten years. And then, Ruthie got released, went home to Mama and Daddy for a bit. Then, one night, they came home from work and she was gone. Up and vanished. Mama was devastated."

"Did you try to find her?"

"I did. For Mama. My husband and I hired a private detective and the only name we found was Emily Kason. Some birth certificate she stole, I guess. After that, nothing. Trail went ice cold. I told Mama she had to let it go, that if Ruthie wanted to talk to us, she would."

"How do your brother and sister feel?"

"Ed, you know, he and Ruthie were the closest and it just destroyed him. He tells people he only has two sisters. Alice, being the oldest, she was hurt, but tried to be the good sister and keep the peace and all that." Patricia shrugged. "She's forgiven her and would welcome her back with open arms because she's a much better person than I am."

"What about you?" Ava asked, fingering the invitation still sitting on the table. "How do you feel about your sister, what she did?"

"You know," she chuckled. "I don't think anyone ever asked me that before."

Ava tilted her head to the side. "Now's your chance."

Patricia was silent as she contemplated the question, absentmindedly bending the top of her straw with her index finger. "I feel bad for Mama," she finally said. "She used to blame herself, thinking she'd failed Ruthie somehow, that she should have worked harder to give her things, you know, stuff. Crying all the time about how she lost her baby."

"And you?" Ava prompted again.

"Honestly, I don't lie awake at night boo-hooing over her. If I feel anything about her, it's anger for what she did to Mama." Patricia tapped the table with her index finger. "So. You never answered my question. You think Ruthie's daughter killed this other girl?"

"As I said before, it's really not for me to say."

"So, Ruthie's married with a daughter, huh?"

"Two daughters, actually. She … uh, she's done very well for herself." Ava picked up her phone and found a picture of Jay online. "That's her husband and he's quite wealthy. I mean like gangsta wealthy, as my kids would say."

"Dang, he's a big one, isn't he?" Patricia said as she studied Jay's picture.

"Yeah. He and Erica look funny standing next to each other." Ava swiped until she found the pom squad photo from last year. "And this is Jordan."

Patricia took the phone back, tears springing to her eyes as she moved her fingers across the screen to zoom in. She looked up at Ava, her face wet.

"Oh, she looks just like Mama. My God." Patricia rummaged through her own purse, extracting her phone, swiping and tapping until she found what she was looking for. She slid the phone across the table to Ava.

"Wow." Ava shook her head over the eerie resemblance between Jordan and her grandmother. "She's the spitting image."

"This would be too much for Mama," Patricia said, patting her face once again with napkins. "This would send her over the edge."

"Kennedy looks more like Jay," Ava said, showing off a picture of Erica's youngest daughter.

"She's adorable," Patricia said as she passed the phone back. She looked down at her hands balled up together in front of her and shook her head. "Well, Sweets, you sure have sent my top spinning this morning."

"Are you okay? Can I get you anything?" Ava asked.

"It's funny, Ruthie calling herself Erica now. She used to love *All My Children*. And boy, did she love Erica Kane. She and I shared a room and she had pictures of her all over her side."

"Really?"

"Oh, yeah. Like an obsession. I guess in some way, Ruthie is starring in her own little soap opera. All in her head." Patricia looked at her watch. "Well, Sweets, I got to put the brakes on this stroll down memory lane. Like I told you, Mr. Davis and I and another couple are leaving for an Alaskan cruise tomorrow and I got a lot to do."

"Did you ... were you interested in reaching out to Erica?"

Patricia sniffed. "For what?"

Ava nodded, understanding. "Of course. Never mind."

The woman stood, swinging her purse over her shoulder. "What are you going to do now? About Ruthie, I mean."

"Keep digging."

"I hope to God Ruthie's daughter didn't have anything to do with this. And if she did, I hope she has the decency to have some got-dang remorse about it."

Ava frowned. "Why do you say that?"

"Because Ruthie was never really sorry for what she did. She was only ever sorry she got caught."

Patricia winked as she picked up her plastic cup, now down to a few melting squares of ice, and deposited it in the trash as she walked out of the coffee shop, not once looking back.

79

RUTHIE

R uthie tapped the steering wheel of her mother's car, borrowed for the occasion, a decrepit midnight blue Honda Civic. She'd taken it to the car wash that afternoon, using some of her babysitting money to splurge on the deluxe package, which included two coats of wax, a vacuum job, and her choice of a complimentary air freshener in evergreen, vanilla, or springtime bouquet. She chose springtime bouquet.

The car wasn't the only thing to get a makeover. She'd been practicing pressing and curling her hair like Shannon's, sweeping the pitiful curls into a low ponytail, with high bangs in the front. Her sister, Patricia, lounged on her twin bed flipping through a *Cosmopolitan* and cracking her sugarless Chewels gum, rolling her eyes at Ruthie's attempts. Ruthie had also done her best to copy an outfit she'd seen in *Seventeen* magazine that month, generally pleased by the way the faded jean miniskirt, aquamarine tee with the knotted hem, and white faux leather rhinestone belt looked on her somewhat pudgy frame. She almost looked cute. The crowning touch, of course—*of course!*—was filling in her lips with the lip gloss Shannon had gifted her. Ruthie felt as special as a princess as she put it on. How Shannon probably felt every day.

The only car in the driveway was Shannon's. She looked at her watch again before letting her eyes drift up to the house, remembering the vases bursting with fresh cut flowers, the wonderful smell she couldn't place, but would never forget, the bedroom masquerading as a closet. She knew the soft light emanating from behind the filmy sheers was from one of those pretty lamps with the multicolored stained-glass patterns. She wondered how many Diet Cokes Mrs. Kendall had had from the bottom drawer of her refrigerator that day and whether Dr. Kendall had played golf.

The front door opened and Shannon appeared. Ruthie recognized the Benneton print minidress from the discard pile that one day, that one magical afternoon in the sanctuary of the Kendall home, a dress she'd never seen otherwise. It made her smile being privy to that secret knowledge. The blue-black curls were swept into a low ponytail and the cherry red lipstick was back.

She sauntered toward the car, her gold heart charm bracelet dangling from her wrist. She frowned a little when she spotted Ruthie inside.

"Ruthie, hey, what's going on?" she asked, confusion lacing her words as she peered inside the open passenger window.

"Ms. Grazoli sent me to pick you up for the initiation dinner for drama club."

"Oh, you're—Ms. Grazoli asked you to be in drama club for next year too?"

"Believe it or not, she did." She laughed. "I know I'm not as good an actress as you, but Ms. Grazoli thinks I could be good for supporting roles. You know, the next-door neighbor, the best friend. That kind of thing."

"Oh." Shannon bit her bottom lip. "And Ms. Grazoli said you were the one who should come pick me up tonight?"

"She knows we live kind of close, so she said I should pick you up and bring you straight over to the dinner." Ruthie put a finger to her lips. "Top secret," she whispered.

"I thought you didn't have a car?"

"It's my mom's car. She lets me borrow it sometimes."

"You know, I could just follow you in my car," Shannon said. "Then I'm not stuck there if it turns out to be lame, but you want to stay."

"No, really, it's okay," Ruthie said quickly. "Besides, all those times you drove me home, I—I want to."

Shannon's arms were folded across her chest and she squinted, the beginnings of a frown tugging at the corners of her mouth. She looked around, mumbling to herself as if she couldn't quite decide what to do. Ruthie licked her lips and held her breath as she watched Shannon, afraid her plan was about to collapse around her like a deflated tent.

Finally, Shannon sighed and slid into the passenger seat. "All right, I guess since Ms. Grazoli specifically asked you to come pick me up." She fastened her seat belt. "I wonder why she didn't just tell my mom you'd be the one to come pick me up? She knows we know each other."

Ruthie shrugged, her heartbeat returning to normal as she backed out of Shannon's driveway. "I don't know. I guess she wanted it to be a surprise."

"Look, if it's totally ill, we're not staying, okay?"

"Sure, okay."

"So, what's tonight all about anyway?" Shannon giggled. "What do we learn, the secret handshake or something?"

"I don't know. Ms. Grazoli didn't tell me much. Just that I should pick you up."

"Huh." Shannon fingered the ends of her ponytail. "So where is this top secret whatever anyway?"

"Ms. Grazoli's house. She lives over in Braeswood."

"Ugh. God that's far. How long's this gonna last anyway?"

Ruthie shifted in her seat, irritation rippling through her. Why did she have to ask so many questions? Why couldn't she just be quiet and enjoy the surprise?

"She didn't say," Ruthie said as she merged onto the freeway. "All she said was I should pick you up at seven and bring you straight to her house."

"Huh." Shannon said again before she fell silent as she dug into her purse and pulled out a cube of Blueberry Bubblicious.

"Whatever it is, I'm sure it will be fun," Ruthie said to break the silence. "I bet it'll be kind of like a sorority. We'll be like sisters."

"Can you turn on the radio?" Shannon asked as she popped her gum into her mouth.

"Oh sure, yeah." Ruthie fiddled with the knobs until she got Power 104, embarrassed she hadn't thought to have the radio on when Shannon got into the car.

"I'm so sick of this song," Shannon said as the stuttering sounds of "Rock Me Amadeus" filled the car. "So overplayed."

Ruthie straightened up in her seat, her throat tightening as she turned down the offending song. "So, what's been going on? I feel like since the play ended, I haven't seen you at all. Before that even."

"I've been super busy with pom squad and tennis and finals coming up. I still have to finish reading *The Scarlet Letter* and the stupid report's due on Tuesday." She flipped her ponytail over her shoulder. "I have to power read the rest of it tomorrow and pull an all-nighter on Monday to finish the paper."

"It was a pretty good book. I finished my paper a few days ago." She pursed her lips, sneaking a glance at Shannon. "I can help you, if you want. I mean, I can tell you all about it. Give you some tips."

"I'm cool. I always wait until the last minute. I think better that way. And I always get an A. Thanks though."

"It's really no big deal," Ruthie said. "I'd be happy to help you."

"That is so sweet. But seriously, though, I got it."

Ruthie beamed at her actions being called 'sweet.' "Of course. That's what friends are for. We are friends, right?"

"Huh? Oh, yeah, sure. Like totally. You're a super sweetheart."

"I'm wearing the lip gloss you gave me. Do you like it?" Ruthie turned to her and smiled. "Does it look okay on me?"

Shannon glanced over then flicked her gaze back out the passenger window. "Oh yeah. Looks great."

The heat of Shannon's approval raced through Ruthie and she

smiled shyly. It was all finally happening. Ruthie and Shannon. Shannon and Ruthie. "You really think so?"

"Oh yeah." Shannon nodded enthusiastically. "Totally."

"That means so much to me, Shannon. Really. I can't tell you how much."

"That's so sweet," Shannon repeated as she adjusted her air vent.

"So, what happened with you and Mikey that day?"

"What?"

"That day I was at your house," Ruthie said. "And you left to go meet him at Sharla's? Did he ask you to junior prom?"

"Ugh, no, he and Chad never even came over, so, totally missed him and I've been so busy the past few weeks, but Skip Lane is throwing a party next weekend and Mikey will be there." Shannon smiled. "I'll get my chance then."

"That's great," Ruthie said. "He'd be seriously stupid not to ask you out."

"Oh, he'll ask me. I can feel it." Shannon twisted around in her seat to look out the rear window as Ruthie exited the freeway. "I thought you said Ms. Grazoli lived in Braeswood?"

"She does. We just have to make a stop first."

"A stop? Stop where?"

"It's a surprise."

"What kind of surprise?" Shannon asked.

"You know, I've always liked you. Ever since junior high."

"What are you talking about?"

"You remember they used to sell those carnations and you could buy them and it was like a secret admirer thing?"

Shannon stopped chewing her gum as she looked at Ruthie. "Yeah?"

"I've never told anyone this, but I used to buy you carnations every year." Ruthie bit her bottom lip. "All through junior high."

"You bought me carnations?"

"I just always thought you were so sweet and pretty and nice and I just wanted you to know." Ruthie giggled nervously. "I mean, even though you didn't know it was me, or who I was even, because I always did it anonymously. Not that you would have known it was me. Anyway, I still thought it was a nice thing to do. Sending flowers to someone. That's nice, right?"

"Um, actually, it's a little weird."

Ruthie blinked. "What?"

"I mean, it's not like we were friends or anything, so yeah, kind of weird." Shannon made a face. "Like, who sends flowers to another girl and you're not even friends with that girl?"

"I told you, I thought it was a nice thing to do."

Shannon flopped back against the seat, folding her arms across her body. "Okay, whatever. It's totally weird, but fine."

"I'm not weird, Shannon," Ruthie said. "You just said I was a sweet person."

"Yeah, okay, fine, whatever," Shannon repeated.

"No, not whatever. You said we were friends. You said I was sweet. You just said it. 'You're super sweet.'"

"Okay, girl, you seriously need to take a chill pill."

"I just ... I want us to be friends, all right? And we were. We are. That day at your house and all those times you drove me home and we sang along to the radio and the lipstick you gave me. We're friends, Shannon. You and I are friends."

"Okay, this is getting super creepy." Shannon blew a bubble, then punctured it with her finger. "Can you just stop the car? Now. Like right now."

"I can't do that. You'll ruin the surprise."

"Stop the car," Shannon repeated, her voice rising.

"It's a—"

"I swear, if you say it's a surprise one more time—"

"I'm taking you for a picnic, all right? Just the two of us." Ruthie smiled as she exited off the freeway and followed the road around to the entrance of her destination. "Isn't that nice?"

"You're doing what?"

"Taking you for a picnic," Ruthie said.

"Taking me for a picnic? You're joking, right?"

"This park, my dad's boss lives close by and we came to a party over here last summer and it's so beautiful. All I could think is how much fun it would be to come here with you."

"Oh, my God. You called my mom, didn't you?"

"I—"

"You called my mom and told her some bogus story about a secret drama club dinner and not to tell anyone so you could get me alone. Right?"

Ruthie squirmed. "I wanted to do this nice thing for you—for us—and I had to be sure you'd come."

"You are seriously twisted if you think I'm going anywhere with you. God. I had no idea you were a fucking freak."

"Stop saying that." Ruthie gripped the steering wheel as she parked the car. "I'm not weird. I'm not a freak."

Shannon laughed. "Yeah, okay, sure. Not at all."

"I'm not. You know I'm not. I'm a nice person who likes to do things for my friends. Like you."

"I knew I should have driven myself." Shannon shook her head. "This is—you know what? Turn around and take me home, right now."

"Take back what you said about me. Take back what you said about calling me a freak."

Shannon rolled her eyes. "Okay. Done. I'm out of here. I saw some houses back there. I'll just call my parents at the restaurant to come pick me up," she murmured before she jumped out of the car.

Ruthie flinched as Shannon slammed the door and stalked off in the direction of the park entrance. She pinched the steering wheel, Shannon's words squeezing her brain as she thought about school on Monday. She could see Shannon now, sauntering down the hall toward Chip, Mikey, Sharla, and Lyz, furtive, giggly whispers escaping those cherry red lips as she pointed Ruthie out, telling them what a freak she was, how she'd sent her flowers and tried to take her on a picnic. They'd all laugh at her, call her all kinds of names, point at her. And they'd each tell another person, who'd tell another person, who'd tell another person. It would creep across school, slow and insidious, like an infestation, growing deep and purple and ugly with each retelling. Even the few friends she had would desert her. It would stain her, brand her like the scarlet letter pinned to Hester Prynne. Every time she walked past a group of girls, they'd laugh. Every time she walked past a group of boys, they'd laugh.

Everyone would laugh.

She'd finally be the outcast she always suspected she was meant to be, but tried so desperately to avoid.

Ruthie pursed her lips, shaking her head. She'd have to convince Shannon not to say anything, that she had it all wrong. Beg, plead, throw herself on her mercy, be her slave.

No one would understand if Shannon told them about tonight.

No one would understand anything except Ruthie Stowers was a weird freak. Avoid at all costs.

She turned the key in the ignition, determination sluicing through her veins, her eyes flitting across the dancing shadows of the park. Shannon couldn't have gotten far in the dark.

Ruthie chewed her bottom lip, her palms slick on the steering wheel as she drove toward the residential neighborhood on the other side of the park, scanning relentlessly for the bouncing blue-black curls of Shannon's ponytail. As she crept through the quiet streets, she never even noticed the stately homes with columns, big expensive cars in the driveways, rose bushes guarding against and inviting prying eyes all at once. All Ruthie could do was knead her forehead as she muttered Shannon's name to herself over and over, anxiety seizing her.

Her gaze swiveled left then right, sitting straight up as she spotted Shannon coming down the brick steps of a house and heading toward the street in pursuit of another house whose door she could knock on, whose phone she could ask to use. Ruthie parked the car, flung the door open, and ran toward Shannon.

"Okay, you have to get away from me now. I'm totally not kidding," Shannon said, speeding up her walk, not even bothering to look at her, as Ruthie caught up to her.

"Shannon, please, please don't say bad stuff about me at school," Ruthie's breath came in short puffs as she struggled to keep up with her. "Please don't tell everyone I'm weird or a freak."

"Leave me alone," Shannon said, jogging now.

Ruthie ran after her, grabbing her arm and swinging her around. Shannon instinctively pulled back, as Ruthie clutched at her. "I'll take you home, okay? Just—"

"Oh, my God, just stop." Shannon backed away. "I'm not going anywhere with you, do you get it?"

"Shannon, please—"

"Look you little freak, I just want you to get away from me—"

Ruthie's hand closed around the hard orange plastic handle of the sewing scissors hidden behind her back, the ones her mother kept in the side pocket of the driver's side door for emergencies, like the time she was in a car accident and had to cut the seat belt to get out. The ones Ruthie found her hand sliding around as she watched Shannon bound down the brick steps of the empty mansion in search of another door to knock on.

The ones that would keep Shannon from saying horrible things about her to the whole school.

The ones that would silence her.

That's all she wanted to do. Keep Shannon quiet.

Ruthie whipped the scissors around and Shannon gasped, pulling away, poised to bolt down the street.

"Oh, my God—"

Ruthie plunged the scissors into Shannon's neck.

Her chest.

Her shoulder.

Her stomach.

Her cheek.

Her temple.

Her stomach.

She didn't hear Shannon gasp or see her face crumple with pain or tears slide down her cheeks.

All she saw was the hallway on Monday morning, absent Shannon's arrogant, gum-cracking stroll, cloud of Liz Claiborne, the tap of her pink jellies across the shiny yellow tiles. She wouldn't huddle with Sharla or Lyz or Abby or Skip or Mikey or anyone to excitedly relay that they'd never *believe* what happened to her that weekend, what an *awful* Saturday night she had because of that *gross freak* Ruthie Stowers.

There'd be no stares, no whispers.

Because Shannon Kendall would not be there to tell the story.

Ruthie gripped the scissors in her bloody hand as Shannon sank to the ground, clutching her stomach, blood gushing from her wounds, coating her arms, legs, face. The crazy thing was, Shannon didn't even scream. She just looked shocked, as though she couldn't believe what Ruthie was doing.

She stared at Shannon for mere seconds, before she noticed the Tiffany charm bracelet glinting in the moonlight. The beautiful gold charm bracelet that swung around that slender wrist every day. Without thinking, Ruthie bent down, struggling with the slippery lobster clasp before finally it fell free from Shannon's bloody wrist and she stuffed it into the pocket of her jeans. She'd be surprised to find the links of gold crusted with blood in her pocket that night when she got undressed for bed.

And then she ran, pumping her arms and legs until she reached the car, the driver's side door hanging open, waiting to welcome her back. She threw the scissors down onto the passenger seat and peeled out of the neighborhood, her eyes focused only on the clear square of window in front of her as she hurtled toward the safety of home.

She didn't look at her rearview mirror until she was out of the neighborhood. She never once turned around. She didn't see Shannon writhing on the ground. She didn't see her struggle to her feet, and stagger across the street to a white house with a red door, pounding on it, hoping someone would let her in.

She wouldn't hear the furious bleating of sirens storming down the quiet street moments later. She wouldn't see neighbors flooding out of their homes, running toward the white house with the red door, now ringed with yellow and black crime scene tape. She wouldn't hear the gasps at the pools of blood glistening under the streetlamps, also surrounded by tape.

She wouldn't know until later she'd stabbed Shannon Kendall seven times. Or that the woman who opened the door to a bloody, breathless, and dying Shannon Kendall rode in the ambulance with her to the hospital, for she, too, had a sixteen-year-old daughter and couldn't bear the thought of this young girl drawing her last, agonizing breaths alone.

She didn't know until later that Shannon Kendall's parents didn't make it to the hospital in time from their jovial dinner across town with another couple. She didn't know until later that at the precise moment she and her mother sat down at their kitchen table at eleven-forty-seven that night to munch on the last two pieces of pepperoni pizza from Friday's dinner, Shannon Kendall would be pronounced dead.

The only thought tearing its way through Ruthie Stowers's brain as she raced home that night, her heart pounding, sweat drenching her body, the steering wheel hot and sticky with Shannon Kendall's blood, was pure relief—relief she wouldn't have to see Shannon Kendall in the hallway at school on Monday morning.

80

AVA

Nothing about one of the supposedly wealthiest suburbs of Houston impressed Ava as she exited I-45 at Rayford/Sawdust and headed toward Lake Woodlands. Strip malls, fast food drive-thrus, and of course, a Walmart, all bisected by a winding ribbon of freeway, which, in the short amount of time she'd been in town, seemed perpetually choked with pickup trucks, SUVs, and eighteen wheelers.

However, once she passed the drive-thru Starbucks on the corner, bland, overcrowded suburban sprawl gave way to tranquil streets shrouded in trees. In fact, a building was hard to come by, because all Ava could see were trees. Tall, thick, protective trees, hiding the homes, the people, their daily lives.

Her phone called out directions to Dr. Mason Kendall's home. She'd been less surprised by his agreeing to speak to her about Shannon than Patricia's willingness to talk about Ruthie. It was a burden he would always live with, a memory he would always want to share.

Ava drummed her fingers on the steering wheel as the trees morphed into still more trees and finally, a gorgeous expanse of blue lake, the surrounding bank dotted with the type of stately, staggering mansions Lake Forest had groomed her for, what she had expected from this lush Houston-area zip code.

She pulled up to the house and cut the engine, staring at the home for a minute, drinking it in. Two stories, majestic columns, crystal chandeliers blazing behind the all-glass front, even in the early afternoon. A cobalt blue Mercedes was parked in the driveway and the sight of an abandoned red tricycle in the front yard a jarring reminder to Ava that seventy-something Dr. Kendall had started a new family with his younger wife.

Ava gave herself one last look in the visor mirror before she gathered up her bag and headed up the front walk to ring the doorbell. In the distance, she could hear the loud, carefree laughter of kids out on the lake and the low buzz of water skis. She looked around at the quiet street, wondering if she should ring the doorbell again.

Just as she lifted her finger to do so, she could see the blur of a figure behind the beveled glass moving toward her. The door opened to reveal a tall, trim man in blue khakis and white button-down with the sleeves rolled up. A gold Rolex twinkled from his wrist, the liver spots of age that dotted his otherwise golden-brown hands and forearms somehow making him more distinguished, not less. He pushed back a lock of thick white hair from his forehead, which disobeyed and stubbornly sprang back into its former position.

"Dr. Kendall?"

"Please, call me Mason," he said, his voice no less booming than it had been on the phone, the faint southern accent wobbling ever so slightly. "Have any trouble finding us?"

"Not at all," Ava said as she stepped into the foyer, complying with his wave of the hand to follow him through the living room, which reminded her of her own house, filled with obviously expensive, though comfortable couches, a marble-topped coffee table, and decorative sculptures and lamps. Family photos, interspersed with massive oil paintings, dominated the rust orange walls. "You have a beautiful home."

"My wife always wanted to live out here," he said as he kicked a multicolored beach ball out of his way and turned to smile sheepishly. "I prefer the city, but you know, happy wife, happy life."

"How many kids do you have?" she asked as they sidestepped a tower of stuffed animals that toppled over as they walked past.

"Three," he said as he pointed her to what looked to be a den with its wood paneled walls, built-in bookshelves, and fireplace that Ava doubted saw much action. "Two with Nikki. And Shannon. Of course."

Ava nodded as she accepted his offer of a bottle of water, taking a minute to observe the photos on the shelves of Mason Kendall, his considerably younger wife—at least a twenty-year gap if she had to guess—and their two young children, miniatures of each parent. Tucked next to a hulking medical journal was the color version of one of the grainy black and white versions of Shannon's photo that Ava had become all too familiar with over the past few months. Mason smiled as he handed her the bottle of water from the mini fridge next to the mahogany desk.

"You have a beautiful family," she said.

Mason glanced at the pictures, almost as if he were surprised to see himself in the frames. "Thought I'd be playing Grandpa by now, not fending off funny looks when people find out I have an eight-year-old and a ten-year-old. Hell, sometimes I'm tempted to say they're my grandkids."

"How long have you been married?"

"Fifteen years. Nikki was thirty-two when we met. I was zooming toward fifty-five. Took me a long time to agree to have more kids." He shook his head. "Still takes a bit to wrap my head around."

"As my grandmother would always say, the heart wants what it wants," Ava said before she took a hearty gulp of her water.

"Julia—my first wife—she used to say that all the time. Of course, she and I were the same age," he said almost sheepishly before he clapped his hands together. "I hope you don't mind, but I invited two of Shannon's friends to come over in a bit, since I figured you'd probably want to pick their brains too."

"That would be great, thank you," Ava said. "I had actually

planned to ask you if you might be able to put me in touch with anyone."

"Lyz—that's L-Y-Z as she'll tell you—and Sharla were Shannon's best friends, so I know they'll have a lot to say."

"That's fantastic. Thank you."

"So, what would you like to know about Shannon?" he asked as he settled onto a brown leather chair.

"What was she like?"

A slow smile spread across Mason's face as he drowned himself in the memories of his lost daughter. "Confident. Smart. So, smart. Straight A's, honor roll. Without even trying. I mean, this girl could pick up an algebra book once and know how to solve every problem. I wanted her to follow in my footsteps, go into medicine, but she had kept saying she wanted to go to UT for undergrad then law." He shook his head. "She would have been outstanding."

"Do you have a favorite memory?"

"Day she was born," he said without hesitation. "I had been on call for I don't even know how long. Days. Days and days. And we were expecting her any minute, and I had my pager at the ready, just wait-ing. Then I decide, well, I'm just going to grab a quick minute in the on-call room. No sooner than I put my head down, my pager's going nuts. I'm racing to get down there and Julia is moaning like crazy. I'm trying to get her to do the breathing and she smacked me in the nose."

"I kind of wish I'd done that with my husband."

Mason chuckled. "Well, for a first baby, she came quick. Just a few pushes really and she was out. She just couldn't wait to get here. And the minute I looked at her, she just had me wrapped around her finger. I couldn't believe it."

"You and Shannon were close."

"Oh, yeah," Mason said. "We played tennis together every Saturday morning—she only let me beat her half the time—had dinner together just the two of us once a week at Strawberry Patch, which was her favorite. It's been gone for years. Kind of fitting." He fell silent. "Anyway, I used to have her page me when she got home from school or practice or whatever she was doing to make sure she was okay. She had her own code. 56892. I still remember."

"That last day. Tell me about it."

A deep, heavy sigh rumbled through Mason and he was quiet for a moment before speaking. "Normal Saturday. Shannon and I played tennis in the morning, then I saw patients until noon, grabbed a sandwich on the way home and crashed for a few hours. Julia went to the hairdresser then to the mall for something, I can't remember what. We were meeting Julia's co-anchor and his wife for dinner. Shannon said she was going to some drama club thing and someone was coming to pick her up."

Ava shuffled through her notes. "Shannon had her own car, right?"

"Yeah." Mason nodded. "Karmann Ghia. Birthday present when she turned sixteen."

"Did you find it strange that she didn't drive herself?"

"My wife took the call, and the killer, who we didn't know at the time was the killer, but the killer said it was a big thing for the drama club—a surprise dinner—and that she'd been instructed to pick Shannon up and bring her to the teacher's house for the dinner. Julia said the killer was very adamant about that."

"Did your wife find it odd?"

"Not at first, but one of those hindsight things. I think she found it more unsettling as time went on." He sighed. "Anyway, we left before Shannon did and we told her to have fun, be careful. The usual. To page me if she got home before we did." Mason's breath hitched around the last part and he held up his hand for a moment indicating he needed a minute.

Ava waited, allowing her eyes to settle once again on the picture of Shannon. In color, she was even more beautiful—stunning really—than she was in the gritty photos Ava had scraped from the Internet and library microfiche. Even hidden behind a pound of sparkly 80s makeup and hairspray, lost in a mound of ugly oversized sweaters stamped with wild geometric shapes that were the height of fashion once upon a time, the girl was gorgeous.

Mason cleared his throat and Ava swept her gaze back in his direction.

"Are you okay to continue?" she asked.

He nodded. "Yeah. Anyway, we uh, we were finishing up dinner when my pager starts going off. I don't recognize the number, but I call back and there's a man on the other end asking if I know a Shannon Kendall and telling me to get to Bellaire Medical. I found out later Shannon had knocked on his door, that his wife had gone to the hospital with her and that he found my number in her address book in her purse." Mason slumped down in his chair, a tear rolling down his face. "By the time we got to the hospital, she was in surgery and they couldn't get her stabilized. Then she was gone."

"I'm so sorry."

"It's been over thirty-five years and I still remember it like it was yesterday. Hurts just like it was yesterday."

"When you found out that it was … Ruthie … what went through your mind?"

"Shock. Anger. Confusion. How a sixteen-year-old girl could do this. I still don't understand it."

"It's hard to comprehend."

"Julia was never the same. She went back to work for about a year, but the grief was just too much for her and she quit. Well, retired, I guess you could call it. She managed to hold it together long enough for the trial, to see that through, but after that, she pretty much closed up shop. Got into bed and basically never left it." He shook his head. "The house was like death after Shannon. At any rate, my wife died from a heart attack at fifty-three. Really, though, she died the night our daughter did."

The doorbell pealed and Mason wiped his eyes as Ava blinked back her own tears. "That's Lyz and Sharla. Excuse me."

Ava stood and edged closer to the photo of Shannon, snapping a quick picture with her phone before returning to her perch on the couch, the voices of Mason and two other women announcing their arrival. She smiled at the appearance of the two women who were about her age and held out her hand.

"Lyz, Sharla, this is Ava Ewing," Mason said gesturing toward Ava.

"That's L-Y-Z," the woman said on autopilot, her thick Texas accent punching the syllables. Ava and Mason exchanged an amused glance, him throwing an 'I told you so' look her way.

As they all continued to exchange pleasantries, Ava did a brief, incisive inventory of the pair. Lyz's simple yet obviously expensive black suit, hot pink acrylics, and shiny blond highlights screamed high-powered something. Sharla's dark brown ringlets, sprigs of gray threaded throughout, pale, makeup-free face, gauzy caftan, and over-sized crocheted tote amused Ava, as she doubted she'd traipsed through the halls of Willow Branch High School as the resident spiritual healer.

"We brought you a copy of our yearbook from junior year," Lyz said, her Texas twang as pronounced as Patricia's, as she extracted the book from her designer bag and handed it over to Ava, who eagerly took it, opening up the pages. "It's for you to keep," Lyz said. "My sister was yearbook editor so we had extras."

"This is great, thank you," Ava said, sliding the book into her bag, itching to pounce on the pages. "How long were you friends with Shannon?"

"Since elementary school," Sharla said, her hushed little girl voice holding only a breathy trace of a southern accent. "We all grew up together."

"What about Ruthie? Did you know her?"

Both Sharla and Lyz shook their heads. "I think she moved to Willow Branch in junior high, but we weren't friends with her, no," Lyz said.

"I had a math class with her once," Sharla said, twirling her hair around the tip of an index finger. "What math do you take sophomore year?"

"Usually algebra or geometry," Ava said.

"Geometry," Sharla said, seemingly slightly delighted with herself. "I had geometry with her."

"Do you remember anything about her?" Ava asked. "Anything that stood out?"

Sharla shook her head. "No, nothing. Just a quiet girl. Kept to herself. I think maybe she was in band? I have a memory of seeing her carrying a flute or clarinet case in class."

"Did Shannon ever mention Ruthie at all to either of you?"

"Let's be clear," Lyz said. "Shannon and that girl were *not* friends. She was *not* in our crowd."

Ava pursed her lips. "Any reason why not?"

Lyz sighed, almost as though she couldn't believe she had to explain this straightforward concept to naive simpletons. "We were the popular crowd. The cool kids. The leaders. The overachievers. Everyone wanted to be like us, to know what we were doing, what we wore, what we did. That's not who this girl was."

"Oh my God, Lyz, you make it sound like we were horrible snobs," Sharla said, laughing nervously as she swept an embarrassed look in Ava's direction. "We really weren't."

"We were!" Lyz half-snapped, half-laughed. "Sharla, seriously, you're telling me you would have said to that girl, 'Hey come hang out at my pool this weekend,' or 'Let's go to the mall after school.' Come on."

Sharla burned bright red, shooting Ava another flustered look. "It's just that we all grew up together. We all knew each other. We were *comfortable* with each other."

Lyz turned to look at Ava. "I'm not going to apologize that we had privilege or opportunities. Any more than I want my girls to feel bad about the things my husband and I are able to give them. We work damn hard for our lifestyle, same way my parents did."

"Lyz, please," Sharla mumbled as she laughed nervously, her gaze now pinned to her lap.

"I saw that Shannon and Ruthie were in drama club together?" Ava asked, eager to get off this fast road to nowhere.

Lyz rolled her eyes. "It's a stretch to say that. All three of us—me, Shannon, and Sharla—tried out for the spring musical, as kind of a lark. Shannon got the lead, Sharla, you and me got what? Roles in the chorus? So, we dropped out. I think that girl—the killer—was also in the chorus. Shannon told me later the teacher or advisor asked her to join permanently and at first, she wasn't sure if she was going to do it, but then she decided to give it a try."

"That's essentially what she told us," Mason piped in. "She had so many other things on her plate, but ultimately decided it would be fun to do."

"She did come on the class trip to Galveston," Sharla piped up. "I can picture her. She had this kind of red striped bathing suit that didn't really fit right and the rest of us had bikinis. Remember, Lyz? Remember that she was there?"

"No," Lyz said flatly. "I don't. Listen, the point is, Shannon never did *anything* to that girl. Period, point blank."

"Shannon was the sweetest, nicest girl," Sharla said as she grabbed for Lyz's hand, the two women tearing up. "She'd never hurt *anyone*."

And that's when Ava saw it. Or more precisely *them*. She made a face as she abruptly turned to look at Shannon's photo, confirming that she too wore one.

Gold Tiffany heart charm bracelets, dangling from Lyz and Sharla's wrists. An identical one nestled against the sleeve of Shannon's multi-colored sweater.

Just like the one adorning Erica's wrist. The one she fiddled with constantly.

Holy hell.

Ava leaned closer, her heartbeat quickening as she pointed to the two bracelets. "Excuse me, but I couldn't help but notice you're both wearing the same bracelet and I see Shannon is wearing one in her photo."

The two friends glanced at each other, sharing a knowing smile. "All the girls in our group had one," Lyz said. "It was Shannon's idea, for our eighth-grade graduation."

"My wife gave each of the girls one," Mason said. "Shannon contributed part of her allowance."

"We've never taken them off in all these years," Sharla said, her voice catching. "It's like a bond between us."

"They think the killer stole Shannon's when she stabbed her," Lyz said, her voice dark with bitterness. "Shannon would have never taken it off."

"The police searched the killer's house for it," Mason said. "They never found it. My wife was devastated."

Over the next two hours, Ava moved through the rest of her questions, the links of the gold Tiffany charm bracelet tickling the back of her brain the entire time. With occasional interjections from Mason, Lyz and Sharla shared memories of slumber parties, travel trips for tennis and pom-pom, church camps. How brilliant, funny, and beautiful their friend was. How much they missed her. Still.

In the distance, the clatter of the front door opening, accompanied by the excited screeches of children and the exasperated voice of a weary mom commanding them to be quiet while simultaneously ordering them to put their things away and wash up for dinner, pulled everyone's attention away from memory lane. The air in the room shifted. Ava could see a noticeable stiffening in Mason as he shot out of his chair, while Sharla also hurriedly got to her feet, Lyz staying seated as she rolled her eyes.

"I've taken up enough of your time," Ava said, following Mason and Sharla's cue as she gathered up her things. "I really appreciate all of you talking to me."

Mason's wife called out his name as she entered the room, stopping short at the threshold at the sight of the small crowd. Tall and tan, she looked to Ava as though she might have been an athlete at one point. One of those beautiful gargantuan girls who played beach volleyball when she wasn't surfing or paddle boarding. The sun worshipper with saltwater blond hair, her freckled nose and shoulders in a perpetual state of pink and peeling. Mason planted a kiss on her cheek before she uttered a prim hello as she nodded politely in Lyz and Sharla's direction, each of whom responded with their own strained greetings. The woman's gaze settled on Ava, an open, questioning look on her face.

"Nikki, sweetheart, this is Ava Ewing. She's doing a story on Shannon."

Instead of the warm goo of understanding that Ava expected, it seemed as though the new Mrs. Kendall drew up a little too quickly, something cold and dark flashing across her eyes. She awkwardly stuck out her hand as though she had to think about it for a few seconds.

"Nice to meet you," she said, limply shaking Ava's hand.

"I've got to get home," Lyz said as she finally stood and cleared her throat, which caused Sharla to jump and hastily follow her to the front of the house. Mason walked everyone out, shaking Ava's hand, telling her to call him anytime, before Lyz and Sharla hugged him goodbye, saying they'd see him soon, quickly closing the door behind them.

"Good God, I was hoping to miss her," Lyz grumbled as she deactivated the alarm for her Hummer.

Ava glanced back at the house. "Not your favorite person?"

Sharla bit her lip. "She's okay."

"Oh, please," Lyz said. "Total bitch. I feel sorry for him every day being stuck with her. Nothing at all like Mrs. Kendall."

Sharla sighed. "She's Mrs. Kendall, too."

Lyz scoffed. "A bargain basement version."

"She's probably tired of hearing about Shannon," Sharla said as she shot Ava a skittish, worried glance. "It has to be really hard for her."

"It's what she signed up for." Lyz turned to Ava. "When's this going to run?"

"I'm not sure yet," Ava said, her eyes darting around to avoid Lyz's penetrating gaze. "I'll let you know."

Sharla pulled Ava into an embrace, a move that startled, though it didn't necessarily surprise her. Mostly she was relieved to find she didn't smell of patchouli, but rather, vanilla. "Thank you for your grace," she murmured.

After releasing Ava, Sharla got into the passenger seat of Lyz's car, the two women waving to her as they sped off down the street. She slid back into her rental car, pulling up the picture of Erica, shaking her head at the sight of the ubiquitous gold charm dangling from her wrist. Murderers almost always took a souvenir.

What had Erica stolen from Whitney?

81

ERICA

The images on Erica's laptop floated into an indiscernible kaleidoscope of color. Concentrating on her work was impossible. The only thing she could focus on was Jordan.

It had been a little over a week since Erica had pulled her daughter out of East Lake Forest. Her first instinct had been to fight. To crush that smirking principal and her condescending kowtowing, first to the memory of Whitney Dean and then to the vipers who'd flung darts at Jordan's back. Of course, Lauren Dean was the one who put the target there to begin with. Erica could have ground each and every one of them into powder, dust that she'd gleefully blow into oblivion.

She hadn't counted on Jordan being relieved to be out of East Lake Forest. She hadn't counted on Jay suggesting a boarding school in Connecticut and Jordan enthusiastically agreeing to it.

Once again, nothing had gone according to plan.

The bubbles screensaver for Erica's laptop flicked on and she sighed, deciding to take the sign and save work for tomorrow. She closed the lid to the laptop and sat staring at it. Without thinking, she reached for her keys and unlocked the bottom drawer of her desk, extracting a plain white envelope, snug against the lip gloss Shannon had gifted her all those years ago. She turned the envelope over, the yellow ponytail holder falling into her hand. The silky black tresses of Whitney's hair sprouted from the band, reluctant to let go. Just like Shannon's bracelet, she'd been surprised to find it in her purse the following day. Her initial impulse had been to throw it in the trash, as she didn't recognize it right away.

Now felt like the right time to wear it. A reminder of all she'd sacrificed for Jordan.

Even if she'd never know.

Even if she'd never be able to appreciate it.

She slowly gathered the ponytail holder around the strands of her hair.

82

AVA

A rush of icy air enveloped Ava as she hurried through the lobby of her hotel, her mind still numb after spending almost two hours in the heinous grip of Houston rush-hour traffic. She'd always thought the Dan Ryan was the devil; 45 and the 610 Loop had gleefully snatched the horns.

She crowded into the elevator with a group of conference goers, wondering how bad she smelled, the thought of a steamy, soapy shower with the high-end body washes courtesy of the in-house spa almost causing her to collapse with happiness.

Hygiene would have to wait, though, because her grubby little hands itched to paw at the pages of the 1986 Willow Branch High School yearbook.

Ava entered her room, kicked off her shoes, and threw down her bag after extracting the yearbook. She folded her legs underneath her on the bed and cracked open the book, mustiness and ink mixing together as they escaped the pages, making her wince.

It was a typical yearbook, filled with black and white photos of the student body at their best and worst. For every student studying quietly in the library or reading a book under a tree, there were students hanging out of cars, a cluster of football players with pacifiers sprouting from their mouths, yet another group of kids adorned in clown wigs and pajamas running amok in a crowded gym. The classic random pictures that are hysterical at the time, but the further you get away from that oh-so-important four-year span, fade in importance and amusement.

Ava quickly flipped to the junior class and the 'Ks,' Shannon Kendall's bright, smiling visage jumping off the page with little effort. Ava put her finger next to Shannon's activities, finding the pages where the busy junior posed with the tennis team, the track team, the drama club, and the pom-pom squad. She was out front in the snaps for the honor roll, the center of attention as homecoming queen, and the star of the spring musical. Shannon graced other pages, too, the camera managing to find her and her friends at their lockers, welded to the Coke machine, or slathering their faces with makeup while hanging out on the school lawn (Lyz Cox looked exactly as Ava thought she would —blond hair teased higher than even Texas allowed, lip gloss and eyeliner competing with each other for 'most,' while Sharla Ritter's frosted locks, GUESS? jeans and designer sweater gave no hint of the hippy dippy granola goddess waiting down the street). An orange juice carton poised elegantly in one hand as Shannon paused from eating a salad at lunch. Laughing at her good luck at two strapping boys kissing each cheek. In mid-dance during a formation with the pom squad.

The tragic coda, of course, was the all-color In Memoriam insert, the only four pages in the yearbook deemed worthy enough for the splurge. A moving tribute to her sportsmanship, leadership, beauty, and grace, filled with quotes from classmates and friends like Lyz ("We were like sisters. I'll never forget her.") and Sharla ("Shannon was such an amazing and beautiful spirit. I can't believe she's gone.") to effusive remembrances from teachers and coaches about the star athlete and accomplished student.

Ava bit her lip as she thumbed her way to 'S' for Stowers, finally able to see the ghost of Erica floating in the undeveloped features. Ruthie had the weird, shy, uncomfortable smile endemic to so many sixteen-year-old girls. Girls who hadn't yet grown into their faces. Girls who hadn't yet slipped into the confidence that age and simply not caring anymore gives you as you get older and gain your footing in this world. At sixteen, you don't know that those corners are up ahead in the distance. You can't conceive of those glorious signposts. At sixteen, every hurt is magnified by a thousand. Every rejection a catastrophe. Every slight, real or imagined, the end of the world.

Ruthie's activities—art club and flute in the band (good memory, Sharla)—weren't the impressive roster that Shannon's was, though they were completely respectable, completely normal ways to pass the time, make friends, nurture a skill or an interest. Ava didn't see her in any other pictures throughout the yearbook, though as she dove deeper into the pages, it was possible she might appear in a glimpse or two.

Ava closed the book and tossed it onto the bed next to her as she flopped onto her back, drained. She knew it wouldn't be long before she had every page, every picture memorized, but that could wait. She needed a shower, dinner, and an obnoxiously large glass of white wine as she unwound from today and prepared to head home tomorrow.

She was convinced—more than convinced—that Erica, not Jordan, had murdered Whitney. It was only a hunch, a gut feeling.

But how to prove it?

Ava forced herself off the bed and into the bathroom for a quick shower, all the while wondering not only how she was going to nail Erica, but how she was going to save Carly.

83

ERICA

Erica sat in her car, staring out the windshield, the orange sphere of late afternoon sun slashing the rows of black tree branches, still stripped bare, their green leaves stubbornly refusing to come out despite it being April. The unending miles of dry, brown ground stretching across the preserve also didn't appear to be cooperating with spring's arrival, content it seemed with remaining populated with tufts of tough, dead vegetation.

She hadn't been here since that rainy Saturday afternoon, when the grass was still green, when flowers still sprouted from the ground. There had been no pull, no need to return to the scene of the crime, no magnet forcing her here against her will.

Today though, for some reason, there had been. An inexplicable tug during an afternoon run of errands, one of which took her right by the Middlefork Preserve, found her turning down Middlefork Lane and coming to rest in the same parking spot as that day.

She exited the car, shoving her hands into the pockets of her parka as a small, unexpected gust of wind rushed over her, whipping her hair into her eyes. Erica pulled Whitney's ponytail holder from her pocket and stuffed the strands of her own hair inside before she took small, stuttering steps toward the field where she and Whitney had their last meeting. Twigs and stiff leaves crunched beneath the hard rubber soles of her white leather sneakers as she slowly made her way toward what, in the summer and fall, was a cheerful patch of black-eyed Susans, but what was now a bed of sleeping, spindly weeds, waiting for the warmth of spring and summer to rescue them.

"I didn't expect to see anyone out here."

Erica gasped and whipped around at the quiet voice cracking the silence of solitude. She found herself face-to-face with an older woman sporting a sensible graying brown bob, seemingly materialized from nowhere, sorrow appearing to burrow more deeply into the cavernous lines of her face.

"I didn't hear you," Erica said, her hand on her chest, wondering if the explosion of heartbeats were audible.

"Sorry, didn't mean to scare you," the woman said, coming closer, stepping around Erica to stare down at the ground. "Name's Kate."

"Nice meeting you," Erica said, hoping the woman wouldn't pry for her name and wondering what she'd say if she did.

"First time I've been out here myself since October."

Erica drew up. *October.* "Oh?" she asked innocently.

"My husband and I were the ones who found that girl that was murdered last year." She tapped the hard ground with the toe of her shoe. "Right here."

"How awful," Erica said, hoping she sounded appropriately horrified and sympathetic, when in reality, the terror of the moment crept up her insides like slow rising water. Today, of all days, this woman, of all women. Here. Now. "That must have been just terrible for you."

"I haven't been able to stop thinking about it. I have nightmares about it."

Erica ran her tongue across her bottom lip as she attempted to slow her breath. She had to proceed, oh so carefully. "Would you like to talk about it? I know I'm a stranger, but sometimes that's easier."

The woman chuckled ruefully before wincing. "Well, that's true enough."

Erica waited, watched. Wondered.

"Well, we live near here," Kate continued. "Part of the year anyway. We're in Arizona the rest of the time. Anyway, we usually like to take a walk out here. It's so secluded, it's like having our own forest preserve."

"It's very pretty here," Erica said. Still waiting.

"It was just pouring down rain that day and there was a break, so we thought we'd chance it, for a few minutes anyway, get a quick little walk in." She took a shuddering breath. "We were walking, talking about what to have for dinner that night. He wanted fish, I voted for stew. And then, I saw something yellow in the grass. My first thought was that it was those black-eyed Susans. I really didn't think anything of it at first."

Erica nodded, hoping it would prod the woman a little. "Makes sense."

Kate frowned as the memory washed over her. "Except, it was too much yellow to be a flower. Much too much. Solid. I pointed it out to my husband and asked, 'What is that?' and as we got closer, I could see all that yellow was a raincoat." Kate choked back a sob. "That's when we realized it was a body."

Erica sucked in her breath. "She was already dead?"

"Well, we weren't sure, but we rushed over there nevertheless. Then she moaned." Kate stopped and covered her mouth with her hand and took a few ragged breaths. "She was still alive."

Erica gulped. "Oh, really?"

"I screamed at my husband to call 911 while I turned her over and that girl was just drenched head to toe in blood. I mean, just—" Kate waved her hands up and down her body. "There was not a spot on that poor girl's body that wasn't just blood. All that blood. All that yellow."

"How terrible."

"I couldn't even think. All I knew was, we had to try to save her."

"Of course," Erica whispered as she stared straight ahead.

"We called 911 and it started raining again. Took them forever to get to the hospital. I put my coat over her. Held her hand. She was so out of it, but I was hoping. Oh, boy, was I hoping."

"And she was still alive?" Erica asked.

"Yes. She squeezed my hand back at one point, so that made me think, all right, everything's going to be okay."

Erica's heart lurched. "Did you ride in the ambulance with her?"

"Absolutely, I did. I didn't think she should be alone." Tears welled up in Kate's eyes. "Nobody should die alone."

"No," Erica said quietly, her gaze wandering in the direction of the sun, starting its sink below the horizon. "No, they shouldn't."

"Anyway, I was in the ambulance with her, they took her back to work on her, and then ... a few hours later, she was gone."

Erica pursed her lips, still staring off into space. "Was she unconscious the whole time? Did she say anything?"

"No, she—" Kate frowned as if a memory were poking her brain. "Actually, she was trying to say something, now that you mention it."

Erica straightened up, her entire body going cold. "Oh?" she asked, flinching at the wobble in her voice.

"J. She was stuttering. J-J-J. Like she was trying to say something, but she couldn't quite get it out."

The cable that ran from Erica's heart to her shoes snapped, sending the elevator crashing to the ground, imploding into a million little pieces as it smashed into its destination.

Jordan. She tried to say Jordan's mom. Damn, damn, damn.

"How strange," Erica said, her throat closing around the boulder of fear lodged against her larynx.

Kate shrugged, clearly troubled. "To tell you the truth, I'd forgotten all about it until now. I wonder if it means something, if I should go to the police. Now I just have to remember what I did with that detective's card."

Erica took a deep breath. She had to cut this woman off at the knees. Even if the police couldn't connect the dots to her, they'd beeline straight for Jordan. Neither scenario was acceptable. "I know you didn't ask, but would you like some friendly advice from a total stranger?"

"Sure."

She turned to face the woman, sliding behind a mask of concern. "It doesn't sound as though it would serve much purpose. It might even upset the girl's family, stir up feelings, emotions about what she might have been trying to say."

Kate twisted her lips around. "That's a good point."

"And the police, well, doubtful they could do much with a single letter. Sounds like a real rabbit hole." She shrugged as nonchalantly as she could. "Seems to me it would be best to let it be."

Kate sighed and looked away from Erica. "You're probably right. For what purpose."

"Exactly." Erica made a big show of looking at her watch as she slowly backed away. "Well, it was nice to meet you, Kate."

"Oh, yes, thank you, Miss...?"

"Have a good evening," Erica called out, almost to her car, smiling and waving as she slid behind the wheel, fighting the urge to peel out of the parking lot.

84

AVA

A va mindlessly stirred the spaghetti sauce simmering in a pot on the stove in front of her, Kyle chattering behind her about his workday while he tossed a simple green salad, Carly somewhere upstairs, probably on social media instead of doing her homework.

She was back in Houston, still sitting across from Patricia Davis. Still sitting in Mason Kendall's study with Lyz Cox and Sharla Ritter.

She'd gotten home late last night, the sensory overload of the trip keeping her eyes focused on the ceiling for the better part of the night until she drifted off briefly around two, only to zombie her way through work. The shock of the resemblance between the Stowers sisters, Erica's lies stacked upon lies, Patricia's cunning observation about her sister's likely lack of remorse over her crimes, those gold Tiffany bracelets ripped through Ava like a current.

And she couldn't even talk about it with anyone. Not yet.

The overwhelming similarities between Whitney and Shannon's murders shook her like branches in a storm. It was Erica. Erica had stabbed Whitney to death just like she'd stabbed Shannon to death. She was as certain of it as she was that today was Thursday.

But that's all she had. A feeling. Gut instinct. She couldn't exactly go marching into the police station with her gut feeling and demand they arrest Erica for murder. She planned to spend the weekend putting everything together in a binder, hoping that going over the information again would bring forth an ah-ha! moment, an Elementary-my-dear-Watson-Miss-Marple-Jessica-Fletcher-explains-it-all revelation.

It wasn't enough, though. She needed solid, irrefutable proof.

Ava sighed and smiled at Kyle as he bent over for a quick kiss and rubbed her shoulders.

"You okay, Mate?" he asked.

"Fine. Just tired."

"You seem even more knackered from this trip than usual."

Ava offered him a feeble, lying smile. "It's all Psycho Kitty. You know, same shit, different day."

He nuzzled her neck. "I was thinking, maybe after your brother's wedding, let's take a proper holiday this summer."

"That sounds great," she said with feigned cheer.

"I'll get going on some research, then, come up with a few ideas."

"Yeah. That sounds great," she repeated. "Can you call Carly down so she can set the table?"

Kyle complied and Ava mechanically drained the noodles into the strainer before dumping them into a bowl and setting them on the table. Carly bounded down the stairs and set the table before they all took their seats and said a quick grace.

"How was school, Lamb?" Kyle asked Carly.

"Fine."

"How are the kids feeling about Whitney?"

Ava's ears mildly perked up. Carly shrugged. "I mean everyone thinks Jordan did it. I totally think she did."

"We don't know that Jordan did anything," Ava murmured. "You need to stop saying that."

"Why?"

"Because nothing has been proven," Kyle said. "Besides. If it turns out it wasn't Jordan, that would be a real cock-up."

"What do you mean?"

"Saying false things about someone is called slander and you could be sued for it."

Carly looked down at her spaghetti. "Mrs. Dean thinks she did it. She said so in her interview. Aren't the police going to arrest her?"

Ava sighed. "It's not exactly the same thing."

"Well, it doesn't matter anyway, because Jordan got kicked out of school."

Ava's head flipped up. "What?"

"What happened?" Kyle asked, frowning.

Carly squirmed in her chair. "The principal just thought she shouldn't go to school at East Lake Forest anymore."

Ava dropped her fork and it clanked against her plate. Something about Carly's face flashed complicity of some sort. "Why?"

"Because of Mrs. Dean's interview," Carly repeated. "Mom. Everyone knows she did it especially after the party and the tweets—"

"What tweets?"

Carly's jaw clamped shut, clearly having said too much. She hunched over her plate. "Nothing."

Ava leaned closer. "What. Tweets."

Silence descended as Ava continued staring a hole into her daughter, Kyle at the head of the table, his gaze swiveling between the two, seemingly unsure of what was unfolding in front of him, but almost sure not to like it.

"Caroline Gene, so help me—"

"All right, all right." Carly gulped. "Right after school started, there were some tweets about Jordan and how she couldn't be trusted."

"And?"

Carly looked down. "And some people called her some names."

The bomb was ticking. Ava envisioned her head exploding like confetti. "What. Names."

Carly cleared her throat, clearly uncomfortable. "Like ho. Skank. That she stole Whitney's man and that's why she was mad at Jordan."

The confetti cannon detonated. "Oh, God."

"It was just a bunch of stupid tweets. I didn't think Jordan would kill Whitney over it."

Tweets. The tweets.

I didn't think Jordan would kill Whitney over it.

"Let me see them," Ava said.

Carly shrank inside her shirt. "I think they got deleted."

Ava threw down her napkin and pushed back from the table, not caring that she knocked her water glass over as she grabbed Carly's phone.

"Oh, my God, Mom! What are you doing? Are you crazy?" She looked at Kyle. "Dad, are you going to let her do this to me?"

"Don't even think about going there, Carly," Ava said as she unlocked the phone, invoking their parental deal that she have access to it whenever she wanted. She'd never called in that chit until today.

Ava tapped the Twitter icon on the home screen, then Carly's profile, relentlessly scrolling through mindless tweets about pop stars, Lifetime movies, and what she ate on any given day.

"This was before Whitney's party, right?"

"Mom—"

"Right?"

Carly slumped down in her chair and scoffed. "Yes."

The pad of Ava's index finger burned as she kept attacking the screen, until she landed on the first one.

Hey, @itsJordanBaby Who'd you bang?

Tweet after tweet after tweet of the vilest words, the most horrific of attacks. Red danced in front of Ava's eyes as she read the evidence of girls turning on girls, friends attacking friends.

Ho. Skank. Slut. Trash.

She kept scrolling, rage tearing through her like a bullet.

Ava grabbed the chair next to Carly and swung it around until she was face-to-face with the girl. "Who or what started these tweets?"

"Mom—"

She held up her index finger and took a deep breath. "Carly, so help me—"

"It was because of me, okay?" Carly sobbed. Ava and Kyle glanced at each other, their jaws slack.

"What does that mean?" Ava asked.

Carly sniffed and grabbed her napkin from the table and blew her nose. She continued sniveling for several more minutes before she gulped and took a deep breath. "Whitney said that Jordan couldn't be trusted and I told Dionne and I don't know who Dionne told and the next thing I know, it was all over Twitter. I swear, that's all I did."

Ava let this information sink in. She couldn't move, couldn't think. Her daughter, the fucking ringleader. The class A instigator.

"So, you went gossiping to Dionne about some stupid comment that Whitney made and she started this smear campaign against Jordan on social media. Right?"

"I mean, I didn't think Dionne would do something like that—"

"Yes, you did." Ava slammed her hand down on the table, causing Carly and Kyle to jump. "That's exactly why you did it."

"Mom—"

"Why?"

"Dad—"

"Don't look at him!" Ava screamed. "I asked you a question!"

Carly sniffed a few more times before blowing her nose into the linen napkin again. "I didn't want Whitney and Jordan to go back to being friends. And if Jordan came to Whitney's party, then they'd— that's what Mrs. Dean said, Mom. She said Whitney and Jordan would probably make up at the party. And I couldn't let that happen. Then Mrs. Mitchell had to go and make Jordan come to the party and if she'd just stayed away from Whitney, if she'd just stayed home, none of this would have happened. Whitney would still be alive. She'd—"

Bile forced its way up to Ava's mouth, but she swallowed it back. She slumped down in her chair, her skin tingling, words and images sweeping across her brain like errant, swirling debris.

"Go upstairs," she whispered.

"Am I in—"

"Up. Stairs."

"Can I have my phone?"

Ava's jaw fell open in disbelief and indignation, and Carly, who, it seemed, thought better of pushing back against her, instead slunk out of her chair to scurry upstairs.

And the social media, the tweeting. You wouldn't believe some of the tweets I've seen. Absolutely disgusting. Teenage girls can be so vicious.

This was it. That night out with Erica, she'd mentioned tweets.

She knew about these tweets.

Believing they originated with Whitney.

And if she knew Carly was the one behind it—

The bile pushed its way back up. Except this time, Ava couldn't swallow it back. The faint tickle of Kyle's voice in her ear receded as Carly's phone dropped from her hand and clattered to the ground. She bolted for the powder room just off the kitchen and threw up in the sink.

85

RUTHIE

The police first called to talk to her eight days after the murder.

Ruthie wasn't scared when that detective called and asked if she could come down to the station to answer a few questions about Shannon Kendall. They were talking to all the junior class, along with most of the seniors, so she knew it was coming.

She wasn't even nervous about it.

Shannon's murder had made the front page of both daily newspapers, topped every half hour on the news radio stations, and was the lead story on all the newscasts. Probably because Shannon's mother was a celebrity in town.

Probably because it was so vicious.

Ruthie's mother had been the one to tell her, having heard it on the radio as she was getting ready for work that Sunday morning. With teary eyes, she knocked softly on her door and sat on the corner of her trundle bed as she stroked Ruthie's leg and relayed the stunning news. Ruthie couldn't explain it, but it was as though she didn't have any idea, as though her mother telling her was really the first time she knew something horrible had happened to Shannon Kendall. Her hand flew to her mouth and she gasped, a raspy, "What?" pushing past her lips. Her mother slid her arms around her shoulders and held her as she cried, soothing utterances slipping from her lips. She didn't want her to go to school on Monday, but Ruthie *had* to be there. She had to be at her locker, watching and waiting, assuring herself Shannon wouldn't come floating down the hallway.

And indeed, as she stood at her locker that morning, her heartbeat quickened a little as she looked for Shannon, bizarrely forgetting momentarily she wouldn't be walking down that hallway anymore. Lyz and Sharla were absent that day, and Skip Lane and Mikey Gold leaned against their lockers in a daze. Tears actually ran down Mikey's face. The whole school was in a trance of grief, clouds of disbelief and sorrow hovering over all of their heads.

There was no school that day. Students went to class and teachers stood in front of chalkboards, but there were no lessons scrawled across the blackboard, no meaningful discussions about symbolism in literature, no pop quizzes, no reminders about papers due. Instead, there were clumsy invitations from shell-shocked teachers for students to share their thoughts and feelings in class or to visit their guidance counselors instead. Classes were turned into study halls. Girls who'd never shared so much as a hello with Shannon Kendall wept. Boys whose teenage dreams starred Shannon Kendall sat sullen and stunned at their desks.

Ruthie didn't cry. Her eyes got a little misty and a hard lump of panic lodged itself in her throat for most of the day. She commiserated with her friends at lunch. Sandwiches were left wrapped in baggies, cartons of milk grew warm, and apples sat smooth and untouched as they all huddled together shaking their heads, disbelieving utterances slipping out of someone's mouth every few minutes. She fielded a few questions from the group, since she'd sort of been friends with Shannon. That made her special somehow in their eyes.

But she never cried. Not one time.

The whispers in the hallways over the ensuing days were that the police were on the hunt for any enemies Shannon may have had. Girl fights, love triangles, boy troubles. She'd say the same thing as everyone else. Everyone loved Shannon. No, of course she didn't have any enemies. Who in the world would want to hurt Shannon the Beautiful, Shannon the Sweet, Shannon the Most Popular Girl in School?

The interrogation room was a lot nicer than she thought it would be. She guessed she imagined it would be like the *Barney Miller* reruns her father laughed his way through every night at eleven on channel thirty-six, or *Hunter*, which her brother obsessively watched on Saturday nights if he wasn't out with one of his buddies or on a date.

No, the room was clean and small, marked only by a rectangular wooden table, two metal chairs with padding on the seats, the plain white walls, stark and bare except for a clock whose numbers peeked out between sturdy metal strings. One detective brought her in and told her to have a seat, smiling as he offered her a paper cone of water, while another detective joined them, bearing a yellow legal pad and black pen.

The questions were all as she expected:

How well did you know Shannon?

We had some classes together and then we were in the spring musical together. Well, she was the star and I had a nonspeaking role.

How long have you known Shannon?

Since junior high.

Do you know of anyone who would want to hurt Shannon?

No, nobody. I mean, she was really popular. Everybody loved her.

When was the last time you saw Shannon?

In class on Friday.

Where were you on Saturday night when Shannon was murdered?

I was at a party across town. It was kind of boring, so I came home early.

As Ruthie dutifully answered their questions, she didn't think about the orange-handled scissors and how she'd washed the bloody blades in her bathroom sink that night, scrubbing at them with the same dark green scouring pad she used to clean the bathtub. She didn't think about hurriedly wiping Shannon's blood from the steering wheel of her mother's car with a dish rag. She didn't think about how she snuck into the house, tiptoeing past her father snoring on the couch, the end of the ten o'clock news droning in the background, and hurried to her room to strip out of the blood-encrusted jeans and top, stuffing them into a plastic bag she threw in the dumpster behind the Whataburger down the street the next day.

She only thought about how she got away with it.

86

AVA

Ava flipped her sunglasses to the top of her head as she exited her car and inserted her credit card into the gas pump, shoving the nozzle into her greedy tank. She wasn't usually one to ride on fumes, but she was beyond distracted. It shook her foundation to its singular core to realize that her daughter was a mean girl, cut from the same cloth as her own schoolmates from decades ago, the ones who'd tortured Laney into lashing out and taking a girl's eye.

She'd convinced herself she was well aware of Carly's problems and had thrown platitudes at them to solve them. In reality, she'd done precious little to address the issues plaguing her daughter.

The stark white reality was that Ava had to accept a modicum of responsibility for this version of Carly, a girl who bullied, a girl she could even believe to be capable of murder. She wasn't around enough, her job consuming all of her emotional bandwidth, leaving next to nothing for her daughter.

If Carly was going to change, Ava had to, too.

Of course, Carly wasn't all that was keeping Ava up at night. Even after compiling her notebook on Ruthie Stowers, combing through the mountain of paper and pictures, she was still only able to draw a wobbly, jagged line between Erica and Whitney's murder. She needed an undeniable link of steel before she went waltzing into the police department, pointing a finger at Erica Mitchell. Besides being laughed out of the building, if Jay Mitchell caught wind of what she was prepared to accuse his wife of, he'd come after her with the force and venom of a bull seeing red. It wasn't so much that Ava was afraid of Jay, though his deep pockets and mean streak were certainly reasons enough. It was that she was smart enough to know that if she came after one of his own, she'd better have all her ducks lined up with military precision. She couldn't stand on a leg of jello; she needed a pillar of stone firmly beneath her feet.

"Ava?"

She glanced up at the sound of her name, the source Marcy Samuels, the Dean's across-the-street neighbor having pulled up to the pump next to her. The passenger door spit out Britt, Marcy's surly pre-teen dressed in black leggings and a ripped black shirt, alternating stripes of hot pink running down the length of her jet-black bone-straight hair. She never looked up from her phone or said a word as she walked into the gas station.

"How are you?" Marcy asked Ava as the two women met in the front of the pump.

"Okay. Busy. You?"

"Same, same. How's Carly?"

Ava bristled internally at her daughter's name. "Um, she's fine." She cocked her head in the direction of the gas station. "Looks like you're about to enter my world."

Marcy rolled her eyes. "I might have been nicer to my mother had I known."

"Have you talked to Lauren at all?"

"Just a wave over the mailbox on occasion. They've been keeping a pretty low profile over there." She shook her head. "All these months. I still can't believe they haven't arrested anyone yet."

Ava ran her tongue across her bottom lip. "Were you home that day?"

"No, with the power and the Internet being out, I took the kids to Old Orchard and we went to the movies. I wish I'd either been home or that the storm hadn't knocked the cameras out, because they might have caught something, or maybe I would have seen something. Nobody's cameras were working that day."

"Oh, my God, Mom."

Ava jumped at the silent, sulky reappearance of Britt, a look of incredulity on her face.

"What?" Marcy asked.

Britt rolled her eyes. "We don't run our cameras through the home router. We do it through the cloud on our phones. It stays backed up for a year," she heaved, her own exasperation pouring from her. "Like, why don't you know that?"

"Wait." Ava turned to Britt, the realization hitting her like a blast of bricks. "You mean it's possible you might have footage from the day Whitney was murdered?"

The girl made a face and shrugged. "Probably."

Ava's heart leapt. "Can you show me?"

"Sure." The girl shrugged again as she started scrolling, swiping, and tapping across her screen. "Mom, I totally can't believe you didn't ask me."

"How was I supposed to know?" Marcy asked, looking just as stymied as Ava would have in her shoes.

"What day was it?" Britt asked, as she calmly bit into a protein bar she'd purchased in the gas station. The same brand Carly ate. The same brand Whitney ate.

Ava gave her the date and she waited, her eyes flipping back and forth between Britt and the phone. Britt nodded as she came to a stop and held the phone out toward Ava.

"This is everything from that day if you want to look at it," she said.

Ava had to refrain from snatching the phone from the girl's hand in eagerness, instead taking it calmly and tapping the screen. The camera was pointed almost directly at the front door of the Dean's house, allowing her to see all the comings and goings of the family on that fateful Saturday. The kind of mundane entering and exiting that happened with a busy family on the weekend: Lauren walking outside with Parker, loaded down with swim gear, to meet an SUV likely filled with his teammates in the early morning darkness. Lauren and Steve leaving two hours later, she dressed in Chanel, no doubt for a long day of showings, he wielding a briefcase, but clad in khakis and a polo, the corporate man's standard weekend uniform. Ava gasped silently at the sight of Whitney dashing out late that morning, climbing into her brand-new car and backing out of the driveway.

Whitney was the first to return, a Coffee City cup in her hand. Ava fast-forwarded past where there was no movement at the Dean house.

Then. Two o'clock. At the timestamp of two o'clock in the afternoon, Ava saw exactly what she needed to nail Erica Mitchell to the wall.

87

DETECTIVE MAGGIE DIEHL

Detective Maggie Diehl set her pen down while she stretched and cracked her cramped, stiff knuckles. She rolled her head around, the joints in her neck popping like firecrackers. Fortunately, it had been a quiet day, allowing her to catch up on reports and files and not think about the stalled Whitney Dean case.

Cold cases were part of the job. Witnesses disappeared, evidence was inconclusive—it went with the territory.

It didn't make it suck any less.

The Whitney Dean case was as big a puzzle as Maggie had run into in her fourteen-year-career with the PD. Not that you got much practice (read: none) with homicide in Lake Forest, crime in the quiet, tranquil suburb mostly confined to people attempting to pass bad checks at Starbucks, DUIs, a multitude of folks driving on suspended licenses. The occasional pot bust.

Murder was not in the Lake Forest wheelhouse.

Still, the circumstances of this girl's murder were baffling. Worse were the logjams. Her phone was missing, her carrier only keeping text message logs a period of three days (Maggie was still kicking herself for not having jumped on that right away). They kept calls for a year, but that didn't do any good because she hadn't talked on the phone to anyone that morning. That wasn't something teenage girls did a lot of these days. So different from her own adolescence.

And then there was the thunderstorm. The pounding, relentless thunderstorm that Saturday that knocked out surveillance cameras, Internet, and electricity for a good chunk of the day across many parts of Lake Forest. No video doorbell footage in Whitney's neighborhood. No red-light cameras. No physical evidence, no sexual assault, no witnesses, no discernible pattern matching any homicides committed in any of the surrounding suburbs—the city, even.

Everywhere she turned was a dead end. No pun intended.

The pressure to solve this case was like a vise around her hand. Pretty young girl from a wealthy, high-profile family in an affluent community. The constant community and media chatter wondering why there hadn't been an arrest. The girl's mother upping the ante with her explosive TV interview. The social media conspiracies.

The vise squeezed itself tighter every day.

Out of the gate, her money had been on Jordan Mitchell, the former best friend. She'd leapt for joy when they found the one working surveillance camera that Saturday capturing Jordan leaving the library that morning (seriously, she'd wanted to cry because finally, she had *something*). Except, the five different people backing up her rock-solid alibi that day had smashed that theory to pulp. It was a simple story, one as old as time. Her boyfriend had picked her up from the library that day, a blue-collar boy Mommy and Daddy wouldn't approve of and she didn't want them to know. Case closed.

Then there was the Ron Byrne debacle. She hadn't wanted to bring him in, but her Lieu had pressed the issue, desperate to show movement, progress being made toward closing this case.

For all the good it had done.

She jumped when her phone rang internally. "Yeah?"

"Ava Ewing is here to see you."

"Who?"

"Ava Ewing. Says it's important. About the Dean case."

She sighed wearily, not up to dealing with the hysterics of yet another outraged mother demanding to know what they were doing to catch Whitney Dean's killer. Screeching missives flooded into the department email on a daily basis, its Twitter feed and Facebook page littered with high-pitched calls for justice. Maggie had been bitched at more on this case than on any other in her law enforcement career.

"All right, tell her I'll be right up."

She rubbed her eyes, blinking them rapidly in a woeful effort to look alive, sharp. Aware. Not beaten down and exhausted.

Ava Ewing sat perched on the edge of one of the cloth chairs lined up beneath the window facing the parking lot. The blurry features of the woman's daughter, Carly, floated beneath the surface. She clutched a hefty white binder filled with paper, the accessory somewhat out of step with the sleek black pantsuit, red-soled stilettos, yellow purse, and the type of simple, chunky gold bracelet that graced the pages of the glossy, high-end magazines her sister read like they were crack. Maggie smiled dully as her eyes met Ava's and she extended her hand to the woman.

"Mrs. Ewing? Detective Diehl. How can I help you?"

"Is there somewhere we can talk privately?"

"Of course. We can go into one of the interrogation rooms."

Ava Ewing traveled dutifully behind her, the soles of those expensive shoes striking authoritatively against the gray concrete floor. She didn't look like the typical harried suburban housewife, but rather had the sheen of a no-nonsense corporate bigwig. A high-ranking executive at a global conglomerate with missions and objectives Maggie would never understand if she had ten MBAs.

She opened the door to one of the empty interrogation rooms and told her to have a seat. "So, what can I do for you today?" she repeated as she sat down across from Ava.

Ava laid the binder down on the table and plucked a piece of paper from the front inside pocket. She slid it across the table.

Maggie looked at the image—copied out of an ancient yearbook from the looks of it—of a young girl with glasses, crooked teeth, beak of a nose and shrugged, nonplussed. Irritated.

"What am I looking at?"

"The girl who killed Whitney Dean."

88

RUTHIE

Rumors about what happened to Shannon Kendall ripped through the halls of Willow Branch High School like an inferno. Shannon had been stabbed thirty times. It was a crazed ex-boyfriend. A disgruntled patient of her father's, someone obsessed with her mother and who wanted to get to her through her daughter. A satanic cult who'd sacrificed her for some crazy ritual. An escaped serial killer.

On and on and on, the loop of salacious gossip wrapped itself around the student body, who all now eyed each other with weary, suspicious contempt. The police had questioned some students and teachers multiple times, particularly all the members of the pom-pom squad and tennis team. Ruthie herself was questioned twice. The first time had been because of drama club in general. They didn't even ask her about the party on the other side of town she told them she'd gone to that night—who went, if anyone could verify she was even there. She'd held her breath, certain she would say something to trip herself up, that they could smell her fear and anxiety, could see the sweat pooling inside her shirt, would question the constant fiddling with the elastic hair tie in her hand. To her surprise and relief, they, like so many others in her lifetime, seemed utterly disinterested in her. Merely checking a box.

Despite the brief focus of attention on members of the drama club, the police's interest always seemed to meander back to Lyz, Sharla, and Abby, the bros Skip Lane, Mikey Gold, and Chad Warner, as though the answer to what happened to Shannon lay within the confines of that glitzy, tight-knit circle. Shannon spent more time with them than anyone. It very well could have been one of them. Not that anyone seriously thought someone in Shannon's circle did it, but then again, no one was completely ready to rule them out either, especially since the police hadn't made an arrest. They were all up for grabs.

That is until a viable, concrete suspect emerged for everyone to turn their ire onto.

One of the newspapers reported on the mysterious phone call Mrs. Kendall told the police she got about a top-secret drama club dinner that Saturday night, the one that caused Shannon to leave the house. Ruthie, along with the other drama club members, was called in for a second round of questioning. They'd pressed her a little harder that time, asking if she'd heard anything about the call, could she think of anyone who would make that call, if there were any dustups with Shannon and any other members of the club. She shook her head, affecting wide-eyed innocence that she didn't know anything about it, reiterating how beloved Shannon was.

While that news lit the match, what really ignited the inferno was the unsubstantiated rumor the drama club planned to stage *The Children's Hour* in the winter (Ms. Grazoli had actually decided on *Our Town*). The drama club being used to lure Shannon out of the house, coupled with the mere suggestion of a play with homosexual themes tarring the lily-white image of Willow Branch High, rankled the community and they turned their wrath onto Ms. Grazoli, fingering her as the culprit.

She was a made-for-TV suspect. A New Yorker—a divorcée to boot—with a penchant for chain smoking and head-to-toe black. The close-cropped bleached blond hair, and studded dog collars for bracelets made her a thorn among the roses of big hair, frosted eye shadow, and Jessica McClintock dresses. First were the whispers she was actually a lesbian who'd tried to convert Shannon, savagely murdering her when she couldn't have her way with her. Then it was decided she and a gang of lesbians had done it. Mingled with those whispers were the titterings that Ms. Grazoli actually had a boyfriend and they were swingers who'd kidnapped Shannon for perverted sex games, murdering her after savaging her. Each day brought new, more bizarre claims against Ms. Grazoli that she did little to defend herself against, likely believing the brouhaha would blow over. Her colleagues avoided her in the teacher's lounge, students went silent when she walked down the halls. Some hissed at her retreating back. The drama club, once a thriving after-school activity, became a fungus, as all but the most diehard of theater geeks dropped out in droves. Students who were able transferred out of her class into art or music. Those who couldn't get an official transfer stopped going altogether, taking an incomplete.

Eventually, there would be no more Ms. Grazoli, as the target on her back swelled. Her car was egged, rocks thrown through the windows of her house, followed by spray-painted epithets, and trash strewn across her lawn. The administration did little to stem the waves of vitriol, claiming their hands were tied. Finally, Ms. Grazoli quit and ran home to New York, eventually landing a job teaching acting classes at a theater school in Brooklyn.

Everyone thought that was the end of it.

Ruthie especially.

She had no idea the police were closer to her than she knew.

89

CARLY

"I can't believe how hot it is," Madison said as she took a sip of her iced latte.

"So hot," Lexi agreed as she bent the tip of her straw with her finger. "I think my skin is melting."

The three girls launched into mindless chatter about the end of the school year and the yearbooks scheduled to come out next week. The yearbook editors had interviewed the pom squad about Whitney and rumor had it there would be a full color spread taking up half the book. Carly doubted it would be that much, but she knew it would be a lot. Girls like Whitney Dean didn't fade into yearbook obscurity.

Jordan flashed across Carly's mind, as she often did, the creeping guilt she always squashed down prickling against her neck, trickling down her spine like ice water. None of the girls had ever talked about their role in Jordan's banishment from East Lake Forest. For bullying Jordan out of school. In fact, they'd patted themselves on the back for getting rid of her. Carly had gone along with the smug victory, but the truth that she couldn't quite admit to herself was that she was mortified at how she'd acted. Spreading gossip, bullying, lying. A mean girl. That's not who she was.

She just wanted to be liked.

Madison looked at her watch. "I've got to get home to babysit my brother. You guys want to meet up tomorrow morning to work on some pom routines?"

Carly and Lexi nodded as they gathered up their things and deposited the nearly empty plastic cups into the trash. They continued their small talk about what they would do when they got home, what books they were reading over the summer, what time they should get together tomorrow. The girls said their goodbyes and departed to their individual cars, Carly grateful for the light traffic as she made the short drive home. She was surprised to see her mom's car in the driveway, as she could have sworn she was supposed to be out of town today. Not that Carly could keep up with how often her mom was gone.

She didn't call out for her mom as she entered the house, as she was likely in her office on a conference call or a Zoom or whatever she did. Instead, she grabbed a sparkling water from the fridge and a protein bar from the pantry before heading upstairs.

Carly did a dead stop at the threshold of her room, blood pounding in her ears at the sight of the neatly folded sweatshirt, the spatters of blood still visible, the X-ACTO knife on top, the blood of that Saturday long since crusted over.

"Where were you that Saturday?"

Carly gasped at the sound of her mother's voice behind her before she whirled around to face her. "Mom, I—"

"I just want the truth."

Tears flooded her eyes. "Mom, please. Please don't make me."

"Carly, I promise, whatever it is, we'll figure it out together."

She shook her head. "It's too much, it's—I can't."

"Did you see Whitney that day?"

Carly shuddered. She had to come clean. She had to stop pushing her feelings of guilt and shame deep down inside her. She gulped and nodded. "Yeah. I saw Whitney that day."

"What happened?"

"She said some really horrible things to me."

Her mom was silent. Waiting.

"She said I was erased, over, that she was going to ruin me at school, get me kicked off pom." Tears pushed out of Carly's eyes. "I thought my life was over, so I ... I was going to kill myself."

Her mom's façade cracked as she shook her head slightly. "Oh, Carly."

"I bought an X-ACTO knife and I went down to the lake because I'd read that if you drown yourself after you do it, like in a bathtub, it goes faster." She shook her head. "Jimmy called me that night about something stupid and if he hadn't ... I had a bandage around my wrist for a whole week and nobody even noticed."

For several minutes, her mom didn't say anything. Just stood there, the quiver of her bottom lip the only movement on her face. The silence was deafening. Her mom hated her. She knew it. In that moment, Carly knew her mom would never love her the same.

"I've failed you, Carly," she finally said, her voice hitching as a single tear slid from one eye, followed by another and another. "I never knew how much until right now."

"Mom—"

"I'm going to take a leave of absence and we're going to therapy."

"You don't have—"

Her mom held up her hand. "No more traveling. No more late nights, no more early meetings. No more insanity."

"But, Mom, you love your job. Like, love."

"And I've let you think I love it more than you."

Without a word, her mom grabbed her, pulling her into a hug as they both cried.

90

DETECTIVE MAGGIE DIEHL

A dmittedly, when Ava Ewing marched into the station a month ago floating a ridiculous assertion that Erica Mitchell, wife of the richest man in town, had murdered Whitney Dean, Maggie's first inclination was to laugh. The childish fit of giggles had simmered in her cheeks, danced on her lips, quivered in her bones. She managed to keep her composure and the semblance of a professional demeanor throughout the woman's calm and careful explanation as to how she'd arrived at this crackpot theory. It was ludicrous. Beyond ludicrous. The work of a true crime enthusiast/wannabe amateur detective, which, God knows, anyone with an Internet connection thought they were these days, proffering an absurd notion about a grown woman murdering a teenager over some tweets.

Tweets.

Until Ava Ewing played her trump card.

Maggie couldn't believe what she was seeing, but it didn't matter. She was off to the races.

As she'd pored over the material Ava Ewing had provided, spreading everything across an interrogation room table—scribbled notes, timelines, photocopies, reams of computer printouts—it was more than enough to hold up a giant magnifying glass to the anonymous Erica Dane and the clean slate of her past. She was highly impressed with the depth and breadth of the information Ava Ewing had provided, rivaling any investigation Maggie had seen. She had called Houston PD, getting a Commander Murphy on the phone, the original investigator on the Shannon Kendall case, just days away from retirement, but more than happy to rhapsodize about Ruthie Stowers and arrange to get her the case file, which had proved to be fascinating reading.

The tangled origins of Erica Dane had proven the most laborious. She'd first stolen the birth certificate—a time-honored scam of ex-, current, and future cons—of an Emily Kason, who'd died in childbirth in 1954 Louisiana. From there, she obtained a state ID card from Florida, where she stole yet another birth certificate—three-year-old Melinda Stokes, who'd died in a fiery car crash with her family in 1965. Another ID card, this time from Massachusetts under the name Violet Ford. She was even issued a social security number. Finally, in a Chicago courtroom, some three months after she'd walked out of Huntsville Prison, Violet Ford legally changed her name to Erica Dane. Four different stolen identities. Maggie couldn't fathom how in the pre-Internet age, Ruthie Stowers had managed to successfully navigate this quagmire of identity theft without raising one hackle of suspicion. Of course, she'd been in prison for ten years, so someone on the inside had probably left a hearty trail of breadcrumbs for her.

As if Ava Ewing's trump card wasn't enough, a minor detail, mentioned in passing by Jordan, woke Maggie up in the middle of the night, yet something else to kick herself over for not picking up on it at the time: Erica Mitchell was in possession of her daughter's phone the Saturday of the murder. And unlike Whitney Dean's carrier, the Mitchell's carrier archived text messages for over a year.

And what a story those text messages told.

If that jackpot wasn't enough to get Maggie humming, Erica Mitchell's financials revealed she had traded in her less than a year-old car the Monday after the murder. The dealer had already sold it and they had to impound it from the new owner. Unfortunately, the car had been thoroughly detailed, leaving behind almost no forensic evidence.

Almost.

Her partner, Lucy Prentiss, stood over the glass partition of her cubicle.

"Room's ready."

Maggie nodded. It was time to make the phone call.

91

AVA

Ava stood in front of the colorful boxes of sparkling water, her vision blurring at the choices of cherry, cranberry, grapefruit, passion fruit, and even some combinations her pea brain could not conceive of. Kyle had been on a sparkling water kick the last few months, sucking through a twelve pack a day. She couldn't seem to buy it fast enough.

They'd started family therapy and the revelations at just how low an ebb Carly's self-esteem hovered around was sobering. Coupled with how much harder it was to detox from her job than Ava had anticipated and the wait for something to happen since her march into the police station armed with her evidence, left Ava more drained at the end of each day than a month of red-eye flights.

She was sure that after she laid out her case to the detective that it would be a matter of hours—days at the most—before Erica was walked out of her house in handcuffs. She'd ignored the look of skepticism smeared across the detective's face as she'd plowed through her evidence with aplomb.

That is, until Ava had dropped her bomb. It, as her grandmother would have said, made the cheese a little more binding.

And yet still, she waited. She kept her eyes pinned to the ceiling each night as she waited. She still had copies of everything and had contemplated anonymously sending just enough of what she had to the media and let them put the pressure on the police. Something would need to move the needle and if Detective Diehl wouldn't, Ava's finger was twitching to do the honors.

"Well, hello, Ava."

She jumped at the shrill bell of Erica's voice, blinking rapidly as she forced herself to turn around to face the woman bearing down on her with a grocery cart.

"Erica. Hi." Ava croaked.

"It certainly has been a while, hasn't it?" she asked, leaning over to give her a hug, having no idea how startled Ava was by the affectionate move. "I was starting to think you'd moved away and didn't tell me."

Ava chuckled uncomfortably. "I'm so sorry I disappeared. We've just had a lot going on at home lately."

"We never did get the second round of drinks we talked about." A shadow passed across Erica's face. "Of course, we've had our hands full."

"Carly told me about Jordan transferring schools."

Erica scoffed. "We sent her to a boarding school in Connecticut. Thanks to Lauren and her nonsense, that stupid interview. The principal actually had the nerve to say Jordan was 'distracting.' Can you believe that? A distraction."

Ava flinched, her knowledge of the role her daughter played in helping to eject Jordan from school pinching her like a rubber band.

And that was just the stuff she knew about.

"I'm sorry to hear that."

"Well, I will tell you, Jay and I are not going to stand for it. No, we're just going to get through the rest of the school year, then we have the whole summer to get that woman out of there. I've always thought she was a terrible principal anyway. Then, Jordan will go back, she'll get back on pom ... everything will go back to the way it was."

Ava's mouth went dry at Erica's glee over crushing Principal Bain in her palm. And even now, she remained obsessed with Jordan ruling East Lake Forest.

Would she come for Carly next?

She couldn't stand it. She had to get away from this woman.

"Well, Erica—"

Erica's phone trilled from her purse and she held up her index finger to indicate Ava should give her a minute. She frowned at the caller ID.

"This is strange."

"Who is it?" Ava asked.

"The police department. What on Earth could they want?"

She answered the phone and Ava searched her face, her own heart pounding with hope.

Dear God, let this be the day.

"Are you sure this can't wait? I'm at the grocery store." Erica rolled her eyes in Ava's direction and shook her head. "All right fine, I'll finish up here and head over," Erica said as she ended the call and threw her phone in her purse. "Well, that certainly is odd."

Ava bit her bottom lip so hard, she was afraid she'd draw blood. "Did they say what they wanted?"

"All she said was they had some new information and they're re-interviewing everyone. I'm sure you'll be getting a call soon. Carly, too, since she was friendly with Whitney."

"Yes, probably," Ava murmured, barely able to hear herself over the pounding of her heart.

"Well, let me finish up here so I can get this over with," Erica said. "I'll text you next week about that drink."

"Okay," she said feebly, as she watched Erica float down the aisle. She wasn't sure how long she stood in front of all those boxes of sparkling water, her breath ragged, her heart thrashing against her chest like a thunderstorm, before she abandoned her half-full cart and collapsed in her car.

92

ERICA

"Thanks for coming in, Mrs. Mitchell."

"Of course. You said you were re-interviewing everyone. Is there a new lead?"

"We're just following up on a few things. Shouldn't take long."

Erica flipped her hair over her shoulder. "All right."

"How long have you lived in Lake Forest, Mrs. Mitchell?"

"About eighteen years. We moved here before our daughter, Jordan, was born."

"Where were you before that?"

"In the city. Ravenswood. Well, I lived in Ravenswood. Jay lived downtown."

"And you worked for an advertising agency, is that right?"

"I did, yes—I'm—I'm sorry, but what does that have to do with anything?"

"Oh, we're just building profiles on everyone Whitney was in contact with. Routine stuff."

"Well, I wasn't really in contact with Whitney, but go on."

"So, you did graphic design at this ad agency, right?"

"Yes."

"You go to school for that?"

"Yes."

"Where did you go? For school, I mean."

"It was an art academy."

"Mrs. Mitchell, what's your maiden name?"

"Dane."

"Erica Dane." She seemed to mull this over. "That's a very pretty name. Very glamourous."

"Thank you."

"So, Mrs. Mitchell, where are you from originally? Your hometown?"

"Bay Village. It's a small little town outside of Cleveland."

"You know that's funny, because I thought I detected a little bit of a southern accent."

"I don't know why that would be."

"Huh. And how old were you when you moved to Chicago?"

"Twenty-three." Erica crossed her legs. "Again, detective, I really don't understand—"

"Mrs. Mitchell, I want to show you something." She flicked open the bulging manila folder and extracted a piece of paper. She placed it on the table and pushed it over to her. "Do you know who that is?"

Erica glanced at it, her heart plunging like a roller coaster.

Instead, she shook her head. "Should I?"

"Her name is Ruth Ann Stowers. Some people call her Ruthie."

"Okay…?"

"I want to read you something," Diehl said, thumbing through the stack of papers inside the manila envelope, extracting a yellowing sheaf of pages.

Even from a distance, she recognized those typewritten pages, the official FBI seal affixed to the top. Erica blinked, hoping the tears wavering behind her eyes didn't come spilling out. She swallowed.

"Detective—"

"It's fascinating reading, Mrs. Mitchell. Really. I was up all night. Couldn't put it down." She flipped through the pages and cleared her throat. "Ah, okay, here it is. Here's the part I was looking for."

Erica stared straight ahead, her lips pressed into a hard, thin line, bracing for the words she'd worked a lifetime to bury, but would never forget.

93

RUTHIE

The summer of 1986 was an unremarkable one for Ruthie.

Her neighbor across the street, Mrs. Falk, hired Ruthie to babysit her eight-year-old daughter three afternoons a week while she did volunteer work for the Junior League and on the occasional Saturday night when she and Mr. Falk went to dinner or a party. It was an easy gig, as the girl was a bookworm who spent all her time curled up on the hot pink beanbag in her room, her nose barely peeking over the pages of Judy Blume, Roald Dahl, or Beverly Cleary, even while Ruthie fixed her a peanut butter and jelly sandwich and cut up carrot sticks for lunch every day. She kept her head bent over her book at the kitchen table as she shoveled the food into her mouth, expertly navigating her way back to her room when she was finished without even so much as a glance up. It was the same thing when Ruthie took her to the library. The little girl would beeline for the kids' section, her arms instantly bulging with the maximum stack of books her library card allowed. Or when they went to the community pool, her charge huddled up on a deck chair, a floppy hat obscuring her face, book glued to her hand while the other kids played Marco Polo or cannon-balled into the clear, blue, overly-chlorinated water.

Mostly, Ruthie reclined on the beautiful white leather sofa in Mrs.

Falk's plush living room and gorged on *All My Children* and *General Hospital* while indulging in ice-cold cans of Coke, Jiffy Pop popcorn, one of Mrs. Falk's Lean Cuisines, and Little Debbie Snack Cakes, the kind of food her mother would never buy. The lemony floral scent of Mrs. Falk's house smelled almost as nice as Shannon's. Almost. During *One Life to Live*, Ruthie cleaned the kitchen and vacuumed and dusted the living room, finishing just as the insistent sirens of *General Hospital's* theme song roared across the screen, going home shortly after Mrs. Falk fluttered through the front door at three-thirty.

Her off days were mostly spent hanging around her house, which she typically had to herself, as both her sisters had jobs at the mall and boyfriends to keep them busy, while her brother and his buddy built a thriving landscaping and maintenance business that took them all over town from sunup to sundown. She'd wake up early, lingering in bed until she heard everyone leave, then take a quick shower before eating two bowls of Frosted Mini-Wheats while she watched reruns of *Dallas* followed by *Sale of the Century*. At eleven-thirty, she'd walk four blocks to the Whataburger or Del Taco for a to-go order so she could be home in time for her soaps, which stretched into afternoon court shows and sitcom reruns until peace was shattered by the one-by-one returns of the Stowers family by early evening. Shannon's mother had come back to do the news two months after the Shannon died. The few times Ruthie had watched her, before it had become too painful, too shameful, she marveled at how cool and calm Mrs. Kendall was while she reported the day's news.

You'd never know.

Sometimes, Ruthie and her friend, Dawn, went to the movies. They saw *Top Gun* (she preferred Iceman to Maverick), *Back to School*, *American Anthem*, *One Crazy Summer*, and even snuck into *Ruthless People* one busy Friday night. On occasion, she and Dawn hung out at the community pool or took the bus to Memorial City Mall, trying on clothes at Foley's, splitting oversized sugar cookies smeared with thick, hot pink frosting, and reading magazines at the Walgreens.

Sometimes, Dawn's mom loaned her the car and they ventured out to the much nicer Town & Country Mall, wandering around Nieman

Marcus, afraid to even brush up against the racks bulging with expensive clothes. She invited Dawn to the small family dinner they had at home for Ruthie's seventeenth birthday that June. Every few weeks, Ruthie slept over at Dawn's house. The girls would slather their faces with ninety-nine-cent mud masks from Eckerd's and paint their toenails in garish reds, purples, or pinks, then giggle hysterically as they took the quizzes in *Cosmopolitan* and *Seventeen* ('Are You Easily Manipulated?' 'How Tactful Are You?' 'What's Your Lovemaking IQ?'). They filled out multiple Columbia House Music Club cards, quickly losing track of the names they made up in pursuit of those twelve tapes for a penny (as the tapes kept coming, they ultimately realized they'd filled out no less than six separate cards each).

Occasionally, they talked about Shannon. Ruthie never squirmed outwardly. At least she didn't think she did. She would merely agree that it was sad and scary all at once and share tidbits from their brief time in drama club or from her one and only visit to Shannon's house. She took some of her babysitting money and bought Madonna's new album, *True Blue*, which she'd dedicated to her husband. Ruthie listened to the title track over and over, wondering sometimes if Shannon would have called Power 104 to dedicate it to Mikey Gold.

It was a quiet, sluggish summer.

Until the last Wednesday in August, right before the start of her senior year, when the kitchen phone rang right as the delicate swell of *All My Children's* theme song rolled across her TV screen. It was the police sergeant she'd talked to twice before, calling to ask if she would come down to the station because he had some more questions for her.

Her heart had plummeted, all the moisture in her mouth evaporating like water into a dry sponge. It had been months since that night with Shannon, months since the police had questioned her, months since the story had even been in the news.

Why were they calling her now?

She'd agreed, hoping they couldn't hear the quiver in her voice, that she'd sounded nonchalant and carefree about the whole thing, happy to provide any additional information she could.

Ruthie didn't tell her parents the police wanted to talk to her again.

And she was too scared to ask any of her friends or anyone from the drama club if they'd also gotten a call.

Instead, Ruthie told herself that it would all be okay.

They arranged for her to come in two days later, a day when she didn't have to babysit for Mrs. Falk. She didn't want to ask her mother to borrow the car, not wanting to raise suspicion, so instead, she took the bus to the police station, her bowels knotting and unknotting themselves the whole time. Her footsteps seemed to thud against the concrete sidewalk as she struggled to open the heavy glass door and timidly walked up to the officer at the front desk, telling her that she had an appointment with Sergeant Murphy. She knew her hand was limp and sweaty inside his strong, dry one when he came out to collect her and usher her into an interrogation room. She tried not to be intimidated by his barrel chest or towering height, the military-grade blond buzzcut, or the gleaming black gun holstered on his hip. The quarter-sized grease stain on his tie, bouncing against the dome of his stomach, made him a little less intimidating, but not much. She tried not to glance at the manila folder he tossed onto the battered green-gray table, afraid she'd see her name on it.

There were pleasantries at first—an offered paper cone of water, which she declined, banal commentaries about humid Houston summers, an anecdote about his daughter's swimming league, queries about how she was spending her days. All while that manila folder sat carelessly on the table in front of him, silent, yet damning somehow. Ruthie answered him carefully, cautiously, reminding herself to speak above a whisper, to smile. To not be nervous.

Finally, Sergeant Murphy's smile receded into a deeply etched frown as he pulled that manila folder even closer to him.

"So, Ruthie, I called you to come down today because we've got some new information about the case with Shannon that I wanted to share with you."

She didn't trust herself to speak in the moment. She knew she needed to, but couldn't make herself squeak out anything but a faint, "Okay."

He flipped open the folder and looked down at the stapled sheets of paper inside. "In trying to figure out what happened to Shannon, we talked to a lot of people who knew her—friends, classmates—we talked to you twice."

"I know."

"And we just couldn't come up with anyone who would want to hurt Shannon."

"Everyone loved Shannon."

He smiled. "We heard that over and over. Everyone we talked to all said how wonderful she was. That she was a beautiful girl. Sweet. Talented. A real star." Sergeant Murphy sighed, his face slumping back into a disturbed frown. "The other problem we had was, it just didn't seem like a random attack by a stranger, either."

Ruthie gulped, wishing she'd taken the water. "Okay."

"Tell you the truth, we were kind of at our wits end about what to do, about how we could solve this case."

"Okay."

"And sometimes, when that happens, we call for outside help, you know, other law enforcement agencies and officers and agents who have different types of expertise, access to different types of tools than we have here."

Ruthie licked her lips, afraid to breathe, afraid to speak. She took a few shallow breaths through her nose and nodded again. "Okay." Why did she keep saying that?

Sergeant Murphy cleared his throat and Ruthie jumped. She shifted in her chair in a lame attempt to cover, hoping he hadn't noticed, though she knew he had.

"Like I said," he continued, as though she hadn't made a move, "we were having a real tough time trying to figure out what happened to Shannon, so we reached out to the FBI and they came up with something for us."

Ruthie could barely hear him over the blood pounding in her ears. Something about the FBI.

"Okay," she said. Again.

"What they did is, they came up with a psychological profile of Shannon's killer. And what they do with that is, they look at the crime scene and examine similar crimes and figure out things like personality traits, family background, stuff that will tell us who the killer is." He cocked his head. "Would you like to hear what they came up with?"

She screwed each nail of her finger into her palm, those pinches of pain being the only thing she could feel aside from the gallop of her heart, the thrum of blood thrashing around in the canals of her ears. The insides of her mouth gooey and dry all at once.

"Okay," Ruthie said quietly. *Damn it.*

He cleared his throat again and picked up that stapled sheaf of papers with one hand, his eyes scanning that front page until he licked his thumb and forefinger before catching the bottom corner of the top page between the pads and flipping it over, the rustle of the pages screeching against Ruthie's ears. He nodded and whispered to himself, as though he'd found what he was looking for.

Sergeant Murphy cleared his throat. "The perpetrator is likely known to the victim," he read, tapping the sides of the pages with his index finger. "Perpetrator and victim are likely peers, members of the same class at school. While the victim is popular and outgoing, the perpetrator has few friends and is shy and introverted, considered quiet and agreeable by their peers. The perpetrator envies the victim's social status, accomplishments, and natural talents. The perpetrator is likely the youngest member of a large family and often feels inconsequential, inferior, and inadequate. Perpetrator sometimes vacillates between feelings of wanting everyone to notice and like them and a desire to fade into the background where no one will see them. The perpetrator is a female between the ages of fourteen and seventeen. Perpetrator is impulsive, prone to unprovoked outbursts, yet typically displays an outwardly calm manner that is in keeping with their pacifist nature. In fact, perpetrator likely harbors dissociative tendencies, able to easily compartmentalize or disconnect from events around them, particularly the more chaotic those events are. They will distance themselves emotionally from the act of violence to the point of believing they did not commit the crime, and may even display genuine surprise when confronted with the facts of their involvement. Perpetrator's attack on the victim was unplanned, messy, and impulsive, a burst of rage. Therefore, no staging of the crime scene and/or body was present."

Sergeant Murphy put the pages down on the table and looked up at Ruthie. "What do you think?"

Ruthie swallowed over the hard lumps in her chest, afraid, so afraid to open her mouth, to say a word.

"It could be a lot of girls." She finally said as she looked down at her lap. "Like half the junior class."

"You're absolutely right, Ruthie. It could be a lot of girls."

"Who do you think it is?" she whispered, her gaze still locked downward.

"Ruthie … I don't think. I know. It's you."

94

ERICA

"I don't understand what your bedtime reading has to do with me," she said as the detective finished reading selected portions of the psychological profile on Ruthie Stowers, words she would never forget.

"Oh, I'm not quite finished yet, Mrs. Mitchell. Just a few more things." She shuffled through the stacks again, pulling out a pile of papers bound by a big red rubber band. "Now this ... oh, yes, here we are. 'Ruthie Stowers Released After Serving Ten Years.'" Diehl looked up at Erica. "Sound familiar?"

"No."

"Okay. I'll keep reading. Ruthie Stowers, the quiet introvert who longed to be accepted by her peers, one peer in particular, was released yesterday after serving ten years for the vicious murder of her class-mate, Shannon Kendall. She served her sentence, the maximum allowed under state law, in the Texas Youth Commission, after fatally stabbing sixteen-year-old Shannon Kendall in 1986. Stowers was denied parole in 1991, with one parole board member citing the inmate as possessing a trigger temper she has trouble controlling as the reason for the rejection. She said, quote, I strongly believe there is every possibility she—Stowers—if provoked, could very easily do this again.

I believe she remains a danger to society. I pray I'm wrong, end quote."

The detective looked up at Erica. She wondered if the woman could see the crack in her façade, if she could see mousy little Ruthie Stowers cowering inside her.

"Should I go on, Mrs. Mitchell?"

"You're right, Detective Diehl. A very interesting read."

"Do you know Emily Kason?"

Despite herself, Erica flinched. "No."

"What about Melinda Stokes?"

"Should I?"

"Violet Ford?"

"Detective, I have no idea who any of these women are."

"No?"

"No. No idea."

Diehl nodded as though she were contemplating this. "Hmm. Well, how about this?"

She laid down two pieces of paper: her most recent DMV photo and her instantly recognizable junior year class photo, her uncomfortable smile poorly masking all of the anxiety and inadequacies twisted up inside of her.

Ruthie and Erica next to each other.

One and the same.

She looked down at the images, the tears no longer having any place to hide. It had been so long since she'd looked at herself at sixteen. She'd tried to forget that ugly, awkward little girl with the greasy hair, crooked teeth, and dumpling bottom. She'd banished ugly little Ruthie Stowers to the trash heap, choosing to be reborn as the glamorous Erica Dane with the slimmed down frame, new teeth, contact lenses, and sleek, shiny hair that billowed in the wind.

The detective tossed another stack of papers onto the table. "Your daughter told me you had her phone because she was on punishment. We got the logs of your daughter's text messages from the carrier and she was texting with Miss Dean the day of the murder. Except it wasn't her. It was you."

Erica fell silent, afraid to speak now.

"You lured Miss Dean out of the house by pretending to be your daughter," the detective said.

She continued her stony silence.

Diehl picked up her tablet. "I have some video doorbell footage from that day that I'd like you to take a look at," she said as she swiped and tapped at the screen before coming to stand over Erica, placing the tablet in front of her.

Erica's eyes flicked down at the sight of her cream-colored SUV pulling into the Dean's driveway, sheets of rain beating against the roof, her license plate in clear view.

Moments later, Whitney runs out of the house in her yellow rain slicker then does a dead stop. Hesitating. Talking to the driver. Looking back toward her house. Hesitating again. Finally relenting and getting in the car.

"We ran the plates on that car. Registered to Stoneright Global, your husband's company. We can also see, as this car pulls off, a clear shot of you behind the wheel. We ran your financials. You bought a new car the following Monday."

Her stoicism imploded, the déjà vu of being confronted with conclusive evidence too much to keep her upright, apathetic to the house of cards crumbling around her in swift and stunning fashion.

It was over. It was all over.

"You killed Whitney Dean," the detective said, her voice flat. "Just like you killed Shannon Kendall."

She couldn't say anything, the tears having their way with her. She sobbed brokenly, but quietly, into the palm of one hand, ashamed and afraid to look the detective in the eye, to admit that yes, just like that lone parole board member had warned all those years ago, she had indeed snapped again.

Instead, her eyes squeezed shut, she nodded, giving in, giving up.

"Okay," Diehl said. "Tell me about that Saturday."

SATURDAY

95

WHITNEY

Whitney exited out of her photo gallery and headed outside, the rain pounding against the dark green overhang of Coffee City. She held onto her latte with one hand, maneuvering the hood of her yellow slicker over her head with the other as she prepared to dash out to her car parked a few doors down.

"Whitney?"

She gasped then rolled her eyes when she turned to see a pathetic Carly standing next to the front door.

"What, are you following me now?" Whitney asked as she fiddled in her pocket for her key fob.

"I was coming in for a latte and saw your car," Carly said. "I wanted to wait for you."

"I thought because you hadn't been in school all week you'd transferred or something."

"I—I was sick."

"I seriously don't have time for this today," Whitney scoffed as she pulled the fob out of her pocket. "Find someone else to bother."

Carly grabbed her arm. "Wait, please, I just—can't we be friends again? Please? Whatever I can do to make it up to you about the party, about not having your back with Jordan, I'll do it. I got so scared and I froze and I didn't know what to do, but I promise, nothing like that will ever happen again."

Whitney burst out laughing. "Seriously. Get a hobby that's not me."

"Whitney, what do I have to do? Tell me, please, what can I do to make this up to you?"

"You really don't get it, do you?" she hissed. "We're done. You're done. You should stay home another week because there won't be anything for you to come back to at East Lake Forest. You're gonna be off pom, you're gonna have to sit in the library for lunch. You'll be like Jordan—worse. No one will talk to you, no one will want anything to do with you. You. Are. Erased."

Tears crawled down Carly's cheeks, which she frantically tried to wipe away, though they fell faster than she could keep up. "Whitney, please—"

Whitney had nothing left to say, so instead of responding, she darted over to her car, being careful to avoid even looking in Carly's direction, though from the corner of her eye, she could see her still standing there, looking pathetic. What had Whitney even seen in her? She'd seemed cool, she supposed. Worthy of Whitney's attention.

How wrong she was.

She hated to admit that the confrontation with Carly had rattled her and she was already a little nervous about driving in the rain, so she'd have to be extra careful. Fortunately, this was a really good car, with every bell and whistle her mother could stick on it. It would probably even protect her against zombies.

Sheets of rain continued sliding across her windshield as she made the short drive home, Carly receding from her mind with each swish of the wipers. Hopefully she'd scared Carly into leaving her alone. Whitney knew she was a lot of things, but a gossip wasn't one of them. Not like that bigmouth Dionne Cruise. Even though she told Carly she'd ruin her by spreading all kinds of things about her around school, the truth was, Whitney knew silence was deadlier. All she had to do was ice Carly out and be super mysterious about it. The threat would be enough. Let everyone else run their mouths trying to figure out what happened. She'd just smile and say nothing.

The car's dash read twelve-thirty. She had more pressing things to deal with today than the annoying gnat that was Carly Ewing. Mrs. Trent was going to drop Parker at home by two, then she was supposed to feed him something and make sure he took a bath or a shower, then take him to his sleepover a few blocks away. She and Peyton had talked about going to the mall, but with all this rain and running around, the only thing she was in the mood for now was to chill. Maybe she'd text Peyton when she got home and see if she wanted to come over instead, then she wouldn't have to rush home for Parker.

Whitney turned left onto her street then her driveway. It would be nice to have the house to herself. Play her music as loud as she wanted, or just sit and read for an hour without her mom or Parker bugging her.

She took a huge slurp of her coffee as she headed upstairs to grab her book and text Peyton about coming over later, when her phone dinged with a new text message.

The sight of Jordan's face stopped her in her tracks.

Hey, Whit.

96

ERICA

Rain smacked against the bay windows and a crack of thunder shook the foundation of the house. Erica winced as a jagged ribbon of lightening exploded across the purplish-gray sky. The storm had knocked out the Internet, effectively scrubbing all hope of getting any actual work done. At first, she'd thought she'd leave the house to run errands, but had changed her mind, deciding instead to spend the morning organizing her files and making to-do lists. A much more efficient use of her time.

Hunger clawed at her stomach. Erica rubbed her eyes, stretching as she stood and made her way upstairs to grab a magazine from her nightstand to read while she munched on a salad. Jordan's phone beeped from the nightstand drawer with a low battery warning. She pulled it out, turning it over in her hand. At the rate Jordan was going, she was never getting this thing back. She'd have to talk to her again about apologizing to Whitney. This nonsense had gone on long enough.

She sighed, about to slip the phone back into the drawer when it dawned on her.

The phone. Teenage girls documented every waking minute of their lives on their phones. Whatever was going on with Jordan and Whitney was probably on the phone.

Erica carried the phone downstairs, grabbing her charger from her office before heading into the kitchen to fix her lunch. She plugged in the charger and prepared her salad of romaine lettuce, kale, sunburst tomatoes, cucumbers, black olives, and a handful each of mung bean sprouts and edamame, tossing in a little olive oil and lemon juice. She leaned against the kitchen counter, nibbling on a cucumber slice as she picked up Jordan's phone, jabbing the screen with the four-digit code to unlock it, the icons for the social media apps bulging with little red dots announcing new tweets, chats, and Instagram posts.

She speared a tomato with her fork and mindlessly scrolled through the text messages, surprised there weren't that many. Various texts from her and Jay. Benign exchanges with classmates about homework assignments. Some texts with her cousins. Nothing between her and Whitney, the girl's phone number and whatever texts had existed between them in the past scrubbed clean.

Her daughter's Instagram feed didn't reveal much either. Jordan didn't take many selfies, instead posting funny, irreverent pictures of cats, weird street signs, stupid videos. Nothing of real interest.

Erica's eyes flicked over the Twitter icon, which indicated Jordan had close to a thousand new tweets. She jabbed the screen.

Her jaw dropped.

@itsJordanBaby Trash

@itsJordanBaby Skank

@itsJordanBaby THOT

@itsJordanBaby you're such trash

@itsJordanBaby how do you sleep at night? Oh right, you sleep with everyonz man.

HoBag

Trust @itsJordanBaby she will stab you in the back. Just ask @WhitLuv

Erica's heart stopped as she continued to scroll through the mounds of tweets, each one more revolting than the last. Tears stung her eyes and her fingers shook as she continued to poke the screen, no longer even seeing the tweets, the horrible, awful things these animals said about her daughter.

All she saw was rage.

The phone slid from her hand, smacking against the floor, and she dug the heels of her hands into her eyes, her breath ripping through her in short, stuttering bursts. Whitney was behind this. Whitney was the reason Jordan had quit the pom squad, why Jordan was so moody and unhappy.

Because she was upset. Because she was sad. Because she was humiliated.

And it was all Whitney Dean's fault.

Erica kicked the phone as she paced the kitchen, her mind racing with what to do, how to fix this.

Except all she could see was Whitney's smiling face. All that phoniness, dripping insincerity. She'd always been so thrilled that her daughter—*her* daughter—was best friends with the most popular girl in school. All the girls clamored to gain entrée into that exclusive circle and Jordan held the most important spot. Right by Whitney's side.

And this was how Whitney repaid all those years of loyalty. By smearing her daughter's good name, humiliating her in front of the whole school.

Jordan was right. No one knew just how awful Whitney Dean was.

A slick trail of snot ran out of Erica's nose and she bent down to retrieve the phone.

She had to fix this.

Jordan may not have had Whitney's number anymore, but Erica did. She made it a point to have contact numbers for all of her children's friends, in case, God forbid, something should happen and she needed to get in touch with someone. Her mother always had the numbers for all of their friends. Why shouldn't she?

Erica clicked her tongue against her teeth, staring at the seven little letters of Whitney's name. This girl had to learn you couldn't say whatever you wanted about people. You couldn't play with people's lives like this.

Actions had consequences.

Wrongs had to be righted.

Texting from her phone and saying she wanted to talk wouldn't do anything. And forget about involving Lauren with this. It was clear the woman had no control over her daughter. Whitney would be all fake smiles and pseudo-sincere apologies that she would renege on.

No, Erica had to deal with this problem directly. Firmly. Put the fear of God into that girl. Erica sniffed back the mucous, taking several short breaths to try to calm herself. Focus. She picked up Jordan's phone, jabbing Whitney's number into the text function.

Hey, Whit.

97

WHITNEY

W hitney's heart pounded as she read and reread the two little words for what felt like a hundred times. Surges of anger rumbled through her as she turned over in her mind why Jordan would even dare to text her now.

The suspense of wondering was too much. She fired off a text.

What the fuck do you want.

Whitney looked at the black screen, daring it to answer, half hoping Jordan responded, because now, she was itching to get into it with her.

The phone pinged with a new message.

J: Everything's just gone totally nuclear. I don't know how everything got out of hand.

"What the hell?" Whitney grumbled as another message came in.

J: Maybe we can meet up and talk.

New waves of fury rose inside of her. Jordan was up to something. She was never this cool, this blasé.

W: For what?

Whitney threw the phone down and took a slurp of her latte, her patience with whatever bullshit Jordan was trying to pull wearing thin. She snatched the phone back up, those pictures she'd been afraid to delete now truly on the chopping block, fear and uncertainty no longer saving them from destruction.

J: I wanted to apologize ... about the party.

The words hit her like a sledgehammer. She definitely wasn't expecting that. Jordan never apologized for anything. She was always right, practically daring you to challenge her. Even when you proved her wrong, she'd just roll her eyes and huff and scoff and pretend like the whole thing had never even happened.

W: Seriously.

J: Yeah. I totally screwed up.

She sank down onto her couch. This didn't even sound like Jordan. At all. Her mom was always saying people can change and that sometimes you had to give them a chance.

Maybe Jordan was finally changing her ways.

W: You so did.

J: So? Can we talk? Like face-to-face? Just for a little while?

Whitney sighed and chewed on her bottom lip, needing once again to slowly absorb the words in front of her. If she was being honest, she really did miss her longtime bestie. Carly was cool, but kind of a kiss ass. She'd never had as much fun with anyone. And if Jordan wanted to apologize, she could come over here and do it. No reason for Whitney to put herself out.

W: Fine. You can come over for a minute. No one's home.

J: Let's meet at Coffee City instead.

W: I was just there and it's packed. Plus, I'm not really in the mood to drive right now.

J: I can swing by and pick you up and we can go? Or we could go to Ferentino's instead. Grab a quick slice? That probably won't be that crowded. Like ten minutes?

Whitney heaved a sigh. Something was telling her to stick with her original plan and just stay home and chill. But the curiosity got the best of her. Of course she'd meet Jordan.

W: Yeah, okay, fine. Ten minutes.

J: Okay, cool. I have my mom's car. I'll see you in a few.

Whitney's head plummeted to the back of the sofa. She and Jordan.

Talking. Making up. Being friends again. It felt weird, like an out-of-body experience. Maybe she'd even apologize for the whole sugar daddy thing. At the time, she thought it was funny, but it was kind of stupid in hindsight. It would have cost her pom if Coach K found out, since they had a zero-tolerance policy on cyberbullying. To be honest, she never expected Jordan would be that pissed about it. Maybe a little aggravated, but not nuclear. Definitely not end a friendship over it.

She texted Peyton to let her know something had come up, but that she'd fill her in later. Until she knew what was going on with her and Jordan, she'd keep her mouth shut. Then again, she and Jordan might be making it Instagram official later with a selfie of the two of them. Together again.

Whitney peeked out the front window and saw Jordan's mom's car in the driveway. She wound a yellow ponytail holder around her hair, then gathered up her keys, phone, and wristlet before throwing on her yellow rain slicker and running into the thunderstorm.

98

ERICA

The door of the Dean house swung open and Whitney emerged wearing a yellow slicker, her black ponytail flying behind her in a dark blur as she dashed out toward the car. She frowned when she opened the passenger door and saw Erica instead of the expected Jordan behind the wheel. Erica smiled.

"Hi, Whitney."

"H—Hi, Mrs. Mitchell." Whitney's voice shook. "What—what are you doing here?"

"Oh, Jordan's at home. I didn't want her driving in this bad rain, so I said I'd come pick you up and take you back to the house."

"But we're supposed to go to Ferentino's."

"Oh, I know, I know." Erica smiled again. "I told Jordan I'd clear out, give you girls some privacy. You'll have the house to yourselves. That would be better than going to a pizza place, anyway. Right?"

Whitney played with one of the snaps of her yellow rain slicker. "Yeah, but—"

"It's okay, really. Jordan's waiting at the house for you and I said I'd bring you over. Hop in."

Whitney looked back at the house and Erica bit her lip as she waited. "Okay," she said somewhat hesitantly before she slid inside.

"So," Erica said as she backed out of the driveway. "How have you been?"

Whitney looked down at her lap. "Fine."

"We haven't seen much of you this school year. I was trying to remember how long it's been. Summer, I suppose."

Whitney shifted in her seat, the wet slicker squeaking against the tan leather seats. "Yeah, I guess."

"So how has junior year been so far?"

"Fine."

"Jordan hasn't had a very good school year at all," she said as she looked over at Whitney, before turning left and pressing the accelerator slightly. "But I guess you already knew that."

"This isn't the way to your house." Whitney sat up straighter. "Where are we going?"

"Oh, I forgot, I have to run a quick errand first. Then we'll go."

"Um." Whitney scrunched up her face like she'd smelled something bad. "Where?"

"You know, you and Jordan have been friends for such a long time. I can remember how you used to share your dolls with each other, the tea parties you used to have together." She laughed. "That time you girls got into my makeup and smeared lipstick all over each other's faces. How you used to play in your mother's high heels. You remember all of that?"

"I guess so."

"Jordan really, really loved you. Like a sister. Better than her own sister. Didn't you love Jordan?"

"Yeah, sure."

"Yeah, sure." Erica nodded and pursed her lips. "That doesn't sound very convincing, Whitney."

"Mrs. Mitchell, where are we going?"

"And I mean, I know you're both popular, you know everybody likes both of you—a lot—but you, well, I guess you're the most popular girl in school, aren't you?"

"Jordan's popular."

"Oh, I know, I know. But you're the *most* popular, right? I mean, if you say to everyone in school, 'Don't like Jordan anymore,' everyone would listen to you, right? Everyone would stop talking to Jordan, wouldn't they?"

Whitney squirmed in her seat, her fingers dancing nervously over the snaps on her slicker. "I guess."

"And if you said that Jordan was a whore and trash, everyone would believe you, right? If Whitney *Dean* says you're a skank, well, then you're a skank, right? None of the other girls would want to be your friend. Because Whitney Dean said so."

"It wasn't like that, Mrs. Mitchell—"

"Jordan told me you were horrible and I didn't believe her. I thought she was overreacting. But she was right. You're the disgusting one. You're the trash."

"Mrs. Mitchell, I think you should probably take me home. I don't feel good."

"You don't feel *well*, Whitney. It's, 'I don't feel well.'" Erica scoffed. "You may be the most popular girl in school, but you have atrocious grammar. Perhaps you should pay closer attention in English class."

"Mrs. Mitchell, take me back home. Now."

"Jordan is … far superior to you. You know that, don't you? That Jordan is not your equal, she's not inferior to you in any way, but your superior."

"Yeah, Jordan's awesome." Whitney folded her arms across her chest. "Jordan's the best."

"That's right, she is. Way, way better than you." Erica sniffed. "Now. At school on Monday, you're going to let Jordan back onto the pom squad—"

"I don't have any control over—"

"And then you're going to get back on Twitter and apologize for all those disgusting things you said about my daughter."

"Mrs. Mitchell, I didn't have anything to do with that—"

"Oh, shut up. Of course you did." She rolled her shoulders back in indignation. "What do you think, I'm stupid or something?"

"I mean, you might be crazy—"

Erica stomped on the brake, both of them jerking forward, her arm automatically shooting out across Whitney's body to keep her flying out through the windshield, like the metal bars on a roller-coaster. They squealed to a stop, the wheels slipping a little against the rain-bloated street. Thunder shook the car. She grabbed Whitney's arm.

"What did you say to me?"

Whitney struggled against her grip as she narrowed her eyes. "Let go of me."

"Answer me!"

"I said you might be crazy," she spat. "I think you might be straight up cracked in the head." Erica reared up, her ears unbelieving. Was this little snot giving her attitude?

"Excuse me?"

"Making my mom invite Jordan to my party, driving around in the rain, babbling on about pom and tweets, always bothering Jordan about her clothes and her hair. Jordan used to say all the time, 'My mom is nuts.' I never believed it until now, but she's totally right."

Strands of lightening burst across the black clouds rolling over the horizon as Erica gasped. "You nasty little bitch."

"My mom says the only reason anybody cares about you is because of your husband, that nobody likes you, that nobody can stand you—"

Red rage descended across Erica's vision as she blanched, the dagger of Whitney's words knocking her backward. Her eyes slid shut as she took several deep, pronounced inhales.

"You owe me an apology, you entitled piece of garbage," she breathed, fury sluicing through her. "Apologize to me now."

"No way," Whitney scoffed. "I'm not apologizing to you or your ho bag daughter."

Thunder roared as a fresh round of relentless rain pummeled the car. Without thinking, Erica lunged across the armrest and slapped the girl's face. Tears pricked Whitney's eyes as she cradled her cheek, momentarily stunned into awed silence.

"I know all about girls like you, *Whitney*." Erica shot a finger into the girl's face, smugly satisfied when she flinched. "I grew up with girls like you. Pretty, popular princesses. Straight-up nasty, mean bitches. Just like you."

"I can't wait to tell my dad what you just did to me," Whitney half-hissed, half-sobbed. "He's going to destroy you."

Erica laughed. "Whitney. You really think your father is any kind of match for me? You really, *really* think I can't stomp you and your father out like roaches?"

"I'm going to tell everyone about you and how crazy you are," Whitney said, her voice shaking as she seemed to regain her footing. "Everyone is going to know about you."

Shannon flashed across Erica's mind. She shook her head to wipe away the memory.

"Shut up," Erica said, grabbing for Whitney again and catching her wrist. She dug her nails into her skin, which forced a pained yelp from the girl's lips as she writhed against her grasp. "Shut your fucking mouth," she snarled.

Whitney pulled away, tugging Erica with her. She smashed against the door as she attempted once again to yank her arm from the clamp of Erica's hand.

"Let go of me, you freak," she screamed through clenched teeth.

Time turned sideways in that moment, Shannon's ghost, her vicious words rising from the past, swirling around her like a foul wind.

I had no idea you were a fucking freak.

"Take that back," Erica whispered.

"Forget it, freak," Whitney panted. "Get your fucking hands off me."

Before Erica knew it, the scissors that she'd grabbed at the last minute as she left the house were in her hand, hastily yanked out of her purse and pointed at Whitney, the handle blue this time, not orange like the ones with Shannon. The girl gasped, her eyes wide as she pawed at the lock on the car door, finally understanding, it seemed, that actions did indeed have consequences.

"Oh my God, help, somebody, help me—"

"I said take it back. Take back what you said about me," Erica shrieked.

The lock gave way and the door flew open. Whitney tumbled out of the car, dropping to the wet ground. She darted away, whipping her head back once. Erica bolted after her, the scissors warm and heavy in her hand. She pumped her arms, rainwater splashing against her ankles and the backs of her legs as her feet pounded into the shallow puddles. Whitney was screaming, the deafening downpour swallowing her cries as she went slipping and sliding against the slick carpet of grass. She fell, a crater of mud grabbing her foot, slamming her into the spongy ground. Her eyes popped wide against her face as Erica drew closer and she scrambled to her feet, scurrying toward a patch of nearby black-eyed Susans.

Erica drew heavy, frantic breaths as she closed the gap between them, close enough now to see the dots of rainwater sliding down the back of Whitney's yellow slicker. Whitney screeched as Erica grabbed her ponytail and yanked her backward. She pulled Whitney in a bear hug and tackled her to the ground, both of them grunting as they landed in the cold, wet grass. Whitney held her arms over her face, screaming.

"Please, please don't hurt me, please, I'm sorry for everything, please. I don't want to die."

Erica plunged the scissors into Whitney's stomach.

Her chest.

Her stomach.

Her arm.

Her neck.

Her neck.

Her chest.

Whitney's screams soon gurgled in her throat like a bubbling water fountain and her face went slack, her head drooping to one side. Warm, salty blood splashed against Erica's face. Lightning splintered above her, followed by an angry growl of thunder.

Blood continued to pump from the girl's wounds as she whimpered like a distressed puppy. Erica raised the scissors over her head and rammed them into Whitney's chest one final time.

She continued to straddle her, staring as Whitney Dean drew her last breath.

For several moments, it was just the two of them, the rain battering the two very different bodies. One heaving with frenetic breath, her hand clutching the scissors, suspended in mid-air. The other still and eternally quiet, rain falling into the dead, dark eyes. Both bodies drenched in blood.

Another snap of thunder broke the spell and spurred Erica to work, searching Whitney's pockets and extracting her phone, before plunging her hands into a puddle, swishing them around until the blood swirled into the murky water. The yellow of Whitney's ponytail holder against that wet black hair winked at Erica. She extended a shaky hand toward it then jerked it off in one smooth motion. She grabbed the scissors and jumped up, running blindly to her car as the rain pelted her face like hot rocks. She threw the scissors on the passenger side floor and stomped on the accelerator.

Blood pounded in Erica's ears as she drove away, mindlessly dropping the ponytail holder into the inside pocket of her purse. Her mind raced as it frantically unpacked all the tasks she would need to accomplish. Though she thankfully had on all black today, she'd still toss her clothes in the trash bin. She'd find one of those self-car washes so she could quickly wipe down the inside of the car, then trade it in for a new SUV on Monday. Dump the scissors and both phones in the lake, but not before destroying the SIM cards. She'd buy Jordan a new one and would fall all over herself, apologetic about having ruined the phone—how, she didn't know just yet, but it didn't matter. Teenage girls always wanted a new phone.

As always, she had a plan.

She looked at the clock on the dash. Two-forty-five. Hours before anyone would be home.

Her own phone jangled with Jay's ringtone and Erica gasped, vacillating between picking up and letting it go to voicemail. Her eyes flailed uselessly around the car in search of an answer.

Pick up the fucking phone. Act like everything's fine. Smile.

"Hello, darling," she said brightly, forcing the words out of her mouth, hoping they sounded normal and cheerful.

"Babe, I want to do a dinner party tonight with Lance and Gabby and the Deans. About seven—"

Terror shot through her like a rocket and her chest clenched. "Did —did you say the Deans, darling?"

"Look, I could give a shit about what happened at that party. Lance needs an architect, Steve Dean is a good one, and Lance and Steve may need to remember down the line that I put the two of them together. That was personal. This is business."

Erica blinked rapidly, the full weight of what was about to crash down around her starting its descent. A whole evening of playing nice with Lauren Dean after she stabbed her daughter to death.

But by God, Whitney had it coming.

And for Jay, she'd play the charming, gracious hostess. After all, it was pretend. And if there was anything Erica had gotten good at over the years, it was pretending.

She licked her lips. "Of course, darling. Of course. Did you say around seven?"

"Yeah. Seven. And get that caterer, you know the one that does those puff things that I like."

She wanted to pound the steering wheel. Scream at him to do it himself for a change, to jump through the hoops just one fucking time. Once, just once.

Except Jay, like most men, relied on a wife, girlfriend, mother, sister, secretary, daughter to keep the trains running on time. As long as there was a dutiful and devoted woman standing beneath the ledge with a net, there was never a need to worry about the consequences of a fall.

And like the good little wifey she'd trained herself to be, instead of telling him to do it his damn self, she smiled. Always the gracious, perky, carefree wife who could do it all with the biggest, brightest of smiles, the most buoyant wave of her hand. "Consider it done, darling."

"You're the best, babe."

They cooed I love yous before ending the call. Erica came to a stoplight, grateful for the few moments to be still and think. She could do this. She would do it. She had hours and hours to make it all work flawlessly and beautifully. The light turned green and Erica called the caterers, jabbering on cheerfully about the menu for tonight, knowing she'd have to pay triple the rush fee to pull it off. They'd do whatever she wanted, though. Of course they would. Saying no to Jay Mitchell would have sounded the death knell for them.

Erica looked at the clock again as she commanded her phone to find her a self-car wash. By the time she got done with everything, she'd just make it home ahead of the caterers' arrival at the house around five-thirty.

She had hours and hours.

Hours and hours to forget all about Whitney Dean.

99

RUTHIE

Ruthie Stowers was in jail for exactly two thousand, nine hundred and twenty days.

She was sent to Giddings State School, about two hours from home, to serve her sentence. Her lawyer had told her what to expect at the juvenile correctional facility, but it was still like being tossed flailing and screaming into the deep end of an ice-cold pool. There was the indignity of being strip searched and the scalding two-minute shower to 'delouse' her. The wrinkled old Ziploc bag with her hygiene kit: a small blue plastic comb, soft bristle toothbrush, toothpaste, bar of soap, and a small bottle of watery shampoo that smelled faintly of tar. A razor was out of the question and in due course, her legs resembled those of her brother and father. The pair of gray sweats, socks, brown rubber shower shoes she was to wear at all times, a package of plain white underwear, and one beige bra.

The days were long, every minute regimented, every minute documented. Giddings was filled with murderers, drug dealers, burglars, carjackers, and gang members. It was drilled into them every day that they were in serious trouble and any hope of getting out meant they'd better get with the program.

The 'program' meant they were to wake at the crack of dawn and quickly make the worn, scratchy sheets fit with precision over the flat, dirty pad they said was a mattress. She struggled at first with the morning runs and drills, the two-mile obstacle course. Meals were served three times a day, and you had to eat, whether you were hungry or not, whether it was filled with bugs and dirt and fingernails or not. She still had to attend school every day, though unlike some of the other girls, Ruthie didn't labor with that aspect of her day—she'd always been an above-average student, excelling particularly in English and history. She even helped tutor some of the girls. Her afternoons were first spent on laundry duty, then the kitchen. Any free minute of time, which were precious few, she was confined to her cell. Sometimes at night, she was allowed to watch movies in the common area with some of the other girls, usually a corny PG movie or Disney romp that she mostly tuned out.

The only visitors she was allowed were her parents. Her mother came dutifully, every week, writing her reams of letters between visits and filling her commissary with whatever meager dollars she could. In the beginning, her father used to come with her mother every week, but over time, his visits trickled down to once a month, to eventually, a handful of times a year. The visits always left Ruthie drained and miserable. She couldn't look them in the eye, so ashamed of how she'd let them down. Her mother always acted like everything was normal, chattering on about how she'd run into Mrs. Falk at the grocery store and how big her daughter was getting, or Patricia's swanky new job or how she'd heard Dawn was studying abroad in Italy. Ruthie could see the strain in her mother's face, the pained realization of how much her daughter was missing out on. Unlike her mother, her father didn't try to fill the silence with nonstop babble, but rather stiff questions about how she was getting on or the occasional rambling story about the baseball game or boxing match he'd watched on TV the night before.

She never wrote a single letter to a friend. The few she received— opened by the guards—were thrown into the trash by her. Ruthie couldn't bear to read soft pink stationery filled with stories about dances and classes and parties and eventually colleges and boyfriends.

At night was when she cried. Sometimes the tears were silent and unrelenting, other times a flash flood—brief and violent.

Ruthie despised the mandated counseling every Tuesday (individual) and Thursday (group). Her counselor told her she had anger issues, an inability to control her temper, a penchant for lashing out when she didn't get what she wanted. Ruthie didn't think that was true. Everyone had a temper. Everyone got mad. She wasn't an out-of-control barbarian—not like these other girls, the girls who pulled screws out of the walls or made shivs out of combs and toothbrushes. Some of these girls had never been to school, didn't even know how to brush their hair, didn't understand the mechanics of soap and a washcloth, or how to use a fork.

No. She wasn't like these girls.

Ruthie had one bad moment. One. She wouldn't have another.

The only positive she found during those long, miserable days was a talent for graphic design, nurtured in opportunities to leave kitchen and laundry duty behind in exchange for doing jobs for a local printer, though she wondered what the actual clients would think if they knew a convicted felon was designing their birthday invitations and real estate brochures.

As her twenty-first birthday loomed, Ruthie was convinced she'd be sent to serve the rest of her sentence in Huntsville, which terrified her. She'd earned her high school diploma and took as many graphic design courses as she could through the local community college. While she mostly kept her nose clean, there'd been a few skirmishes with other girls that landed her in solitary confinement, another time when she had trashed the meager contents of her cell in frustration, all of which she knew would work against her. Dr. and Mrs. Kendall would oppose any kind of early release. She hadn't even wanted to go to the hearing, but her attorney said she had to and her fear of Huntsville came true. She was transferred to the adult facility where she served out the rest of her sentence and was released at the age of twenty-seven.

Her first night home, it was clear she couldn't go back to being Ruthie Stowers, resident of Houston, Texas, youngest daughter of

Edgar and Grace Stowers. Her mother's fluttering, her father's awkward disregard, the fear of running into Dr. and Mrs. Kendall, Lyz or Sharla—a random stranger—all ready to sear her flesh all over again with 'M' for murderer. She might not have been behind bars anymore, but the longer she stayed there, she'd never be free.

She needed a fresh start.

Which meant she could be anyone she wanted to be.

Ruthie hadn't told her mother her plan. It would be easier that way in the long run. Her father would probably be relieved. She'd called her public defender and asked how she could legally change her name. She'd taken the meager wages she'd saved during her incarceration to become Erica Dane, using the rest to buy a train ticket to Chicago after closing her eyes and letting her finger fall on a map.

On a Tuesday morning in September, after responding to her mother that lasagna for dinner that night sounded great, she waited until her parents left for work, before sliding the suitcase she'd packed the night before from underneath the bed. She left the goodbye letter she'd written propped up against the napkin holder on the kitchen table, before she ducked around the side of the house with the shovel from the garage to dig up the plastic baggie holding the lip gloss and gold Tiffany heart charm bracelet she'd buried in the backyard a few days after taking it from Shannon's bloody wrist. She'd put the soil-covered bag in the pocket of her jeans, picked up her suitcase, and said goodbye to Ruthie Stowers forever.

The pieces fell into place so easily once she got to Chicago. After a week at a fleabag hotel which would have terrified Ruthie, but didn't bother the ten-years incarcerated Erica, she found work as a designer for a small printing company and rented a clean and quiet studio on the North side. She scrimped for a new nose. She scrimped for a shiny set of veneers. She scrimped for a cut and color every eight weeks. The stubborn weight she'd carried most of her life had dropped off her frame in prison and stayed off thanks to obsessive exercise and pecking at bird-like meals, the glorious price of all that scrimping.

And every morning, Erica would look in the mirror and smile at the woman gazing back at her, so thrilled to finally be clutching thin and glamorous with both hands.

The first time someone asked where she was from, without even thinking, she said Ohio. She made the rest up as she went along, inventing the tragedy of dead parents in a house fire, simultaneously weaving fantastical tales about a charmed, wealthy adolescence as the most popular girl in town, a homecoming beauty with the world at her feet. Sometimes, she actually believed she'd floated through this wonderful, enchanted childhood. That was the trick of lying. In order to convince everyone else, you had to take it as the gospel for yourself.

Mostly, she kept to herself. Work, quiet dinners with a handful of close friends, and a giant city to explore.

Over the years, there were a few awkward romances with well-meaning simpletons who worried about their cholesterol and read the *New York Times* on Sundays because they thought it made them sound smart to say they read the *New York Times* on Sundays. Eventually, she gave up on the hope of marriage and a family. And then, when she was thirty (she told him she was twenty-five and to her shock, he believed her), the blindingly wealthy Jay Mitchell dropped from the sky and swept her off her feet to a mansion in Lake Forest and the lavish life she'd always lied about having, outrivaling anything in her *Dynasty-Dallas-Falcon-Crest* fantasies. Money was no object, scrimping a long-forgotten memory, security and comfort her now daily companions. It empowered her, this deep pool of prosperity, emboldened her to do whatever she wanted with no consequences. After all, who would dare cross the wife of a global billionaire?

Five years later, she gave birth to a beautiful baby girl they named Jordan Grace. Eight years later, to her utter shock, came another beautiful baby girl, Kennedy Marie. Jay's business thrived, her business thrived. She had friends, a happy marriage to a man she adored, a beautiful family.

Everything.

And now, it was all gone.

100

AVA

Ava groaned as she ran a finger across the tiny bump in her neck bulging with an ingrown hair, a supplement to the whisker she discovered under her chin yesterday, the hard bristle too short to pluck, yet long enough to make a sharp scratching noise against her fingernail. A one-string banjo.

The clock on her dash told her that despite her best efforts, she would come blowing through the door ten minutes late due to Friday night traffic, as every street in Lake Forest seemed to heave with vehicles. She continued circling for a spot, determined not to valet. About thirty seconds before resigning herself to the inevitability, the white lights of a minivan backing out of a space near the entrance elicited a hallelujah.

As Ava parked, she ran the pad of her thumb against the chin hair, her fingers itching to dig into it with her tweezers, imagining the release when she plucked that sucker. She gathered up her purse, keys, and phone, ready to sprint for Authentico. For the first time in two months, she'd actually read the selection for tonight's book club, and was eager to participate in the discussion.

That she'd found time to do anything the past few months was a minor miracle. She'd been accosted by media, strangers, and friends, both casual and close about how she'd "cracked" the Whitney Dean case. There were offers of book deals, an infinite stream of interview requests, and offers for reality shows of all things. She was inclined to turn it all down flat, but also didn't want to be rushed either way.

Erica's sentencing had been standing room only and Ava had garnered just as much attention as the defendant. No one was surprised by Erica's life sentence, both due to the brutality of Whitney's murder and Erica's status as a repeat offender. She was awaiting transfer to the penitentiary soon and Ava suspected once that happened, that would be the last anyone heard from her. Dr. Kendall had sobbed brokenly as he thanked her for exposing Erica, while Lyz and Sharla seemed determined to make her their new best friend. Lauren had showed up at her house one night and the two women cried for hours, Lauren incredulous that Erica had brought her a fucking casserole.

The trill of her phone in her hand pushed another growl from her lips. She frowned at the caller ID, a blocked number. Probably another reporter. Ava's finger hovered over the ignore button, but something—she would never know what—compelled her to take the call.

She sighed and hit 'answer.'

"Hello?"

"You have a call from an inmate at Lake County Adult Corrections Facility," an automated voice spit into her ear.

Ava stopped in the middle of the street, her heart thumping, terror scurrying beneath her skin like ants.

Erica.

A series of beeps sounded before Erica's voice crackled through the receiver.

"Ava?"

She gulped and nodded. "Erica. How—how are you?"

Erica laughed and heat flamed across Ava's face.

"How do you think I'm doing?"

"Erica, this really isn't a good time."

"Just let me say what I need to say."

A car honked for Ava to move. She jogged to the sidewalk in front of the restaurant, the phone sweaty in her palm, her head swimming.

"Okay," she said. "I'm listening."

"You never liked me, did you?"

Ava blanched. Of all the things she pictured Erica saying to her, their first conversation since that day in the grocery store, asking whether she liked her wasn't one of them. She ran her tongue across her bottom lip. "I always thought you were sweet," she said cautiously.

"But you didn't like me," Erica pressed. "Not the way you liked Lauren, or even that nutjob Regina."

"I don't think it's fair to compare friendships—"

"We're not friends," Erica said. "We never were."

"Erica—"

"You know, in all the time I've known you, you never asked me out for a drink or lunch. Not once. I would always have to ask you. And even then, it was always, 'Sure, let me check my schedule,' or 'I'll get back to you.' But you never did. Ever. Now, if Jay called, you came running. But if it was me? You couldn't be bothered. And the one time, the *one* time, you actually extended an invitation to me, you were setting me up."

"To be fair, Erica, my travel schedule has always been—"

Erica half-laughed, half-groaned. "Oh, my God, enough with the bullshit. Even now, you can't admit that you just didn't like me. For the love of everything, have an honest moment."

Ava clicked her tongue, looking down at the sidewalk, the irony of Erica lecturing her on honesty tickling a rumble of manic laughter in her gut. She was right, though. It was time to drop the pretense. Niceties and the mask of social graces no longer mattered.

"Okay, Erica, you're right. You're absolutely right. I didn't like you."

"Ha! Finally, some honesty."

"Erica, like I said, this really isn't a good time—"

"Why?"

"Why what?"

"Why didn't you like me? What did I ever do to you?"

"Sometimes, you just don't like people."

"But there was something specific about me, wasn't there?"

She sighed. She'd already peeled back the Band-Aid. It was time to rip it off. "To be honest, I always thought you tried too hard." She smiled wryly and shook her head. "Like you didn't know how to be yourself."

Erica scoffed then fell silent. Ava looked at her watch. She was creeping up on twenty minutes late.

"Listen, Erica, I have to go—"

"It was Melody, wasn't it? That day outside of Coffee City? She recognized me, didn't she, told you all about me."

She sighed. Why Erica was pressing about this now baffled her, as she knew that's exactly what had happened. Perhaps the itch of hearing the words from Ava's mouth was all-consuming.

"That's what started it, yes," she said.

"So, you decided to hunt me down. Out me." She snorted. "Ruin my life."

"Erica … you ruined your life."

"Why couldn't you just … leave it all alone?"

Ava ran her tongue along her bottom lip, her eyes floating to the sky. "Because you murdered a girl. Again. Just like they said you would."

"One more minute," the electronic voice said, cutting into the call.

"God, you're just like her."

"Who?" Ava asked.

"So dismissive, so superior. All you pretty girls, all you cool girls, you're all the same."

Ava straightened up, rankled. "What's that supposed to mean?"

"Thirty seconds."

"Whitney, Shannon … you. Ugly little freaks like me … we'll never be good enough for you."

The line went dead. Ava looked at the phone, the sting of tears buzzing behind her eyes. A laughing couple swept past her heading toward The Gallery, while a gaggle of twentysomething girls spotted each other and ran into each other's arms, screaming with laughter. Just another Friday night of happy oblivious people living their lives. She dug into her purse in search of a Kleenex, blowing her nose and dabbing her eyes with the last two in the pack. Erica had all but called her a mean girl, a label she never would have ascribed to herself. Not in a million years.

But it was true. She had shunned Erica, because as the woman said, she just didn't like her. Teased her with promises of drinks and dinner dates, uttered vows she never intended to keep. Wasn't that how the wheels of polite society turned? Feigning interest in people you didn't care for, indulging in vague small talk, engaging in pleasantries and platitudes all to give the shallow appearance of being a 'nice person,' a 'good girl.'

Another laughing couple shuffled past her, chattering about getting tickets for Ravinia, while a harried mother and father shuttled their brood of three toward the front door for a night of family fun. Life going on. Never stopping. Always moving.

And so would she.

Ava blew her nose one last time before squaring her shoulders and heading to the door, ready for her book club discussion. A round of drinks. Appetizers. Another round of drinks. Pouncing on Kyle when she got home. Curling around him in the morning. Kissing her daughter's forehead at the breakfast table.

Her life would go on.

It was time to forget Erica Mitchell ever existed.

Because she never really did.

101

ERICA AND RUTHIE

The long, agitated buzz announcing bedtime sounded, followed by the *clank, clank, clank* of fluorescent lights going black, one by one, like a row of falling dominos. Her cell was dark, except for the slices of bright white floodlight from the yard glaring through the small rectangle of window lined with metal bars.

She'd be transferred sometime within the next forty-five days to Logan Correctional Center in Lincoln, wherever the hell that was, for life.

Life.

Erica rubbed the hard knot of fear and sadness that had blown up inside her like a balloon the day of her arrest, settling in like a phantom appendage, like one of those parasitic twins that grew inside the other, the host forced to lug around bones, teeth, and limbs they had no use for.

And indeed, no one had any use for her. Jordan, unsurprisingly, had refused to see her, spurning all of Erica's overtures to at least hear her side. Letters came back unopened, phone calls sent to voicemail. Not one so-called friend had come to visit or offer thoughts and prayers.

However, the biggest, most stunning betrayal had come from Jay, her warrior, her protector, the man who had always unequivocally had her back. He'd gone apoplectic with rage upon her arrest, his fury exploding in a barrage of blistering attacks upon learning he'd been married to a convicted murderer for all these years, and one who, even worse, had done it again, in almost the same circumstances. And just like that, he'd vanquished her, was granted an uncontested divorce inside of two months, and vowed to keep the girls from her. Her decades as a loving and loyal wife discounted like a puff of smoke on the wind.

Her mind drifted to seeing that woman, Kate, in court a few days ago at her sentencing and the flummoxed, disapproving pinch of her face at realizing Erica was the woman at Middlefork Preserve that day dissuading her from going to the police about Whitney's last words.

But the most astonishing face of all to see was Dr. Kendall, an apparition conjured up from the thin air of the past. Her heart had stopped as he marched toward the lectern to condemn her. She hadn't even heard what he said, she was so stunned by the déjà vu of the moment. Equally stunning had been the glimpse she'd gotten of Sharla and Lyz sitting next to what Erica assumed was Dr. Kendall's new wife, an Amazonian blond clearly decades younger, a stoic look on her face verging on boredom. Nothing at all like Julia Kendall. She would have known Sharla and Lyz anywhere. Lyz looked exactly as she would have expected, the shiny varnish of money and power radiating from her like the sun. It was the bitterest of ironies to her that were it not for this situation, she and Lyz would have run in the same social circles. No, scratch that—Lyz would have clawed and groveled for the chance to run in Erica Mitchell's social circle. Sharla's hippy dippy graying ringlets, pale, makeup-free face, filmy, swirling caftan, and fanny pack were a slap of cold water. No one ever would have guessed this was the future awaiting one of the pretty, prissy princesses who used to glide through the halls of Willow Branch High like she was the High Priestess of Cool.

She lay there in the darkness, her breath slow and steady, as she stared up at the concrete ceiling, listening to the sounds beyond the heavy metal door of her cell. In prison, lights out meant nothing, for the prisoners trapped within these cages could whine and howl until the fluorescents repeated their *clank, clank, clank* at six a.m., demanding they rise and shine. If that didn't do it, the guards barreling down the hallway, barking more pronounced commands shortly thereafter got you moving fast enough.

It was hours and hours until then. And roughly four hours until the guards came to do the first of their two nightly cell rounds to check on the prisoners.

Which meant she had time.

Erica sat up slowly, still holding her stomach, her ear cocked toward the door, almost as if she expected a guard to burst into her cell in some surprise attack to toss the room. It hadn't yet happened to her in the short time she'd been here.

That didn't mean it wouldn't happen tonight of all nights.

Which meant she needed to get on with it.

She bent down to the concrete, cold to her leg beneath the thread-bare cotton of her jumpsuit. She ran her hands underneath the metal grate of the bed, a stray wire poking her index finger, drawing a tiny pinprick of blood. She stopped to suck her finger, before resuming her search.

Finally, her hand closed around the object of her desire and she wrestled it from its prison between the mattress and grate, the metal scraping against her fingers, almost ripping two of them open. She stood, wiping the dust and cobwebs on the front of her pants, before edging across the room toward the door. She stood on tiptoe to peer out of the little block window. It was too small to see much past what was immediately in front of the door, but she did it anyway. Habit, she supposed. You always wanted to look out of a window to see what was coming.

She went back to the bed and sat on the edge of the mattress, which protested at the slight dip of weight with an agonizing squeal. She picked up the item she'd liberated from beneath the bed, turning it over in her hands several times, shoving the hard point into her palm.

It was time.

102

CARLY

C arly tucked a chunk of hair behind her ear as she dug into her purse for her keys, wondering why she was always dropping the fob into the black hole of her bag instead of shoving it in the pocket of her jeans to make it easier to find. Just as her hand made contact with the hard plastic, from the corner of her eye, she saw someone juggling a box from Coffee City as they hurried across the lot. The sharp inhale of breath was involuntary.

Jordan.

Their eyes met and the two girls stared at each other, like animals in the wild, sizing each other up, the duel imminent.

Carly was the first to look away, casting her eyes downward as she unlocked her car before glancing up again, her gaze tentative. Jordan stood still, her head cocked to the side, also unable, it seemed, to tear her eyes away. Finally, she jerked upward and began to walk toward her.

"Hey," Carly said uncertainly as Jordan came closer.

"Hi."

She bit her bottom lip. "How are you?"

Jordan shrugged. "Okay."

"What are you doing here?"

"I live here."

Carly's cheeks flamed red. "I know, I just meant—"

"I'm home for a couple of days. I'm going back to Connecticut tomorrow."

"Do you like it? Connecticut, I mean. The school—"

"It's fine."

Carly looked down again. "Listen, I—"

"So, look—"

The girls stopped and stared at each other, seemingly unsure of who should be the first to give ground. Carly cleared her throat.

"Go ahead," she said.

Jordan sighed, twisting her lips around a little. "Look, you and I, we're never going to be friends."

"I know that," Carly said, her voice both shakier and harsher than she intended. She sniffed. "Of course we're not."

"What I'm trying to say is, I'm not holding anything against you, even though you started all of this by opening your big fat mouth to Dionne like a moron. I should. And I could, I really could, but I'm not. I mean, you didn't make my mom ..." Jordan looked away.

Shame flooded through Carly. It wasn't lost on her that it was her actions that sent Mrs. Mitchell after Whitney. That it could have easily been her body in a rainy field of black-eyed Susans, eight stab wounds littering her body.

She nodded. "I know and I'm—I'm sorry. I never—I never should have said anything to Dionne about anything going on with you and Whitney. I was just trying to ..." She shook her head. "I don't know. I just ... with Whitney I was, I mean, I know it sounds stupid, but I was afraid if you came to the party, you and Whitney would make up and then she wouldn't be my friend anymore. That you'd take my place. Or your place, I guess. You know what I mean."

Jordan clicked her tongue against the back of her teeth. "You're right. That is the dumbest fucking thing I think I've heard in my life."

Carly looked down at her shoes. "I know. Anyway, I'm sorry. For everything."

"If it hadn't been that, it would have been something else. Probably."

"You think so?"

Jordan scoffed. "I mean, it's always something, isn't it?"

"I guess you're right."

"Okay, here's the thing. We're not friends. We'll never be friends. Ever. But we don't have to run away from each other if we see each other. Wave to each other from across the room, say hey or whatever. We don't have to act all weird around each other." She cleared her throat. "Like, let's just be cool and leave it at that."

"I'm okay with that," Carly said.

"Good." Jordan nodded. "Fine."

"So ... what are you up to this summer?"

"Spending most of it with my grandparents in Naperville. I mean my dad's parents. My mom's sister ... my aunt, Patricia, has invited me to Texas for a few weeks this summer so I can meet that side of my family. I think I'll go."

"Are you coming back to school next year?"

A short bitter laugh escaped Jordan's lips. "Oh, God no. I'm never coming back to East Lake Forest." She looked around. "This is probably the last time I'll ever be here."

"Do you miss it?"

"Not even a little bit. I'm glad to be gone." She stared at Carly for a few moments. "You doing pom again next year?"

"I don't know. A lot happened this year. I have to think about it."

"Well, do you."

In spite of herself, Carly giggled. "Yeah. I will."

The silence settled around them as the girls stood awkwardly staring at each other for a few moments, Carly wondering how long this being cool thing was supposed to last.

"Well, I gotta bounce. My dad's making lasagna tonight." She held up the box in her hand. "I picked up dessert."

"Oh. Cool."

"It's totally weird. Turns out he really likes cooking. He's been doing it a lot since my mom..." Jordan licked her bottom lip and shook her head again. "Anyway, I'm out." She jingled her keys in her hands and adjusted her sunglasses. "Have a good senior year."

"Yeah. You too."

Jordan turned on her heel toward her car. Carly did the same, never once looking back.

She doubted Jordan did either.

103

AVA

Ava stared at the explosion of pinks, golds, and whites unfurling across the early morning sky outside her bedroom window. Her cell phone lay dark and silent beside her, having been turned off last night before she crawled into bed. She gripped a steaming hot cup of coffee in one hand, the other hand nonchalantly threading its way through her curls. Downstairs, Kyle, back from his run, slammed the front door. He'd grab a quick coffee and shower while she finished her last-minute packing and then they'd be on their way.

Ten minutes later, the bedroom door edged open and she turned, offering him a tired smile.

"Hey."

"Morning, Mate," he said coming over and kissing her, the warm, sweet coffee still lingering on his lips.

"How was your run?"

"Fine."

"Anything in the paper?"

Kyle pulled his drenched gray Lycra tank over his head and threw it on top of the hamper. "All over the front page."

Ava's head dipped back and she sighed. All the more reason to get the hell out of town.

The tenth anniversary of Whitney Dean's murder.

This being the tenth year, the frenzy had started much earlier than it had the other nine years. It would always begin quietly, a good two months before the actual date. For the ten-year anniversary, the sniffing had started nearly a year ago. The tactics were still the same: eager reporters accosting anyone who lived in Lake Forest who knew the Deans personally or were connected to the Dean family by the slenderest of threads—friends, neighbors, relatives, teachers, clergy. The pitch was always the same. "Hi, I'm from fill-in-the-blank news organization and I'm doing a story on the fill-in-the-blank anniversary of Whitney Dean's murder and how it continues to impact the community."

Then there were the reporters salivating to talk to anyone who knew Jordan or Erica. Same pitch, slightly different wording: "Hi, I'm so-and-so from fill-in-the-blank news organization and I'm doing a story on the fill-in-the-blank anniversary of Whitney Dean's murder, specifically your reaction to Erica Mitchell aka Ruthie Stowers, being the culprit. Can I buy you a cup of coffee?"

Initially, Ava had shied away from talking about her role in the case. At first, it was to shield Carly from unnecessary attention. Then, it was to shield herself. For the first few months, her phone pinged with emails day and night. Messages clogged her work voicemail, and a few crafty reporters had even unearthed her cell number. It had been worse for Carly—tweets, Instagram posts, camping out in front of the high school, following her. Phone numbers and email addresses were changed, social media accounts went private or were deleted altogether. The bloggers and podcasters went year-round, though they seemed less intrusive and more respectful. There were even rumors one of the more popular podcasts would be turned into a movie or TV series. Eventually, Ava relented to a lengthy *Vanity Fair* article and a two-part episode of *Dateline*. That had been enough.

The second year and every anniversary since, Ava and Kyle turned off the phones, packed up the house and went away for two weeks until the storm died down. With Carly living in D.C., ensconced in her teaching career, married with a new last name, going by Caroline to boot, she'd been somewhat isolated from the swirl of the past few years, though Ava still planned to check in with her every hour on the hour.

Eight years ago, after getting his quickie divorce from Erica and selling his house, Jay Mitchell had remarried, pledging his troth to a meek little mouse of a woman named Iris that he'd met through his sister. Ava suspected—it least initially—it had less to do with love than it did with Jay being a man and men replaced their wives. The last she heard he and his new wife lived in Florida, but there was no word if Jordan ever came to visit.

Actually, no one heard anything from Jordan. She'd evaporated into the ether. She got her diploma at the Connecticut boarding school before matriculating to King's College in London. The only sliver of information Ava could find was a small bio on a website for a financial services firm in London stating she was a junior advisor, had an MBA from Cambridge, and had grown up outside of Chicago. No mention of a husband or children. No social media, no online profile whatsoever. Much like her mother, Jordan had perfected the art of vanishing.

The Deans vanished themselves, taking only their clothes, one car, and a smattering of personal effects. They simply left town in the middle of the night without a whisper to anyone, selling their house lock, stock, and barrel through one of Lauren's colleagues. They first moved to a gated community in Arizona, finally settling in New Mexico to be near Janine and her family. For the first few years, there'd been the occasional text in response to Ava's queries about how she was doing. Lauren dutifully responded every time with a breezy rundown on the life and times of the Deans, formerly of Lake Forest, Illinois. Nothing overtly personal, nothing revealing, nothing deeply held. A rote report that everyone was doing fine, she and Steve were enjoying retirement, that his golf game had improved considerably, Janine was expecting her first, then her second, then her third, and Parker was thriving in school. Light, bright, and airy. As though she were updating a casual neighbor she'd run into in line at the coffee shop as opposed to a good girlfriend she'd known for decades, had vacationed with, had laughed and cried with. Over time, Lauren stopped answering, likely because she didn't want even this fragile, faint reminder of a life she no longer cared to remember. Ava missed her, but understood the need to cut ties. She couldn't say she wouldn't have felt the same inclination.

One person who seemed to revel in remembrance was Mr. Ron Byrne. The bottom having fallen out of his teaching career, Regina Knowles's settlement money for mowing him down sustained him while he penned a roman à clef about the case. The book was a smash hit and he became the darling of cable crime shows, blogs, and podcasts, recounting his experience of being falsely accused, offering his insights into the sliver of time he'd been acquainted with Whitney Dean, as though he'd known her since she was yea high. To Ava's surprise and mild disgust, he'd parlayed his fifteen minutes into a successful career as a bestselling novelist, churning out seven books over the last ten years. No doubt, he was splashed across the coverage this year, reluctant to relinquish his grasp on the tragic scandal that had catapulted him out of the classroom and onto the world's stage.

Not much had changed for the Ewings. There was talk of retirement in the next ten years, selling the house and possibly splitting their time between Virginia to be near Carly and her husband and Jimmy and his family in California. She and Patricia Stowers maintained what she referred to as a social media friendship, commenting occasionally on photos and statuses, exchanging the odd text and Christmas newsletter. Same with Lyz and Sharla. Sometimes, Jordan appeared in photos with her aunts and grandmother around the holidays, but it was extremely rare. Though they never spoke of Jordan or Ruthie-cum-Erica in their infrequent communiqués, Ava imagined Patricia was bombarded every year with interview requests and she no doubt granted them. Shannon Kendall had become as much of a cottage industry as Whitney Dean. Patricia didn't seem to hold the pain of Ruthie/Erica's actions. Rather, it seemed she'd resigned herself to forever being intertwined with her sister's troubled soul.

Sometimes, the haunts of her final conversation with Erica hovered over her, the sneering derision in the woman's voice as palpable over these past ten years as it had been that night. She'd often wondered if she was the last person to talk to Erica. Sometimes, she could hear the woman in her dreams, her whispers fluttering against her ear. Other times, her heart would race and sweat would blister across her body when she imagined seeing her somewhere, that rail-thin body, the haughty, condescending smile. It was a mirage of her imagination, of course, these delusional sightings, these waking nightmares. It would sometimes take a few hours to talk herself down from the ledge and remind herself that she didn't have to worry about the woman anymore.

Erica was gone. She wasn't coming back.

Kyle took both their bags down to the car as she finished the last-minute minutiae inherent in a long trip—check the locks, unplug the appliances, set the alarm, text their next-door neighbor a reminder to collect the mail. She'd never been to Bora Bora before. Lying on a beach, submerged beneath innumerable glow-in-the-dark cocktails, a scorching sun, luxuriating against silky white sand, no mention of Whitney Dean or Erica Mitchell ... she might not want to come back.

Ava emerged from the house just as Kyle slammed the trunk shut. The inimitable sound of teenage voices cracking the early morning quiet pulled her gaze up. Coming down the street, linked arm in arm, forming their own miniscule version of a human chain, was her neighbor, Priscilla and three of her girlfriends—giggly, loud, erupting every thirty seconds with, "Oh, my God," and sentences and syllables crashing into each other at warp speed. Ava stood on her front step watching, alternately fascinated, alternately nonplussed. When had she blinked? She could have sworn that just yesterday, Priscilla was the stereotypical awkward pre-teen—scrawny and wild, all braces and hair and pimples.

She was sixteen now, a junior. So were her friends.

Priscilla spotted her staring, before she smiled and waved.

"Hi, Mrs. Ewing," she said, all bubbles and effervescence.

Ava could only return a faint wave as the girls shuffled down the sidewalk, destination unknown, their laughter, accompanying their complex lexicon, a secret code only they knew, rippling across the quartet as they disappeared from view.

As she watched their retreating backs, these best of friends, this inseparable pack of girls, the question she didn't want to ask, wouldn't dare say aloud, didn't want to know the answer to, swirled through her brain. It was a question that, once unleashed, couldn't be stuffed back in the box.

How long would it be before those girls turned on each other?

104

KIMBERLY

Kimberly Mendes wakes every morning at six a.m. without an alarm clock. She's disciplined like that. She starts each day by throwing open the French windows of her miniscule second-floor, one-bedroom apartment in Old San Juan to let the warm, salty breezes of San Juan Bay flood into the living room. She stands on the Juliette balcony as she sips her morning café con leche, her eyes affixed to the gentle swells of white-capped, blue green water, relishing the balmy winds skimming across her skin.

Her apartment is a spartan residence with creaky wooden floors, a utilitarian couch she rarely sits on, a wobbly coffee table, a breakfast nook, a few lamps, and a singular bookshelf filled with trashy romance novels in Spanish. The only artwork is a framed acrylic portrait of Felisa Rincón de Gautier that came with the apartment.

After a quick shower, she slips into one of the multitudes of billowing, multicolored sundresses that are squeezed into her bedroom's matchbox closet. There's a quick swipe of lip gloss and dusting of blush before she runs a careless comb through her hair. She'd long since shed the honey blond extensions in favor of a short black bob of her natural hair and swapped the hazel contacts for light brown ones. She still spray tans, because even here, a golden brown hue is elusive to her naturally pasty skin. Kimberly is thinner than Ruthie, but fatter than Erica, a happy medium facilitated by her endless walks all over the city and eating whatever she wants without worry. It's liberating to have a hearty jibarito or plate of sorullitos de maiz for dinner followed by a thick wedge of bizcocho de novia without the itch to burn it all away on a treadmill.

She works at a cramped bookstore six blocks away that smells of equal parts coffee, musty pages, and the lemon furniture cleaner she swabs the shelves with once a week. As the hard soles of her flat leather sandals slap against the bumpy cobblestones during the short walk, Kimberly smiles and nods to the shop owners opening their stores for business, the hot ball of yellow sun beating down on them, even at the early hour. She is friendly, but keeps to herself, preferring her own company to that of prying, cloying acquaintances.

The bookstore is never very busy, with twenty customers in a day constituting a rush. Kimberly used to wonder how the owner kept the doors open until she learned the woman's wealthy husband kept it afloat for her as a distraction from his many mistresses. In between reading, she restocks the shelves, rearranges displays, and has fleeting, friendly chats with the customers, some of whom are regulars. She doesn't need the paltry sum the woman pays her every Friday, since her money will outlast her, however long that is. Regardless, the work keeps her occupied and gives the appearance of stability.

On her days off, she plays tourist, even after ten years. She goes on helicopter tours, explores the old cathedrals, meanders along the streets of La Perla, strolls through the plazas while spooning a gelato. She visits El Morro often, perching herself on the hulking, jagged rocks as she stares at the ocean, imagining the battles that took place there in the fight for the island's freedom.

It's a metaphor she understands well.

Though she'd lived as Erica Mitchell believing she'd never be found out, she'd prepared for the possibility that she could be. Millions that Jay never missed squirreled away in dribs and drabs over the years into a secret unmarked account (considering the brutal swiftness with which he'd cut her off at the knees, she didn't feel all that bad about taking his money), a new persona with the necessary ID and paperwork on standby.

One of the other inmates she'd befriended had smuggled in a stash of laxatives for her in exchange for a few cigarettes she'd swiped from someone else. She hid the box between the metal frame and flat sagging mattress in her cell until the time was right. It was a matter of a few hours before she was transferred to the infirmary where they were baffled as to why they were unable to stop her intestinal distress. They were just too stupid to notice that she kept slipping herself laxatives. She was eventually taken to the county hospital, where, once she was stabilized, the chaos of a busy, understaffed emergency room and the less-than-attentive cops guarding her allowed her to steal a pair of scrubs, palm the ID of a distracted nurse, and walk out the front door without so much as a raised eyebrow.

Her escape made national news. Of course. Even she had to admit it was quite remarkable that she was able to vanish once again. Who was able to do that twice in one lifetime? Her, apparently. To this day, Erica Mitchell remained a wanted fugitive. With any luck, she always would be. Then again, if she didn't, Kimberly was ready.

Always have a plan.

Only on occasion did she think about Jordan and Kennedy. Fleeting, like those floaters behind your eyes. The girls were part of Erica Mitchell's life, not Kimberly's, and that life was a squashed, almost nonexistent memory. They probably didn't miss her anyway. Besides, she'd learned the hard way that forming emotional attachments was a useless exercise.

Kimberly adjusts her sunglasses as she hands a five to the cashier at her favorite ice cream shop in exchange for a coconut limber, the gold Tiffany bracelet that dangles from her wrist clanking against the cold glass of the display case. She pops the concoction out of the plastic cup, biting into the sweet, frozen creaminess as she steps back into the steamy Saturday afternoon. A slender vein of sweat slithers down her spine, the result of the sweltering sun stubbornly clinging to the clear blue sky. An old man is perched on a milk crate at the corner, gently strumming his guitar as he wails a song of regret and longing in

Spanish. Kimberly flicks the change from the ice cream shop into the rusted-out coffee can at his feet and he tips his battered old fedora in appreciation. A few steps ahead of her, she spots one of the ubiquitous walking tours of Old San Juan. She leisurely catches up to them, matching her steps to the lazy gait of the tourists who stumble around in awe of the candy-colored neon of the buildings, the wondrous cracked blue cobblestones, the enormous swaying palm trees.

She'll just go along for the ride and pretend like she is one of them.

After all, she is good at pretending.

END

AUTHOR'S NOTE

If you or someone you know is struggling with suicidal thoughts, please call the U.S. National Suicide Prevention Lifeline at 800-273-TALK (8255) any time day or night, or chat online. Crisis Text Line also provides free, 24/7, confidential support via text message to people in crisis at 741741.

AUTHOR'S NOTE II

AND WHEN I DIE was inspired by the 1984 murder of fifteen-year-old Kirsten Costas by her classmate, Bernadette Protti. Among the numerous books, articles, documentaries, and online materials I consulted in writing this novel, here are three that might be of particular interest:

- *Rolling Stone, July 18, 1985, p.44 Death of a Cheerleader: An American Tragedy by Randall Sullivan*
- *Ladies' Home Journal, November 1985, p120 The Cheerleader Murder by Carol Pogash*
- *Investigation Discovery, The 1980s: The Deadliest Decade, Season 1, Episode 3, The Cheerleader Murder*

ACKNOWLEDGMENTS

Getting to THE END on AND WHEN I DIE was a long and bumpy road. The idea first sparked after I watched an episode of *The 1980s: The Deadliest Decade* about the murder of Kirsten Costas. I was so intrigued by the idea of what had happened to her murderer, that I asked myself the question, "What if she did it again?" With that premise driving me, off I went to write the story of vicious teenage girls, seething jealousies, and of course, the 80s (of course!). After a lot of false starts (and a few false endings), I finally figured out how to express the story I wanted to tell.

Every book starts with a thank you to First Reader Kathryn, who encouraged me to keep going (while, of course, telling me all the things wrong with the story). Thank you for your wisdom and your insights.

My awesome Beta Readers, Lanee, Kayla (during finals no less!) and Joy, for taking the time to read the manuscript and offering such great and necessary feedback.

To my editorial team, Lydia Jennings and Alison Scotchford, for your sharp eyes.

Thank you to Kate Rock and her team for helping to get the word out.

To all the bloggers, Bookstagrammers, podcasters, and reviewers who have read and reviewed my books, THANK YOU. Your support means so much to authors, especially those of us in the indie space.

There aren't enough words of gratitude to my readers. Your emails, messages on social media, buying, reading, and reviewing my books—it really does help keep me going. Much love!

HAVE YOU READ THEM ALL?

"SLOANE HAS A KNACK FOR DRAWING READERS IN."
-OOSA ONLINE BOOK CLUB

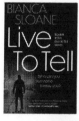  

WWW.BIANCASLOANE.COM

BOOKS BY BIANCA SLOANE

STANDALONE NOVELS

Killing Me Softly (Previously published as Live and Let Die)

Sweet Little Lies

What you don't know

And when I die

THE EVERY BREATH YOU TAKE SERIES

Every Breath You Take

Missing You: A Companion Novella to Every Breath You Take

The Every Breath You Take Collection (Box Set of Every Breath You Take and Missing You)

THE LIVE TO TELL SERIES

Live To Tell

Tell Me A Lie

White Christmas (A Live To Tell short story)

Get **EXCLUSIVE** Bonus Content from **AND WHEN I DIE!**

Join Bianca's Book Club to access some extra-special exclusives including:

- A 24 page digital booklet with the inside story and true crime inspiration for **AND WHEN I DIE,** including archival news clippings and color photos

- Four deleted scenes including author commentary

- A high res digital poster of the book cover, signed by the author

VISIT

https://www.biancasloane.com/and-when-i-die

to access your Bonus Content!

ABOUT THE AUTHOR

Bianca Sloane is the author of the suspense novels *Killing Me Softly* (previously published as *Live and Let Die*), chosen as "Thriller of the Month" (May 2013) by e-thriller.com and a "2013 Top Read" by OOSA Online Book Club, *Sweet Little Lies*, *Every Breath You Take*, and *Missing You:* A Companion Novella to *Every Breath You Take)*. When she's not writing, she's watching Bravo TV or Investigation Discovery, reading, or cooking. Sloane resides in Chicago.
To connect with Bianca:

www.biancasloane.com
Bianca@BiancaSloane.com